ALFRED EBERHARD WAS OBSESSED WITH A DREAM . . . AND CLAIRE EBERHARD WAS OBSESSED WITH HER HUSBAND . . .

It was late at night. Dr. Alfred Eberhard could not sleep. His wife, fighting off drowsiness, stayed awake at his side.

"Alfred," she said, "what is it? Is it the work?"

"No," he answered, rubbing his weary eyes, his expression agonized. "It's—" a groan replaced the words that were not yet ready to come forth.

"Darling, tell me," Claire crooned, stroking his forehead. "Share your thoughts with me, and maybe then you'll be free of them."

Again, Eberhard tried to speak; his voice caught; he tried again.

"Claire," he finally whispered, "I—I want you to have my child."

A wave of joy and relief swept through Claire Eberhard as she heard these words. Was that all that was bothering her husband? How strange that it should be the very thing that she herself was yearning for! The beginning of a family—how odd that it should be so hard for her husband to say.

"Oh, darling," she exclaimed, "of course, of course. Why didn't you ask me sooner? Were you afraid the pregnancy would interfere with my work, or—"

"Claire," said Alfred Eberhard softly, "I don't think you've exactly understood me. I want you to have *my* child. I want you to bear my clone. . . ."

HORROR FROM HAUTALA

SHADES OF NIGHT   (0-8217-5097-6, $4.99)
Stalked by a madman, Lara DeSalvo is unaware that she is most in danger in the one place she thinks she is safe— home.

TWILIGHT TIME   (0-8217-4713-4, $4.99)
Jeff Wagner comes home for his sister's funeral and uncovers long-buried memories of childhood sexual abuse and murder.

DARK SILENCE   (0-8217-3923-9, $5.99)
Dianne Fraser fights for her family—and her sanity— against the evil forces that haunt an abandoned mill.

COLD WHISPER   (0-8217-3464-4, $5.95)
Tully can make Sarah's wishes come true, but Sarah lives in terror because Tully doesn't understand that some wishes aren't meant to come true.

LITTLE BROTHERS   (0-8217-4020-2, $4.50)
Kip saw the "little brothers" kill his mother five years ago. Now they have returned, and this time there will be no escape.

MOONBOG   (0-8217-3356-7, $4.95)
Someone—or some*thing*—is killing the children in the little town of Holland, Maine.

Available wherever paperbacks are sold, or order direct from the Publisher. Send cover price plus 50¢ per copy for mailing and handling to Penguin USA, P.O. Box 999, c/o Dept. 17109, Bergenfield, NJ 07621. Residents of New York and Tennessee must include sales tax. DO NOT SEND CASH.

REPLICA

Lionel Saben

Pinnacle Books
Kensington Publishing Corp.
http://www.pinnaclebooks.com

PINNACLE BOOKS are published by

Kensington Publishing Corp.
850 Third Avenue
New York, NY 10022

Pinnacle and the P logo Reg. U.S. Pat. & TM Off.

First Zebra Printing: June, 1978

First Pinnacle Printing: June, 1997
10 9 8 7 6 5 4 3 2 1

Printed in the United States of America

One

The clock on the wall of the operating room hummed ever so slightly, it seemed to Dr. Alfred Eberhard. It was a muted and distant humming, high-pitched like a far-off siren, just barely audible. And yet the doctor could not escape it. His mind returned to it again and again; it annoyed him terribly, like a persistent toothache. . . . But no, he told himself, the clock did not hum. He knew that perfectly well, as well as he knew every detail of this operating theater in which he had spent so many hundreds of hours, performing surgery, lecturing, overseeing the work of his subordinates. . . . The humming, then, was within himself, the muffled but inescapable voice of conscience. He could not shout it down, could not block it out. It persisted, a shrill nerve-fraying hum that assailed him as he contemplated the bizarre, clandestine operation he was preparing to perform.

"Is everything ready, Jean?" Dr. Eberhard heard himself say.

"Yes, Alfred, everything." The husky female voice broke through the buzz, at once comforting and goading. "The anesthesia has taken effect.

Brain waves and pulse are normal. Respiratory functions are satisfactory. The freezing mechanism has been activated and is ready to receive the organ as soon as it's been removed. We can begin whenever you are ready."

For several moments, Dr. Eberhard stood perfectly still, only his eyes moving restlessly in their deep sockets. Piercing and driven and infinitely sad, his eyes scanned the room greedily, as if wishing to preserve forever the images around him at this very instant. He knew that soon—as soon as he touched his scalpel to the numbed flesh of the body laid out before him—everything would become irreparably different, the entire moral universe would be turned upon its head, and he yearned for one last clear-sighted vision of how things were *before*.

He glanced at the surgical instruments, laid out in perfect order on the tray in front of him. The cold steel glistened eerily in the shadowless light of the operating room. Dr. Eberhard could *smell* the steel, its icy crispness burned his lungs like freezing air. He regarded the scalpels, razor-sharp, which sliced through human flesh as easily as a knife moves through a ripe melon. He appraised the shears whose blades were of a metal hard enough to cut through cartilage or even bone, to sever a rib or split the sternum if one wished to approach the heart or lungs. Swiftly, his expert eye ranged over the clamps, the sponges, the tubes, the sutures. All the tools by which the interior of the human body could be probed or manipulated—or robbed. . . .

Dr. Eberhard winced slightly, and his glance sprang away from the glinting instruments. Now he looked quickly around the room, naming to himself the various machines arranged around him—the oscilloscopes, the respirators, the apparatus that cleansed the blood, the cooling device that preserved organs to be transplanted. . . . How he had admired those machines! How he had rejoiced in their ingenuity! Why, then, did they horrify him now? Why, at this moment, did they appear to him not as benevolent human aids to human well-being, but as diabolical tools for man's relentless quest for power, his pathetic groping toward an unnatural and impossible permanence?

His eyes fled the image of the machines, just as they had fled the sight of the shears and scalpels. Unconsciously, primitively, his gaze turned upward, as if looking for comfort from heaven. But there was no heaven above him: only the emptiness of the darkened gallery behind its shield of germ-proof glass mocked his stare. . . . Yes, the gallery was empty now. This operation was not to be observed—unlike so many of Dr. Eberhard's previous surgeries, with the eyes of the medical world looking on with highest regard, perhaps with awe. . . .

No, this operation was secret, as sin is always secret.

"Alfred, are you all right?"

Jean's voice brought him back to himself. He squeezed his eyes shut for a second, and then he opened them and regarded her. He regretted that the cool white light of the operating room was not more flattering to her: had she appeared more ideally beautiful, more perfect, it would have been easier to convince himself that he was undertaking his grim task purely for the sake of her love. And yet he did love her, as much as he had ever been able to love anyone or anything that existed outside of his own body.

He looked at her now, and saw her truly. She was only twenty-eight, half his age. And yet, already, certain signs of mortality had begun to mar her. The soft skin surrounding her flashing black eyes was beginning to be edged with wrinkles, as were the corners of her mobile and full-lipped mouth. The muscles of her chest were beginning to stretch, and her breasts were starting to fall. The firm flesh of her thighs was loosening . . . and yet he did love her, and did desire her. He loved her thick black hair, coarse and almost scratchy against his face. He loved the cold incisiveness of her scientific mind, her unyielding, shameless logic, which contrasted so fascinatingly with the footloose abandon of her passions.

"Yes," said Dr. Eberhard. "I'm all right. Just let me collect myself for a moment more, and then we'll begin."

Dr. Eberhard rubbed his forehead, trying to dispel the droning hum that still tormented him. He raised his eyes once more to the electric clock built into the wall, Time—how it mocked him! How it mocked everything. He watched, rapt, as the second hand swept along through a quarter of its arc. How even its movement was, each second precisely as long as the one before it. How maddeningly indifferent! Time knew neither hurry nor hesitation, nor fear of death nor greed of life. Time was calm, and yet it was the factor that made calm impossible for anyone who prized existence. It was time that caused obsessions and crimes—crimes against the natural order, the order that ordains one life per individual, a life of just so many sweeps of the second hand, and no more.

Eberhard decided to memorize the time. He wanted to recall the exact moment at which he approached the body on the operating table: 2:34:18 A.M., of Monday, the second of September, 1991: Labor Day.

He sighed and moved forward bidding his conscience to be still. Now he must be the supreme technician, the consummate surgeon. Coolly, he glanced at the instruments which monitored the patient's metabolic processes. All was as it should be. The brain waves moved smoothly and gracefully across the gridded screen of the scope; the metal pen traced out the rhythm of the patient's heart on a silently turning drum. Next, the doctor turned his attention to the welter of tubes going in and out of the patient's body; he examined the straw-colored plasma that was trickling into a vein in the patient's arm; he appraised the urine that was being drained out through a catheter.

Only then did he turn his expert gaze upon the body itself. The body was covered with two pale green sheets. One of the sheets hung down over the patient's feet, and came up as far as the tops of his thighs. The other sheet began near the solar plexus, and was draped neatly across the patient's forehead. Thus, there was a naked area ranging from the patient's groin to the base of his ribcage; it was here the surgeon would strike.

Dr. Eberhard looked down at the smooth expanse of bare flesh in front of him. The abdomen raised and lowered ever so slightly with the patient's shallow but even breathing. The torso had been shaved, and the skin seemed preternaturally smooth. The navel seemed a peaceful crater. The genitals, mature, adult-sized, but stripped of their covering of pubic hair, seemed vulnerable and inexplicably poignant. . . .

Gently, the doctor began to palpate the abdomen. His expert fingers worked independently now, without the intrusion of his mind. They traced out the locations, the shapes, the sizes of the various internal organs. They hunted out swellings, abnormalities—and they found none. The patient was perfectly healthy, healthy with all the bursting, taken-for-granted health of youth. A moment of inexpressible sadness swept over Eberhard, entering him through his fingers, the fingers that played over the youthful skin and taut muscles of the young man on the operating table. . . .

He reached out his hand and his colleague, his lover, instantly slapped the handle of a scalpel into his palm. Even through his surgical glove, Dr. Eberhard could feel the coldness of the metal as he measured the weight of the scalpel in his hand, all the while staring at the torso in front of him. How beautiful its lines were!

Beads of sweat appeared on his forehead and Jean instantly mopped his brow with a cool cloth—

her fingers were a comfort, and yet . . . how they goaded him!

Slowly, his fingers closed around the handle of the scalpel, his eyes fixed on the naked, helpless torso in front of him, tracing out the place where he would strike, measuring the arc that he should cut to gain entrance to that torso, that rich repository of organs, of youth.

As his scalpel-wielding hand edged forward toward the body, the hum rang out in Dr. Eberhard's brain, echoed by the harsh glare glinting off the blade of his knife. The point of the scalpel encountered the first resistance of the skin, the paltry defense of the body against the intrusion of the steel, then Eberhard felt in his fingers—all through him—the slight elastic yielding that precedes the tearing of the flesh—

But something was wrong, some small detail troubled him, some small matter of procedure had been mishandled. . . .

Eberhard abruptly drew back. "Jean!" he said in a professional, mechanical tone. "Why have you covered the patient's face? The face should not be covered in abdominal operations—it interferes with breathing."

"But Alfred!" said Jean. "The face—it . . ."

"I know very well," said Dr. Eberhard. "It's kind of you to try to spare me. But we must not violate surgical procedures. Uncover the face, please."

At this demand, Jean's vast composure seemed to slip from her. Her eyes, previously so cool, so unflinching, now flashed terror. Her hands, so immensely competent, now seemed unschooled, awkward, as she reached out for the pale green sheet folded across the patient's hairline.

Slowly, as if wishing every second that the request might be rescinded, she began to draw the sheet down across the patient's face. First, the forehead appeared, noble, broad, enormously intelligent. Then came the eyes, now lidded and deep-set, but piercing and sad beyond their sixteen years when open. Then the nose and cheekbones were exposed, the nose broad and straight, the cheekbones prominent, high, sloping downward toward a strong, square jawline. The mouth was uncovered, broad and strangely wry. Then came the final handsome feature, the chin just slightly cleft. . . .

Jean spent a long time refolding the sheet under the patient's chin. She dreaded the instant when she would have to look up and meet the doctor's eyes, confront his face as *he* confronted the placid, drugged countenance of the figure on the operating table.

After some moments, when she could no longer find reasons to delay, she slowly turned her head to gaze upward at the surgeon. He stood there, the scalpel still poised in his clenched hand, and in his face there was a look of such anguish, of such turmoil and pure gut terror, that she herself was immobilized by it, and could do nothing but dumbly stare up at her tormented lover, teetering between immortality and madness.

The room reeled around Eberhard; the humming rose to a rending shriek. His left hand reached out and he grabbed the edge of the operating table to steady himself. His mouth fell open and he stared down at the sleeping face with a recognition so intense as to undo itself, to make everything unrecognizable, to call into question the very existence of Self. It was his own face he stared down at, his own countenance, feature by feature, from the deep-socketed eyes to the sensually curling mouth to the barely clefted chin! It was his face as it had been forty years ago, before age had grayed and then begun to thin the jet-black curly hair, before the firm, set planes of cheeks had begun to slaken into jowls, before the nose and ears had become glutted with the rampant growth of old man's hair.

How he loved that face! How he yearned to recover it, to replenish himself with the youthful tissues that lay underneath the youthful skin. And yet, how filled he was with primitive horror at the mere beholding of it, as if it were a ghost of Self, a mirror-image detached and deadly. . . .

"Jean," gasped Eberhard, "I don't know if I can do it. I don't know if I can go through with it—"

"You must!" said Jean, in a voice as cold and piercing as the instruments gleaming on the surgical tray. "You are old, Alfred! Twice as old as I. Three times as old as him. Your organs are wearing out. You will become weak. . . . You will die. . . . You must take what you need. . . ."

"But Jean," he was almost pleading, "what of *him?*"

"There is no *him!*" said Jean insistently. "There is only you! This," she said, deprecatingly sweeping her hand across the figure on the table, "is only your shadow, an imprint you once made. *You* are the mold! *This* . . . what is this but a mass of jelly that bears your stamp! Nothing more. Not a son, not a person—a clone! An image that has put on flesh, an image derived from you, and from you alone—unshared! You created it, and you have the right to use it. That body is yours. That body is *you!*"

"Yes, of course," the doctor said, his voice wracked with doubt and confusion. "But what of his personality, his dreams, his emotions?"

"Those things are phantoms, Alfred-accidents," hissed Jean. "What else are they? Can you hold them in your hand? Can you weigh them? Where do they come from? What shape are they? They don't exist. Bodies exist! Tissue exists! Organs exist . . . and they get old, they wear out. And people die. But *you* can live, Alfred! You have your very own organ bank! You have a supply of extra parts, genetically coded to yourself. You can have transplants certain of success. And you can extend the process for as long as you wish!"

"And what if it is not my wish to extend it?" said Dr. Eberhard, a note of tremulous defiance entering his voice. He was suddenly overwhelmingly weary of his life; he suddenly realized that the prospect of death was not a terror but a consolation. . . .

"It doesn't matter if it is your wish or not," said Jean, with furious finality. "It is your destiny! You have come this far—further than any man before you has come. You cannot stop now. Get hold of yourself, Alfred! Steady your hand. Make the incision!''

Dr. Eberhard made no reply. He had no will left. Jean was right, he knew. There could be no turning back.

He glanced down at the hand that held the scalpel—it was steady now, as steady as it had ever been. But something was different, the humming inside his head had stopped. The crisis, then, the moment of indecision was over. . . . Dr. Eberhard was grateful for the silence.

He again prepared to incise the waiting torso. Again he checked the oscilloscopes and graphs—their concreteness reassured him. Yes, he told himself, the body was mechanical, consisting of parts that could be probed and measured—nothing more. No ambiguities, no phantoms.

Breathing deeply, again he leaned in toward the naked section of the body before him. Again he measured the curve of his cut, and moved the blade toward the skin. Again he felt the skin's resistance, its futile pushing back against the encroaching steel. But this time Dr. Eberhard did not draw back. He pushed ahead with the scalpel, gently but relentlessly, and finally there came a tiny moist popping sound as the skin was punctured and the point of the scalpel forged on toward the softer flesh beneath.

A thin line of blood appeared on the torso at the place where Dr. Eberhard had cut into it. At first, the blood simply traced the line of the cut, as if seeking to seal it. But within seconds it had begun to overflow, thin trickles of it streaming down. Jean's hand, clutching a sponge, reached out to mop the life fluid away, but Dr. Eberhard clutched her wrist, restraining her.

For several seconds he watched the blood trickle down in scarlet rivulets, wonderstruck by the sight of it, though it was something he'd seen thousands of times. It was only blood, a fluid of the body, a soup made up of water and various chemicals. . . . But now those red trickles brought back to him a long fought-off awareness of the ultimate mystery of life, a painful pondering of that secret and perhaps sacred realm of thought that starts where science ends, where all of science's brash conjectures crash against that which cannot be known.

As Dr. Eberhard watched the flow from the wound, down over the handle of his scalpel, onto his surgical glove, the blood began to coagulate. The body was already striving to heal. Life had become mysterious again—and mocking. Everything had turned into such a gruesome travesty of what he had hoped and planned. . . .

Two

From the very beginning, it was clear that Alfred Eberhard was an extraordinarily gifted individual. He began speaking at the highly precocious age of nine months. By the time he was a year and a half old, he had mastered the rudiments of sentence structure. By three and a half, he was reading, and by the time he'd entered kindergarten, he understood enough of the process of language to enable him to teach other children to read.

His intellectual precocity was not limited to the linguistic sphere, he exhibited a similar facility in mathematics. He had mastered the principles of addition and subtraction earlier than the average child learns to count, and at the time most children were wrestling with their multiplication tables, Alfred was moving on to algebra.

His early teachers marveled at the ease with which he learned, and at some point it was decided that the remarkable boy should undergo a special series of intelligence tests—no one doubted that he was brilliant—the question was, *how* brilliant? The tests, however, failed to answer the question finally. Alfred solved all the puzzles, found just the right way to arrange all the blocks, traced out all the subtleties in the problems on mechanical and abstract reasoning. He finished all the parts of the exam long before the allotted time was up, and though the mental strain of all that problem solving was known to be enormous, Alfred did not seem the slightest bit fatigued. . . .

It was the woman who administered the tests who appeared exhausted!

"I'm sorry," she said wearily, upon emerging from the testing room, "but I'm afraid there's no way of computing the boy's I.Q. on the basis of these tests."

"What do you mean?" the principal of the school demanded. "Surely you must know the results!"

"I'm afraid you don't quite understand the way these tests are scored," explained the psychologist. "The scores are determined on the basis of how far one deviates from certain norms. As one gets further and further away from the average, in either direction, it becomes more and more difficult statistically, to pinpoint the score. At some point, the scores go off the scale entirely—and that is the case with Alfred. His intelligence is too great to be measured by this test."

"Well then," asked the principal, feeling rather exasperated, "how *do* we know just how smart the lad is?"

The psychologist, equally exasperated, replied that she could say nothing more than that he was too smart for her tests.

Alfred's gifts, however, seemed to go beyond the

realm of mere academic brilliance. He was something of a musical prodigy as well. He began to play the piano at the age of four, and by the time he was six, was proficient enough to be playing Bach and Mozart. His long, slender fingers—those fingers which were destined to grow into the preternaturally skilled appendages of a consummate surgeon—developed strength and coordination at an unusually early age.

Young Alfred's musicianship was not simply a matter of precocious technical achievements, either, it seemed. He also appeared to have a genuine *feel* for the music, an esthetic sense that seemed inborn. His fantastically quick mind grasped the abstract structure of music as readily as it had grasped the structure of language, and by the time he was eight, Alfred was composing short pieces of his own. His fugues were as balanced and mathematically precise as those of the baroque masters.

It may be supposed that Alfred's physical development in some way suffered as a function of his early intellectual and esthetic growth. This, however, was not the case. Alfred was, in fact, an early walker, a physically vigorous toddler, an energetic and athletic boy. The stereotype of the bookworm—bespectacled, puny, weak of limb—did not apply to him at all. His physical reflexes were as acute as his mind; his musculature seemed to develop at a pace scarcely less impressive than his intellect. Nor was he lacking in external beauty. He was not classically handsome—too intelligent-looking for that, with his enormous forehead, and eyes which, even as a child, seemed already to have seen everything. But he was undeniably attractive, his features regular and strong, his hair curly and black, the slightly cleft chin adding one more note of incongruous maturity to the boyish face.

In short, the child was something of a miracle of nature, a fortunate freak in whom each and every genetic possibility had worked out for the best. The foundations for his manifold excellence were to be found, of course, in the capabilities of his parents, who were both bright, well-educated, musically adept, and sound of body. But, whereas their attainments were relatively modest, their off-spring's were prodigious. Credit for this can only be assigned to *chance*.

Out of the literally billions of ways in which their chromosomes might have merged, only the most felicitous linkings were effected. The different placement of one infinitesimal molecule of protein might have made Alfred a bit less adept as a mathematician; the slightest rearrangement of a single step in the ladder of nucleic acids might have resulted in his having a less astounding musical sense; the most minute shifting of an invisible strand of DNA might have deprived him of his sure, athletic sense of motion and balance. But none of those things happened. In Alfred Eberhard, Nature, working at random, in her own ineffable but inevitable way, had chanced upon a near-perfect formula for a human being.

Perhaps it is understandable, then, that the mature Alfred Eberhard, a man of science, as well as a mortal man with mortal vanities and the mortal fear of death and oblivion, should have become obsessed with the notion of *preserving* that formula, of making sure that his fortunate genetic combination should not be undone by mingling with other chromosomes, by making other, less optimal, pairings. . . .

In any case, in spite of all his gifts and talents, Alfred's childhood was not a time of unmitigated happiness. To some degree, he was victimized by the scourge of all exceptional people: loneliness. It was not that he was unpopular—quite the contrary. In addition to its other bestowals, nature had given Alfred what is perhaps the rarest gift of all in highly intelligent people—charm and ease of manner. His peers flocked around him and instantly recognized him as a leader. In later childhood and adolescence he was a veritable magnet to the prettiest girls. He never wanted for friends or for dates or, later, for lovers. No, his loneliness was of a different sort, a more poignant sort as he came to realize that other people's minds could not go as far as his, that, though he might begin a conversation in the company of several people, by the end of it, he would be alone in a realm of understanding and conjecture where the others could not follow.

At first, this surprised him—a child assumes that everyone perceives things in the exact same way he does. Later, it became a disappointment and a burden, a realization that his most profound dialogues could only take place within himself. Over time this awareness hardened into a kind of self-absorption and conceit—a conceit that, to some degree, compensated him for his intellectual aloneness.

So then, as a youth, Eberhard was sociable and charming, but his most important thoughts remained always inward. This, perhaps, is what led to the striking originality of many of his ideas. Since he discussed things so little with others, he had no need to bring his views into line with their expectations. He went his own way, and went much further than more temperate minds would have dared to. This was the quality that gave the stirring note of boldness to all of his research, which lifted him above the herd and made him a great scientist. But it was also the quality which led him to the hubris of tampering with nature, of trying to be father unto himself. . . .

As the boy moved from youth toward manhood, he began to narrow his range of interests, and finally, midway through his first year at M.I.T., he made the decision that, to a large degree, was to determine the entire future course of his life. He decided to go into medicine. He had toyed with other notions: the poetic abstractness of pure mathematics and the exciting mechanics of physics. Ultimately though, he decided that the study of the bewildering organism called the human body, was the one that most intrigued him.

Once that decision had been reached, Alfred Eberhard never wavered from it, and his academic career was one long stream of awards and honors. As an undergraduate, he topped his class, and then went on to Harvard Medical School. Here, too, he graduated first. More important, however, he was admitted into the regard and confidences of his professors, who, recognizing his potential, treated him more as a colleague than a student.

And, more important still, was the fact that Alfred Eberhard made a friend while in medical school, the best friend—and perhaps the only true friend—he was ever to have in his life.

John Goodwin was a serious but cheerful youth, tall and rather lanky, with reddish hair and green eyes that were fringed by pale, sparse, birdlike lashes, giving him a perpetually surprised look. His complexion was pale, and given to flushes. In the midst of an intense discussion with Alfred or among the other students, his face would sometimes turn a burning pink, and his birdlike lashes would flutter in tense concentration. Though not as prodigiously gifted as Alfred Eberhard, John Goodwin was a brilliant student in his own right, far better equipped to converse with Alfred than most of his peers. But it was not mere intelligence that first drew Alfred to John—it was something subtler.

There was a thorough humanity about John, though his thoughts could range into the abstract, though his mind was capable of carrying him into the most rarefied realms of speculation, his emotions and his moral sense were always firmly rooted in the earth. While other scientists might become so enraptured with their theoretical flights that they would lose sight of the human implications of their notions, John Goodwin would cling passionately to common sense and to a certain ethical caution. He could be brash in his thinking, but he staunchly insisted upon the distinction between the theoretical and the actual. . . . It was in this regard that he fundamentally differed from many dyed-in-the-wool scientists, Alfred Eberhard among them, for whom theory and practice were one, for whom any idea, however much it flouted conventional morality or went against the working of nature itself, cried out to be tested in practical application.

In any case, the two young men met during their third year of medical school, and very soon became nearly inseparable. When it was time to arrange for their internships, they managed to find posts at the same hospital—any facility in the country would have been more than happy to have them. They passed the years of internship and residency together, having both elected the most rigorous course available—that of surgeon. When in 1962, they had completed their residency and were accredited as full-fledged doctors, they were of a single mind about what they would do next. Private practice, they agreed, was the refuge of money-hungry mediocrities, pill pushers and quacks who hadn't bothered to *think* since their last exam in med school. Clinic work was socially useful, but it was horribly limiting and depressing. No, the only real scientific work was in research, where the mind had free play, where one could be a thinker, and not a mere functionary. Research was what *mattered*.

Accordingly, the young doctors decided to eschew the morbid glamor of the hospital and the cushy prestige of the private office, and to work instead within the austere and spartan confines of the laboratory. They would work on puzzles yet unsolved—and they elected to work on the most baffling puzzle of all, the puzzle on whose solution the greatest number of lives hinged: cancer. They would bring their skills and their ambitions to bear on this most mysterious of killers, and—like every bright young scientist who has ever pitted himself against disease—they had no doubt that they would prevail, that they would solve the awful riddle.

They sought, and found, research positions at one of the nation's most prestigious laboratory facilities, and they eagerly plunged into their work. They did not, after a time, discover the cure for cancer, though much of their work was useful, and opened doors for further exploration, but one of the things they began to explore was the mysterious means by which a single cell, *unaided,* began to reproduce, gave rise to a huge mass of neoplasm, genetically coded only by itself. What prompted the cell to begin stamping its own image on everything around it? And must such rampant growth lead only to a harmful end, to a tumor? Why shouldn't such reproduction produce a useful growth, a whole new individual?

Dr. Eberhard spent many hours studying this remarkable process. The process was known as cloning. It was a subject that would grow to obsess the man more and more as time went on.

Three

It was at one of the Brookside Research Institute's staff meetings that Alfred Eberhard was first exposed to the idea of cloning.

These meetings were held every week, and as a rule they were pretty dry affairs. Everyone who worked at the research facility was required to attend: the senior researchers sat in the first several rows of the modern lecture hall; the junior researchers—Eberhard and Goodwin among them—sat in the following rows; in back of them sat the technicians, assistants, and, on occasions when some news of possible consequence was to be discussed, members of the press.

The scientists who were to speak at the particular meeting were arranged on a dais. Surrounding them was a tangled heap of audio-visual material—charts, diagrams, projectors, tapes. One by one, the distinguished men of science would hobble up to the lectern, always accompanied by a polite round of applause, say what they had to say—which invariably ended in the sad conclusion that the mysteries of cancer still eluded them—and

then they would sit back down, amid another polite but lifeless ovation.

Young Dr. Eberhard loathed these meetings.
Their avowed purpose was to allow for the sharing
of ideas, but, as the young man saw it, precious little
was ever *shared*. Rather than allowing for the genuine interplay of ideas, each researcher would *cam-
paign* for his particular point of view, would strut
and boast about the infinitesimal sphere of knowledge in which he was supreme, the one thing about
which he knew more than anybody else. It was a
tiresome, rather pathetic business. Aside from that,
there was a dreadful amount of repetition involved
in the presentations. One would always hear
phrases such as, "As my distinguished colleague has
already said," or "As my dear friend Dr. So-and-So
has just implied. . . ." It went on and on, and Dr.
Eberhard's swift mind, which grasped every idea at
the first mention of it, groaned and prickled at the
plodding pace.

As a rule, he barely listened at the Friday meetings. He took in only the first several sentences
uttered by each speaker. Generally, he could get
the gist of an entire theory on the basis of that
alone, completing a thought in his own mind
much faster and with greater economy than the
man on the dais could ever say it. After that, the
doctor would let his mind wander. He would sit
still, polite and seemingly attentive—seeming to be
assiduously taking notes in fact!—but his "notes"
consisted of nothing more than a series of doodles
in the margins of his notebook pages. His doodles
ran the gamut from mathematical puzzles to cari-

catures of the speakers to obscene drawings of some of the female technicians. Occasionally, John Goodwin, sitting next to Dr. Eberhard would glance down at his sketches, and he would turn a bright pink from the effort involved in holding back a roar of laughter.

The Friday meetings, then, were not usually a terribly useful time at the laboratory. On one particular Friday, however, when the subject of cell cloning was brought up, the entire assembly—especially Dr. Eberhard—perked up their attention to an unprecedented degree.

The presentation in question was given by Dr. Emanual T. Schreiber, a hoary-headed old microbiologist who despite his age, still had the fierce gleam of the crusader in his eye. Years ago—decades ago!—Dr. Schreiber had been regarded as one of the most acute minds in the entire field of cancer research; now, though, it was thought that his powers were fading. He was regarded more as an honored patriarch than as an active thinker. His presentations were generally accepted with a kind of wry indulgence—as if no one really believed that old Dr. Schreiber had anything more of value to say. But, in fact, he did . . . much more than the smug young researchers gave him credit for.

Dr. Schreiber was greeted by the usual lukewarm applause as he walked slowly to the lectern. He waved his arms, silencing the clapping—he didn't like to waste time. He cleared his throat once and began speaking.

"Ladies and gentlemen," he said, "one of the ways that cancer may be regarded, is as a confusion on the part of the body as to what properly belongs to itself, and what does not. In short, it is a failure of the body to distinguish correctly between Self and Other. The mutant cell, which does not properly belong to the body's chemistry, is not rejected, as the body *should* reject it. The body, rather, *accepts* it as part of itself—and it is this acceptance that allows the cancer to grow and become deadly. The mutant cell feeds off the body's chemistry, *as if* it had a rightful place. It usurps the place of other cells, it outgrows them. It goes its own way—and it kills!"

Dr. Eberhard had listened to Dr. Schreiber's speech thus far, and he now decided to shut off his attention. Dr. Schreiber's explanation was interesting enough—the first time that one heard it. It was a succinct way of describing cancer, but it was part of every researcher's basic education, and Alfred Eberhard could not guess the value of repeating it yet one more time. Suddenly, however, Dr. Schreiber's remarks took an unexpected turn—unexpected even to Alfred, who could usually anticipate every twist in an argument.

"I now propose an analogy, ladies and gentlemen," continued Dr. Schreiber, "which may perhaps provide a useful way of studying the process by which the body fails to recognize the distinction between Self and Other. The distinction I propose, is between cancer and sexual reproduction!"

A buzz went up in the lecture hall as Dr. Schreiber pronounced these words. Here and there one heard a stifled laugh. Some of the researchers looked at each other with secretly raised eyebrows,

signaling that old Dr. Schreiber had finally become
senile. . . . Some of the more imaginative doctors,
however—Eberhard and Goodwin among them—
were not so quick to dismiss the microbiologist's
notion. It was a bold line of thinking, a truly radical
one, to draw a connection between the body's most
fruitful capacity and its most morbid one.

Dr. Schreiber waited for the noise to die down
before he continued. Now it was *he* who wore an
indulgent look. He was accustomed to the closed-
mindedness of many scientists—he'd been battling
against it all his life. . . .

"Does my analogy seem farfetched to you?" he
asked rhetorically. "Consider: In the case of cancer, a cell which is somehow foreign begins to reproduce at a much faster rate than any of the other
cells in the body; in the case of sexual reproduction, a foreign cell—a sperm—is introduced into
the body, triggering a growth which *also* proceeds
at a much faster rate. Now, my point is this: Might
there not be a common chemical factor involved
in the triggering of both the cancer reaction and
the fertilizing reaction? And, if that factor can be
identified and synthesized, might not its chemical
inhibitor be of great possible use in the prevention
of cancer?"

Again, a buzz went up among the audience. Now,
however, it was not a derisive disturbance, but
rather a thoughtful hum. Clearly, Dr. Schreiber's
analogy was intriguing. But would it hold up under
closer scrutiny. After some seconds, a hand shot
up in the first row of the lecture hall.

"Dr. Kenton," said Dr. Schreiber, "You have a question?"

"Yes," said Dr. Kenton, rising. Dr. Kenton was a small, stoop-shouldered man, intelligent but unimaginative who had a nasty penchant for deflating the ideas of others. The assistant director of the research center, he owed his job more to his skill as a political in-fighter than to his excellence as a scientist.

"Your notion is a fascinating one," Kenton said in a voice which made it clear that he didn't really find it so, "however, I can find no justification in support of your suggestion that there must be some unknown chemical factor which triggers the growth of cells in sexual reproduction. We already know perfectly well what it is that triggers that growth: it is the combining of the male and female gametes, each of which contains only half of the chromosomal material required to generate a new individual. Combined, they form a complete genetic package, and it is this presence of the full number of chromosomes which sets off the fertilization process. There's no need to appeal to the agency of some unknown chemical to explain it— it's already explained!"

Giving the audience a sour little smile, Kenton contentedly sat down, confident that he had taken the wind out of his colleague's sails. Dr. Schreiber, however, was not to be so easily defeated. Again he waited for the buzzing to subside, and then, with a master orator's precise timing, he simply said:

"You are right, Dr. Kenton. The process of sexual reproduction *has* already been explained, in just the way you outlined for us. The problem, however, is that that explanation is not adequate."

"Not adequate?" Dr. Kenton sprang up feistily, ready to do battle over the aspersion that his explanation fell short. "How so, not adequate?"

"It is very simple," said Dr. Schreiber, knowing that his audience was hanging on his every word now. (Even Alfred Eberhard, he noticed, usually so blasé, leaning forward in his seat, straining to hear every syllable.) "The mere presence of a full complement of chromosomal material cannot be regarded as sufficient means to start the process of reproduction, because *every cell* in the body—except the gametes—has a full supply of chromosomes. If nothing more were required, every cell would reproduce!"

"But Dr. Schreiber," exclaimed Dr. Kenton, "every cell *does* reproduce! It's called mitosis, and every freshman biology student learns about it!"

The sympathies of the audience were clearly with Dr. Schreiber now. Dr. Kenton's sarcastic jibe earned him nothing more than a number of angry glances.

Dr. Schreiber, always the gentleman, held his temper and answered in a calm and masterful voice. "You seem to miss my meaning, Dr. Kenton. I am well aware that every cell in the body is capable of reproducing *itself*. That is not what I am saying now. I'm saying that, if nothing more than a full stock of chromosomes were required, every cell in the body would be capable of reproducing *an entire new organism!*"

The excited buzz which had greeted every one

of Dr. Schreiber's previous revelations was absent now, and in its place was a shocked and thoughtful silence. Could it be true? Every element in Dr. Schreiber's theory seemed rigorously logical, and yet . . . the idea was so startling, so . . . unnatural! How was one to respond? The silence persisted for several moments, then was finally broken when Dr. Kenton, still vainly trying to wrest the upper hand from Schreiber began in a studiedly skeptical voice, "Dr. Schreiber, are you suggesting that under suitable conditions, in the presence of your mysterious unknown factor, any cell in the body could play the part of a sex cell? That any cell at all—a muscle cell, a bone cell, a liver cell—could step in and play the part of a gamete—a unique kind of cell that has been worked into its own specialized function over the course of countless generations?"

"I am saying that it is theoretically possible," said Dr. Schreiber with quiet insistence. "More than that I cannot say. There is still far too much we don't know about cell development, to assert its practical possibility or impossibility. But in theory, at least, I believe it could happen."

"Very well," Kenton continued, "since you will not go further than theory, let us drop that part of the question and return to your earlier assertion. In just what way do you think that the analogy you have drawn might be of use in cancer research?"

"Ah," said Dr. Schreiber, "that is where we get down to the nuts and bolts of my presentation. You must understand that what I have to say is based only on the most embryonic research—I feel that I may be on to something important, but for now

I am only groping along. But enough disclaimers. . . .

"Ladies and gentlemen, I have discovered a chemical substance—heretofore unidentified and, as far as I know, unobserved—which exists in the nuclei of cancer cells and also in the nuclei of normally fertilized reproductive cells. At present, I know very little about this substance. Of certain basic things, I am certain—the substance is a protein, and it is slightly acidic. That is all I know. I do not even have a name for it, but for my own purposes, I have been calling it the O+ factor.

"I stress that my work on this substance is in the most rudimentary stages. My thesis is that this O+ factor may serve as a sort of 'master switch,' a chemical messenger that triggers reproduction in both cancerous and normal cells. But that thesis may very well be wrong. It may perhaps be coincidental that the substance exists in both types of cells. Or the substance may in fact perform a function totally different from the one I suggest. In either case, I shall be continuing my research into this substance, and I hope to have more to report to you in due time. Are there any further questions?"

Dr. Schreiber peered nearsightedly out over the lecture hall but no hands were raised. His presentation suggested many questions, but they were questions too complex to be phrased and discussed on the spur of the moment. After a few seconds, Schreiber thanked the audience for their attention and as he turned to resume his seat, he was greeted by a hearty round of applause—not the usual lukewarm ritual, but an outpouring of genuine admiration.

Several other speakers followed, but their presentations were only a long tiresome denouement after the exciting climax of the old microbiologist's speech. Their "revelations" dealt with the usual stuff—radiation and laboratory rats and endless series of inconclusive experiments. They had no theoretical fire, and the meeting soon fell into its usual stifling dullness.

Though Alfred Eberhard went back to his doodling, his mind no longer wandered at random. Focusing on Dr. Schreiber's radical theory, he turned it every which way, savoring its every implication. Schreiber's brash but irrefutable logic gave him a high, and the idea raced through him like wine, tickling him, intoxicating him. He thought it over as he doodled, and his doodles consisted of a long series of O+'s, neatly arranged in the margin of his notebook page. . . .

After what seemed like an interminable time, the meeting was over. As soon as the last speaker had said his final word, the restless audience sprang to its feet, stretching and chattering amid a great rustling of notebooks and loose papers and sighs and yawns and small talk about the upcoming weekend.

Turning to Dr. Goodwin, Eberhard asked, "What do you make of it, John?"

"Of what?" Goodwin sounded distracted.

"Of Schreiber's notion, of course. What else at the meeting was worth discussing?"

"I'm not quite sure what I think of it," John admitted. "It's a seductive theory, that's for sure and has a certain elegance to it. And if Dr. Schreiber says he's isolated that substance, I believe him—he's still the top analyst around here. But still, there is something a little . . . bizarre . . . about the whole notion of non-sex cells reproducing, and about linking cancer with reproductive processes."

"That may be," Eberhard interrupted, "but you can't discount a scientific idea just because it isn't pretty."

"I'm not discounting it," Goodwin countered. "I'm only saying that I'm a little uneasy about it. It strikes me as a theory that might be *too* rich in implications—and who knows where you could go with a theory like that?"

"Well," Eberhard said, "I'd like to find out."

"All right." His friend smiled. "That's healthy scientific curiosity. But how do you propose to find out?"

"I'd like to work with Schreiber on his project, if he'll agree to take me on."

"But Alfred," John asked, "what about the project we're involved in now? Will you just drop it? I've never known you to be so impulsive."

"Ah," Eberhard said, a look of impatience and discontent on his face, "the project we're doing now is worthless. It's non-science! What will it accomplish? A few more dead rats and another stack of useless data? Another inconclusive statement that such and such a substance *may* cause cancer—you can't even say what does or doesn't *cause* it, let alone *cure* it! No, all these projects are nickel-dime stuff. They keep the technicians busy, but they haven't got any real theoretical backbone.

"That's what I like about Schreiber's idea—it's a new departure, a new direction. Who knows? Maybe it's totally wrong, maybe it's a dead end, but at least it's a different dead end for a change! I'm going to talk to him on Monday. Will you join me?"

Four

That following Monday a bright spring morning in April of 1963, Drs. Eberhard and Goodwin approached Dr. Schreiber in the laboratory lounge as the latter was sipping his way through his morning cup of tea. The hot liquid steamed up the thick lenses of the old doctor's glasses, giving him, somehow, the look of a blind, aged mouse. (It was something of a standing joke—and a subject of wonder—that Schreiber, with his weak, squinty eyes, should be such a marvel with a microscope. "Perhaps," Eberhard thought the first time he saw Schreiber crouched over the eyepiece, "that man does not exactly see—could it be his vision is of a slightly different sort?")

"Ah," Schreiber said cordially as the younger men moved toward him, "Dr. Eberhard, Dr. Goodwin, good morning. What can I do for you?"

"If you have a moment," said Dr. Eberhard deferentially, "we'd like to speak with you about your presentation of last Friday."

"Yes, of course," said Dr. Schreiber, his eyes widening with pleasure. And then he added with a surprising sly wink, "It certainly seemed to upset certain members of the staff, didn't it?"

"It's a very bold idea, Dr. Schreiber," said John Goodwin.

"And, I think, a brilliant one," said Dr. Eberhard.

"Gentlemen, you flatter me," said Dr. Schreiber. "I am taking a guess, that is all. Perhaps, at my age, one shouldn't take guesses, or not such wild ones at least. Maybe the chances of guessing wrong increase as one gets older . . . In any case, what was it you wished to talk about?"

Dr. Eberhard felt a moment of unprecedented shyness as he attempted to phrase his request to work with Dr. Schreiber in search of the O+ factor. Here was a man he respected so much, one of the few men he regarded as his intellectual and intuitive equal. . . .

"Well," Alfred began, "I—we—If you have room on your staff, Dr. Schreiber, Dr. Goodwin and myself would consider it a privilege to assist you in this project."

"Dr. Eberhard," replied Dr. Schreiber, "I am honored, truly. I am not intimately acquainted with the work of either of you two young men—so many young doctors come and go, it is simply impossible to know what each and every one is up to. However, one does form first impressions—hunches about the qualities of those who surround one. And I regard the two of you—on a hunch; another guess!—as two fine young scientists. If it can be arranged, I would be more than happy to attach you to my staff. With the understanding, of course, that I may very well be leading you along on a wild goose chase."

"Dr. Schreiber," said John Goodwin with a wry smile, "if we were worried about being on a wild goose chase, we wouldn't have gone into cancer research in the first place."

With the proper pulling of strings and a number of persuasive arguments (including a somewhat unpleasant confrontation with Dr. Kenton, who was still smarting from the one-upping he had received at the hands of Dr. Schreiber) Drs. Eberhard and Goodwin had themselves transferred to the staff of the admired microbiologist. They plunged into their new project with intensity and enthusiasm—but, as always, progress was agonizingly slow. In an all too brief a time, the original heady invigoration of the O+ factor had begun to wear off, and in its place came the quiet, sober, plodding day-to-day work of the laboratory scientist.

Dr. Schreiber's flights of erudite imagination—his "guesswork," as he modestly referred to it—now gave way to the nuts-and-bolts business of preparing and examining microscopic slides, interpreting the growths and changes in the various cultures, neatly labeled and arranged in seemingly endless rows of petri dishes. The three scientists spent hundreds of hours in the cramped laboratory, their sparkling lab coats billowing around them like cassocks, their rubber-soled shoes squeaking ever so slightly on the polished floors. They seemed always to be squirming around each other, standing aside to let each other pass, putting their heads very close together, each impatient to have a shot at the eyepiece of a microscope. . . .

Their experiments were divided into two basic categories. One set dealt with studies of cancerous cells, gleaned from biopsies on the tumors of laboratory rats; the other with normally developing fertilized fish eggs which were used because, even in nature, they are fertilized outside the body, and therefore do very well in incubator situations. In keeping with Dr. Schreiber's notion that there was a chemical "master switch" triggering reproduction in both cancerous and normal cells, the procedure involved close observation of the nuclei of both types of cells, in search of a common factor—the O+factor, if Schreiber's hunch was right.

The experiment moved slowly at a pace determined by nature. For months they would observe the progress of a single culture—a mass of nameless protoplasm living a bland and seemingly motionless life in a glass dish in an incubator—hoping that it would give up its fearsome secret. How did it grow? What prompted it to become cancerous? What was the chemical agent that triggered the development . . . was it the O+factor? (If, in fact, there was such a thing, as Dr. Schreiber was always quick to caution.)

But the various cultures jealously guarded their atom-sized mysteries. The cells seemed to be teasing the scientists intentionally! Now, for a moment, a new molecule would form—a protein chain, slightly acidic, as Dr. Schreiber had described. The molecule would seem to flirt with the scientists, giving them just a glimpse of itself, like a woman rearranging her skirt. . . . And then, mysteriously, for no apparent reason, the cells's metabolism would break the molecule down again! It would be sundered into its constituent parts before its function, or even its precise makeup, could be determined. . . . A frustrating business indeed!

The three scientists maintained their good humor as well as could be expected under the cramped and frustrating conditions of their work. Old Dr. Schreiber, with nearly fifty years of laboratory experience—thirty-five of them in cancer research—was well acquainted with setbacks and with waiting. He yearned passionately for a successful upshot of his theories—and yet, he could regard failures with an astounding equanimity. If one of his most promising cultures suddenly became inactive, if a molecule he'd been chasing around for weeks turned out to be a total dead end, he would just look up from the microscope and shrug—a disarmingly boyish shrug, complete with a comical turning outward of his palms and a wry twisting of his mouth—a gesture that often made Drs. Eberhard and Goodwin laugh out loud. Schreiber would laugh along with them, and for some moments, at least, the awful tension of the laboratory would be broken.

Then the three men, refreshed, would go back to their hunting. Their quarry, if elusive, was constantly fascinating. The nuclei of cells are amazing places, microcosmic factories where all the building and production of the living world goes on. Within the miraculously thin nuclear membrane—a band of jelly a million times thinner than the edge of the sharpest razor, which, with unerring selectivity, allows the passage of useful substances and blocks the entry of harmful ones—there were an astounding assortment of processes always going on. . . . Ions were always coming and going, enzymes were always breaking down the complex proteins, allowing them to be rebuilt in a thousand different combinations. . . . And, most fascinating of all, was the endless surge and duplication of chromosomes.

The chromosomes were easily recognizable: they were brightly hued (the word comes from the Greek *chromos,* or color), strung together like tiny beads on a necklace. For a time, they would exist at random within the nucleus, ebbing and flowing with the rhythm of the nuclear tides. At some point, however, they would line themselves up along the midline of the cell (How? Why?). . . . Like expert dancers, the chromosomes would align themselves in precise formation, every one— and every part of one—knowing its exact place. Most miraculous of all, was when the chromosomes—and the entire cell around them—would begin to split. Slowly the halves would move apart, becoming gradually elongated, like soft dough in a baker's hands. At some point, when the protoplasmic "dough" had been stretched too thin, the chromosome necklaces would tear—precisely in half!—one half remaining in each of the new-formed nuclei of the two new cells.

And yet, the miracle is not yet completely told. The chromosomes had not merely divided, but also *replicated,* so that each of the two cells had the exact same amount of chromosomal material as the original, single cell had! Where did the extra matter come from? And what was the chemical agent that "taught" the chromosomes their complicated, vital dance?

Sometimes Dr. Eberhard became almost dizzy in the contemplation of these mysteries. The questions were too immense, there was simply too much to know. As his thoughts plunged into the abstract, he would begin to feel that he was standing on the very top of a high mountain—the very highest place, higher than any man had come before. . . . There was nothing above him to give him shelter, nothing alongside him that he might hold on to. . . . He felt horribly alone on his eminence, buffeted by winds, by mind-storms, liable to the most horrible catapulting falls, into oblivion, into madness. . . . When these spells came upon Dr. Eberhard, he was grateful to have the plodding, mundane slides and petri dishes to return to.

It was a relief to deal with the simple, concrete facts of fish eggs and fish sperm. It was restful to the mind to let the hands perform the functions of preparing slides, to let the fingers automatically play over the complex focussing devices of the high-powered electron microscopes. It was relaxing to be taken away from the mind-boggling implications of one's work, and to operate in the physical realm—weighing things, looking at things, using the apparatus.

And it was also relaxing to sip a beer with his two colleagues in the lounge at the end of the working day. This was a habit that the three doctors had gotten into very early in their shared research. And in a short time it had become a ritual, a ritual that each of them looked forward to.

The threesome would leave the lab together and walk down the long, fluorescently lit hallway to the lounge, the younger men flanking Dr. Schreiber, his short, slightly stooped form providing a touching counterpoint to the lean, self-assured strides of the assisting doctors. Once in the lounge, John Goodwin would make a beeline for the refrigerator, while Drs. Eberhard and Schreiber settled themselves into a pair of brightly colored vinyl chairs. (Dr. Eberhard would throw himself down with abandon, with all the unconscious zest of healthful youth while Dr. Schreiber would settle in slowly, his old man's physical cautiousness pervading his every movement.) John Goodwin would pop the beers and ceremoniously present them to his colleagues, and then he would sit himself down and cross his legs—his long calves and king-size feet always looked a bit incongruous poking out from between the panels of his lab coat—making him appear a bit like an overgrown boy.

How good that first long swallow of cold beer always tasted! How delightfully the grainy tang of it swept away all traces of the sharp unnatural odors of the laboratory!

That first swig of beer—coupled with the inexpressible pleasure of sitting still in a comfortable chair for five minutes—invariably put the three doctors in a convivial mood, and they talked animatedly among themselves. In the early part of their association, their talk was generally connected with their research, or with related fields. They might gratefully put fish eggs out of their minds, yet find themselves returning again and again to the mysteries of cell structure, mutations and reproduction.

As time went on, however, and the two younger men became more comfortable in the presence of their older colleague, their conversation ranged further and further away from the mysterious O+ factor, until finally, they could discuss any subject as peers. Old Dr. Schreiber may have had an immense dignity and a terrifically august presence, but he was no prig, and he was not so far removed from the ardent impulses of his own young manhood that he'd lost sight of the needs and inclinations of others.

One afternoon, in a particularly relaxed and even mischievous mood, he came right out and asked them how they were making out at the facility.

"How do you mean?" Alfred asked, though he knew perfectly well how the question was meant.

"You know," said Dr. Schreiber, "with women, with sex."

Alfred was as embarrassed by the question as if it had been put to him by his own father. John Goodwin positively blushed, his birdlike eyelashes fluttering a mile a minute. Neither of them managed to speak for some seconds.

"Come, come, boys," continued Dr. Schreiber, "it's not such a difficult or unreasonable question, is it? Are you afraid that I'm going to move in on your territory? Listen, I'm interested in a purely scientific way, in a spirit of detached psychological and sociological inquiry. I want to know what happens when the government decides to plop down a research facility in the middle of nowhere and stocks it with a predominantly young and single group of men and women. The nearest town is thirty miles away, and its residents have practically nothing in common with the people who work here. Now, what do you do? Do you seek a change of pace in the arms of the town women? Or do you stick close to home and go after the technicians and women doctors here?"

Alfred and John looked at each other and couldn't help smiling, like boys who have been caught at something naughty—but something they're proud of nevertheless.

"Well," Alfred said, breaking the silence, "since you're asking in the name of scientific inquiry—we do a little of both."

"Ah, good," Dr. Schreiber said. "Now our little survey is getting somewhere. Well, I guess the next question should be what similarities and differences are there between the two."

"Well," John piped up, "the similarities are pretty obvious! So I guess we should concentrate on the differences?"

"Very well," said Dr. Schreiber. "What, then, are the differences?"

"First of all," Alfred mused, "when we go into town, we're considered exotic."

"Exotic?" Dr. Schreiber echoed.

"Sure," Alfred said. "The townspeople regard Brookside as a different world, and they think of us as practically a different species. They mistrust us in a way, but they're also intrigued by us. The women like us because they think we're wonder workers."

"So then," said Dr. Schreiber, "it is easy to get them to go to bed with you?"

"Sometimes," Alfred said. "It goes to extremes—either it is very easy, or it's impossible. If it's easy, it can be very nice—making love with a woman from the town is like taking a brief vacation—a quick jaunt down to the tropics, as it were. If it seems like it's going to be impossible, you give up and try elsewhere."

"Just like that?" said Dr. Schreiber, a look of mock-offended gallantry on his lined, expressive face. "But what of true desire, of devotion, of love?"

"That's not what we're talking about," said John Goodwin.

"True enough," said Schreiber. "A clear-headed distinction—the hallmark of a good scientist. Well, what else can be said about the women from the town?"

"They have a strong leaning, all in all, toward matrimony," Alfred reported. "They have somehow formed the rather bizarre notion that it's an honor to be married to a doctor."

"How do these absurd rumors get started?" Schreiber smiled.

"I don't know," said John, "but they certainly can be an inconvenience. That's one of the major advantages of playing around with the women at the facility. They know the *real* story about doctors. A lot of them *are* doctors. So you don't have to work your way through all the layers of myth to get down to the skin."

"As it were," put in Schreiber, coyly clearing his throat. "But, in any case, I would expect that the sex to be had among the staff would be far more interesting than the sex to be had in the town."

"Why would you expect that?" Alfred asked, though the look on his face made it clear that he agreed, and perhaps even had a theory of his own about the subject.

"Because," began Dr. Schreiber, "I believe that working in the biological sciences does interesting things to people's sexuality. You know, I'm sure, all those crude old jokes about gynecologists, about what they do when they get home and so forth—well, gynecology is obviously an extreme example, but I think that, to some degree, the same principle pertains to all sorts of biological work. You enter into a very intimate relationship with the body and with biological processes. You examine every aspect of it. You study the way the body works. You become obsessed with it."

"I think you're right," Alfred concurred. "Very right. In fact, I think you're so right that I can't help wondering if you're speaking theoretically, or out of actual experience."

"Well," Schreiber answered with a nostalgic but sly wink, "I wasn't always an old man, you know. I may only be a theorist now, but I've done my first-hand research along the way. . . ."

"I agree with you, too," said John. "I've found that among science people, nothing is forbidden. I guess if you spend your days experimenting, you may as well carry it over into the nights!"

"True enough," said Dr. Schreiber. "But I think

there's more to it than that. I feel that the sexual abandon of scientists—of women scientists, in particular—has to do with a yearning to recapture mystery, to get beyond what they already know about the body and how it works, and to plunge headlong into the realm that they don't know about, that *nobody* knows about."

"Exactly," Alfred said. "If I may carry the discussion into the more specific: A woman biologist, say, knows exactly what causes the penis to become erect; for her, the occurrence is not a miracle, but a perfectly logical consequence of various physical and chemical events. Similarly, she knows exactly what is going on—biologically, that is—when her vagina grows wet, or when her nipples become aroused. Those things make *sense,* and sense, whatever else it's good for, is not terribly good for sex. So, to get beyond the point where things make sense, men and women of science have to up the ante, so to speak. They have to make things so heightened, so abandoned, that they *forget* that they know what's going on! They have to work harder to lose themselves. . . ."

"Bravo, Dr. Eberhard!" Schreiber cried enthusiastically. "Well put! And perfectly correct! That's why nurses have the sort of reputation they do. Do you think it's an accident? Not at all! They're in intimate contact with bodies all day long—and much of that contact is none too pleasant. That's why, when they have sex, they have to go at it like crazy! They have to get so lost in it that they lose sight of the fact that it is in fact a body they're getting pleasure from, not so very different from the other bodies. . . ."

Dr. Schreiber suddenly broke off, surprised and perhaps a little abashed at his own eloquence and fire. There were several moments of amused silence, as Drs. Eberhard and Goodwin smiled broadly at their elder colleague. With his face flushed, his white hair tousled and mussed—he truly resembled a sly and spunky satyr.

"Dear me," he said, after a pause. "Don't tell me that, at this late date, I'm becoming a typical dirty old man!"

"Not at all." Eberhard winked. "It was all in the name of scientific inquiry, just as you said."

"Er, yes," said Dr. Schreiber. "The sort of scientific inquiry that generally goes on in locker rooms. . . . Well, no harm done in any case. I'm glad to hear that you two fellows are taking care of yourselves. It's bad enough to be frustrated in our work—we shouldn't be frustrated in our play, too. Well," he sighed, "I'd best be going. I could use a little nap before dinner."

"Will you have another beer with us first?" asked Goodwin.

"No thank you," Dr. Schreiber said. "I need sleep more than alcohol. I'll see the two of you tomorrow."

The three men exchanged farewells, and as Dr. Schreiber left the lounge, John Goodwin opened another beer for himself and his friend.

"He's a remarkable man," John noted.

"Yes," Alfred agreed. "A fine scientist, a magnetic personality. . . . We sound like we're eulogizing him—let's not be so solemn! What do you intend to do this evening, John?"

"I don't know. I'm pretty knocked out. I may just do some reading and try to sack out early. What're you doing, Alfred?"

"I think I'll pay a call on Sharon," Eberhard mused. "That 'survey' of Dr. Schreiber's has made me rather horny—it's remarkable the way the mind affects the body sometimes."

"It's equally remarkable the way the body affects the mind," said John Goodwin with a smile. "But do you think Sharon will have you?"

"Why not?" asked Dr. Eberhard innocently.

"You know why not," said John Goodwin, the barest trace of censure creeping into his voice. "She doesn't really like the way you treat her. She's spoken to me about it."

"Really?" said Dr. Eberhard. "What has she said?"

"Nothing she hasn't already told you directly. She feels that you see her for sex. She's resentful that you practically ignore her the rest of the time. It frustrates her that you don't accept other things from her, other sorts of affection, and that you don't offer her any either."

"For God's sake, John," Eberhard said. "What does she want? A romance? A love affair? An engagement ring, maybe? You know, it's one thing to have to go through nonsense like that with the town women, but it's another thing to have to go through it with the women here, with *scientists*. Why can't she just accept the thing for what it is? Doesn't she enjoy the sex?"

"How should I know?" said John Goodwin. "I suppose she enjoys the sex—why else would she agree to see you at all? But it's not fair to just disregard anything else that she might want out of it."

"I'm not disregarding it," Alfred protested. "I'm just saying that I'm not in the market for whatever it is she wants to have with me. I haven't got the time for it, and frankly, I haven't got the inclination."

"What do you mean, you haven't got the inclination?" asked John Goodwin. "What does inclination have to do with it? Either you're in love with a woman, or you're not."

"Isn't that a bit naive, John? I think it works quite differently. I think one has to have the inclination to be in love, before one even begins to think in terms of whether a woman is lovable or otherwise. Sharon may very well be thoroughly lovable, but I'm not inclined to be in love. I'm inclined to have sex with women I find desirable. And I find Sharon very desirable. Is that such a dastardly way of looking at it? I don't force myself on her, do I? I offer myself on certain terms, and she is free to accept me or to turn me away."

"Well," said Goodwin, "for your sake, I hope she accepts you. But I can't help thinking it would be better for her if she mustered the discipline to turn you away."

As it happened, however, Sharon did not turn Alfred Eberhard away. When she answered his knock that evening, her face was the face of a woman who knew she should refuse, but who knew she would not. Her expression was partly expectant, partly sad, partly angry—and partly proud of herself. Her pride stemmed from overcoming her own compunction—she had admitted to herself, weeks ago, that a relationship with Alfred Eberhard meant nothing more than sleeping with him now and then. She finally had overcome her scruples about the matter-of-factness of the setup and could just now let herself enjoy it—though of course, she still resented Alfred, just as she desired him. She was thoroughly ambivalent about him, just as she was thoroughly ambivalent about her own participation in this lovely but loveless affair.

"Hello, Alfred," she said, trying to sound casual. "What brings you around, as if I didn't know?"

"I wanted to see you," he said. "May I come in?"

"Sure," Sharon told him. Already she knew that she would yield to him again. But she didn't know if she would win or lose by yielding or even if there *was* anything to win or lose with this strange, cold attractive man. "Hard day at the lab, huh?" she said. "Coming to good old Sharon for a winder-downer, eh?" It made her feel better, somehow, to goad him, to be coarse with him. And yet, in some part of her, she realized that the irony was aimed at herself.

"You could put it that way if you like," Eberhard answered. "I wouldn't put it quite as crudely, but what the hell. Don't you ever need a winder-downer at the end of the day?"

"Of course I do," she said. "You know I do."

Despite herself, she smiled. Her smile was no less ambiguous than her opening scowl had been—but it was a good deal prettier. Sharon Ferguson had a soft and mobile face, and when she smiled, she looked very girlish, more innocent than she in fact was. Her forehead crinkled up, her brows raised, her wide-set gray-blue eyes sparkled with an impish gleam. Her arched lips pulled back from her small and perfect teeth, strands of sinew stood out in her thin and graceful neck, as if her entire body was being pulled upward toward that smile.

"That's better," Alfred said. "You look more convincing when you smile than when you pout. You're not a very convincing pouter, you know. Well, what's new?"

"Do you really want to know, Alfred? Do you really want to hear what's new in the life of your favorite gamma ray technician and easy lay?"

"Well," he said, "if you put it that way, I guess I don't really want to know. I was just asking to be polite."

"Well, let's not be polite, Alfred. Let's not be polite, and let's not be romantic, and let's not pout."

"All right," he said. He enjoyed Sharon's feistiness. It lent a certain perverse air to their lovemaking—a perversity he did not require, but which he could not deny relishing. "What, then, shall we be, if not polite or romantic?"

"Let's not *be* anything," said Sharon. "Let's just screw."

Sharon moved toward him suddenly, intent and unrestrained. He watched her eyes close, saw her lips part as she lifted her face up toward his. Slowly, he brought his mouth down onto hers, but even before their lips had touched, her hand had reached out to caress his groin.

If it was to be pure sex, she thought, let it be free of all conventions, let it be a raw and undisguised appetite for each other's genitals. . . .

They kissed, their tongues exploring the warm canyons of each other's mouths, but the depths of the kiss was only a backdrop for the more insistent sensations of the ample member now swelling against the pressure of Sharon's eager hand. Through the fabric of his trousers, as she traced the shape of his rising sex, he felt the heatless, insulated grasping of her fingers. His arms wrapped around her back, and he felt the soft collapse of her breasts against his ribs as he pulled her close. He reached into her slacks, letting his fingers work their way under the elastic waistband to the small of her back which was moist with coital sweat. His hand, moving down over the curve of her rump, encountered the thin film of nylon panties. The panties were pasted over her damp flesh, clinging to her deliciously. . . .

Frenziedly, Sharon attacked the buttons of Eberhard's shirt. She ran her fingers greedily through his chest hair when his torso was exposed. Her fingers played about his belt, now plucking at the buckle, then opening the trousers. She dropped to her knees, following the pants as they fell, untied his shoes, tugging at the laces with her fingers while her mouth worked elsewhere.

Her own clothes were stripped off in a minute and she stood vulnerable before him, her collarbone beautiful with shadowed hollows, her breasts full, nipples taut and beckoning. . . . Her belly, flat and strong, showed just the slightest bit of roundness at the navel, at the place where the abdomen began its slope downward to the pubis, which was covered with a downy mask of chestnut hair.

She grasped him roughly by the elbow, taking him over to the bed. He allowed himself to be led, reveling in the passive role, the role of one sought after. Sharon tugged his arm and he tumbled onto the mattress as if he had been thrown.

Her body was alongside his now, the heat coming off her in humid summer waves. Alfred lay still against her, waiting, forcing her to act. . . .

Sharon hesitated—was it a victory to be the aggressive one, or was there defeat in being forced to be the leader? It didn't matter, she couldn't let it matter. She reached down for him and found him ready, grasping at the heat of his hardness. She pushed him over, onto his back, and rose up on him, using him, using herself on him, taking to fend off being taken, being taken by herself. . . .

Later, Sharon's pout returned.

"What's wrong?" asked Eberhard.

"I don't feel so good about it," she said. "I love it and I hate it, and each time I tell myself I'm not going to do it anymore. But I do."

Yes, thought Dr. Eberhard sleepily, you do. Women generally do. It was not vanity, but only history, which made Eberhard think this. He'd been in similar situations before. With similar results. Women enjoyed him, whether or not they liked him. But he was fortunate. Nature had overlooked no detail in her bounteousness toward him.

Five

It was now 1965. Two years had passed since Drs. Eberhard and Goodwin joined the staff of Emanuel Schreiber. During that time, certain things had changed, while others had not.

Sharon Ferguson had passed out of Alfred Eberhard's life, and her place—quite literally—had been taken by a succession of other women, all of whom had, in turn, faded out. Dr. Joseph McQuinn, who had headed Brookside when Eberhard began his career there, had retired, and in his place was Dr. Kenton—who, as always, had proven to be a master politician and manipulator in the power struggle which followed Dr. McQuinn's resignation.

Another change that had occurred very, very gradually, almost imperceptibly was that Dr. Schreiber had gotten older and wearier. His mind still retained its spectacular acuity, but his body was deteriorating; there could be no question of it. Day to day, his younger colleagues watched with concern and compassion as his steps grew more labored, his speech thickened with the failing of motor processes.

One thing that had not changed, however, was

that cancer remained uncured. Research followed many avenues—and every avenue seemed to lead to the same dead end. The work of Drs. Schreiber, Eberhard and Goodwin was no exception in this regard. The O+factor still eluded them. The mysterious acidic protein still flirted with them, appearing for a moment in the nuclei of various cells, only to dissolve before it could be caught.

Foxlike, it showed its face only as a decoy, before it scampered off in some new, unpredictable direction. Thousands of hours had been spent in the minutest examination of the cancer cells and the developing fish eggs, though not one conclusive bit of evidence had been found. However, it could not be said that all the work was fruitless—far from it. In the course of their studies, Drs. Eberhard and Goodwin had discovered several previously unknown facts about the passage of certain ions through the cell membrane; in addition, though they failed to locate the *specific* protein they were searching for, they learned much about how proteins are broken down by the nuclear enzymes. Both men had presented several reports on their findings, and the importance of their work was not unrecognized—it was already rumored that they were in line for promotions to the status of senior researcher—a nearly unprecedented honor for men who were just turning thirty. In fact, their research was so productive, it had became something of a joke at Brookside. Eberhard and Goodwin were known as the two men who could find out anything about the cell, except what they were looking for.

But, it was still the O+factor they were after, and its continuing evasiveness was understandably discouraging. Dr. Schreiber had begun to doubt that his original analogy—so bold, so persuasive!—had any real validity whatever.

"I don't know," he said during their afternoon beer-break in the researchers' lounge. "I just don't know. The idea seemed so good, so right. But if it *was* right, I can't imagine that we would have come this far without finding *something*. . . . I don't know, I'm beginning to be afraid that I've been wasting the time of two very talented young doctors, and spending millions of dollars of the taxpayers' money—all in support of the last wild guess of a pig-headed old man—an old man who maybe should have stopped making guesses years before. Well, I guess I'm just like a quarterback who doesn't know when to get out of the league. I'll have to get knocked on my ass a few times and throw a couple of key interceptions before it'll get through my head."

"Now, hold on a minute, Dr. Schreiber," said John Goodwin. "First of all, I still think your idea is a sound one—regardless of whether it leads anywhere or not. *Nobody's* getting anywhere, in terms of hard and fast results. Everybody's just guessing. And I feel as strongly now as I did on day one, that your guess was more imaginative, and had more of a backbone in sound, scientific thinking, than nine-tenths of the so-called research that goes on here."

"Well, thank you, John," said Dr. Schreiber. "It's kind of you to say so. I don't mean to run myself down, or to sound self-pitying. It's just that—well, let's be frank—I'm not going to live much longer. One needn't look at me under a microscope to know that. Dying doesn't bother me that much— I'd prefer to go on living, of course—but I'd had such great hopes for this project. Maybe it was just my vanity. You know—wanting to go out in a blaze of glory. . . ."

There was a silence, and the younger men did not know what to say. They felt that any pronouncement would be a cheapening of the high unpitying sadness they felt at the prospect of Dr. Schreiber's passing. The silence lingered until it seemed that the subject could be changed.

"Dr. Schreiber," said Eberhard, "I, too, feel that your idea is basically a sound one. But, for the past several weeks, I've been thinking about a slight but significant refinement of it. I hadn't intended mentioning it until I'd thought it out more fully—but, since the subject has been raised, I thought . . ."

"Yes, yes?" said Dr. Schreiber, his voice suddenly animated, a trace of his youthful vigor evident in his expression and his forward-leaning posture. "Tell me, please, what it is you have thought?"

"Well," began Eberhard, "the connection you drew between cancer and reproduction was based on the fact that both phenomena entail a rampant growth of cells, and in both cases, the growth results in a new entity—tumor or fetus—which, strictly speaking, is foreign to the organism in which it develops. In both cases, or so we believe, the growth is triggered by the action of some unknown chemical agent on the chromosomal material of the host cell. So far, the analogy holds."

"Yes, fine," said Dr. Schreiber, his face pinched in intense concentration. "But go on, where does the refinement come in?"

"Well," said Dr. Eberhard, "it seems to me that the analogy, though valid, is not precise, for the following reason: In cancer, whatever happens, happens in the chromosomes of a *single* individual; in sexual reproduction, the chromosomal structure becomes a mixture of the genetic material of *two* individuals. Now, we can't really expect a single set of chromosomes to act the same way as a *blend* of chromosomes."

"I see what you're saying," Goodwin exclaimed. His hand was on his forehead, as if he were massaging his brain into peak activity. "You're saying that the mixed chromosomes might affect *each other,* so that there'd be no need for another chemical agent."

"Either that," said Eberhard, "or the chemical agent may be present, but in a different role. There's no way of knowing. But the point is, we're confusing matters by trying to compare a *pure chromosome* situation with a *mixed chromosome* situation—it's like adding apples to oranges."

"I see," said Dr. Schreiber, after a thoughtful pause. "You're absolutely right—it is a definite weakness in the entire framework of the research we've been doing. . . . But, Dr. Eberhard, what is the alternative?"

"The alternative?" Eberhard said, almost to himself, wishing to be absolutely certain of the question being asked before he uttered his radical answer.

"Yes," said Dr. Schreiber. "You say that the analogy between reproduction and cancer is basically sound; but you also say that a double-chromosome configuration cannot be studied alongside a single-chromosome configuration. How, then, can those statements be reconciled?"

"There's only one way," said Dr. Eberhard softly. "We must try to generate a fetus asexually. We must try to create a new individual from a single set of chromosomes! Only then will the analogy be rigorously correct. Only then can we feel confident that the O+factor—if it exists at all—will be brought into play."

There was a long silence as the other two doctors pondered Eberhard's startling but perfectly logical theory. After some moments, John Goodwin pursed his lips and let out a long slow whistle.

"Jesus, Alfred," he said, "that all makes perfect sense—but somehow, it's a disturbing idea."

"Why disturbing?" asked Dr. Eberhard.

"Well," said Goodwin, "I don't suppose it's something that can be put in scientific terms. It's just disturbing, that's all. The whole idea of *generating* a fetus. . . ."

"Well, look," said Eberhard. "The whole idea of sexual reproduction, of chromosome-sharing, is a pretty new one, biologically speaking. Originally, all life reproduced by simply replicating itself, by cloning. If anything, it's the idea of sex that's disturbing."

"No, Alfred, I don't agree," John said. "Nature had a reason for moving away from cloning and into sexual reproduction. It's the sharing of chromosomes that gives rise to variety within a species, that allows for advances and useful hybrids. And, if we carry it a step farther, philosophically, it's the whole idea of gene-sharing that sets the stage for love and for loyalty among people. And aside from that, it's the dilution of one's own genes that spares man the ultimate confrontation with himself—and, if we can trust the literature on the subject, that confrontation is neither pleasant nor healthy."

"For God's sake, John," cut in Dr. Eberhard, "I'm talking medicine, not philosophy."

"Are you sure you can detach the two?" asked John Goodwin.

"I can for now. Besides, I'm not talking about cloning people—I'm talking about cloning laboratory animals—fishes!"

"But still," insisted Goodwin, "the process, once explored, would be the same."

"Gentlemen, gentlemen," interrupted Dr. Schreiber, "one thing at a time. No doubt the subject has all sorts of ethical ramifications which may have to be dealt with eventually. But before we worry about moral implications, let us try to determine if this procedure is even practically *possible*. Are we even sure that it can be done? Has it ever been done before?"

"As far as I know," said Eberhard, "an actual clone of a many-celled animal has never been accomplished, though there has been a bit of writing on the subject, and several procedural schemata have been proposed. It seems to be the consensus, though, that cloning is definitely possible. There is no strong theoretical evidence against it, and there's a good deal for it."

"Such as?" asked Dr. Schreiber.

"Well," said Dr. Eberhard, "for one thing, the cytoplasm of a fertile egg is sufficient unto itself for the support and nourishment of a developing embryo. The sperm contributes nothing—or so it's believed—and so, in that respect, the sperm is incidental—it could be replaced by any other cell. Further, the phenomenon of parthenogenesis suggests that, in lower animals at least, the egg is incapable of distinguishing between pure and blended genes. If the right amount of chromosomal material finds its way into the egg at the proper time, the egg begins to develop, regardless of the source of the chromosomes. Now, of course, those are only theoretical arguments. Whether they will hold true in a laboratory situation is quite another question."

"Of course," said Dr. Schreiber. "But tell me, Dr. Eberhard, do you personally believe that a clone of the sort you're describing can actually be achieved?"

"Yes, Dr. Schreiber, I do."

"Well then," said Dr. Schreiber, "I suggest that we try to do it! What the hell? We can't do any worse than we're doing now! What do you say, Dr. Goodwin? Do you agree?"

John Goodwin spent a moment gazing at the enthusiastic faces of his colleagues. They had not looked so vibrant, so eager, in months. "Yes," he said in agreement, though his own face was somehow wistful, as if he foresaw where this tampering with nature might ultimately lead. . . .

Six

From that day forth, the research of Schreiber, Eberhard and Goodwin was embarked on a radical new path. The men ignored the cultures on which they had worked so long. They discarded the petri dishes which had been the object of their attention for two years, they destroyed the naturally fertilized fish eggs which had been growing in the incubators, and they began studying unfertilized eggs, trying to discover how the eggs might be prepared for the introduction of the foreign cells which, it was hoped, would develop within them, as if it were a natural growth.

The three doctors were now involved in true ground-breaking work. There were no precedents for them to look to for assistance or advice. There was no record of *any* laboratory studies, only the sketchiest theoretical treatises. Every procedure had to be invented from scratch, every operation performed upon the eggs had to be intuited.

In principle, the researchers' method was elegantly simple. All they had to do was to remove or destroy the chromosome-containing nucleus of the egg, while leaving intact its embryo-supporting body; this accomplished—in principle—they had to inject the egg with the nucleus of a body cell from a living fish—keeping the cell alive through the process of removing one nucleus and injecting another. From that point on, it was simply a matter of waiting to see if the injected nucleus would "take," if the egg would respond to the presence of a full set of chromosomes and begin to develop. It was as simple as that, in principle.

In practice, however, the task was monumentally difficult, with every step of the process presenting nearly insurmountable obstacles. It proved impossible to remove the nucleus. How could they probe the interior of the egg without damaging the cytoplasm, rendering it incapable of supporting an embryo? And even if they could scan the interior, what instrument was fine enough, precise enough, to locate and pluck out only one microscopic element, leaving the rest intact?

The obvious alternative to removing the nucleus, was to destroy it, but this, too, posed problems. The nucleus could be destroyed with radiation, but could it be done without also destroying or contaminating the cytoplasm? Just how far could the egg be tampered with, before it would lose its fertility?

Even assuming that the operations that needed to be performed on the egg could be successfully accomplished, there was still another entire set of hurdles that had to be topped in dealing with the isolation and injection of the "fertilizing" cell. *That* cell would have to be kept alive through the entire trauma of its removal from the body, its handling and transfer to the ultra-fine hypodermic through which it would be injected into the egg.

If it survived all that, it would still have to adjust itself to the chemistry of the new environment in which it found itself—and there was no way of foreseeing whether or not that adjustment would take place. The slightest shift in pH might be sufficient to destroy the foreign cell; the presence of an unfriendly enzyme might very well dissolve it! And even if the injected cell were not actually killed by all of that, who could say what all the handling and transplanting would do to its metabolism. Perhaps it might lose its capacity to reproduce altogether.

Further, as if all those contingencies were not enough to thwart the most avid researchers, there was the final daunting possibility: What if the egg could be de-nucleized, the body cell transplanted, and then, when they were put together, the results were a big zero.

This was a very real possibility, and an agonizing one. There was no assurance that a successful clone would occur, even if all conditions were optimal. What a grim irony it would be if all the work involved in preparing the cells, in keeping them healthy, in combining them, should be directed to no purpose, should be done in the service of a "mating" that would never take place in a million years. . . .

Yet in spite of all these obstacles, the trio plunged into their new project with amazing energy. Their enthusiasm, drained out of them by the two years of goose chasing after the mysterious acidic protein, was now restored. They were once again confident of victory, though victory, if it came, would necessarily be won slowly. Six months passed in the mere *designing* of procedures. Half a year was gone before the first foreign cell was even introduced into the naked cytoplasm of an egg.

In the course of those six months, there were several important political occurrences at Brookside, which, over time, were to have a great impact on the future of Dr. Schreiber's project, and on the subsequent careers of Drs. Eberhard and Goodwin.

Shortly after the initiation of the second phase of their association with Dr. Schreiber, both Alfred Eberhard and John Goodwin were promoted to positions of senior researchers. This promotion came as a surprise to no one—although few members of the staff expected it to happen quite so soon. The two men were barely thirty, and, brilliant or otherwise, was it proper that they should be raised above the level of so many of their seniors?

As far as Dr. Schreiber was concerned, the answer to that question was a resounding "Yes." In fact, he had been instrumental in securing the advancement of his two young colleagues. Shortly after beginning his investigation into the possibility of producing a laboratory clone, Schreiber had given another of his Friday afternoon presentations. At that meeting, in the presence of the entire staff, he generously announced that Drs. Eberhard and Goodwin should be considered not assistants or subordinates in the project, but full and equal associates. Further, he acknowledged that it was Dr. Eberhard, and not himself, who had provided the new and—in Dr. Schreiber's phrase—unquestionably brilliant, theoretical impetus to the undertaking.

In light of praise such as that, from a source as universally respected as Dr. Schreiber, the directors could not fail to promote the two young researchers.

As stated, their promotion was remarkable only in terms of its timing.

The other political event, however, was nothing short of shocking, and it caused a hubbub which did not die down for some time.

Dr. David Sims, who had been promoted to administrative assistant when Dr. Kenton ascended to the directorship, suddenly resigned. All sorts of polite reasons were brought forth, but the real reason, known to everyone, was whispered freely among the gossip-loving staff: David Sims could not stand Dr. Kenton, could not bear his pettiness, his snide attitude toward anyone who differed from his starched and lackluster opinions.

Sims had taken the job of assistant director in the hope that he might have some buffering effect on Dr. Kenton's arbitrary use of power, that he might make himself heard on questions of policy. Though Sims was the better scientist and the better man, Kenton was the better politician, and he had control of the purse strings. Kenton had the friends in Washington, Kenton decided who got funded and who didn't. Sims had found himself helpless in the face of Kenton's machinations. . . .

Compromise had failed, confrontation had failed—and so Sims had resigned.

Sims' resignation was something of a black eye to Dr. Kenton, but, as with any situation, there had to be a way to wrest some gain, some advantage from it—and no one doubted that the wily Kenton would find it. The assumption was that he would appoint one of his cronies to the vacant post—a move which would further consolidate his unpopularity, as it further cemented his power.

When the time came for Dr. Kenton to announce his choice of a replacement, however, he surprised everyone by offering the post to Emanual Schreiber. A less likely choice could hardly have been imagined! Not that Dr. Schreiber was not qualified for the job or deserving of the honor—indeed he was. But it was well known that he and Dr. Kenton were long-standing enemies. Dr. Schreiber made no effort to conceal his slight opinion of the man who was nominally his "superior"; and Dr. Kenton had just enough sensitivity to recognize Dr. Schreiber as a worthy man who despised him. What, then, could have been Kenton's reasoning in selecting Schreiber for this high post? Was it an attempt at a reconciliation? Was it a swallowing of Kenton's pride, an acknowledgement of the merits of a man he had made a show of underestimating for so long?

The entire staff discussed the question long and hard, but no unanimity of opinion could be reached as to Kenton's motives. It was Dr. Schreiber himself who pinpointed them.

Drs. Eberhard and Goodwin approached him in

the lounge, as soon as they had heard he was being offered the post. As a matter of form, they congratulated him, though they could see in his face that he was not happy about the offer.

"Congratulations my ass!" said the spunky old microbiologist. "The offer of that job is an insult, a ploy, a malicious joke—"

"How do you mean?" asked Dr. Eberhard.

"Look," said Schreiber, "Matthew Kenton hates my guts. I've known that for years. It's never bothered me—as a matter of fact, I've taken a certain pride in it. He's not offering this position as a favor, you can bet on that."

"Then why is he doing it?" asked John Goodwin.

"Probably for a number of reasons," said Dr. Schreiber. "I've known this man a long time, I know how he operates. Look, he offers me the job, and that makes him look like a nice guy—one point for him. Now, if I take the job, I'm working *under* him, and he'll make my life as miserable as he can—that's two more points for him. He'll try to load me down with administrative nonsense, and at my age, I simply don't have the strength to be both an administrator and a scientist, which is to say, he'll be in a position to deprive me of my work, my *real* work. It's his way of stopping our research. Aside from which, he knows I'm not going to last too long, so he'll put up with me for a year or two, after which he'll feel free to put one of his chums into the job. And all of that means, that I'm not going to take the job."

"You're not?" said Dr. Eberhard.

"Of course I'm not!" said Dr. Schreiber. "I have

nothing to gain from it. I'm an old man—do I need the prestige? Do I need the post to advance my career? That's absurd. I want to be left alone to finish up whatever I can finish up in the laboratory.

"But let's try to figure out what will happen when I tell Kenton I don't want the assistant's job. He'll still look like the nice guy for offering. Perhaps I'll look like an ingrate for refusing—not that that bothers me. But then Kenton will probably just go ahead and appoint one of his dull bureaucratic puppets to the post. If anyone protests, he can always say that he offered the position to me first, and what else was he supposed to do? And I'd feel indirectly responsible for the installation of still more mediocrity in high places. Damn! I wish there were some way around it!"

Dr. Schreiber knotted his old hand into a fist and pounded softly on the arm of his chair. His face was red and his mouth twitched slightly at the corners.

"Don't worry about it so much," said John Goodwin consolingly. "Look, you'll turn the job down, Kenton will do what he pleases, and there's an end to it. We'll go back to the lab and mind our own business. We've managed to ignore him this far, we'll ignore him a little longer."

"Yes, you're right, of course," said Dr. Schreiber. "But still, it's maddening to be used as part of that bastard's schemes! There has to be a way we can turn this thing around, a way we can get some good out of it."

Dr. Schreiber again fell silent and drifted into

thought, clutching the arms of his vinyl chair. His eyes seemed far away behind his thick glasses. He did not speak for some moments, and when he did, his voice came forth with a startling suddenness.

"Alfred," he said, "do you want the job?"

"I?" said Dr. Eberhard, unable to utter more than a single surprised syllable.

"Yes, you!" said Dr. Schreiber, his excitement at the idea gathering force. "Why not?"

"But Dr. Schreiber," spluttered Eberhard, "I'm so young. I've been here only a few years, I've only just been made a senior—"

"So what?" said Dr. Schreiber vehemently. "What does any of that matter? You are very likely the most brilliant man at this facility, and one of the most dedicated. You're one of the few people who seems to have enough intellectual verve to handle both administration and research. And you seem to have enough force of character to be able to stand up to Kenton's power plays. Look, Alfred, you're at the beginning of your career. A post like this now, and you can be anywhere in ten years. You can be head of your own facility—you could be in Washington, helping to determine policy. You could do things that really mattered. Would you accept this post if it was offered to you?"

"Well," said Dr. Eberhard, uncharacteristically flustered, "yes, of course. But it hasn't been offered to me! It's been offered to *you*, and, though I'm flattered by your idea, I don't really think you have the power to pass it on."

"That's true," said Dr. Schreiber. "I don't *offi-*

cially have the power to pass it on. But if, at the assembly at which I'm scheduled to announce my decision, I decline, and follow my declining with an enthusiastic plea that the post be offered to you—do you think, at a moment like that, with audience sympathy unquestionably with us, that even Matthew Kenton would dare to deny me my request? He'll *have* to go along with it. What a victory! I will have done my part to advance the cause of science over that of politics, and you, my dear Dr. Eberhard, will be launched in fine style."

And so it happened that, at an unprecedentedly early age, Dr. Alfred Eberhard came to be second in command at Brookside. His youth and relative inexperience caused quite a stir, though, in terms of ability and dedication, no one could quibble with his qualifications—not even Matthew Kenton, who rather grudgingly offered him the post amid a noisy acclamation. It was, in fact, a spectacular victory though an equivocal one. Dr. Eberhard had earned Dr. Kenton's barely disguised enmity, and could expect only hindrance from him in the future. . . .

Meanwhile, back in the laboratory, the trio's research was progressing slowly—but it was progressing. They were still very far away from producing the clone "birth" they were after, but they had learned much about the handling of the egg and body cells, and their eventual goal seemed at least technically attainable.

In the course of the long months of designing

and preparing their experiments, the three scientists had decided on a seemingly small but very significant change in their plans—instead of using fish eggs, which had given them so much trouble in the beginning, they switched to frog's eggs, with which they were having better luck. The frog's eggs were much larger, and so, in a purely mechanical way, they were easier to work with. In addition, the amphibian egg seemed to be more durable. The membrane which surrounded it was more pliable and resilient than that of the fish egg. It was possible to puncture the egg with a hypodermic for the insertion of the body cell, causing only a minimum of damage, the membrane would seal itself immediately, allowing only the smallest loss of protoplasm.

So then, things were going better, but it would not be quite true to say they were going *well*. Drs. Schreiber, Eberhard and Goodwin had gotten their techniques down to the point where they were able to inject a frog cell into a de-nucleized frog egg, keeping both cells alive in the process—but still, once they were together, no fertilization occurred. One of two things could have accounted for this failure: Either the cells, though living, had undergone a significant chemical change or vitiation because of their handling, and had lost their ability to procreate; or, for some other reason that the scientists could have no notion of, cloning was a chemical impossibility—some rejection reaction of chemical blockage simply would not allow it to happen.

The men fought against acknowledging this latter possibility. If it were true, all their work would have been in vain, they would have been doomed before they'd even started.

And so, for another half a year, they continued to hone their techniques, in the hope that, with gentler handling, the cells would in fact begin to reproduce. Gradually, encouraging signs started to appear. The transplanted body cell began to *grow* within the egg. It did not yet *reproduce,* but at least it grew within itself. This indicated that the radiation the egg cell had undergone had not poisoned its cytoplasm.

And several weeks later, the first cell division occurred. It was not a sexual division, but simply a mitotic one. The cell was not moving toward the development of a new frog, it had simply replicated *itself.* This, however, was still a hopeful sign, an indication that normal metabolic processes could be carried on by the transplanted cell within the hosting egg.

Then, in the summer of 1966, fourteen months after the three doctors had begun this new phase of their work, the first rudimentary but definite signs of a successful clone finally appeared. It was Dr. Goodwin who first saw the amazing sight.

Every morning, the scientists would begin their work by micro-examining the frog's eggs that had been incubating. One by one, they would take the translucent spheroids and place them in a special "vise"—probably the most delicate such device ever designed—which held them stationary under the lens of the microscope. The eggs would be cross lit by beams of polarized light, making their interior visible and shadowless. Thus, they could be scanned for signs of growth and development. Usually they showed nothing—a cell in suspended animation, or dead.

On this particular morning, however, when Dr. Goodwin focused in on the inside of the frog egg—seemingly no different from the so many thousands he had already examined—he saw something he had never seen before except in studies of *normally* reproduced frog embryos. He could not believe his eyes. He looked through the eyepiece for a long time, but the long-sought image did not disappear. He stood away from the microscope and waited a full minute, rubbing his eyes and wondering if he had really seen what he had seen. Slowly, fearfully, he went back to the scope. The image was still there, as clear and unmistakable as the light of day.

And now John Goodwin's excitement triumphed over his restraint. He let out a yell, a whoop of victory that echoed metallically through the whole hushed laboratory. His voice bounced off of the polished chrome machinery, it rang up out of beakers and alembics. . . .

"What is it, John?" Alfred asked. "What's going on?"

"Alfred!" said John Goodwin, "I think we've got ourselves a blastula!"

In an instant, Alfred Eberhard had sprung to the side of his friend. Hungrily, he pressed his eyes against the microscope; greedily, he peered in. And he saw what John Goodwin had promised— the chambered ball of cells known as a blastula, the first phase of a developing embryo. Each of the cells looked exactly the same, but even at this stage, Dr. Eberhard knew, they were beginning to differentiate, to develop into the specialized tissues of a whole frog, a creature which would be the exact genetic duplicate of the amphibian from whom the body cell had been taken! The ball of cells was hollow—already the embryo had an outside and an inside—the beginnings of skin and viscera!

In another moment, Dr. Schreiber, his walk painfully slow and labored, though his mind and heart were racing, had arrived at the scene of the prodigious sight. Dr. Eberhard stepped aside and let the older man peer in.

Dr. Eberhard put his arm around Dr. Schreiber's shoulders as the microbiologist treated himself to a long appraising look. At length, Dr. Schreiber raised himself from his crouch over the microscope. There were tears in his eyes behind his thick glasses, and he was smiling like a boy as the three scientists embraced.

Seven

The artificial generation of the blastula of a higher animal was an astounding achievement, and was recognized as such by the research community. This accomplishment was regarded as the crowning glory of Dr. Schreiber's already monumental career, and as a stunning opening for Drs. Goodwin and Eberhard. Both men were now universally acknowledged to be front-rank researchers, and special credit was given to Dr. Eberhard, as he had provided the theoretical framework through which the practical victory had been reached.

The entire Brookside staff seemed genuinely pleased and proud at the progress of the three men's work. Only Dr. Kenton's enthusiasm seemed to be absent—but then, he never could get very enthused about the hard-earned victories of others.

In any case, the successful generation of the blastula, though it was a huge step forward, was also the source of further frustrations: For some reason, unknown to anyone, the embryo failed to develop further.

For days, the scientists anxiously scrutinized the clone-bearing egg, waiting for the moment when the cells within the blastula would fold over on themselves, signaling the next phase of the embryonic process, the phase in which the three distinct tissue layers—ectoderm, mesoderm, endoderm—began to differentiate. At first, the hopeful scientists had no doubt that this would happen. . . .

But it didn't happen. The developmental rate fell far behind the pace at which normal development took place. The scientists told themselves not to worry about that—perhaps the clone pace would be slower, due to the absence of certain hormones. Metabolic processes within the individual cells still seemed to be normal. There was no reason to expect that the embryo wouldn't continue the push toward maturity it had started so felicitously.

But development was arrested at the blastula stage. And then, after a time, the blastula died. One by one, the cells within it switched off, as the scientists watched helplessly. They kept observing the ball of cells long after it had become inactive, vainly searching for clues as to what had gone wrong. They found nothing, and yet, with baffled insistence, they kept peering at the hollow sphere of dead cells.

Finally, the cell membranes began to deteriorate. . . . The cells broke up and decomposed, literally dissolved inside the harsh dead chemistry of the egg. There was no trace left of the victory that had seemed so stunning.

The scientists were depressed. How maddening

it was to come so close, and then to be thwarted, defeated, crushed, by a microscopic ball of cells which, like a bratty child, stubbornly refused to cooperate—and for no good reason under heaven!

Nevertheless, they persisted. With the constant refinement of their impregnation techniques, they were soon able to generate another blastula. But again, the blastula failed to develop. It stalled, and then died. The scientists generated another, and another. In time, they became so expert at impregnating the eggs, that they might have as many as a dozen blastulae alive at any given time. This allowed them to perform all sorts of experiments on the developing eggs: they were incubated at a wide range of temperatures; they were submerged in nutritive solutions designed to aid in the "feeding" of the growing cells; they were injected with hormones extracted from living frogs.

But nothing worked. The cloned specimens followed an agonizingly changeless pattern of growth, arrest, and death.

One afternoon, after a particularly frustrating day, John Goodwin suddenly slammed the butt of his beer bottle against the arm of his chair.

"Goddamit!" he exclaimed to his colleagues. "Those blastulas make me furious! You know, when I look at them under the microscope, they seem to be about the size of a baseball—just perfect for fitting right in the palm of your hand. And sometimes I'm so mad that I'd like to just reach in and squeeze the little bastards to death!"

"But that's just the problem," said Dr. Schreiber

with a wistful smile. "You don't have to squeeze them to death—they die on their own."

"Yes," said Dr. Eberhard, "that is the problem, isn't it? But why do they die? What do we have to do to them to keep them going, to move them on to the next phase of development? I look at those cells, and I can visualize everything that *should* happen, clear up to the tadpole stage. I can see it, but I can't bring it about—it makes me feel helpless and enraged."

"Gentlemen," said Dr. Schreiber, after a pause, "rest assured that I share your bafflement and your frustration, but, you know, it occurs to me that we may be losing sight of the original purpose of our research."

"How do you mean?" asked Dr. Goodwin.

"At the beginning of this project," said Dr. Schreiber, "our avowed intention was to try to locate and identify the O+factor, which—or so I theorized—might be common to the development both of tumors and of embryos. At the outset, the notion of cloning did not even figure in our research scheme—that wrinkle—a very useful one—was added later, at Alfred's suggestion. But my point is this: The *end* we are after, is some new insight into cancer; our study of the process of cloning is, properly speaking, only a *means* toward that end, and I wonder if we are not spending a disproportionate amount of time and energy on it."

"But Dr. Schreiber," Alfred countered, "what is the alternative? You acknowledge that a study of cloning may perhaps be useful. We know from

long experience that the study of normal reproduction was fruitless. If we discard the notion of
studying the chemistry of the cloned embryo,
where, then, do we turn?"

"Alfred," Schreiber said softly, "I'm not suggesting that we discard our idea of studying the chemistry of the cloned cell—I still stand by that idea.
However, of late, all our attention has been trained
on the problem of bringing the clone *past* the blastula stage—but it occurs to me now that, if the O+
factor is in fact present, it must show itself from
the very beginning of embryonic development. In
terms of cancer research, there is no reason to take
the embryo farther."

"Dr. Schreiber," John said, unable to keep the
disappointment out of his voice, "are you suggesting that we give up our efforts to bring the cloned
egg to maturity, and instead, that we simply study
the blastula, and leave it at that."

"Yes," said Dr. Schreiber, with quiet but firm resignation.

There was a long silence, during which none of
the three colleagues could meet each other's eyes.
When the silence was finally broken, it was broken
by Dr. Schreiber, speaking in an almost apologetic
voice.

"Listen, John, Alfred—I know that working on
the embryos is a good deal more exciting than
plodding on in search of that damned evasive protein. I'm not denying that. The whole concept of
cloning is fascinating, intoxicating, mind-boggling.
The thought of creating new life in a new way—it's
an awesome idea with awesome possibilities, and I

fully understand your interest in it. But I can't help feeling certain ethical qualms about all the time and money we're spending on it. It's not what we're being paid to do. We're being paid to do cancer research. We're technically accountable to the government, and morally accountable to the people of this country, and what the people want, perhaps more than anything in the world, is for cancer to be cured.

"If we try to cure it, and fail, we've made an honest effort. But if we allow ourselves to get side-tracked, however fascinating those side tracks may be—I feel that we'd be shirking somehow. . . ."

"But Dr. Schreiber," protested Eberhard, "you can't deny that research into cloning may also be of value, and that the entire subject may someday have an impact even greater than a cure for cancer."

"Don't misunderstand," said Dr. Schreiber. "I'm not denying that the research we are doing now is of value. Nor am I denying that the process of cloning may someday have an enormous impact—though I'm less than certain that its impact would be beneficial. I'm simply saying that it makes me feel somehow dishonest to be doing a job other than the one I'm supposed to be doing, and therefore, I suggest that, rather than trying to *advance* the blastulae, we simply try to keep them alive as long as we can, and search for the O+factor in them. That is my suggestion—that is what I feel is the right thing to do. However, we are all equal associates in this project, and I won't force my opinion on you. If both of you want to go ahead with the work on cloning, I'll go along with you, though I sincerely urge that we don't. . . . Well, what do you say?''

There was a long tense silence as Drs. Eberhard and Goodwin thought over Dr. Schreiber's argument and made ready to respond. They had to mediate between their own desires and their high regard for the older man's unimpeachable integrity; they had to decide whether to defiantly go their own way or to follow the wishes of the man who had been their mentor and, in many ways, their benefactor.

Dr. Eberhard was determined not to be the first to speak. He would wait to hear what Goodwin had to say. If John Goodwin showed the slightest spark of resistance, he, Dr. Eberhard, would chime quickly in support of him. . . . If there were a way to salvage the cloning project, Dr. Eberhard would do it, even at the cost of offending Dr. Schreiber.

"I think," began Dr. Goodwin slowly, "that . . . that Dr. Schreiber is right. The cloning work *is* exciting, but perhaps it isn't what we should be doing. I go along with the idea of studying the blastulae.''

Dr. Eberhard was silent for some moments. He feared that if he spoke, a certain note of bitterness would be audible in his voice. The bitterness he felt surprised him—he hadn't realized just how thoroughly engrossed he'd become in the cloning project. But now that the project had been suddenly and unexpectedly terminated, he felt that he had been deprived of something intimate, as if a part of him had been cut out. He felt a sudden and unprecedented burst of anger toward Dr. Schreiber—the sanctimonious old fool! For a moment, he despised his friend John Goodwin—just like him to be swayed by the first argument that was thrown at him!

And now an ugly thought imposed itself on Alfred Eberhard, a thought that came unbidden but which he could not disclaim: Dr. Schreiber would be dead soon. He wouldn't last another year. What did it matter if he was humored in the meantime?

Finally Alfred Eberhard spoke, prodded by the expectant eyes of his colleagues upon him.

"Well," he said, trying to make his voice sound pleasant, "that's a majority right there. I guess that decides it."

"But you're still entitled to a vote, Alfred," said John Goodwin. "Just so we know, how would you have voted?"

"But that's the nice thing about going last," Alfred said. "One doesn't have to say."

Eight

And so Drs. Schreiber, Eberhard and Goodwin stopped trying to coax further development from the stalled frog blastulae, and began analyzing the dormant cells for traces of the O+factor. After the heady excitement of the cloning experiments, this backtracking seemed deflating and demoralizing; the work seemed colorless and dull. The younger men could muster no enthusiasm for it.

"Discipline!" Dr. Schreiber would urge them. "You don't need to be enthused, you don't need to be inspired—you need only to be disciplined!"

Drs. Eberhard and Goodwin *were* disciplined. The long years of medical training had taught them to be, yet there was no denying that some vital element had been lost in their attitude toward their work. There was no sense of adventure in it. They felt let down and somehow disappointed in themselves, as if they had been climbing a mountain and then began descending before getting to the top. At every moment, they yearned to turn around and begin the climb again.

They did the work that needed doing: They prepared the samples, they examined the cells; they interpreted their findings. But there was a certain listlessness in all their movements, even in their thoughts. They moved around the lab like automatons—competent, but nothing more. . . .

After a time, John Goodwin started pulling out of this subdued state of mind. The search for the O+ factor became exciting to him again. The invigoration of the clone experiments lost some of its edge in memory. The whole business of watching eggs, of waiting for them to develop, of being enraged when they didn't, seemed like a distant episode now. It had been very interesting, and many interesting ideas had been raised and left unanswered, but, then, that was always so with science. One had to move on, to immerse oneself in whatever project was at hand.

Alfred Eberhard, however, was far less successful in putting the cloning experiments out of his mind; in fact, he made no attempt to do so. He still lingered over the unresolved questions—why had the embryos stalled in their development? What other measures could have been taken to make the development continue? And then, if the development *had* been made to continue, what would the matured fetuses have been like? Would they have been normal? Would they have become healthy tadpoles, and then healthy frogs? Would they, in turn, have been able to reproduce normally?

These questions played continually in Alfred Eberhard's mind, even as he went about the more mundane tasks connected with the search for the O+ factor. He was brilliant enough to be able to do his job, preoccupied or not, but anyone who knew him could tell that his thoughts were elsewhere. When he scanned a blastula, his *eyes* were attuned to the slightest clue about the presence of the mysterious acidic protein—but his *mind* regarded the ball of cells quite differently. *This,* he thought, might have been the one that would have developed, that would have become an adult, that would have gotten us somewhere. . . .

The months went by slowly. The O+ factor still remained cloaked in mystery. From day to day, it became increasingly apparent just how mortally Dr. Schreiber was fading. It became more and more obvious that his final project would end inconclusively. It seemed to Dr. Goodwin that working on this project had become a sort of sacred ritual, accompanying a great man to the very edge of the grave.

Dr. Eberhard, however, had no time for such sentimental thoughts; he was too wrapped up in his inward conjectures about the clone experiments, conjectures which grew bolder and more obsessive the longer he held them inside, secret, abstract, removed from the moderating influences of scientific caution and ethical restraints.

Then, on Christmas night of 1966, Dr. Schreiber died. He passed in his sleep, without disease, without suffering—at least that anyone knew about—without the manifold humiliations of a lingering death. His body was simply worn out.

Dr. Schreiber was sincerely mourned by the entire scientific community. The surgeon-general himself flew down from Washington to deliver the microbiologist's eulogy. The staff at Brookside, however, did not need the bloated words of an outsider to make them mindful of their loss. They knew what kind of scientist, and what kind of man, Emanuel Schreiber had been. Many could recall warm anecdotes about him, many could remember words of advice so valuable that they had changed the course of entire careers. And all could remember the man's unassailable kindness and generosity of spirit.

There were few dry eyes at the assembly held in honor of the deceased. Dr. Goodwin cried heartily and without shame. Dr. Eberhard stood next to him through the long moment of silence, wrestling with the contrary feelings within him. His sense of decency told him that he should mourn this man—and yet he could not help feeling a kind of joy—with Schreiber gone, he could return to his clone experiments as soon as the new year began.

As it happened, however, Dr. Eberhard was not to return to his clone experiments after the year-end break, or for quite a while thereafter. . . .

When he entered the laboratory on the first working day of January, 1967, he was curtly informed that the entire O+ project had been cancelled. There would be no more funds for frog eggs, no more time spent in examining moribund cells, in search of a substance which, in all likelihood, did not exist. Drs. Eberhard and Goodwin would be reassigned shortly. Thus said the brief memorandum which Dr. Eberhard found in his office mailbox. The memorandum was signed, M. Kenton, Director.

Shocked and enraged, Dr. Eberhard stormed into the office of his superior. He found Kenton sitting at his desk, a small phony smile on his face. Clearly, he'd anticipated Dr. Eberhard's entrance, though he studiously attempted to appear surprised.

"Yes?" he said in a smooth voice. "What is it, Dr. Eberhard?"

Dr. Eberhard was beside himself. He could barely speak. He strode up to Dr. Kenton's desk, leaned over it, and rustled the memorandum in his face.

"This!" he finally managed to say. "What is the meaning of this?"

"Isn't the wording of the memorandum clear?" asked Dr. Kenton innocently. "It says—"

"I know what it says!" Dr. Eberhard interrupted. "But why? You can't just cut the project off like that!"

"Oh, but I can," said Dr. Kenton. Certain of victory, he had the luxury of allowing himself to remain calm. "That's my job, in fact—to see that government money is not squandered on crank research."

"Crank research!" hissed Dr. Eberhard. "How can you call that crank research? Dr. Schreiber's notion was one of the few original ideas ever to come out of this facility, and it provided one of the first possible new directions to come along since radiation."

"Your loyalty to Dr. Schreiber's memory is touching," said Dr. Kenton, with elaborate emotion. "But let's not allow personal allegiances to cloud our thinking. Dr. Schreiber's idea was a poor one, a very poor one indeed. Some of us here"—Dr. Kenton cleared his throat and adjusted the knot of his tie—"knew that from the very beginning. However, we felt that, owing to Dr. Schreiber's prestige and to the very real contributions he had made in the past, we should bear with him—in light of his, let us say, infirmity. But now that he is dead, there seems little reason to carry on with this fruitless and expensive charade."

Dr. Eberhard took in Dr. Kenton's words with an ever-spiraling anger. By the time Kenton had finished his pronouncement, Eberhard was livid, swept past all sense of tact and protocol.

"Listen, Kenton, that is some of the most pathetically transparent nonsense I've ever heard! Schreiber's idea was sound, and you know it. You're jealous of him—you always were. You were jealous of his popularity, and of the respect he generated among the younger doctors—a respect that never attached to you. . . . And aside from that, you were jealous of his mind. He was a scientist, you're a functionary. You're cutting off this project to spite his memory, and to spite me personally."

"Dr. Eberhard," said Dr. Kenton, struggling now to remain calm, "I see no reason to bring this discussion down to the level of a personal attack. I excuse your childish outburst on the grounds that you are overwrought and have not had time to sufficiently think things over. However, the facts are clear—three years have been spent in search of the O+factor; nothing has been found. The project is therefore terminated."

"But how many years have been spent shooting rats full of dyes, bathing mouse tissue in baths full of carcinogens, spraying radiation on guinea pigs? And what concrete results have those things yielded?"

"Dr. Eberhard," said Kenton, his patience and his zest for confrontation clearly fading, "it is neither my obligation nor my wish to justify myself to you further. I have told you my reasons—you do not accept them. That changes nothing. The project is cancelled."

Dr. Eberhard felt himself suddenly close to tears as he realized the full helplessness of his position. There was no one to appeal to, no chance of changing Kenton's mind. Never in his life had he felt so frustrated. For some moments he stood perfectly still, silent, immobilized. Finally, talking more to himself than to Kenton, he said, "But then, what of the cloning research?"

Dr. Kenton leaned forward in his chair at the sound of these words. His hands were folded and his face was set—his enjoyment of an unfair fight had returned.

"Ah," he said, "now we're getting down to the real reason you're upset. It doesn't have anything to do with Schreiber, does it? No, you've got a project of your own in mind."

"Yes," said Eberhard, his defiance rising again. "Is there anything wrong with that? It is my own project, and it could be a very important one!"

"Perhaps," said Kenton indifferently. "But I'm

afraid it hasn't got much to do with cancer research, so my advice to you is that you forget it."

"You *are* trying to spite me, aren't you?" said Eberhard. "You have no other reason for turning me down."

"Dr. Eberhard," said the director patronizingly, as if talking to a recalcitrant boy, "since you insist on carrying on our discussion on such an inappropriate plane, I'll tell you a couple of things—off the record, of course.

"I don't like you, Eberhard. I don't like the way you were forced on me as an assistant. That ploy was a victory for Schreiber—it cost me a lot of embarrassment and inconvenience in fact—but I will see to it that it is not a victory for you. As my assistant, you are essentially powerless. You have no jurisdiction, except that which I delegate to you, and I don't intend to delegate any—or none but the most trivial. You'll have projects to work on, of course, but I'll make sure they're nothing too pivotal, nothing that might swell your already inordinate pride."

"I see," said Eberhard. "Well, it's nice that we at least know where we stand. But, Kenton, if you're so determined to thwart me, why don't you just get rid of me? Why don't we just split up somehow?"

"That's easier said than done," the older man said. "I'd be tickled to get rid of you if I could. But how? I'm afraid I have no grounds for firing you. That could lead to an inquiry, and I'm afraid I'd come out of it looking worse than you. But on the other hand, you really can't quit—doing cancer research isn't like working in a gas station, where, if you don't like your boss, you go to work for the guy across the street. There are maybe three or four places in the whole country where you can do the kind of work you want to do—and positions in them are awfully hard to come by. No, Dr. Eberhard, it seems that we're stuck with each other. We'll just have to make the best of it—or *you'll* have to make the best of it. I'll make of it whatever I like."

"All right, Kenton," said Eberhard with grim control. "Thanks for letting me know what to expect. But can you tell me one more thing? If you're killing the O+ project, what do you intend to assign me to next?"

"Well," said Dr. Kenton, "as it happens, all the actual lab projects are adequately manned right now. But we do have a rather troublesome backlog of paperwork."

Nine

If one is to fully understand the eventual virulence of Alfred Eberhard's obsession, one must take into account the immense and constant frustrations of the next several years of his life.

Under the malevolent authority of Dr. Matthew Kenton, every attempt was made to stifle the probing creativity of Eberhard's scientific mind. Much of his time was wasted on meaningless administrative chores—chores which should have been delegated to bureaucrats, not researchers. When Dr. Eberhard managed to get into the lab at all, he found himself assigned to the most workaday projects—doing biopsies, checking data, dissecting cancerous rats—medical school stuff, of no theoretical interest whatever.

Vexed though he was, he seemed to have no recourse, no means of gaining fairer treatment for himself. By casual but searching inquiries, he learned that he could not expect any very strong support from the staff at large if he tried to fight Dr. Kenton directly. Kenton had too many of his cronies in pivotal positions, and besides, Alfred Eberhard, unintentionally and unknowingly, had made a number of enemies, simply because of the swift pace of his ascent.

Ascent, indeed! The ascent had certainly back-fired. As a junior researcher, he had been allowed to do pretty much as he pleased in the lab—he had been considered a novice still, nothing great was yet expected of him. In a sense, he had been turned loose among the apparatus, free to educate himself, to prepare for the vital work that might, perhaps, come later. No one watched junior researchers all that closely—that was when Dr. Eberhard had been happiest.

As a senior researcher, he began to be taken more seriously—and also to incur the first barbed bits of professional jealousy. And then had come Dr. Schreiber's well-intentioned but disastrous ploy—and now, *this,* a desk full of papers, a brain teeming with frustration . . . Ascent, indeed. . . .

To escape the excruciating tedium of his days, Dr. Eberhard turned inward on himself to a greater and greater degree. Though never one to form facile friendships, he had always been a sociable man; now, however, immersed in thoughts of his own, often seeing nothing but the shimmering phantasms of his own imagination, he would often brush by clusters of his colleagues without so much as a casual hello. He had never been warm in his sexual dealings—but he had made an effort to be charming, at least in the early stages of a courtship; now, however, even those painless gestures of gallantry seemed more trouble than Dr. Eberhard cared to take—when he needed release, he sought refuge with the prostitutes of the town, contenting himself with those quick and wordless linkings.

He was even beginning to find it difficult to maintain his friendship with John Goodwin. Goodwin, though he hadn't been assigned to any terribly exciting projects since Schreiber's death, still had, at least, free access to the lab—and Dr. Eberhard was finding it harder and harder not to show his jealousy, not to take it out on his friend.

John Goodwin, however, was, to some degree at least, aware of what a difficult time his colleague was going through, and he tried to be indulgent at these times when Dr. Eberhard would become sullen and unreachable.

"Alfred," he said on more than one occasion. "There has to be a way around some of this."

"There isn't," Eberhard would reply. "I've thought it over a hundred times—there's nothing I can do."

"You can leave," Goodwin had suggested.

"Yes," said Eberhard. "I can leave, and get out of cancer research. Maybe I should go into private practice—play golf, read magazines—wouldn't a life like that be just terrific?"

"Look," John had said, "I don't know if anything could be much worse than what's happening to you here. I don't know exactly what's going on in your mind, Alfred, but I can't imagine that it's healthy. You're always preoccupied, it's obvious that you're terribly angry. I'm worried about you. I really think that maybe you should leave. I would leave with you if you liked."

"That's good of you, John," Alfred said, trying

to find some real gratitude within himself, "but I'm not leaving. There's work I want to do, and one way or other, I *will* do it. The work will take a lot of time, a lot of equipment, a lot of money—it has to be done here. I've just got to wait."

And so Alfred Eberhard waited, though he didn't know exactly what he was waiting for, what event would in time free him to embark on the work he was so eager to do. . . .

That work—as only Drs. Goodwin and Kenton knew—was the continuation of his research into the process of cloning. Dr. Eberhard thought about the subject constantly. The idea had *entered* him, had become a part of his being. Strictly speaking, it was not a mere idea anymore—for ideas are of the mind. Cloning, now, had become a part of Alfred Eberhard's very flesh. . . .

It was strange, the manner in which the subject had taken hold of him so totally. At first, it had only been a sort of intellectual diversion. Eberhard turned to it to distract himself from the duller tasks of his wretched days. He pondered the lingering mystery of the arrested blastulae, he carried the process many steps further in his mind. It had been a kind of game. . . . But now it had become so much more. Theories, possibilities, implications—they consumed his waking mind, they visited him in dreams. And Eberhard told his thoughts to no one. He kept them all inside, subject to no one's scrutiny but his own.

Inevitably, Dr. Eberhard's obsession became entangled with the rage he felt toward Dr. Kenton. His work on cloning would be more than just a personal project, it would be a kind of revenge against the sniveling mediocrity who had tried to hold him down so long; it would be the amazing burst of creativity that would undo the memory of all these endless days of desk work, of boredom, of impotence.

For nearly three years, these powerful thoughts and emotions percolated within Dr. Eberhard, gaining in intensity with every passing day. The outside world lost its palpability; the obsession grew more real. Cloning, in Dr. Eberhard's mind, was no longer a merely theoretical subject but a concrete entity, something that could undoubtedly be done, something that *must* be done, that *he* must do. . . . That thought was the only thing that made his dull days bearable. Perhaps, then, one can understand the manically single-minded way in which Dr. Eberhard pursued his goal when, by a grimly ironic circumstance, the opportunity finally afforded itself.

Alfred Eberhard could not help himself from laughing aloud when he learned that Dr. Kenton was dying of cancer.

John Goodwin recoiled from the sound of that laugh. It sounded hollow and cruel and more than a little mad.

"Alfred!" he said. "How can you laugh? I know you hate the man—but still, he's dying. And he won't die easily. There's tremendous agony in store for him, and he knows it."

"I'm sorry, John," said Eberhard, "but I'm

afraid I can't get myself to play the hypocrite for the sake of that son of a bitch. I'm glad he's dying. And I don't care one way or the other about his suffering. But it's so perfect—I mean, the way it's happening. It's enough to make me believe in a metaphorical interpretation of disease."

"What are you talking about?" asked John Goodwin, clearly uneasy at the rather bizarre behavior of his friend.

"You know," Alfred said, "it's the whole idea of cancer as a symbol for the spiritual corruption of modern man. The ugly growth within the body corresponds to the hateful tumors within the soul. It fits Kenton to a tee, as if that carcinoma in his brain was the residue of every contaminated thought he's ever had in his whole stinking life—"

"Alfred!" Goodwin interrupted. "The man is dying! He's got terminal inoperable cancer, already metastasizing all over his body. Can't you lay off him?"

"Why?" asked Eberhard. "Why should I lay off him? Because he's dying? Everybody dies! Does that make everybody a good guy in the end? Does that undo every lousy thing they've done in their whole lives? That's a lot of pious nonsense! You might as well suggest he'll go to heaven if he converts on his deathbed."

"All right, Alfred," John said. "I understand your feelings, though I can't agree with them. But let's not argue about it. The fact is, though, that he'll be dead within three or four months, and he'll have to retire almost immediately. You'll move into his position, I suppose."

"Yes," said Eberhard. There was no joy in his voice, but there was a certain note of carefully restrained relish, as if he had wanted to scream out the single word. "I'll move into the directorship—that's pretty much a *pro forma* proceeding. And I'll be my own man again. I'll be able to make my own decisions. It'll be up to me to decide where the resources flow, how the brainpower is allotted. And I've got ideas, John! There are things I want to do, things that have never been before—"

"Do you intend to reinstate the cloning project, Alfred?" John asked.

Dr. Eberhard froze at the mention of the word. It sounded mystically strange in his ear, like a magic incantation. Why? Then Dr. Eberhard realized that he had not *heard* the word in almost three years. He had discussed his feelings with no one—not even John Goodwin. The word had been in his mind always, yet never had he heard it said. And now it assailed his ears—its sound excited him. He sensed the roundness of the word, the shape of it. It came at him like a dream incarnate.

"Yes," he said. "Immediately."

John Goodwin looked at his friend with concern and a certain wistfulness. He hardly seemed to know him anymore. He looked into the dark, deep-set eyes, and he saw that they were sealed, though wide open. He stared down at the long and graceful surgeon's fingers, which drummed nervously on the desk in a secret and somehow fearful rhythm.

"Why are you looking at me that way?" asked Alfred Eberhard.

"It's nothing," said Goodwin. "It's only that . . . that I'm a little worried about you."

"Ah, John," said Eberhard, trying to make his voice sound buoyant and convincing, "there's no need to worry about me now. I've been depressed, it's true. But now the weight is off me. I feel fine; I feel like I can do anything!"

"That may be just the problem," said John Goodwin.

"That's never the problem!" said Alfred, a mood of genuine good cheer suddenly overtaking him. "It's always good to be working, and to feel that one's work will succeed—always! Listen, John, will you help me on the project?"

"Sure," said Dr. Goodwin, with a single nod of his head. Alfred's sudden cheerfulness made him hopeful. Perhaps it would all work out after all.

"And John," continued Alfred, "the number two spot will be vacant when I move up—will you take it?"

"Only if you promise not to load me down with three years' worth of paperwork," said Dr. Goodwin.

"I promise," said Dr. Eberhard. "Well, shall we drink a beer on it, like in the old days?"

Ten

It was early in 1970 when Dr. Alfred Eberhard officially seized the reins of power at Brookside Research Institute. Dr. Matthew Kenton, though not yet dead, was thoroughly debilitated, and able to offer no assistance whatever in the bulky bureaucratic process of installing a new director. Dr. Eberhard, therefore, aided by his friend and new assistant, John Goodwin, had to take care of all the details—from the major ones, such as learning all the ins and outs of writing grant proposals and dealing with the powerful men in Washington, to the most trivial: the changing of the letterhead on the official director's stationery, the painting of the new name on the inner office door.

In addition to this welter of official chores, there was the added strain of a personal move. Dr. Eberhard had to move his things out of the apartment he'd occupied as second-in-command, and take over residence of the more sumptuous director's suite. This involved the packing and labeling of dozens of cases of books, ledgers, sheafs of laboratory notes, as well as the more usual domestic baggage. Dr. Goodwin, in turn, had to move his things out of the dormitory-style researchers' quarters and into the more spacious and private assistant's apartment.

All in all, it was a herculean task, one which, under normal circumstances, would have taken months to complete. Dr. Eberhard, however, working with a preternatural energy, effected the entire transition in a mere three weeks. In that short space of time, he had accomplished everything necessary to begin the smooth functioning of his regime. Time enough had been wasted, he thought, frittered away in those awful years under Kenton. Now there was nothing to do except to move swiftly and directly toward the goal, the project that had been put aside so long.

Accordingly, Drs. Eberhard and Goodwin straightaway set about to recreate the experimental scheme they had used in their earlier cloning experiments. Having been away from the project for three years, Dr. Goodwin was understandably vague in his recollection of the finer points of the procedures; he often needed to refer to his old notes to remind himself just how the eggs should be prepared, what temperatures should be maintained in the incubators, how much radiation the nuclei should receive, how and when the body cells should be injected.

Dr. Eberhard, on the other hand, seemed to remember every detail of the experiments as if he had just been working on them the day before. And in fact he had: Mentally, secretly, he had been reviewing and refining those same experiments every day for three years.

It was not surprising, therefore, that in a matter of several weeks, the men had succeeded in bringing the experiments up to the same point at which they had been stymied in their last attempt. Again, they had managed to bring about the early development of a cloned frog embryo—they had artificially produced a blastula.

And again the blastula died. Dr. Eberhard watched the arrested ball of cells slowly decompose, and as he watched, he felt an awful sense of *déjà vu*, as if this disheartening image would never stop tormenting him. But, though disappointed, he was not daunted.

"Come here and take a look at a familiar sight," he said wistfully to Dr. Goodwin.

Dr. Goodwin bent over the eyepiece of the microscope and peered in, knowing in advance what he'd see: The cell membranes beginning to break apart, turning the neatly geometric chambered ball into a blurry mass of lifeless protoplasm, the bright-colored necklaces of chromosomes shriveling and becoming brittle, like dried out worms.

"Oh, well," said Goodwin, "back to the old drawing board."

"Indeed," said Eberhard. "But John, I've got some ideas."

"Already?" John asked.

"I've had them for some time," said Dr. Eberhard, a fiercely concentrated gleam in his eyes. "John, do you recall our use of hormones in attempting to get the blastula to develop further?"

"Yes, of course," the other man said.

"Do you remember what sort of hormones we used?"

"Well," said Goodwin, "not offhand. But I can look it up in the notes."

"Don't bother," Alfred said. "I'll tell you. We used female hormones, female sex hormones. Now think about it, John—wasn't that idiotic of us?"

"I'm not sure I follow you," he said. "Why is it idiotic? It's the female sex hormones that are needed to activate the egg."

"Precisely," said Eberhard. "But the egg is *already* activated, or else we wouldn't even have gotten as far as the blastula. No, if there's anything missing hormonally, it has to be male."

"Ah," said John Goodwin. "Now I see—since we're using a male body cell, rather than a male gamete, you're saying it may be a deficiency in male hormones that is causing the arrested development."

"Exactly," said Eberhard. "Now, this is just a guess. As far as I know, the subject has never been studied: But perhaps male hormones are needed to pick up where the female hormones leave off."

"That's an interesting idea, Alfred," said John Goodwin. "It makes sense. Shall we give it a try?"

And so the scientists began injecting minute doses of male frog hormones into the de-nucleized eggs at the same time as they injected the male body cells.

The results, at first, were discouraging. The male hormones, far from assisting the egg in its development, seemed to inhibit it, as if the male hormones in some way cancelled out the female, and effectively de-fertilized the egg. No blastulae formed in the hormone-injected ova.

"Well, so much for that," said John Goodwin with a sigh, after several dozen experiments had confirmed the same infelicitous result. "It was an elegant idea, Alfred, but it doesn't seem to work."

"I'm not so sure we've exhausted the idea, John," Alfred said thoughtfully.

"But Alfred," said John Goodwin, a touch impatiently, "we've tried out nearly a hundred eggs. Now, without hormones, we've been averaging better than one blastula in every ten tries—statistically, even if the hormones did *nothing,* we should have gotten around ten takes. We tried injecting hormones from the same frog that donated the body cell, we tried using hormones from a different frog, we tried using synthetic hormones—what haven't we tried?"

"For one thing," said Alfred Eberhard after a thoughtful pause, "we haven't tried varying the time at which we inject the hormones. We've always injected the hormone right along with the body cell—maybe it would be better to wait."

"But Alfred," John said, "in nature, where the hormones are actually part of the gamete, they enter the egg at the same time. There's no delayed action then."

"No," said Eberhard, "there's no *mechanical* delay—but perhaps there's a *chemical* one."

"How do you mean?" asked Goodwin.

"Perhaps, in nature, there's some sort of chemical buffer which prevents the male hormones from acting on the egg until the early stage of development is over. Perhaps nature provides a sort of time-release effect, allowing the male hormones to come into play only at the moment they're needed."

"I see," said Dr. Goodwin. "You're suggesting, then, that we hold off on injecting the male hormones until the blastula stage has been reached."

"Yes," said Dr. Eberhard. "Though of course I realize that there may be problems with that, too. For one thing, we've seen time and time again that the blastula begins to lose its vitality very soon after the growth is arrested—that'll make the timing of the injection very tricky: Too soon, we inhibit the egg; too late, we may already have moribund cells. And aside from that, we have no way of knowing how the egg will respond to a new injection process *after* development has begun—going in there with the needle may really disrupt things. So, this whole idea may very well be another dead end. But I think it's worth giving it a try before we leave off with the idea of male hormones."

Accordingly, the two researchers made a slight but significant change in their tactics. They kept an almost constant eye on the developing frog eggs. As soon as an egg showed the slightest signs of a take, it was put under intensive surveillance. Mounted in the tiny, cushioned vise, it was gently lit and thoroughly examined. Drs. Eberhard and Goodwin watched the splitting cell as it moved toward the blastula stage: The single cell became two, became four, eight, sixteen, thirty-two, gradually forming into the hollow ball which would, if all went well, eventually invaginate into the folded mass from which the body's tissue layers would arise.

Trusting to intuition, Eberhard and Goodwin tried to gauge the exact right moment to inject the tiny but potent dose of male hormone. Should the injection take place *before* cell division actually stopped? Or just after? But how was it possible to know just when cell division *would* stop? . . .

The men tried various timings. Keeping the egg under the electron microscope all the while, they injected the hormone through the gelatinous membrane which covered it. Under the microscope, the ultra-fine hypodermic looked like a huge, fearful lance, an immense drill that penetrated a soft and yielding globe; the micro-drop of hormone that the hypodermic contained, seemed to gush into the egg like a tidal wave, a viscous surge of intrusive fluid.

The hormone having been introduced, the scientists observed its action carefully. They could see it diffusing into the cytoplasm of the egg, could see it slowly spreading toward the egg's core, where the blastula existed and struggled for growth. They could see the hormone's fibrous strands of protein stretching out like ropes in water, flowing and subsiding, reaching into everything. But what would their effect be when they reached the blastula?

From the very beginning, this phase of the clone experiments offered encouraging, though inconclusive, results. The hormones, injected at the proper moment, did in fact encourage growth—but the growth they encouraged was not normal.

The blastulae, rather than symmetrically turning inward on themselves, as occurs in natural gastrulation, would become misshapen, lumpy, grotesque. They would develop further than they had, but the further development took place in a useless and unnatural direction.

Nevertheless, Dr. Eberhard was excited. If growth—*any* growth—was taking place, then there was reason to believe that with refinement in techniques, with greater exactitude in the timing of the injections, the growth could be made to occur along more natural lines. This discovery was the first bit of concrete encouragement that Eberhard had had since the original generation of the blastulae, three and a half agonizing years before.

John Goodwin was also intrigued by the abnormal growths engendered by the presence of the added male hormones. The thrust of his interest, however, was in a slightly different direction, a direction which Dr. Eberhard, in his fierce single-mindedness, had not overlooked so much as chosen to ignore.

"Alfred," John Goodwin said one afternoon, after examining a particularly misshapen but vital mass of cells, "has it occurred to you that we may be on to something quite important here—quite important in terms of cancer, I mean? There seem to be a lot of resemblances between the growth patterns of the hormone-treated blastulae and the early development of carcinomas."

"Of course, it's occurred to me!" Eberhard responded, with surprising impatience and even defiance. "But we haven't got time to allow ourselves to get sidetracked now."

"Sidetracked?" John Goodwin responded. "But Alfred, cancer research is what we're here to do. How can you call that a sidetrack?"

"I call it a sidetrack," said Dr. Eberhard firmly, "because this project has to do with other things."

"But Alfred," John began. He did not finish his statement, however. The look on his friend's face assured him that all protest would be useless.

Suddenly, a cold wave of queasy misgiving broke over John Goodwin. Suddenly, he was afraid. He recalled the conversation he had had with his friend a number of months ago, the conversation in which Alfred had assured him that he was no longer depressed and that everything would be all right. It was true that Alfred no longer seemed depressed—his energy, his attention, his vigor, provided ample evidence to the contrary—but it was not true that everything would be all right, like it used to be. No, Alfred had changed. . . . He seemed to have lost sight of certain things, certain ethical concepts, a certain sense of proportion.

It seemed, then, to John Goodwin that Alfred Eberhard's fierce dedication had crossed the thin line into monomania. . . . Frightened, he warmly placed his hand on his friend's shoulder, striving for a reassuring contact: He felt the flesh grow tense beneath his palm, as if the touch were more than Alfred Eberhard could bear.

After this incident, there could never again be the same implicit unanimity of purpose that had linked the long-standing friends and colleagues.

John Goodwin sensed that the cloning project was at the very center of Alfred Eberhard's universe, that devotion to it would displace all other loyalties, all other thoughts and feelings. He realized that Alfred might become very difficult to work with, implacable and arbitrary. Nevertheless, he resolved to stay with the project, to stand by his friend, and to assist him in whatever manner—scientific or psychological—he was able.

The two men continued to hone their techniques for the post-fertilization injection of hormones into the frog eggs. Seeking to eliminate the abnormalities in the growth patterns of hormone-treated blastulae, they tested various refinements. They halved the hormone dosage; they doubled it; they injected it from two sides at once, hoping to correct the asymmetrical diffusion of the chemical agents. Still the blastulae developed in a warped and useless manner.

Then, finally, Dr. Eberhard lighted on the notion of subdividing the tiny dose of hormones, and of injecting it in several installments, spaced out over the entire developmental period of the egg. This method, reasoned Eberhard, would provide the closest analogy to the "time-release" idea, if such a thing did in fact exist in nature. The delicate chemistry of the egg would have time to acclimatize itself to the presence of the foreign male hormone. Hopefully, the infinitesimal dosage administered in the early stage would be insufficient to inhibit the initial cell divisions; and hopefully, the final dose, injected when the embryo had reached the blastula stage, would be well enough prepared for, that it would not lead to the distorted growth of the first cells it affected.

Dr. Goodwin acknowledged that the logic behind this new approach was sound; but then, Eberhard's reasoning was always sound. That did not necessarily mean, however, that it would lead to concrete results. By this time, Goodwin could not help feeling somewhat skeptical. And beyond feeling skeptical, he could not help half-hoping that Eberhard's idea would be one more dead end. He had come to feel that the success of his friend's project might ultimately be more devastating than its failure. . . .

But this new idea of Eberhard's did not turn out to be a dead end. On the contrary, it provided a dramatic breakthrough, a result more positive and irrefutable than even Dr. Eberhard would have dared to hope!

From the very beginning, it was clear that the gradual introduction of the male hormone rendered the chemistry of the egg more hospitable. Cell division took place at an accelerated pace. The blastula formed in just over half the time it had taken in the absence of the hormone. . . . The real gain, however, was in the behavior of the embryo *after* the blastula stage had been reached: The embryo continued to develop, and, as far as could be microscopically determined, its development took place along perfectly normal lines!

Rapt, barely able to believe their eyes, the scientists traced the daily—the hourly!—development of the embryo. It was astonishing how closely the cloned specimen adhered to the normal schedule

of gestation. Within days, the blastula had begun
to invaginate. In place of the hollow, simple sphere
of cells, there now appeared the double-ringed gas-
trula—the miraculous first phase of cell differen-
tiation! The interior of the embryo was no longer
the simple blastocoel, but rather the more complex archenteron—the cavity that would develop
into the gut of the mature frog—if the process held
good that long.

Dr. Eberhard concentrated all his mental energy
on hoping that it would; had he been capable of
praying, he would have prayed. He was in a state
of restrained frenzy for as long as the embryo developed. He wanted to hold it in his hand, to in-
cubate it with the moist heat of his own
interior. . . . Despite himself, he gave thanks to
some mysterious power as the embryo continued
to flourish. He could now see the formation of the
mesoderm, the last cell layer to form, evolutionar-
ily the most advanced. Eberhard was exultant.

But the period of watching the embryo develop
was a maddeningly tense time for him. He could
not sleep. His eyes would not stay closed. In his
bed, alone, in the middle of the night, he would
imagine horrible things—something had gone
wrong with the incubator; a filter had failed, the
embryo would be exposed to toxins; someone had
sabotaged him, someone at this very moment was
prowling in the lab. . . .

Sweating, his heart palpitating, wearing a bath-
robe and slippers, Alfred Eberhard would leave his
suite and stalk into the dark and empty laboratory.
Ghostlike, he would move between the empty

aisles of idle machinery. The lab would be silent except for the eerie hum of pumps and filters which kept the samples alive, and for the scuffling of Alfred's slippers along the cold stone floor.

Anxious, full of dread, expecting to find his embryo dead, Eberhard would switch on the cool, precise lights which rendered the gelatinous egg translucent, and he would peer through the scope. He would see that all was well, and he would sense a tremendous relaxation in himself. Staring at the growing fetus, he'd be comforted and, for a lucid moment, he would realize the madness of his behavior, the disproportion of his fears. Then he would make his way back to his bed, and perhaps, shortly before morning, he would drift off to sleep. . . .

But in the morning the awful tension would begin again. The life of the growing embryo seemed infinitely fragile to Alfred, as that which is precious always seems fragile. He felt that any disturbance, any annoyance, might destroy it. Loud noises enraged him, he worried about drafts. . . .

In point of fact, however, the cloned embryo, developing steadily inside its protective envelope of yolk, was far sturdier than Alfred Eberhard gave it credit for. Insulated by its gelatinous wrapper, the embryo knew neither cold nor heat nor sounds. . . . It followed its genetic course, oblivious to all the fanatical attention that was being paid to it.

By now, neural folds—precursor of the brain—had begun to rise up, visible as two oblique ridges near the embryo's top. The spinal cord had begun to form; the skin had begun to differentiate itself. All signs indicated that this artificially fertilized egg, this birth effected with the chromosomal material of a single individual, this *clone*—would develop into a normal adult frog! Indeed, the tadpole stage was only a matter of days away! But would it happen? If it did, it would mark the first time in history that such a birth had been brought about in a higher animal. Truly, it would be a victory!

And yet, what sort of victory would it be? What would the accomplishment mean? Eberhard could not have said. He yearned, with his entire being, for the success of his experiment, but he could not have adequately explained why, not even to himself. It was just something that *had* to be done. (Later, of course, he would find a highly personal, and bizarre, application for his research—but at this stage of his obsession, he did not even think of practical applications. He thought only of the theoretical grandeur, the prideful unnaturalness of what he had imagined and brought about. . . .)

Through the latter stage of the egg's development, Alfred Eberhard peered through the microscope with an intensity very like madness. He was not content merely to *see*, it was as if he longed to *feel* the growth, to become a part of it.

John Goodwin also did a good deal of frantic observing during this epoch-making time—but his observations were divided between the embryo and his friend. Eberhard's behavior frightened him. Goodwin was horrified by his colleague's shadowed eyes, bloodshot and sepulchral in their deep sockets. . . . He was shocked at Eberhard's extreme irritability, at his morbid immersion in his work. Worst of all, Goodwin realized that whether or not this embryo lived, the project would go on. It would not end here; perhaps it would never end.

And now, miraculously, the clone had become visible to the naked eye! It appeared as a tiny, translucent, fish-like creature breaking free of the egg: a tadpole, the larval stage of the frog, in which breathing still occurs with gills. The creature, having emerged, was now transferred to a tank well stocked with the unicellular organisms on which tadpoles thrive.

Then came the final test, in some ways the most grueling. Would the cloned tadpole, having outgrown the cozy environment of the egg, having been cast out of the optimal chemical bath which the egg provided, be able to function and survive? Had the cloning process produced merely a genetic curiosity, an embryo which was ill-fitted to the world because of the unnaturalness of its generation, or had it produced a real *individual*, a creature having all the resources of its species?

Again, there was a tense period of waiting as the early progress of the free-living tadpole was scrutinized. At first the tiny creature languished, but this was not uncommon, an understandably difficult transition to the rigors of the outside world. But then, gradually, the tiny larva began to come around. It swam; it grew. . . . It fed on the algae that had been provided for it. It excreted normally.

Alfred Eberhard watched the erratic and seemingly pointless movements of the little creature for hours on end, enthralled with the very existence of it. Only he knew how much time, how much will, how much agony, had gone into the production of this unique specimen.

Eberhard's exhausted eyes grew bleary as he watched the tadpole swim. Finally, his eyes filled with tears—tears of fulfillment, but not of restful fulfillment—they were tears of a fulfillment that knew it was fated to keep pushing on and on. Yet those tears were also joyous, seeing the tiny creature swim, healthy, well-established, the first such cloned being ever brought to life. Dr. Alfred Eberhard laughed and cried at the same time.

Suddenly, his joy and his exhaustion took voice. He did not know that he was about to speak, but the words came out of him, midway between a shout and a howl, a cry of pain and a religious chant: "I did it, I did it, I did it!"

John Goodwin stood by, and was not even surprised at his friend's insensitive use of the singular pronoun. Dr. Goodwin had realized long ago that this project had come to belong to Alfred Eberhard, and to Alfred Eberhard alone. That was too bad, thought Goodwin, too bad for Alfred's own sake.

Dr. Eberhard brushed by him and left the lab, his steps labored and unsteady. He went to his suite and fell into an exhausted sleep for thirty-six hours. . . .

Eleven

By the time Dr. Eberhard woke through from his long, recuperative sleep, the cloned tadpole had nearly doubled in size. Dr. Eberhard's first act upon awakening had been to visit the special tank in which the creature swam, to confirm that it really did exist, that the experiment really had succeeded. . . . When his eyes had feasted and his mind had been satisfied, he called John Goodwin into conference in his office. Next steps had to be discussed.

John Goodwin came in and regarded his old friend a trifle warily. Goodwin was willing to make all sorts of excuses for Eberhard's recent behavior—he had been working under an enormous strain, pushing himself very hard on very little sleep—but still, the manic single-mindedness he had displayed could not wholly be dismissed. Goodwin hoped that, having caught up on his sleep, having had time to put things back in their proper proportions, Eberhard would calm down.

Now Goodwin scanned his friend's face carefully. It did seem more relaxed, the eyes were not so eerily shadowed. But Alfred seemed to have aged. The aging did not seem to have been the effect of physical processes, but rather of *mental* ones, as if Eberhard had gone so far in thought, had seen so much in his own imagination, that he had taken on the ancient aspect of a sage or shaman.

On the other hand, John Goodwin now appeared younger to Dr. Eberhard. He appraised his colleague's smooth, unwrinkled face, his rampant shock of reddish hair that never seemed to stay in place, his light eyes, naive and winningly shy behind the birdlike lashes. To Eberhard, Goodwin now seemed to be a perpetual boy. Eberhard felt a genuine fondness for him, but no longer regarded him as a peer. Who, then, were Alfred Eberhard's peers now?

"Hello, John," Alfred said, trying to put these troubling perceptions out of his mind.

"Hello. How are you feeling?"

"Much better," said Eberhard. "I really needed that sleep. . . . John, I'm sorry if I was unfair or unkind during the course of the experiments."

John Goodwin did not respond immediately, but searched his friend's eyes. He did not doubt the sincerity of Eberhard's apology, but would it really mean anything over time? Would it carry over to the next time Alfred found himself in an analogous situation? John Goodwin did not wish to be judgmental, but he could not help doubting. Still, what was there to be gained by being ungracious?

"It's all right, Alfred," he said, finally. "I think I understand how you were feeling. But listen, all that's over. The experiment was a success—and now we've got more pleasant things to worry about."

"Like what?" Alfred asked, wanting to find out Goodwin's thoughts before baring his own intentions.

"Well, for one thing," John said, "I suppose we should decide how we're going to publicize our results—whether we want to just write up a report or maybe bring the media in . . . it *is* a big enough discovery for the media. And aside from that, now that we've got the cloned frog, I think we should back up a step and see what the developmental process of it can teach us about cancer."

Dr. Eberhard said nothing for some moments, but sat there drumming on his desk, framing his reply to John Goodwin's suggestions. Eberhard had correctly anticipated what Goodwin would say. It was, after all, standard procedure—standard, unimaginative procedure. The publicity would be good for the Institute. It was the kind of thing that assured that the federal dollars would keep flowing in, that know-nothing laymen across the nation would continue to marvel at the supposed ingenuity of science. They would discuss it over breakfast, as if they had anything to say about it!

As for backtracking and looking for connections between cloning and cancer, that was Goodwin's old argument all over again. Didn't he yet understand that the great scientist never backtracks, but only pushes forward, ever forward? If some other drudge wanted to handle that side of things—scavenging through the debris that had been left bobbing in the wake of Eberhard's racing progress—that was up to the drudge. Eberhard himself wanted no part of such lackluster mopping-up operations.

"John," said Alfred thoughtfully, "I disagree with you on two counts. First of all, I don't think we should publicize our findings at all. Not yet, at least. If we start getting hungry for a Nobel Prize, *then* we'll go publicity-hunting. But for now, what good would it do us? If the media *did* pick up the story, the whole Institute would be turned upside down. There'd be cameramen plodding through the lab, disrupting things. Our own time would be wasted on interviews. I just feel that it wouldn't be worth it."

"All right, Alfred," Goodwin said. "I'm not sure I agree, but I understand your point—as regards the media, that is, but how about the idea of publicizing the work through the journals? What we've done here is something that's never been done before. Don't you feel that the scientific community, at least, should be informed of it?"

Alfred Eberhard realized that he now had to choose his words very carefully. The issue of scientific disclosure was a perennially touchy one—secrecy was considered contrary to the best interests of science, as it withheld data from the very minds which might advance it. And yet, weren't there some instances in which secrecy was justified? If a scientist had done pioneering work in a certain field, mightn't he be justified in keeping that work a secret until he had brought it to its fullest fruition? Should he simply give away the information that he had worked so long and hard to obtain, providing essentially a four-year head start to other scientists who might plunge headlong into the project?

Eberhard felt justified in withholding news of the cloned frog. The problem was enlisting the support of Goodwin, who, Eberhard expected, would be inclined toward full disclosure.

"Don't you think," Alfred asked, "that reporting our findings now might be a little premature?"

"Premature?" said John Goodwin in surprise. "The tadpole has hatched; we've got a dozen notebooks full of the steps by which we finally managed to get it hatched—what more do we need? Compared to most of the stuff that gets published in the journals, our work is exceptionally conclusive."

"Yes and no," Alfred said. "True, we've got notebooks and we've got the tadpole. But what do we know about what sort of frog that tadpole is going to turn out to be? Do we know, first of all, whether or not that tadpole is even going to *develop* into a normal frog? Do we know if the mature frog will be fertile or sterile? If it is fertile, will its offspring be normal? Will the frog's senses be functional? And what is that frog going to look like on the inside? Those are the *really* interesting questions— and it's going to take a whole frog generation to answer them. After this frog has reproduced—if it can—after we check out its offspring, and dissect the clone after it dies—*then* we'll have something to report."

John Goodwin did not quite believe his colleague. His trusting nature had been pushed just a little too far. True, the questions Dr. Eberhard had raised *were* interesting, and true, they *would* take time to answer—but still, the mere process of cloning the frog was fascinating too, and it provided more than enough material for a journal article. Eberhard was stalling for time, of that Goodwin was fairly certain. But why? Goodwin felt that his chances of finding out were better if he let the subject drop for now, and proceeded by indirection.

"Okay, Alfred," he said. "I think we've got a helluva article on our hands *right now.* But if you want to wait, we'll wait. Anyway, you said you disagreed with me on *two* counts. . . ."

Again Alfred Eberhard paused. Again he realized he was on ethically shaky ground, almost certain to incur the implicit censure of John Goodwin, his colleague and former friend. He did not find it pleasant to argue with Goodwin—not that he couldn't outmaneuver him consistently. But that was just the point. Goodwin didn't *maneuver.* He simply spoke his mind, and his thoughts were unassailably proper and reasonable. No matter, Eberhard told himself, if he had to argue with the man, he would argue, he would persuade. . . .

"I—er—disagree with your notion that our next move should be to backtrack."

"But why?" John asked. "Those abnormal growths from the hormone-treated blastulae provided a tempting analogy to cancer. There might be something very valuable there!"

"I don't think so," Alfred said. "I think that, if we go back to those stunted cells, we're essentially heading out after the O+ factor again—and hasn't enough time and energy already been spent on that brilliantly conceived but useless project?"

"But Alfred," protested John Goodwin, "I don't think we'd be doing that at all. Look, in the old O+ experiments, we never had signs of abnormal growth. This is a whole new element in the experiment. If there is a common factor between reproduction and cancer, if there is a shared chemical agent between the two, we might very well find it among the by-products of the actions of those hormones! Who knows how those hormones are broken down? Maybe one of them resolves itself into the acidic protein that Schreiber said he'd caught glimpses of!"

"Listen, John," Alfred said, losing patience, "those experiments would be a dead end, just like all the others. There's nothing really new in them."

"How can you say there's nothing new?" John exclaimed, losing patience in turn. "There's the male hormones—that's new. There's the cancer-like growth—that's new! My God, Alfred, the courses of whole sciences have been changed by the introduction of less new input than that!"

Dr. Eberhard's argument was now stalled. John Goodwin was right, and both men knew it. It was a matter of simple scientific logic, not to be gotten around. And yet Alfred had to get around it—or if not around it, *through* it. He felt an immense frustration building up in himself, a terrible need to have his way at whatever cost, and so his sense of tact was overwhelmed and he ended up saying far more than he'd intended to say.

"All right, John, all right. There may be something worth looking into in those growths. But can't you see that's not what I'm interested in?"

"Alfred—"

"What I'm interested in is carrying those cloning experiments further. I'm not interested in backtracking, dammit! I'm interested in going forward, moving up the phylogenetic chart! Who the hell cares about a cloned amphibian? What do frog genes matter? I want to carry these experiments up to the level where they mean something, where they're more than just a fascinating laboratory game!"

And now it was John Goodwin who was stalled. He was stalled not by logic, but by the sheer manic force of Eberhard's outburst, and by the dizzying implications of what he had said.

Eberhard had half-risen out of his chair as he spoke; his eyes had the horrible fixity of a sleepwalker. And what had he meant by saying he wanted to carry the clone experiments up to "the level that mattered"? It could only mean one thing—and the thing it meant was mind-boggling.

John Goodwin made several attempts to speak. His mouth moved and no words came out. He stared at Alfred Eberhard, who slumped back in his chair as if exhausted by his own vehemence. . . .

Finally, Goodwin managed to say, "I assume that you have already thought out the possible consequences of what you seem to be pursuing. In any case, that's too huge a topic to go into for right now. We'll try and discuss it at a calmer moment. But that aside, Alfred, we're stuck with the same ethical issue that we dealt with four years ago:

We're not here to do what we want. We're not here to pursue whatever project happens to intrigue us. We're here to try and find a cure for cancer. That's what the facility is for, that's what the equipment is for and that's what *we're* for!"

"Jesus Christ, John!" Alfred said, a note of impatience and even disgust in his voice. "If you only knew how tired I was of hearing that self-righteous drivel! We're not here to do cancer research—we're here to do *science*. Cancer research just happens to be the catchword that makes the money flow. Cancer is the emotional issue, the villain that every legislator has to pledge to fight against with votes for new appropriations. Be realistic! It's political. That's one thing I learned from Kenton—you've got to make a cool-headed appraisal of the political situation. Then you can go ahead and do what you want."

"Oh," said John Goodwin, the distaste clearly evident in his voice, "so is Kenton your model now, your hero? I think I liked you better when Schreiber was your mentor."

"Schreiber was never my mentor!" said Eberhard savagely. "Neither is Kenton, and neither is anyone else! I take credit and responsibility for my own ideas. Whatever I am—whatever I think, do, feel, accomplish—I have mapped out for myself, on my own. Do you understand?"

"Yes, Alfred," Goodwin said, his voice soft and sad now. "I understand. I understand better and better."

The two men sat in their chairs on opposite sides of Alfred Eberhard's mahogany desk. Their faces were flushed, their breathing came heavily, as after a physical skirmish. They regarded each other with a poignant blend of mistrust and remembered affection. Their conflict clearly stated, they felt again a yearning toward friendship—a friendship that could no longer be. Perhaps the most that each could hope for from the other now was a benign non-interference, a distant respect founded on remembrance of a time when their goals and methods had been the same.

After a long pause, Goodwin said, "Enough arguing. Why don't you just tell me what it is you intend to do, and we'll see where or if I fit into it."

"Fine," said Eberhard. "I intend to do two things. First of all, I intend to keep a close eye on our cloned tadpole, to follow him to maturity, and try and breed him. In short, I want to look at every aspect of his life and see if it is normal. At the same time, I want to try to begin developing techniques for the eventual cloning of a rat."

"A rat!" said John Goodwin, impressed despite himself at the ambitiousness of Eberhard's plan. "You're jumping straight into mammals, eh? Do you think you can do it? You'll be dealing with a microscopic egg—you won't be able to use our old rather primitive injection techniques. And then you'll have to worry about implanting it in the uterus. Do you think it could work?"

"Theoretically it can," said Dr. Eberhard. "Theoretically, the only differences are differences of scale—mechanical differences. And those can always be gotten around—theoretically. . . . It won't be easy, though, that's for sure. In any case, that's what I intend to be doing. If you want to continue on the project, I would be delighted to have you."

John Goodwin thought it over for a long moment before answering. He stared down into his lap at his folded hands. He closed his eyes and rubbed his forehead.

"I'm very tempted, Alfred," he said at last. "It sounds like a fascinating project. And the whole concept of cloning is a seductive one, an almost irresistible one. But I really feel that I have to bow out. Perhaps I take my ethics too literally, or perhaps I'm just naive—but I can't quite square it with my conscience. I feel I ought to be working on something directly related to cancer. And I feel that if I worked with you on this project, given my reservations about it, it's inevitable that we'd end up becoming enemies. And we've come close enough to that already."

"Yes, that's true," Alfred said with a small smile and nod—the most sincere gestures he had made in as long as he could remember. He felt a genuine warmth for John Goodwin at that moment—and yet the warmth was brought about, in part, by the relief he felt upon learning that Goodwin was stepping out of the project. His troublesome voice of conscience would be stilled, and Eberhard would be spared the unwanted distraction from his single-minded efforts. "Well, then," continued Eberhard, "if you leave the cloning project, what would you like to work on?"

"If it's all right with you," said John Goodwin, "I'd like to do the backtracking. I think there might be a lot worth looking at in those poor warped blastulae.''

"Fine, John,'' said Alfred Eberhard. His conscience was salved. Goodwin would have his project, the cancer-like growths would not go unexamined—and he himself would be free. "I'll see to it that you're funded and furnished with an assistant right away.''

"Thanks, Alfred,'' said Goodwin. "I hope you'll keep me posted as to your progress on the rats.''

"Of course I will,'' said Alfred Eberhard contentedly. "I may even use you as a consultant!''

"I'd be honored,'' said John Goodwin.

"Oh, hell!'' said Alfred Eberhard suddenly, "I'm awfully sorry about this conflict between us, John. You know, I sometimes feel that these researches of mine take me so far out of the sphere of the normal, that I just can't maintain any normal contacts. . . .''

"It's courageous of you to admit that,'' said John Goodwin. "Perhaps you should ask yourself if you might not be trading away more than you could possibly gain.''

"I *have* asked myself that, John. Many times. And I don't know the answer. But the answer is, I'm afraid, irrelevant. I'll pursue the experiments anyway. It's just the way I'm built.''

"Well, then, Alfred,'' said John Goodwin, warmly extending his hand across the desk, "I sincerely wish you the best of luck. Where will you begin?''

"First step, I suppose, will be the futile task of trying to replace you. I shall have to get myself a new assistant.''

Twelve

Claire Rogers had been at Brookside just over a year. She was one of the youngest members of the entire staff, having been hired directly upon her completion of graduate studies at Johns Hopkins. She was a microbiologist, a very bright young woman and a promising scientist.

She was not, however, terribly happy at Brookside. She chafed at her lowly status of junior researcher, a status which, combined with the rampant prejudice against her sex, seemed to preclude her from getting in on any of the really serious work. She felt that she was being misused, regarded as a mere technician. A thorough discontent and seething anger grew in her as she again was assigned the chores of rinsing the test tubes, of arranging the alembics on their shelves. . . .

She resented many of the men she worked with, particularly her own contemporaries. She felt that she was smarter than they were, which, in most cases, was true. She tried to downplay her femininity while working in the lab. She wore a baggy lab coat which obscured the contours of her breasts and hips. She wound her hair tightly into a bun. She wore glasses which she only marginally needed. She could not mask the fact that she was very pretty—smooth-complexioned, even-featured, big-eyed—but she could at least make it clear that she wished to be regarded, during working hours, as a neutral creature, not to be patronized or flirted with.

These annoyances in her working situation were not, however, the only factors in her unhappiness at Brookside. Paradoxically, she was lonely. Though she insisted on neutral treatment during work hours, she missed the gallant attentions that might have been lavished on her in the evenings. It was not that Claire Rogers had no eager seducers—far from it. There was simply no one who interested her. She did not like men her own age. They struck her as half formed and silly. In her entire stay at Brookside, she had consented to go to bed with only one, and only once. The experience had been, purely and simply, unsatisfying. Claire Rogers had no moral qualms about it—it just hadn't been much fun.

Since that first joyless attempt at among-the-staff lovemaking, Claire had stayed pretty much to herself. She did a lot of reading. She did a lot of daydreaming about the things she would accomplish when the males finally stopped holding her down. She did a lot of masturbating, passionless but very pleasurable probings of her own body, which afforded her respite from her preoccupations and brought her much needed physical release.

Claire's loneliness was exacerbated by a rather severe case of homesickness. She was loath to admit it, though, as homesickness seemed a rather unfitting malady for an intelligent and sophisticated young woman to be suffering from. Yet she missed her family. They were from Baltimore, and, though she had insisted on living on her own as soon as she entered college, she had always stayed within easy access of them. She had seen them a couple of times a week, had always known that they were available. It was not a lack of independence that made her miss them so, Claire told herself, but rather a genuine and wholesome love, a love based on a mutual regard that few families ever attained.

She particularly missed her father, with his gracefully graying hair, his reassuring voice, the clean smell of witch hazel that always emanated from him. She always felt like her own person around him, strong and competent—at the very same time that he made her feel protected, cared for, shielded by his warm maturity.

Burdened by these several different strands of discontent, Claire realized that she was not nearly working up to her capacity. She made errors sometimes in the lab, simply because her mind was elsewhere, daydreaming her way out of an unpleasant situation. ("But how that must vindicate *them,*" she would think angry with herself, "to see a woman botch an easy calculation!") She was not doing the job she knew she should be doing, and it preyed on her conscience—even though (she argued back) it wasn't really her fault.

This being her state of mind, her first thought, upon being told that Dr. Eberhard wished to see her, was that she was to be reprimanded, perhaps even dismissed! But was it possible? She had made no big mistakes—she was never allowed to *do* anything big—how could she make big mistakes? No, it couldn't be that. Well, why worry, she told herself. Maybe it was just a routine interview, a "How are you and how do you like it here?" type of thing.

She told herself to be calm as she introduced herself to the receptionist outside of Dr. Eberhard's office. But she could not be calm. She had heard too much about what a brilliant man Dr. Eberhard was, how surely he saw through people and situations. She had heard him speak at staff meetings, and had been too impressed with his assurance and maturity. She could not be calm. She didn't even think she'd be able to tell Dr. Eberhard what was bothering her, even if he asked. . . .

The receptionist pushed a button on her intercom and told Claire that she could go in now. Claire almost asked the receptionist if she looked all right. But she stopped herself. She tucked her glasses into the pocket of her lab coat and knocked on Dr. Eberhard's door.

"Come in," the even timbered male voice said from inside the office.

Claire Rogers opened the door and meekly stepped into the office. It was some seconds before the man seated behind the big desk, his head buried in a sheaf of papers, even looked up at her. "Sit down, sit down," he said, without acknowledging her presence, absently motioning her into a chair across from his own.

Claire furtively studied the distracted director.

She had never been so close to him before. She had never realized how handsome he was. She noticed especially the wisps of gray hair that mingled with the black near his temples. She admired the deep-set eyes, serious and mature, the grave furrows at the edges of the mouth. She looked down at Eberhard's hands and was vaguely excited by their rugged, expert look, the network of manly veins that crisscrossed them, the muscular knobbiness of the fingers, the black hair that crawled down over his wrists. Dr. Eberhard struck her as a man fully formed, an adult. . . .

Finally he looked up at her. His eyes having been trained on the close-work in front of him, he did not immediately see her clearly. She drifted into focus only gradually. Slowly he could define her features—the rich chestnut hair pulled severely back from her high and handsome forehead, the gracefully arching brows, the sea-green eyes, intelligent and searching, the slender and slightly upturned nose, the mouth, innocent of lipstick, yet slightly pink, the texture of the lip-skin alluringly crinkled. . . .

Dr. Eberhard looked at her, and registered all these things with scientific precision—and with scientific disinterest. In some detached way, it must have gotten through to Alfred Eberhard that the woman before him was exceedingly lovely, but he saw her, truly, as nothing except a scientist, a potential assistant. It was not that Dr. Eberhard was preternaturally equipped to separate business from pleasure, nor could it be said that he was terrifically enlightened in his attitude toward working with women. No, it was simply that the doctor was so utterly preoccupied with returning to his ~~cloning~~ experiments, that everything else in the world—faces, bodies, appetites—had merged into one dull blur, barely visible, infinitely less real than the huge plans which loomed up in his mind.

"Now, uh, Dr. Rogers," began Eberhard when his eyes and his mind had cleared, "I suppose you're wondering why I called you in."

"Well, yes," she said, trying to keep the nervousness out of her voice. But she liked Dr. Eberhard already: He had called her Dr. Rogers, as was appropriate, rather than presuming to use her first name, as men so often thought they had the right to do.

"I've been working on a certain project," he continued, "which I believe to be a very important one. And I've been involved with it for quite a while—close to five years in fact, although there was a regrettable hiatus of nearly three years in which I was kept busy with other things. In any case, just recently there has come a breakthrough, which makes the continuation of the project all the more vital. Now, from the outset, I had been assisted in this project by Dr. Goodwin. He, however, has instituted a project of his own, a spin-off of something we came across in the midst of our researches. I therefore find myself in need of a new assistant."

Claire Rogers could hardly believe her ears! For months, she had been relegated to the dreariest chores, the most debasingly non-creative jobs. And now, out of nowhere, the director of the entire facility, a brilliant man, was speaking to her about becoming his personal assistant in an important long-term project! Relax, she told herself, he hasn't offered you the post—who knows how many people he's interviewing. . . .

"Now, then," continued Eberhard, "that's *my* situation. Now I'll tell you why I specifically called *you* in. The project I'm engaged in is rather different from most of what goes on here. Which is to say, it's not directly connected with cancer—or not in the short run, at least." (Dr. Eberhard could not have said how his cloning experiments might have connected with cancer even in the long run, but professional discretion dictated that he temper his frankness with a kind of hedging on certain matters.) "The project, strictly speaking, has to do with embryology—a field in which very few cancer researchers seem to have strong backgrounds. I have been checking over the profiles of nearly everyone on the staff, and I find that very few have studied embryology at all, beyond the basic courses required for a degree, that is. You, however, seem to have studied the subject a great deal, and that is why I think you might be a good person for the position."

Claire Rogers nodded with professional gravity, trying to hide the rather unprofessional excitement she was feeling. So *that* was it! It was those embryology courses that gave her the inside track, that provided a way out of those dull jobs among those dull men.

"I see," she managed to say. "Well, I have studied embryology rather intensively, as I'm sure you've seen from my dossier. I considered majoring in it, in fact, but I switched to micro, as embryology seemed too narrow a field. Before switching, however, I did a lot of work in it."

"Yes," said Dr. Eberhard, "and compiled quite an impressive record, according to your transcripts."

Claire Rogers almost blushed with gratification. How long had it been since she last received a compliment on her *intellectual* attainments?

"Well," continued Eberhard, "as far as I'm concerned, you're the person for the job—if you want it, that is."

If she wanted it, indeed! She would have given anything to be working on this project, under these conditions, with this associate—this man. Nevertheless, she felt that professional dignity required that she make inquiries before giving her reply, that she not appear too overeager.

"Dr. Eberhard," she said, "I'm flattered that you've offered me the post, and I confess that the entire situation is a very attractive one. But could you tell me a bit more about this project, about what it is and what you hope to learn from it."

"I'm afraid," said Dr. Eberhard, "that there's very little I can tell you about it at this time. Given the project's special nature, I do not wish to have it broadly known—the possible to-do and its incumbent publicity would, I fear, be horribly disruptive. If you do accept the post, therefore, I would insist upon your total discretion. I would ask you to regard the project's every detail as classified information.

"If you choose not to accept the post, then it is

best all around if you do not know more than you already do. I don't wish to be unfair or to place you in an uncomfortable position, Dr. Rogers, but I'm afraid that your decision will have to be based only on what I've told you thus far. I've told you that the project is, in my estimation, a very important one. I hope that you'll trust my judgment on that point and decide accordingly."

If there was one final element needed to cap Claire Rogers' excitement, this note of secrecy was it! What could the project be? Something vast, no doubt—something which would carry her into the very vanguard of science. And in the company of Dr. Eberhard, so solemn, so masculine-voiced, so mature. . . .

"Dr. Eberhard," she replied, trying to match the magisterial seriousness of Eberhard's tone, "I understand your intentness on keeping this project a secret, and though I would be easier in my mind if I knew more about it, I'll accept the post on the terms you offer."

"Ah," said Dr. Eberhard. "Good. I'd hoped you would accept. Well, we'll begin tomorrow, and I'll brief you on what's been done on the project so far, and what I intend to do from here. We'll meet in the private sector of the lab at nine o'clock."

Private sector of the lab! How intriguing it all was!

"All right," Claire said, rising gracefully from her chair. "I'll see you then."

Alfred Eberhard had gallantly risen from his own chair as Claire Rogers was alighting from hers, and the two now faced each other across the director's desk. Instinctively, Eberhard examined his right hand, offering a handshake which would seal the terms of their new association. Claire Rogers extended her own hand in turn, and the two of them linked in a firm sturdy clasp.

Now his attention focussed in a new way by the soft warmth of Claire Rogers' fingers and palm, Alfred Eberhard actually *saw* her for the first time. He saw her as a flesh and blood woman, a potential partner in other things besides lab experiments. He was close enough to see the pores in her skin, the follicles of her hair, the ever-so-slight quiver in her lip as she smiled. . . . Suddenly, Alfred Eberhard recalled things he had ignored for too long. He recalled pleasures, places of secret warmth and inexpressible comfort, he recalled the feel of another person's skin against his own. . . .

Claire Rogers melted as she looked at him. The melting feeling frightened her, and she somewhat awkwardly (or so it seemed to her) withdrew her hand and turned to leave the office.

She had reached the door when she heard Dr. Eberhard call her name.

"Yes," she said, turning back toward him, suddenly, inexplicably breathless.

"You'll need a key to get into the private sector of the lab. Here, let me give it to you now."

Strangely unaware of her own steps, she walked back toward the man and took the key from his extended hand. This time their fingers barely touched.

* * *

On several occasions that afternoon, Dr. Eberhard found his mind wandering. This did not, as a rule, happen to him, and he found it rather annoying. He did not connect his daydreaming, however, with his interview of that morning. Consciously, Claire Rogers was already out of his mind. He did not have time to remember her, or to linger on the strange and unexpected feeling which had usurped him in that moment when they shook hands. Besides, his daydreams had nothing, directly, to do with her. He did not daydream about her face, her shape—he did not even daydream about sex. He daydreamed about being outside, in the open air. He daydreamed about the cool shade of trees on hot days. He daydreamed about the pleasure of napping on sun-warmed earth. . . . And he actually did not realize that all these daydreams were metaphors for the woman he had met that morning, were sly ways that his unconscious mind found to remind him of what he'd been slowly starving for the lack of. . . .

Claire Rogers was slightly more honest in admitting to herself the impact of that morning's meeting—but only slightly. She told herself that she had met a fine scientist, a brilliant man who had treated her with professional respect and who had offered her an exciting and flattering position. She admitted to herself that Dr. Eberhard was an attractive man, that she felt safe and somehow exalted in his presence. But she was reluctant to acknowledge any more than that. She was reluctant to admit the sensation that had flooded her when Eberhard's hand had clasped her own. She wouldn't acknowledge the dizzying, fleeting fantasy that had crossed her mind when Dr. Eberhard called her back from the office door.

And even that night, when she undressed and prepared to climb into her narrow bed, she was reluctant to admit that she was feeling any differently than she felt on other nights.

She lay in bed awhile, letting her unrelaxed body settle in, letting her thoughts drift where they would. And, soon, when her body had settled comfortably against the yielding mattress, when she had gotten accustomed to the presence of herself between the sheets, her fingers wandered down between her legs. . . . She felt no differently than she felt on other nights, she told herself—the same wry acceptance of what she did, the same wry pleasure of doing it. Her body felt the same, she had the same moistness, neither more nor less, she went through the same progression of sensations and peaks, her fingers traced out the same tender zones. Only, on this night, when she was finished, she felt a sort of discontent, a discontent that gnawed at her even in the face of her physical satiety. She found that she was yearning for the fullness of a man—and that was something she hadn't desired for a long, long time.

Thirteen

Dr. Alfred Eberhard had already been in the lab for an hour when, at precisely nine o'clock the following morning, he heard the key turning in the lock of the frosted glass door.

Looking up from the tank in which the good-sized tadpole was frolicking, he saw Claire Rogers enter. Had he not been so enthralled with the progress of the cloned amphibian, had his thoughts not returned so totally to the continuation of his project, he might have noticed that Dr. Rogers' lips were a little pinker today, that the color in her cheeks had perhaps been heightened, that the lab coat she wore was considerably better-fitting than the one she'd had on yesterday.

"Good morning, Dr. Eberhard," she said cheerily. "I'm not late, am I?"

"No, not at all," said Dr. Eberhard. "I decided to come down a little early, to make sure that things were set up properly. I'm very eager to begin."

"So am I," said Claire Rogers enthusiastically. "And even more than that, I'm curious—I still haven't been told what this project is all about."

"Well," said Eberhard, "you're about to be let in on it. Dr. Rogers, in your studies in embryology, were you ever introduced to the concept of cloning."

"Of course," said Claire Rogers, wondering if she should be insulted that Eberhard had even needed to ask. She decided she'd better let him know immediately that she knew her subject. "Cloning is asexual reproduction, the creation of a new individual from a single genetic source. It's the means by which unicellular animals procreate. The sum total of all the descendants of a single organism is known as a clone—linguistically, the word is probably related to the word *clan.*"

"Brava!" said Dr. Eberhard, impressed with Dr. Rogers' expertise, and rather amused at her eagerness to show it. "But do you have any acquaintance with the subject of cloning as it pertains to higher animals?"

Dr. Rogers didn't exactly know what to make of this question. As far as she knew, cloning did not pertain to higher animals at all—except theoretically, of course. But in practical terms, the reproductive processes of higher animals were too complicated, the chemistry too subtle, the necessity of both sperm and egg too ineluctable, for the concept of cloning to have any application—or so she had always been taught.

"I don't exactly know what you mean by the question," Claire Rogers grudgingly admitted after a pause.

"Dr. Rogers," said Dr. Eberhard, steering her attention toward the glass tank perched in a corner of the lab, "I want you to take a look in here. Back there—see, behind that clump of algae—there's a tadpole. Take a look at it and tell me what it looks like."

Dr. Rogers obediently peered through the glass of the tank, seeming to be gladly following Dr. Eberhard's instructions. Secretly, however, she was beginning to be annoyed at the cryptic way he asked his questions. Was he trying to trick her? Was he trying to make her look bad? Why didn't he just come out and say what he had to say? In any case, she peered into the tank, and there, zig-zagging among the algae, tickled by the bubbles that danced out of the filter, was a tadpole—a very healthy, ordinary-looking tadpole. What was all the mystery about?

"Well, it's a tadpole," said Claire Rogers. "I don't know what else you want me to say. It looks like any other tadpole. To my eye, it's only a couple of weeks away from metamorphosing into a frog—its gills are shrinking, the legs are developing, the tail is being drawn in."

"That's very good," said Dr. Eberhard. "You have a good eye. And now, I'll ask you to forgive me for the perhaps baffling way I've been questioning you. I hope you'll understand that I had to proceed the way I did, so that the full weight of the discovery would hit you: Dr. Rogers, the tadpole that you just appraised and described, is a clone."

For some moments, Dr. Rogers could not decide how to react. Her first impulse was to laugh. It was such a bizarre notion. But Dr. Eberhard didn't seem to be joking. Was he, perhaps, still trying to trick her, still stringing her along? If he was, it wasn't very nice of him. But why would he do that, or lie about a cloned tadpole?

"Ah," continued Dr. Eberhard when, after perhaps half a minute, Claire Rogers still hadn't spoken. "I see by the skeptical look on your face that you aren't quite convinced that what I've told you is true. Oh, don't protest—it's a good, healthy scientific skepticism that I see there. I compliment you on it. But what I've said *is* true, I assure you. I've got stacks of notebooks to corroborate it—and even the testimony of Dr. Goodwin, if you should require it."

"Oh, no, that's all right, really," said Claire Rogers, slightly embarrassed about her original mistrustfulness. "I believe you, Dr. Eberhard, it's just that—well, it's something of a shock—I never would have thought it possible."

"Few people *would* have thought it possible," said Eberhard. "At the beginning of the project, I'm not so sure that even I thought it was possible! But I did think it was worth a try, and"—indicating the tadpole pressing itself comically against the glass wall of the tank—"there you have it."

"Well," said Claire Rogers, a relieved smile taking hold of her now that the initial mystery had been cleared up, "I'm impressed, I really am. How did you do it?"

"Lots of trial and error," said Eberhard. "To go into all the details would take up too much time for now—although I do hope you'll familiarize yourself with the notebooks, as they'll be very useful for the next phase. In principle, though, our method was very simple. We destroyed the nucleus of a fertile frog egg—"

"Chemically, or with radiation?" asked Claire Rogers. Immersed in the subject now, her early shyness left her, and her mind worked quickly and confidently.

"With radiation," said Dr. Eberhard. "Then, we took a body cell from another frog, and implanted it into the egg—"

"I see," Claire interrupted. "You need a body cell because it has the full number of chromosomes, rather than half, the way the gametes do."

"Exactly," said Eberhard with a smile. "But who's telling the story, me or you?"

"Oh, sorry," said Claire Rogers. "It's just that . . ."

"Not at all, not at all," said Dr. Eberhard. "I was only teasing you. In fact, I'm quite impressed at the way you pick up on things—you're thinking through the entire process as quickly as I can tell it. Anyway, where was I? Ah yes, we took a body cell from a donor frog, and injected it into the de-nucleized egg . . ."

". . . Hoping that the presence of a full set of chromosomes would be enough of a chemical trigger to get the development started," put in Claire Rogers.

"Yes," said Dr. Eberhard, smiling despite himself at the enthusiasm of his new associate.

"Well, was it?" Claire Rogers asked impatiently, eager to get to the end of the marvelous story.

"Yes," said Eberhard, "but then we ran into

problems. The development began, but it became arrested at the blastula phase."

"Why?"

"That's exactly what we asked ourselves for several years!" said Dr. Eberhard. "We finally realized that the developing egg was hormone deficient."

"But if it was hormone deficient, how did development get started at all?" asked Claire Rogers.

"Well, that's what baffled us," said Dr. Eberhard. "It turned out that it had plenty of *female* hormones—and they were the ones that kept the ball rolling as far as the blastula stage. But it was lacking in *male* hormones, hormones that would normally enter the egg along with the sperm. And it turned out that the male hormones were needed to trigger the *further* development of the egg."

"Hmm," said Claire Rogers thoughtfully. "Now that's interesting."

"We thought so, too," said Dr. Eberhard, amused.

"So," said Claire Rogers, "with the introduction of the male hormones, development continued and produced the tadpole."

"Eventually," said Dr. Eberhard. "Until we got the dosages of the hormones down just right, we had a lot of abnormal growths—growths very like cancer. That's the project that Dr. Goodwin is doing now—the study of those abnormally developing blastulae. In any case, we finally produced the little fellow you see swimming around in that tank—and that, in a nutshell, is how I've spent the last five years of my life."

"Well," said Dr. Rogers, "You could have done far worse. Even without knowing all the details of your experiments, I know enough about frog embryology to realize what an extraordinarily difficult feat you've accomplished. It's never been done before, has it?"

"If it has," said Dr. Eberhard, "it's the best kept secret in the biological sciences."

"Hmm," Claire said, still marveling over the reality of the cloned tadpole. "It really is amazing. But now that you've done it, what do you intend to do next?"

"Well," Eberhard said, "the frog as you know, occupies a rather privileged place on the phylogenetic scale. He's low enough down so that he's relatively simple and relatively uncomplicated to work with—that's what makes him such a prime subject for student dissections. On the other hand, he's high enough up, so that he offers valuable insights into how things may work in higher animals. Morphologically, of course, he has little in common with the higher vertebrates, and yet he is a veritable storehouse of analogies: If something can be done with a frog, then, theoretically at least, it can be done with a mammal! And I intend to put that theoretical assumption to the test.

"The next phase of this experiment will be to try and generate a clonal rat. And that is where you fit in—that is where I need an expert embryologist. I can design the experiments, but I need someone with the specific expertise of knowing what is going on inside the uterus of a rodent. I confess I have very little experience with them."

Dr. Rogers' eyebrows raised and her mouth fell slightly open as she heard of Dr. Eberhard's plans.

It was one thing to graft a body cell into the egg of an amphibian—an egg which was easily manipulable and fertilized outside the body. But it was another thing entirely to try to pull off the same trick with a *mammal*—where the egg would have to be plucked from the fallopian tube of a living creature. "It will be very difficult, Dr. Eberhard," she said. "Quite a trick, in fact. We'll be up against a whole different set of hurdles. There are many more factors involved. Not only will we have to worry about keeping the egg and the donor cell healthy, but we'll also have to worry about keeping the mother rat healthy. And with everything we may have to put her through, that will be a trick in itself.

"Besides, even getting the body cell and the egg together in the first place will be a feat. A body cell can't locomote the way a sperm can, and even if it could, it hasn't got the enzymes needed to make an opening in the egg membrane. . . . I don't know, Doctor, if it will be possible, in practical terms."

"Well," said Eberhard, "I have an axiom which underlies my entire feeling about science, and about the nuts and bolts of lab work in particular: If it's possible in theory, it's possible in practice— the only obstacles are human clumsiness and lack of ingenuity. And those are obstacles that can be overcome."

"Let's hope so," Claire said. "Well, where do you suggest we start?"

"Well, to begin with," Alfred said, "why don't you give me a quick refresher course on the embryology and the reproductive system of a laboratory rat. That'll give us some notion, at least, of how we should proceed at the mechanical end."

"Okay," she agreed, rummaging through her mind for the precise information about the laboratory rat.

"Well, like most mammals, rats are oestral. Their cycles are quite frequent though. They go through a fertile stage just about every two months. Ideally, then, they can bear up to six litters a year, although the average number is three or four. The ovaries are paired, of course, and the eggs migrate from the ovary, down the fallopian tube to the uterus, as in any other mammal. They stay in the uterus for a brief time, and if they aren't fertilized, they lose their vitality and are expelled through the vagina."

"Ah," said Dr. Eberhard. "So the process is exactly the same as in any other mammal, up to and including man."

"Yes," she said. "With the exception that in rats, egg development is multiple. The average litter size is five to eight."

"I see," Eberhard said. "And what is the gestation period? How long will we have to wait to see the offspring—if we're lucky enough to get any?"

"Only three weeks," Claire told him. "The young are born hairless and blind, but other than that, they resemble adult rats from day one."

"That's good," he said. "Patience has never been one of my virtues. I would hate it if we were trying to clone something with a year-long gestation period."

"Well," said Dr. Rogers with a warm smile, "you must have more patience than you give yourself credit for, if you spent five years on the development of that cloned tadpole."

"Ah," Alfred sighed, with a grim little laugh, "I'm not sure you can call that patience. That may be something slightly different. In any case, Dr. Rogers, the thing to do from here, is to get ourselves a couple of hundred white rats. I'll go requisition them from the breeding department. In the meantime, why don't you start looking over the notebooks."

Dr. Eberhard left the private sector of the lab, letting the self-locking frosted glass door click shut behind him. As he strode along the long, fluorescently lit hallways that led to the breeding department, he noticed, with his usual scientific detachment, an unusual feeling within himself. It seemed to be happiness. It was a feeling slightly different from, though related to, the heady elation he felt when his work was going particularly well. Again, the feeling had certain things in common with the warmth he had sometimes felt toward John Goodwin, back before their friendship had become so entangled with professional disagreements—but again, the feeling was different in certain ways, too.

Alfred Eberhard tried to analyze the feeling as he strolled along the corridors. Did it have to do with the prospect of beginning the next phase of his project? Perhaps, but that didn't seem an adequate explanation. . . . Did it have to do with his new associate?—Ah ha. Now it seemed that he was on to something. Her mind was wonderfully sharp, her scientific enthusiasm was refreshingly genuine. But come now—Eberhard cajoled himself—wake up! It wasn't only her scientific enthusiasm, but it was also the face that registered that enthusiasm!

Alone in the empty hallway, Alfred Eberhard suddenly said aloud, "No, it can't be . . ." But his face suddenly broke into a smile, a big boyish smile more unguarded than any smile he had smiled in as long as he could remember.

In a moment, though, the smile was erased. Its place was taken by a sober look, a resolute setting of his strong square chin. "Unprofessional," he muttered to himself. "And a threat to the project. I shall have to be careful. . . ."

Dr. Claire Rogers perched on a high lab stool and pored over several of Dr. Eberhard's lab notebooks. She was very impressed. She was impressed by the bold theoretical framework which underlay the entire project, and she was impressed by the ultralogical and tireless way in which Dr. Eberhard had brought his theory to practical fruition. . . . And she was very impressed with Dr. Eberhard himself. The man had presence. He generated a certain warmth—not a facile, sentimental warmth, to be sure, but a more substantial, noble warmth— the heat of an ever-active mind, of an imagination passionately given over to the wish to put flesh on its imaginings.

Dr. Claire Rogers still felt that warmth now, even with Dr. Eberhard gone from the lab. She felt it in her own middle, under the skirt she wore beneath her lab coat. Yes, she said to herself, Alfred Eberhard was a man of substance. It was a privilege to work with him—even if *only* to work with him. Her mind began to drift away from the notebooks in front of her. . . .

In twenty minutes, Dr. Eberhard returned to the lab. Claire Rogers was brought back to reality by the sound of the key turning in the lock of the frosted glass door. Alfred Eberhard entered, followed by a technician, who wheeled in a huge counter full of tiny cages. The cages were teeming with white laboratory rats, hundreds of them, the raw material for Eberhard's next set of experiments.

Fourteen

Drs. Eberhard and Rogers lost no time in getting down to the nuts and bolts of their project. By the very next morning, they had begun to run blood tests on the laboratory rats, trying to determine, on the basis of estrogen levels in the bloodstream, which of the rats were about to ovulate. This in itself was a rather complicated and time-consuming procedure, as the estrogen levels differed rather widely from individual to individual. Further, the blood tests were found to be inadequate as a means of determining exactly *when* ovulation would take place. And, given the surgical procedure that Drs. Eberhard and Rogers had decided upon, precise timing was of the essence.

The trick was being able to isolate the egg during the brief time it spent in the fallopian tube. It could not practically be removed while it was still in the ovary—chances were it would be immature, aside from which, there was too great a danger of damaging the delicate organ and rendering the rat useless. On the other hand, it was not practical to wait until the egg had reached the uterus—once the egg had attached itself to the uterine wall, it would be almost impossible to remove it without damage. The researchers found, therefore, that out of the entire oestral cycle of the rat —approximately two months in duration—there was a period of perhaps several hours during which the egg might be successfully extracted!

Needless to say, the highly unfavorable time proportions added yet another frustrating circumstance to the scientists' already monumental task. But the period of "tube fertility" was determined by nature, and there wasn't a thing that Eberhard and Rogers could do about it—except to try and refine their techniques for pinpointing the time when the egg would leave the ovary and begin its all-too-brief migration.

The actual removal of the eggs was a highly delicate operation. Unlike the frog, which had been cooperative enough to "lay" its eggs, the rodents hoarded theirs. There was no way to get at them, except surgically. Dr. Eberhard was, of course, an expert surgeon—but his skills were extended to their utmost in trying to deal with the tiny organs of the rat. Manipulating human organs was delicate enough—but the precision involved in coping with organs that we've scaled down to one-thousandth the size was staggering!

In a short time, Dr. Eberhard had evolved a maximally efficient method for going on his "egg hunts." He and Dr. Rogers would isolate approximately a dozen of the rats which seemed the most likely to be ovulating at a given time. These dozen rats would all be anesthetized and set up on a sort of assembly line. Claire Rogers would take the anesthetized creatures and arrange them side by side on a countertop which served as the operating table. (There was something vaguely comical, and terribly poignant, about the sight of the furry little bodies, one barely distinguishable from the other, laid out in a row. Dr. Rogers always made sure the row was perfectly straight. The rats would be on their backs, their little feet sticking up into the air. To allow Dr. Eberhard room to operate, roughly six inches would be left between each rat—their whiskers, however, would fill this gap at the level of their heads!)

One by one, Dr. Eberhard incised the soft, pink shaven bellies of the rats. Claire Rogers assisted him, sponging off the blood that interfered with the surgeon's vision. The incisions were made in the lower abdomens of the rodents, and, once the severed flaps of flesh had been withdrawn with tiny clamps, the entire uro-genital tract of the animals could be discerned. The brownish kidneys could be seen nestled on either side of the backbone; thin tubes—the ureters—led from the kidneys to the bladder, which appeared as nothing more than a tiny cellophane pouch, infinitely thin and fragile; from the bladder extended the urethra, winding down toward the vulva.

It was the reproductive organs, however, on which Dr. Eberhard's attention was focused. There were the miraculous ovaries, appearing as tiny nodules, smaller than a pea, and yet capable of producing the eggs that were the carrier of all future life; extending from the ovaries were the fallopian tubes, the short conduits that conveyed the egg to the uterus, where, in most cases, it was fertilized; then there was the uterus itself, that marvelously muscular organ, strong enough to stretch to ten times its normal size in the course of pregnancy, and yet delicate enough, subtle enough in its chemistry, to provide for all the needs of a developing fetus. Moving down from the uterus, there was the vagina, that clever sheath which lured the sperm out of the male and conveyed it toward the waiting egg.

It was the fallopian tubes which were the target of Dr. Eberhard's surgery. With infinite care, being cautious to disrupt neither the ovary nor the uterus, he made a small slash in each of the tender tubes. The tubes were so fine, that Dr. Eberhard had to use his sharpest, most thin-edged scalpel—a scalpel whose edge made the cutting surface of a razor blade seem coarse by comparison. So keen was the blade of this scalpel, that, by the slightest error, the slightest tremor, the entire fallopian tube would be irreparably severed. What Eberhard had to do was to cut through only *one* surface of the tube, leaving the other—only a fraction of a millimeter behind it!—perfectly intact!

This being accomplished, Eberhard would hold the slitted tube open while Claire Rogers delved into it with a tiny "scoop." The scoop—similar in design to the implement with which the dentist explores the spaces between teeth, though much finer—would come away with a small scraping from the lining of the fallopian tube—among which; hopefully, would be an egg. As soon as the scoop had been withdrawn, Dr. Rogers would place it into a previously prepared bath which duplicated the chemistry of the fallopian tube itself, and which would therefore preserve the egg—if the egg, in fact, was on the scoop.

This entire exacting process had to be repeated for each rat that was opened up—and, on the average, two dozen rats were opened up each day—one batch in the morning and another in the afternoon.

The work was tedious and exhausting, and the results, at first, were anything but encouraging. Only one rat in ten yielded an egg—the other scoops contained nothing but the epithelial cells that lined the inside of the fallopian tube. Of those eggs that Drs. Eberhard and Rogers did manage to isolate, the majority had become inactive by the time they could be examined; either the chemical bath in which they were kept was somehow inadequate, or the trauma of removal from the body had weakened them irreparably.

In any case, by the end of their first week of research on the rats, Eberhard and Rogers had, in concrete terms, accomplished nothing. They had hoped to be able to study *living* eggs, so that they might begin devising methods for de-nucleizing the eggs, and, eventually, for impregnating them with body cells drawn from other rats. But they had been able to isolate no living eggs to study. They had gone scavenging through the interiors of over one hundred rats and had come out empty-handed. It was indeed discouraging. . . .

The discouragement was partly alleviated, however, by the harmonious working relationship that was growing between Claire Rogers and Alfred

Eberhard. With each succeeding day, they became more effective as teammates. They anticipated the turns of each other's mind; they fit into the shape of each other's movements in the cramped space of the lab.

Alfred Eberhard barely understood how, even in the face of his stymied experiments, the good mood he had been in on the first morning of working with Dr. Rogers could persist. Dr. Rogers, for her part, barely took time to think about the paradox of how she felt in Alfred Eberhard's presence—so much her own person, and yet also so protected, so watched over by a mature man whom she revered. Dr. Eberhard did not at first perceive the slight modification of his eagerness to reach the lab in the morning. It did not occur to him that it might not be only his charts and samples he was so eager to get back to. Claire Rogers only half admitted to herself that she was taking more care of how she looked, that she lingered now over her choice of what to wear, that she left her lab coat open so that Dr. Eberhard might see the clinging cloth of her soft blouse against her torso. They worked together, that was all, they were both at pains to remind themselves. Their association was a purely professional one. . . .

At the end of their first week of working together, Alfred Eberhard and Claire Rogers became lovers. The way it happened surprised them both, and yet, in retrospect, there was a simple and fierce inevitability to their linking, as perhaps there always is.

It was Friday, something after five o'clock. The two scientists had had another frustrating day. The last batch of anesthetized rats were just waking up, kicking their tiny legs in the air, trying to regain their sense of place and balance. Dr. Eberhard was cleaning his surgical instruments, arranging them in the autoclave, where they would be sterilized. Dr. Rogers was rinsing out the trays which held the chemical bath—they would try a different formula next week.

There was no conversation in the laboratory. . . . The only sounds were the slight tinkle of the surgical instruments in their tray, the scuffling of the rats in their cages, the cool sound of running water in the sink.

Suddenly, Alfred Eberhard was terribly weary. His fierce optimism had temporarily deserted him. His eyes ached from all the incredibly exacting work he'd been doing. He allowed himself to lean back against one of the lab counters for a moment. How sweet even that tiny bit of rest was! He closed his eyes, intending to rest them only for a moment, and raised his hand to his brow and massaged it, coaxing some of the tension out of his overused brain, trying to relieve the pressure that throbbed within his skull.

Claire Rogers caught sight of him at that moment. How vulnerable he looked! How tender, how handsome . . . how much he seemed to need her! Should she go to him? There was no time for a decision—only time enough for an instinctual response, a response based on her own yearning and her sure womanly knowledge of his.

Alfred Eberhard felt cool fingers against his temples. He felt a certain tension leave his body at the first touch of those soft, embracing hands; he felt a different sort of tension begin to grow. He marveled at the sweet releasing feel of those massaging hands—they seemed to caress his very mind, to soothe his very thoughts. The touch seemed more intimate than any he had ever known.

His hands reached out and held her waist, resting lightly on the shelves of her hips. He felt the warmth of her, the young resiliency of her flesh. He drew her toward him into an embrace, and she did not resist, but moved in gracefully, seeming to flow against him with the smooth inevitable current of warm and fragrant water. And yet she was solid, she was flesh, her breasts pressed against his ribs, her belly undulated against his own, her loins, secret and yearning to make their secret known, nestled against his thighs. Wordlessly, he brought his mouth down onto hers. Her lips were parted, the kiss was deep and there was no turning back from it.

The kiss ended, their lips parted, their eyes opened. The lighting of the lab, the cold metal gleam of the instruments, were a sudden cruel intrusion, a grating incongruity in the waking dream they had entered together. There they were, suddenly, in laboratory coats, at the end of the day, rather than in the naked timeless placelessness of their first embrace. But no matter, there would be no turning back. . . . The dream was planted in their loins, there was hunger there, a stubborn desire that exalted them and put them beyond the reach of distractions, of incongruities.

Alfred Eberhard straightened himself from his

leaning posture. He kept one hand tightly clasped around Claire Rogers' back, and with a movement that was almost rough, almost frenzied, he wheeled her around toward the door of the laboratory. Quickly, never letting go of her, he opened the frosted glass door and ushered her through.

Claire had no thought of fleeing—she walked close to Alfred, rejoicing in the feel of his firm side against her own, aching for the feel of the front of him.

It seemed an eternity of walking down the empty, strangely lit hallways of the facility. The walls, the low ceilings, seemed to be pressing in on them, and yet the corridors went on and on, cold tunnels leading to the completion of a warm and ancient ritual. Their breathing came harder as they walked, Alfred held Claire tighter and tighter around the waist, feeling her flesh coming up between his grasping fingers. . . .

At last they reached the wing in which the director's suite was located. Eberhard fumbled in his pocket for the key, fumbled again to fit the key into the lock—how clumsy he had suddenly become, how unsteady his fingers!

Claire preceded him into the apartment, and only now, here, in his place, did the awesome mystery of what she was about to do break over her. To welcome him into her own body, to open up before him, to make a sanctuary of herself . . . How eternally strange it was, this business of male and female! (In her mind, for an instant, was an image of the incised rats, their sexual apparatus exposed and probed—very little different than she, those tiny mammals, with their tubes, their tunnels, their alluring hollows, their nature-driven cravings. Very little different than she, with their periods of hot and cold, their chemical tides, and their melting but fierce desires, their times when nothing in the world existed except that female yearning to be filled. . . .)

Alfred Eberhard had come up behind her now. He embraced her and pressed himself against her buttocks, and she knew the force of his desire, his own fired blood urging him on toward the same age-old goal as hers. She swiveled in his arms and clung to him, her hand around his neck. Then she pulled his face down toward her own into another passionate kiss, a kiss not to be interrupted this time, but to move them inexorably toward the consummation.

Drifting, barely aware of their movements, they entered the bedroom. They longed to be naked now, to be freed of those fabric constraints, and yet they could not let go of each other long enough to slip out of their clothes. They feared that the embrace, once lost, might be gone, fled, impossible to recover, the moment of sweetness spent. They could not let go, but clung to each other's body as if to stay afloat in the unfriendly currents of their lives. They struggled out of clothes, groaned against the pressure of sleeves, shoes, trousers, skirts, the minimal but vital sheathing of undergarments.

Finally they had achieved nakedness, had reached it with gratitude, a pleasant destination. Eberhard realized suddenly that he had deprived himself too long—his throat closed with yearning, his eyes burned. He buried his face against her breasts. He wanted to cry against them, but no tears came. He was hungry, he sucked, he searched, the nipples came up taut and pliant in his mouth.

Closing his eyes, he drifted, nowhere, everywhere, the sound of Claire's sighs and moans of pleasure were whispers coming from the center of the earth. He cupped her breasts, the feel of her flesh was too perfect to quite take notice of, it had the inevitable perfection of air, of water, giving life so basically its gift is never thought of as miraculous. . . .

Her hands caressed his torso, brushed over the smooth black hair that covered his chest and belly. She reveled in the strength of his lithe and graceful muscles, knotting her fingers in the virile fur of his body. She reached for his sex now, wanting to feel it in her hand. She had to know it so that she would know what it was she welcomed. . . .

Her fingers probed and locked around the cylinder of flesh, and her breath caught.

. . . Again, for an instant, she saw the viscera of the female rats, so delicate, so small, and in her mind she saw a crazy image of her own insides, those insides burning now and eager. She saw tubes and channels, saw fierce red tissue quivering and pulsing, saw the fibrous sac that was the uterus, saw the duct-rich glistening hollow that was the vagina— and all these things she measured against the girth of the thing that was in her hand. It would not yield, she knew, and so she must yield, she must stretch and move and accommodate herself to the heedless shape and volume of the phallus.

Given up wholly to her desires now, Claire Rogers, never letting go of that to which she clung, stretched herself out full length along the bed, urging the doctor down on top of her. Their eyes were open as she guided him in: They had to see each other's face, acknowledge their complicity in this simple and miraculous act. Claire winced with pleasure at the first rending contact. And Alfred Eberhard sighed at the discovery of her readiness. . . .

And now began the long slow journeying together, the rhythmic pace of hips, of breath, carrying them further and further away from themselves, deeper and deeper into the relieving placelessness of passion. Claire Rogers held her lover tightly around his back, her legs wrapped around his, her feet bearing down in the hollows of his knees. Her face was tight and lovely, small tears escaping at the corners of her eyes.

Alfred rose up above her, strong, steady, composed in the midst of frenzy. But now the letting go was near, the restraints had shriveled, the needs had struggled to the very surface and screamed themselves like raw nerves. Alfred felt himself about to burst, to gush the seed which he had kept inside for too long and let turn acrid and toxic within him. But now it was about to be released, he was about to be cleansed of it, cleansed through the body of Claire Rogers. . . . But not only through her body—Alfred Eberhard found that, despite himself, he could not hold aloof at this final moment—not like he had always done, being stubbornly alone in the very midst of this fiercest embrace. . . . No, he was *with* her—he sensed it, experienced it and knew it had never been like that before.

Then Claire Rogers sensed it, too, felt the full, exploding, unwithheld presence of the man who mingled with her now, felt the throbbing thereness of every part of him, and that presence triggered her release, that pulsing around him, that churning and tumbling within herself, the wonderful crisis of muscles suddenly locked in crazy spasm, taking all the tension out of her, squeezing all the tension out in the final wracking clenches of her walls around the encroaching virile flesh.

Afterward, they laughed together, from sheer relief, from sheer gratitude. They laughed like lunatics. Alfred Eberhard could never remember laughing like that.

Fifteen

Needless to say, the atmosphere in this private sector of the laboratory changed after the first sexual encounter of Drs. Eberhard and Rogers. And yet, the tone of things did not change as much as one might have expected. Alfred Eberhard and Claire Rogers were both intently professional, determined to maintain the cool-headed distance so essential to their work. This distance was to become harder and harder to maintain as time wore on, as their ecstatic linkings were repeated, as their need for each other ripened. But in the beginning, they were able, with an almost weird shifting of the psychic gears, to resume their staid work relationship, almost as if nothing at all had happened.

The research, meanwhile, was progressing slowly, although certain advances were being made. Dr. Rogers became increasingly acute at judging the precise time when a rat would begin to ovulate. This led to a significant increase in the percentage of fallopian tubes which did, in fact, yield eggs. Similarly, by varying the composition of the chemical bath in which the eggs were preserved—a little more sodium here, a little less phosphorous there, a slight increase in the temperature of the bath—the researchers were able to keep the eggs alive longer. This gave them the time they needed to study the extracted eggs.

The study of the extracted eggs was in itself a subtle and laborious task. Unlike frogs' eggs, which were large enough to be manipulated—held in the hand, supported in the surgical vise, and so forth—the rat's eggs were microscopic. They could only be studied on a slide, and the preparation of the slide was a tricky operation. How could the egg be prevented from drying out? How could one be certain that any data gleaned about the egg in this bizarrely unnatural context, would have any validity when the egg was again returned to its natural habitat? And *could* the egg be returned to its natural habitat? After having been removed, exposed to light, air and various sorts of handling, could it possibly be re-implanted in the uterus and be expected to grow normally?

These were the crucial questions—and they could only be answered one at a time. Each phase of the experiment could give clues to only one tiny part of the huge riddle which Drs. Eberhard and Rogers confronted. And every clue they unearthed raised a welter of new questions.

So, then, the two researchers had to work at an agonizingly slow pace. Fortunately, their entire scientific training had been an education in patience, in restraint. Again and again they repeated the mass operations on the ovulating rats; again and again Claire Rogers delved in with her scoop, while Alfred Eberhard parted the tissue of the fallopian tube;

again and again, they studied the withdrawn eggs, looking for conclusive information about what to do next, information which never seemed to offer itself. And, again and again, this intimate delving into the sexual parts of the tiny mammals suggested an analogy to Claire Rogers and Alfred Eberhard, an analogy which kept them subliminally excited, and which led them to reach eagerly and gratefully for each other at the close of the day. . . .

Then, finally, there came a breakthrough. It was only a first step, but an important one: Claire Rogers discovered a way to keep the eggs alive for a much greater period of time—long enough to study them, and, it was hoped, long enough to enable them to be micro-injected with a donor cell—when all the details of that incredibly delicate process had been developed.

It was an elegantly simple insight which led Claire to her valuable discovery. It occurred to her one afternoon as she was examining the "scoops" to which the extracted eggs adhered. As usual, most of the eggs had already become inactive; the ones that were still alive, seemed to be in a thoroughly vitiated state. Claire Rogers and Alfred Eberhard looked at each other with discouraged expressions on their faces.

"There has to be something wrong with that chemical bath, Alfred," Claire reasoned. "Something is missing, or something excessive is there. And it has to be something that we can correct."

"But Claire," Alfred said, a note of impatience in his voice, "what could possibly be wrong with it? We've exactly duplicated the chemistry of the fallopian tube itself. We've got the same ions in there, the same hormones, at the same temperature."

Claire was silent for a moment. She turned her chin down and rested it against her chest.

Alfred Eberhard looked at the top of her head, admiring the richness of her chestnut hair—but not expecting that she'd come up with anything of startling importance. It wasn't that he doubted Claire's brilliance, but the two of them had been through this same discussion a dozen times before.

Finally, Claire spoke, a sudden exclamation, accompanied by an almost comical slapping of her own forehead. "Of course, of course," she said. "Alfred, why didn't we think of this before?"

"Think of what before?" he said, feeling a little testy about being the last one to be let in on the idea—it was not a feeling he was used to.

"It's not the chemistry of the fallopian tube we should be trying to duplicate! Even in nature, the egg only spends a few hours in the tube—it's not *meant* to stay there longer. The chemistry can't support it for longer! So, of course, our eggs die! Even if they weren't traumatized by being extracted, they'd lost vitality by staying in the fallopian tube chemistry too long. Alfred, it's the chemistry of the uterus we should be trying to duplicate—that's where the egg could be expected to last the longest."

"Ah!" Alfred muttered, mulling over the indisputable logic of Claire's idea. "I think you're right—it makes perfect sense. Damn, we've wasted a lot of time with that other bath! Well, let's set about concocting a uterine bath and see what we come up with."

Accordingly, the two researchers prepared a new chemical bath. The differences were subtle but significant, particularly in the amount of estrogen present. Immediately, it could be seen that Claire Rogers' innovation was a major improvement. The eggs survived nearly three times as long as they had in the first bath. But still, they did not really live long enough; nor did they maintain themselves in adequately healthy condition.

A further refinement of Claire Rogers' notion was required, and this time it was Alfred Eberhard who provided the intuitive leap.

"I don't quite understand it," Claire said. "True, the eggs are doing better, but I see no reason why they shouldn't be doing better still. I mean, in a normal situation, the egg stays healthy for over three weeks—the normal gestation period, plus the period of migration. . . . Ideally, we should be able to keep the eggs alive at least that long."

"Yes, but—" began Dr. Eberhard. But then he broke off, as if his mind had suddenly taken off in a new direction. He lifted his hand to his face and rubbed his chin judiciously. "I think I've got it," he said after a pause. "As usual, it seems almost too simple to believe. But—what we've done is to duplicate the chemistry of the uterus of an *unpregnant* rat—now, eggs don't live for three weeks unless the rat is pregnant—*obviously*. So what we've got to do is create a chemical environment identical with the uterus of a pregnant rat. That'll probably take some extra hormones, some more calcium, and different concentrations of a number of ions. . . . *Then* I bet we'll be able to keep the eggs alive."

And sure enough, this third formula did the trick. The extracted eggs flourished—if their vitality had been sapped by the trauma of their removal, it did not show in any clinically discernible way. The eggs seemed as healthy as could be.

This was encouraging for two reasons: In the short run, it meant that the eggs could be studied in a deliberate and thorough way. Dr. Eberhard could finally begin the search for means of eliminating the nucleus without harming or contaminating the nourishing cytoplasm; in the long run, this vitality of the eggs made it seem increasingly possible that the egg could in fact be re-implanted—that, after having been "impregnated," it could be placed back in the uterus of the rat, where, theoretically, it might be expected to develop normally.

The clearing of this first tough hurdle filled the two doctors with exhilaration. They smiled, they beamed, they silently congratulated themselves and each other on how effectively they worked together. But it was not only as a working team that this tentative victory cemented their relationship. No, it was as lovers, too. . . .

Before this victory, when their project had been only one long series of frustrations, they had taken solace in each other's arms, they had fled to passion at the close of the day as a means of blotting out the failed efforts of their research. But now, victorious, they took each other in joy, they laughed as they made love. It was a new dimension for them, a new tone. And it made their linking seem so much more rounded, so much more *solid*. It was like looking at a sculpture or a painting: When one had observed it from several viewpoints only then did its full power show itself, only then did it take on life.

Several days after the discovery of the fertile-egg uterine bath, Alfred Eberhard finally managed to arrange to meet with his old friend John Goodwin, to drink a beer in the lounge, "like in the old days. . . ."

In the course of the nearly two months since the initiation of the new phase of his project, Dr. Eberhard had neither seen nor spoken to his colleague. There were several reasons for this. Dr. Eberhard was terrifically tied up with his work—and with Claire Rogers; aside from that, his vanity made him hesitant to speak with his friend unless he had something positive to report; and aside from that, Alfred Eberhard was far less than certain that his friendship with John Goodwin had not been irreparably damaged—Eberhard himself had only good feelings about his former friend, now that the pressure of working with him and debating the ethics of his project was off. But still, he had to acknowledge that he had been unfair in certain ways to John Goodwin, and Alfred had to either choose to deal with Goodwin's possible resentment or to ignore him. And thus far he had chosen to ignore him. Now, however, feeling good about the project, feeling benevolent toward the world, he contacted Goodwin and arranged for a chat.

"Have you ever met John Goodwin?" Alfred

Eberhard asked Claire Rogers, as the two of them cleaned the lab and prepared to leave.

"I've met him only briefly," Claire said. "We were introduced at a staff meeting. I don't suppose he even remembers me."

"But you remember him," Alfred teased.

"Well, yes," Claire admitted. "I do remember him, quite clearly. He does have a certain presence, a certain elfish sort of charm, with that reddish hair and those fluttering eyes. And besides," she continued, deciding that perhaps she should give Eberhard's ego a stroke, "everyone knew that the two of you were associates, and friends—that in itself lent him a certain fascination."

"Well," said Dr. Eberhard, not quite certain how to take Claire's final remark, "I'm afraid we're not quite friends anymore. Although I think awfully highly of him and trust him more than I've ever trusted anyone. But the pressures of working together sort of got to us. It's extraordinarily difficult to work with someone and not have it muck up certain other things."

Eberhard noticed Claire's face cloud over as he said these words.

"There, there," he said. "I'm not saying it's impossible—it's only difficult. . . . In any case, I'm meeting him for a beer over in the lounge—would you like to join us?"

"Well," she said, a certain hesitancy in her voice, "I don't know. Are you sure it wouldn't be awkward?"

"Awkward?" Alfred said. "But why? You're my

assistant on this project; we're working together—
why should it be awkward?"

"I just thought that maybe . . . well, does he
know about us?"

"Not at all," Alfred said. "I haven't spoken to
him in months. Besides, what if he did? What difference would it make?"

"Oh, I don't know," Claire said. "I guess I just
find it a little embarrassing. I mean, it just seems
like such a typical setup: The young woman researcher goes to bed with the charismatic senior
researcher, the director no less. It's just too pat. I
think I'd be embarrassed if people knew."

"Well, it *is* a setup!" Alfred said teasingly. "But
that's no reason not to enjoy it. But if you don't
want anyone to know, then no one will know. Now,
will you come along with me?"

"Sure," she said.

The two scientists walked side by side down the
long corridors of the research center. (Yet how different that shared walk was now from what it was
like when they walked together toward Dr. Eberhard's suite, their hearts racing, their skin prick-
ling, their loins preparing heatedly for their
arrival. Now, they walked slowly and calmly, aloof,
posing as mere associates.)

Dr. Goodwin was already in the lounge when
they arrived. Upon seeing them enter, he unfolded
his long legs and rose from his chair.

"Hello, Alfred," he said. "It's good to see you."
His voice was warm, as was the handshake he ex-
tended. Alfred Eberhard concluded with relief that
John Goodwin bore him no lingering resentment.

"It's good to see you, John," he said. "Do you know Dr. Rogers?"

"I believe we've met once," said John Goodwin. (Claire Rogers was flattered and really not that surprised that he remembered her.)

"Dr. Rogers is working with me now," Eberhard explained. "And I must say, if I ever said I'd never find as good an associate as you, I was being too pessimistic."

"Well," said Goodwin, "I'm glad for you. Now, shall we sit down and have a beer? Dr. Rogers, do you drink beer?"

"When there's nothing stronger available," she said with a sly intonation. Why did men always have to *ask* if a woman drank beer? They always took it for granted that *men* drank beer.

John Goodwin fetched three beers, hoping that he hadn't offended Claire Rogers. But he liked her reply—she was spunky. . . .

"So," John said, handing around the cold bottles of brew, "how goes the work?"

"So-so," Alfred said. "We're making some progress. We've succeeded in getting eggs out of the rats. And, thanks to an idea of Dr. Rogers', we're having better and better luck keeping the eggs alive once we've got them. But we're still in the early stages. We haven't yet *done* anything with the eggs— and that's where the real work will come in."

John Goodwin only half listened to Eberhard's words. He was secretly observing Claire Rogers, noticing the way she stared at Alfred Eberhard as he spoke, the way she hung on his every word. "Well," he said, "at least you're making some progress. But what was the idea that led to your success with the eggs?"

"Oh," Claire said, with a deprecating little shake of her head, "it wasn't really anything much. It had to do with the chemical environment that we created for the eggs after they'd been extracted. Besides, it was really only half an idea—Alf. . . . Dr. Eberhard really completed the thought, and that's what made the difference."

"And how is your work going, John?" Eberhard asked.

"It's hard to say," Goodwin admitted. "The growths in those blastulae are fascinating, but they don't seem to be telling me anything conclusive. That damn O+ factor is as elusive as ever—and yet the concept remains as seductive as ever. . . ."

"Yes," said Dr. Rogers, "it is a fascinating idea. I've looked through all the old notebooks—all the way back to when the project was first initiated by Dr. Schreiber. I think the whole thing has been a remarkable broadening out and developing of a single idea. And there are so many directions for the research to take."

John Goodwin looked frankly at the pretty, mobile face of Claire Rogers. He was very impressed with her—only a real scientist would have bothered to trace the experiments back to their inception—a lesser mind would have been content to familiarize itself only with those aspects of the work which bore directly on the task at hand. Clearly, Claire Rogers had a superior mind. And yet something about her disturbed him.

He examined the disturbance, trying to pinpoint

its source. It did not have to do with Claire Rogers herself, he decided, but with her implicit stance toward Alfred Eberhard. Everything she said seemed to have some veiled reference to him, to be indirectly a compliment, an identification. . . .

A somewhat uneasy silence descended when Claire had finished speaking. Where was the conversation to turn from here? It didn't seem like anyone was in the mood to discuss work any further. And yet, there, isolated, with Eberhard's and Goodwin's long and tangled history, and the added weight of Eberhard's and Rogers' present secret, what else was there to speak of? Suddenly, instinctively, Claire felt that she should withdraw, leaving the men to themselves. If they did, in fact, have things worth saying to each other, they would not say them in her presence—not now, at least, not as long as this artificial and perhaps unnecessary charade was being played.

She excused herself, claiming a headache. Eberhard and Goodwin expressed concern, though both were, in different ways, glad that she was leaving. Things had somehow gotten strained. Perhaps the situation could only be grasped in groups of two.

Once Claire had left the lounge, however, the two old friends found that they did not know exactly what to say, where to start. . . . For some moments there was silence. John Goodwin popped a couple of fresh beers. And then, when he finally began, he began bluntly:

"How long have you been sleeping with her, Alfred?"

Alfred Eberhard was rather taken aback at the question. He'd thought he'd been doing such a good job of keeping the true nature of things hidden. He was a bit disturbed, though secretly pleased, that John Goodwin had seen through the ruse so easily. Nevertheless, he did not exactly know how to reply. Would it be roguish of him to tell the truth, since Goodwin had already guessed it anyway? What was to be gained by fabricating? And yet it did seem rather unprofessional.

"Come, come, Alfred," continued John Goodwin when half a minute had passed and Eberhard had still not replied. "You don't have to be coy with me. This isn't a high school locker room, you know— I'm not going to press you for all the juicy details."

"Well, then," asked Alfred Eberhard, "why do you want to know at all?"

"I want to know," said John Goodwin, "because Dr. Rogers strikes me as a remarkable young woman—intelligent, bold in her thinking, intellectually—if not emotionally—mature—and . . . well, I can't help being concerned about the whole setup."

"Well," said Alfred Eberhard, "I don't see that there's any reason for you to be concerned."

Now that the subject had been broached, however, Alfred Eberhard found himself wanting to talk about it. He was flattered by John Goodwin's high appraisal of his lover, and he was curious about his further view of the entire situation. And also, though he was hesitant to admit it to himself, Alfred Eberhard also felt the need of a good air-clearing talk; he himself was none too certain about the implications of his affair with Claire Rogers. It was different from what his other affairs had been—there was no question of that. But how would it turn out? What would it mean to his work? Would it be possible to end it gracefully, when the time for ending it should come.

". . . If you must know," he continued, "we've been lovers for close to two months now. We became lovers at the end of our first week in the lab."

"Didn't waste much time, did you?" John said.

"It just happened," Alfred protested. "Quite unpremeditated. . . . But listen, John, why are you grilling me about it?"

"I don't mean to 'grill' you," John said. "But I tell you, Alfred, I'm concerned."

"Yes," Alfred sighed, his patience beginning to fade, "you've told me that. But just what is it you're so concerned about?"

"That woman is head over heels in love with you."

"Nonsense!" But Alfred was far less than certain it was nonsense—it was the thing he most feared happening, and yet he yearned for it to happen. . . . "We work well together, we screw well together. That's all. You're reading too much into it."

"No, I'm not. And you know it. It shows. It's plain as day. The way she looks at you when you speak, the way she glances at you when *she* speaks, as if she's playing for your approval every minute. She's in love with you, Alfred. And it seems to be a terribly complicated and virulent sort of love. . . ."

"How do you mean?" Eberhard asked. "Are

some sorts of love more complicated or more virulent than others?"

"Yes," John said, "because certain loves are based on a number of different things—each thing contributes its own special power to the love. And look at it: You're the director here, the god figure. You're what?—twelve years, her senior—what a situation that is! You're the initiator of the project she's working on. Plus which, as you say, you screw well together. You've got it covered from every angle, and that makes for a virulent, and maybe a dangerous, kind of love."

"Dangerous?" Eberhard bristled. "That's a strange word to use." (Although it was a word which, in his own ponderings of love, he had sometimes used.) "In what way is it dangerous?"

"Well," his friend said, "perhaps, if you weren't colleagues, it wouldn't be dangerous. But you're working together—you should serve as critics for each other, moderating forces. But if she loves you as much as I think she does, she'll be useless to you in that capacity. She'll follow you blindly, and it could be very dangerous for both of you."

"Really, John," said Alfred Eberhard with a laugh (a laugh, however, out of which he could not keep a certain grim intonation). "Aren't you taking this a little too far?"

"No," he said firmly, "I don't believe I am. And I'll tell you why. I have a theory. I've thought about it a lot—I think about it in connection with what I'd ultimately like to have with a woman. Now, the theory is this: Every man has a certain secret image of himself. And usually that image is out of proportion—a man feels himself to be smarter, stronger, capable of greater achievements than he—or perhaps anyone—actually is. A man has yearnings in accordance with those bloated hopes and ambitions—and if they aren't checked or soothed, the man is horribly unhappy.

"Now, when a woman loves a man—loves him truly, but not blindly—she intuitively reconciles those swollen hopes, that puffed-up but fragile ego, with the realities of situations. She allows a man to come to terms with the fact that there are certain things he can not do, *should* not do. That is one of the central blessings of a woman's love for a man.

"But, in the case where a woman loves a man blindly—'not wisely, but too well,' as Shakespeare put it—she gets duped by the same myth that's duping the man himself! He believes himself capable of anything—and she comes to believe it, too! So, instead of acting as a gentle check on his excesses, she unconsciously begins to egg him on. She feeds the myth, and the myth in turn becomes devouring. . . ."

"And you're saying that Claire Rogers loves me blindly?" Alfred concluded.

"I'm saying that that's my fear," Goodwin admitted. "Listen, Alfred, maybe I am overreacting. But the work you're doing is so powerful, so potentially sweeping in its implications—and, forgive me for saying so, but I know from experience that, intentionally or otherwise, you can become ruthless in the course of your work. That's part of what makes you a good scientist, but it can be a dangerous tendency. *I* was never frightened by it. I knew that

I could hold my own against you, if only by dropping out of the project. But this is different. You have tremendous power over that woman."

"But damnit!" Alfred argued. "I didn't *ask* to have power over her! I didn't even *ask* to go to bed with her. And now you're playing the voice of conscience and laying this grim responsibility on me."

"I'm not saying that you've *taken* power over her—maybe she *gave* you the power. But in either case, you have it. And I just hope you're careful how you use it."

There was a silence. Alfred Eberhard knew that John Goodwin was right. He knew that Claire Rogers was in love with him. He knew that he encouraged that love, even though in certain ways he didn't want it. In other ways he did. In other ways he needed it. And he needed the power he was at such pains to disclaim.

"Alfred," John said after a pause. "We've overlooked one rather important question: Do you love her?"

"Hmm," Alfred mused, as if the question were a totally novel one. "You know, I haven't really thought about it in those terms."

"That doesn't really surprise me," said John Goodwin with a wistful little smile. "But maybe you should."

After a time, the two men left the lounge. Alfred headed toward the residence wing. He knew that Claire would be waiting in his suite, warm, expectant, perhaps already undressed, yet he walked slowly. There were a number of things he wanted to think over. His talk with John Goodwin did not actually tell him anything that he didn't already know, but it forced him to confront certain things that he had long avoided thinking of.

It was true—he did have vast power over Claire Rogers. He was too many different things to her—lover, surrogate father, exalted scientist, savior from her dull routine of technician's jobs. It was true that she supported him in every turn of his thoughts—she never questioned his intentions, she never dared to dissent, as John Goodwin had done. She did not trouble him with questions of ethics, of propriety, of the ultimate implications of his ground-breaking research. She made things very easy for him—but might that very easiness be leading him, leading them both, toward a grim and inescapable trap?

Perhaps, he thought, he was worrying too much. Perhaps he was letting John Goodwin cloud his thinking. After all, John did have a certain tendency toward pessimism. Like the old testament prophets, his heightened sense of righteousness made him see prefigurations of doom in almost everything. What was he doing that was so wrong? He was screwing his assistant—it happened every day! His assistant happened to be a bright and impressionable young woman. Was that his fault? She happened to have something of a father complex, making her prone to emotional blind-spots where her "daughterly" passions were concerned. Again, was he to blame for that?

No, he told himself, John Goodwin was just playing Jiminy Cricket for a change! Maybe he was even jealous! He acknowledged being very impressed with Claire Rogers—and who wouldn't be? But it was Alfred Eberhard who had her, and he intended to enjoy her!

Why think in terms of "danger"? What could the danger be? What's the worst that could happen? Let's follow the work and the affair to their most extreme logical conclusion, thought Alfred Eberhard, and see where they lead. . . .

And now Alfred Eberhard was seized with a bizarre and exciting thought. It *was* the logical conclusion, the *only* logical conclusion. But no, it couldn't be—it was too unnatural, too bold—bold to the point of madness. Dr. Eberhard struggled to get the thought out of his mind. But it did not want to leave. It dug in, its haunting extremeness hooking onto the core of his imagination.

But he had to rid himself of that thought. *There* was the danger. If the thought could not be gotten rid of, it must at least be covered over, be masked with other thoughts.

Alfred began to think of sex. He tried to cover up his other thoughts by imagining the warm moistness of Claire, by picturing her waiting for him back in his suite. He thought of the power he had over her. He thought of the power that both of them needed him to have. He was thoroughly ready to take her now, and he walked faster toward the room where she was waiting.

Sixteen

Now that Drs. Eberhard and Rogers had succeeded in finding a way to keep the extracted rats' eggs alive, the next phase of the research could begin.

This phase entailed the irradiation of the eggs, seeking to destroy the nucleus—thereby rendering inactive the DNA contained therein—while preserving the usefulness of the surrounding cytoplasm. In the case of the frogs' eggs, this process had been relatively simple. Again, it was mere *size* of the eggs that made working with the mammals so much more difficult. With the rats' eggs, it was all but impossible to pinpoint the radiation sufficiently. The entire egg being microscopic, it was not possible to irradiate the nucleus without also irradiating the cytoplasm—mechanically, the radiation could simply not be directed that precisely.

Accordingly, what was needed was to find a type of ray that could be administered to the entire egg, and which would have *different* effects on *different* parts of it, destroying the chromosomal material while leaving the protein-rich cytoplasm intact. Different sorts of rays produced different results—

X rays were found to have almost no effect when administered in small doses. In larger doses, however, the X rays destroyed *both* the nucleus and the surrounding protoplasm. Ultraviolet rays were also tried, but with no more promising result. The ultraviolet rays actually destroyed the cytoplasm more effectively than they destroyed the nucleus! Finally, gamma rays were tried, and here the results began to be encouraging. . . .

The gamma rays, it was found, affected the egg *selectively.* It was impossible to divine the exact cause of this differentiated effect, although it seemed to have to do with the varying densities of different parts of the cell. The nucleus, being more dense, seemed to absorb more of the radiation, and hence, was more strongly affected by it; the cytoplasm, being less dense, absorbed less, and so was less affected. The gamma rays seemed to pass through the cytoplasm very much like sunlight passes through glass—without heating it. The nucleus, on the other hand, became "heated" by the rays, as, say, asphalt is heated by sunlight, and thus was destroyed.

The mere discovery of the use of gamma rays did not, in itself, provide an immediate boost to the cloning experiments. Much refinement in the technique of administering the radiation still needed to take place. Exact dosages needed to be determined, the precise conditions under which the irradiation should be done had yet to be decided. The selection of gamma rays, however, was the central idea from which all these others sprang.

Six months were spent in perfecting the process

of preparing the eggs in this way. By now it was fall of 1971. Richard Nixon was coming toward the close of his first term as President of the United States. Astronauts and cosmonauts were reaching out into space with ever greater boldness and optimism.

But for Alfred Eberhard and Claire Rogers, none of this mattered. The outside world barely existed for them. Cloistered in the research facility, separated even from their colleagues by the secrecy of their project, their universe had shrunk to a tiny size. It consisted of the lab in which they worked and the bed in which they played. It consisted of their feelings for the work, and their feelings for each other. All their experience, all their hopes, were compacted into this tiny realm—and their lives took on a glowing intensity because of its compactness.

Alfred Eberhard was obsessed with his project— more obsessed than he had ever been. And Claire Rogers was obsessed with Alfred Eberhard: She therefore took his obsession unto herself. And during this fall of 1971, the most difficult work began. . . .

The living eggs having been de-nucleized, the next step was the micro-injection of the donor cell—the chromosomally complete cell which would trigger the reproductive reflex of the egg. This micro-injection of the donor cell posed awesome technical problems: How do you inject one cell into another when both are microscopic, a hundred times smaller than even the finest hypodermic?

And it was not only the size of the cells that offered difficulties, it was also their chemical composition. The egg cell of mammals is surrounded by a tough membrane, making it difficult to penetrate. The sperm cell is equipped with an enzyme which dissolves a tiny portion of that membrane, allowing the much smaller sperm a "door" by which it can enter. After the entry of the sperm, the membrane quickly re-seals and, because of a chemical reaction triggered by the presence of the sperm, becomes impermeable, so that no more sperm can enter.

Now, in the case of a body cell, the entire process is different. A body cell does not contain the enzyme that "eats away" the egg membrane. A body cell cannot, therefore, make a "door" for itself. How, then, could it enter?

That was the question that occupied Eberhard's mind for the closing part of 1971 and for half of 1972. At times the problem seemed absolutely insoluble. It was just too delicate an operation. It required instruments finer than any that had ever been produced. At times, Dr. Eberhard grimly thought that he had come up against the final obstacle, the one that simply could not be got around. At those moments he reminded himself of his own first axiom: If something is theoretically possible, it *can* be done. All that was needed was the *means* to do it. . . .

During that frustrating time, Drs. Eberhard and Rogers held many fruitless "skull sessions" in the lab, hoping that, by constant discussion, some new idea would perhaps be unearthed—who knew how scientific discoveries were made? Perhaps something of value could be said by accident, perhaps a new direction could be offered by a slip of the tongue, a mispronounced word! Eberhard remembered the words of one of his scientific idols, Louis Pasteur. Pasteur had spoken of the important role of luck in scientific research—but mere luck was not enough. One has to be ready to *recognize* the luck when it appeared: "Chance favors the prepared mind," Pasteur had said. And Eberhard was at constant pains to keep his mind prepared; his mind trained itself constantly on the subject at hand.

For all that, however, nothing new came out of the skull sessions in the lab. Eberhard and Rogers ran up against the same problems again and again, the body cells had no means of locomotion. They could not "swim" toward the egg, the way a sperm did; the body cells lacked the membrane-dissolving enzyme, so that, even if they could be brought into contact with the egg, they would have no way of gaining entrance. And again, injection was impossible because of the microscopic size of the cells. There seemed to be no way out of these same old problems.

Finally, however, there came a breakthrough. The breakthrough was brought about by a weird but brilliant associative process in the mind of Alfred Eberhard. This association took place not while Eberhard and Rogers were working in the lab, but while they were frolicking in bed—an indication of just how intent Alfred Eberhard actually was on keeping his mind prepared for the chance hint that might point the way out of his dilemma.

"That's it!" he suddenly exclaimed, reaching down and lifting up Claire Rogers by her shoulders.

"That's what?" she said, understandably baffled by such a strange pronouncement at such an inappropriate moment.

"Listen, Claire," said Eberhard excitedly, "we'll *blow* the donor cells into the egg!"

It was some seconds before Claire Rogers could shift her frame of reference and begin to figure out what her lover was talking about.

"Yes," Eberhard continued, "it's perfect! We'll come up with a way to propel the eggs by means of a gentle pneumatic pressure. The motion thus imparted to them will mimic the swimming motion of sperm. Now, if we propel them hard enough, perhaps they'll be able to implant themselves into the egg, bursting through the membrane like a tiny bullet! The trick will be to propel them hard enough to puncture the membrane, but not so hard that they damage themselves, or pass through the egg entirely. Thus, the enzyme action of the sperm will be replaced by a *mechanical* action. Claire, do you understand what I'm saying?"

"Yes, Alfred," she said. But in her face there was a slightly drawn and dissatisfied look. The evening wasn't working out exactly as she had planned.

His optimism renewed by this bold new conception, Alfred Eberhard lost no time in seeking to solve the technical problems which his idea raised.

First and foremost, there was the problem of developing an "air gun" by means of which an infinitesimal body cell might be propelled. Claire Rogers could not help being skeptical about the feasibility of such a device.

"I fail to see that this air gun is essentially any different from a hypodermic," she told him. "I think we'll still have problems because we won't be able to make a device with a fine enough tube—the cell will get lost inside of the cavity, and the air pressure won't affect it."

"But that's just it!" Alfred exclaimed. "The air pressure *will* affect it, even if the cell doesn't fit snugly in the 'barrel.' That's precisely the way in which the air gun idea differs from a hypodermic. Look, I've rigged up a little model which perfectly demonstrates the principle involved."

Dr. Eberhard reached below the counter in the lab, where they were seated, and produced a section of cardboard tubing and a ping-pong ball. Claire Rogers could not help giggling when she saw these objects which, by their very ordinariness, seemed comically incongruous in the laboratory.

"Now, observe," he said. "The diameter of the cardboard tube is considerably greater than the diameter of the ping-pong ball. Correct?"

"Correct," she said.

"Now," he went on, "if I place the ping-pong ball in the tube, hold the tube scrupulously on the horizontal, and blow, the ping-pong ball is *still* propelled through the tube, even though some of my breath is wasted—that is, even though some of my breath goes *around* the ball. Now, I admit it's rather an inefficient gun, but what does that matter? As long as we can generate enough thrust to move one tiny cell fast enough to get it to crash through the merest wisp of a membrane—that's all we need!"

"Well," Claire said, grudgingly convinced by Eberhard's explanation, "I guess you're right. In any case, it's worth a try."

Alfred Eberhard now directed all his energies toward translating his "air-gun principle" into a concrete form suitable for the propulsion of a single cell.

From the beginning, the basic form this new device would take was clear in his mind. The components of it were actually quite simple: An adjustable pneumatic pump, capable of delivering regulated puffs of air; an ultra-fine hypodermic needle, with the plunger removed; ordinary rubber tubing, for connecting the pump with the chamber of the hypodermic. The donor cell would be deposited in the hollow of the needle itself; the pump would then be attached; when all was ready, the pump would provide a quick burst of air, sending the cell hurtling out through the tip of the needle, toward the waiting egg.

In theory, the entire procedure was admirably simple; in practice, however, it proved to be remarkably difficult. Exactly how was the single cell to be deposited in the needle? You couldn't cram it in, like a cannonball into the muzzle of a cannon! How much air pressure was needed to propel the cell? Would the cell be damaged, would its membranes give way like windows in a hurricane? And, assuming the cell could be successfully propelled, how accurately could it be "aimed" toward its microscopic "target"?

One by one, these problems were attacked and overcome by the persistent efforts of Drs. Eberhard and Rogers. They found that they could deposit the cell within the needle by relying on the workings of capillary action—the cell, suspended in a drop of liquid, was attached to a superfine probe—a strand of metal barely thicker than a human hair. The probe was then introduced into the hollow of the needle; the drop of liquid, containing the donor cell, adhered to the inside of the tube, owing to capillary action; the probe was then withdrawn. The liquid-engulfed cell, however, stayed inside. The first part of the problem was solved. . . .

Next, the researchers turned their attention to the question of how the cell would be affected by the strain of its propulsion. To determine this, they arranged their mechanism so that the cell under study would be blown directly into a water drop, the water drop being placed on a slide under a high-powered microscope. Thus, the cell could be observed at the precise moment of its emergency from the "muzzle" of the "gun," and its progress across the water drop could be traced.

The whole thing looked sufficiently bizarre under the microscope! The tip of the needle—just visible at the extreme left side of the microscope's field—looked immense—truly like a cannon! A split second after the pump was activated, a tiny pellet emerged—this was the cell under study. It did not, however, look like a usual cell. It was not round, but almost crescent-shaped, deformed in accordance with the resistance forces acting on it.

Although the cell was actually moving quite fast,

it seemed to be progressing in a weird slow motion, because of the microscope's exaggeration of distances. It seemed to travel through several feet (in actuality, perhaps a millimeter!) before it ran into the drop of water on the slide. When the cell ran into the water drop, another strange visual effect could be seen—the cell seemed to flatten itself momentarily against the rim of the water drop, adopting its curvature. This was owing to the surface tension of water.

Like a diver breaking through the surface of a swimming pool, the cell had to "pay the price" for gaining admission—one could imagine the sting that the flattened cell must have felt, as if it had done a belly flop off the high diving board! Inevitably, though, the water drop admitted the propelled cell. Upon entering the drop, the cell's motion slowed dramatically. It was not flying now, but swimming. Laboriously, it made its way toward the center of the drop, gaining back its normal shape as it slowed down and the forces acting on it diminished. At last, after what seemed an enormous journey, the cell finally came to rest. . . .

And now, with the cell at rest, came the most important observations of all—the observations of the lasting effects upon the cell by the trauma of its transmission. Had the cell membrane been ruptured by its fierce collision with the rim of the water drop? If this had occurred, the cytoplasm would simply have oozed away; the cell would have shrunk and shriveled like a deflating balloon. Had the cell been "scrambled" by its deformation? Was the nucleus intact? Were the chromosomes still distinct and functional? And what of the long-term effects of the cell's transmission? Might there be damage or mutation that would not show itself until the next generation, that would only become discernible in the offspring of the cell?

Drs. Eberhard and Rogers studied the cells carefully and came up with a wide range of results. In some cases, the cell was obviously damaged—sometimes the cell never even regained its original shape. In other cases, though, the cell seemed to come through its ordeal perfectly intact. It soon returned to its healthy roundness; it metabolized normally within the water drop—it even began to resume its normal mitotic rhythm!

These were very heartening signs. They made it appear likely that with refinements in technique—a more exact gauging of the air pressure needed, fuller study of ways to prepare the cell for its journey—a very high percentage of donor cells could be kept intact.

This led the researchers to the next—and the most crucial—question: Even if the donor cells could be kept intact, could they be aimed sufficiently well so that they'd make contact with the egg? And even if they did make contact with the egg, would they be able to penetrate the membrane—penetrate it without damaging the egg?

There was only one way to determine these things—and that was to begin suspending the eggs in water drops, and start "shooting" the donor cells at them!

Accordingly, Drs. Eberhard and Rogers reenacted their air-gun experiments, this time with the crucial difference that, instead of shooting the cell into an ordinary water drop, merely to test its reaction to the various stresses involved, it was shot into a water drop containing a fertile, extracted rat's egg. (The water drop also had to be supplied with various dissolved sugars, ions, and hormones, to keep the egg alive and healthy for the duration of its stay in the drop.)

Things looked slightly different under the microscope now. In place of the clear, slightly gray surface of the pure drop of water, there was now a grainy, viscous-looking fluid—the water plus its dissolved nutrients. Even more important, however, was the fact that there was now an egg suspended in the medium. The egg was yellowish and almost opaque—under the scope, it appeared to be about the size of an ordinary saucer.

Why, then, if it was as large as a saucer, couldn't the propelled donor cells seem to hit it?

Eberhard and Rogers shot cell after cell into the egg-containing brew, but they always seemed to miss. Watching the slide intently, they would see the cell deform, finally crash through the rim of the water drop, and then go scudding right past the egg, close to it, but never *into* it. How frustrating it was! Eberhard and Rogers had to keep reminding themselves that they were not, in fact, aiming a pellet at a saucer, but were dealing with *microscopic* particles—the kind of marksmanship they were striving to attain was unprecedented in all of history!

That knowledge, however, did little to assuage the scientists' frustration. They fired cell after cell, but, as in some diabolically rigged shooting gallery, they never hit the target—the bells never rang.

And yet, if one considered the odds against them, this continued inability to strike the egg would not seem so surprising. First of all, it must be remembered that the water drop, though it appeared two dimensional under the scope, was in fact a three-dimensional space; relative to the size of the egg, the water drop was very "high-ceilinged"—the propelled cell, even if it seemed to be right on target, had plenty of room to go either above or below the suspended egg. Aside from this, it must be remembered that the egg was always *moving;* the water drop had tides all its own, and the egg bobbed helplessly on its slightest currents. Analogously speaking, then, trying to hit the egg with the shot cell was about as difficult as trying, without a guidance system, to torpedo a submarine which might be hovering at any level in the ocean's depths.

Statistically, though, it was inevitable that a certain tiny percentage of cells would strike the egg— if only by chance. And so it happened that, after innumerable misses, a donor cell did make contact with an egg.

Under the microscope, where distances were magnified and suspense was therefore stretched, the motion of the "swimming" donor cell toward the much larger, bobbing egg, was a tense, breath-holding event. Closer and closer it came, advancing by the merest hundredths of millimeters toward its destined collision. The gap grew smaller and smaller; to Eberhard's intensely peering eyes it almost seemed that the egg was bracing itself for the crash. Onward scudded the donor cell, through the grainy morass of dissolved molecules. . . . And finally, *finally* it ran straight into the egg.

But it didn't penetrate the membrane! With long exhalations of disappointment, Drs. Eberhard and Rogers watched as the egg membrane slightly deformed from the momentum of the donor cell—it "gave," the way a fat man's stomach gives under the pressure of a prodding finger. But it didn't open up to admit the cell; rather, it seemed to take a moment to gather up its strength, and then "flexed" the bent membrane, pushing it outward against the encroaching body of the donor cell, sending it back from where it came. The donor cell changed direction like a tennis ball springing off a racquet. And, in a moment, everything was as it had been in the water drop—the suspended ions flowed at random, the virgin egg bobbed freely on the tides. . . .

Alfred Eberhard could not help muttering a curse. Claire Rogers put her hand on his tense shoulder, but it didn't comfort him. The only thing that could comfort him was to plunge directly back into the work, to take what could be learned from this near-victory, and to try and make the next "hit" successful.

"We'll have to increase the force of the air gun slightly," Eberhard said.

"But we've already determined the optimal pressure for the transmission of the cells," Claire said. "If we increase it, they may be damaged, they may rupture when they enter the water drop."

"I know that!" Alfred grated, a tense ferocity in his voice. "But the cells don't do us any good if they can't penetrate the eggs, do they? We'll just have to push them harder, drive them harder. We do it to ourselves, we can do it to them, too. That's all there is to it!"

Claire Rogers recoiled from Eberhard's words, and from the sound of his voice. He had no reason to talk to her like that, she told herself—and no right to. His voice had been annoyed, and somehow mocking. He'd spoken as if Claire Rogers did not understand the subject. It made her angry. And yet, more than angry, she was worried. Alfred Eberhard had spoken of the cells as if they were *conscious,* as if they made decisions, as if they were *trying* to thwart him. He should have laughed at himself for allowing himself to put it that way—he, a scientist!

But he had not laughed—he had not laughed at all for a long time. It was true, he did drive himself hard, too hard perhaps. And yet it was a horrible, dangerous mistake to think that one could push the laws of nature as hard as one pushed oneself. Claire could not help wishing that Alfred would relax a bit, push himself less hard. But he wouldn't—she knew that. That was what she loved him for. Still, it frightened her sometimes.

Seventeen

Alfred Eberhard did not, of course, relax. On the contrary, his near success with the cell-and-egg collision only made him more determined to effect the merger he so obsessively worked toward.

Accordingly, he stepped up the pace at which he labored. He increased the number of operations he performed on the ovulating rats, being sure to always have a full supply of fertile ova on hand. (How many hundreds of rats had he scavenged since the beginning of this experiment? How many thousands of tiny incisions had he made?) Similarly, he refined his techniques for removing donor cells from the viscera of male rats, being certain always to have hundreds of the cells incubating in their petri dishes.

And he continued working with his air gun. He increased the thrust with which the donor cells were projected. As Claire had foreseen, this increase in pressure was more than many of the cells could stand. The cells would often shatter upon hitting the water drop—their membranes would rupture, and their cytoplasm would burst out, seeming literally to explode, like a cat run over by a truck. Whenever this would happen, Claire would involuntarily wince. Alfred Eberhard, however, would simply discard the used slide and replace it with a new one, repeating his experiment with a new cell. . . .

On occasion, Claire would try to offer suggestions. In the past, she had done this often, and her ideas had provided useful new directions in the research. Now, however, Alfred Eberhard seemed to regard any suggestion as an annoyance; he was becoming impervious to all ideas which did not issue from himself. For example, one day Claire suggested that perhaps the cells could penetrate the water drop more easily if some effort were made to reduce the surface tension of the water.

"And how do you suppose we do that?" Alfred asked, a now-habitual edge to his voice.

"Well," Claire told him, her confidence already shaken by the tone of Eberhard's reply, "we know that the addition of certain detergent agents reduce the surface tension."

"Yes," he said scathingly, "and wouldn't the cells be likely to flourish in a detergent solution."

His replies often had that tone now. Claire Rogers was made to feel—just as John Goodwin had been made to feel—that she was no longer a real part of the project. But, unlike John Goodwin, she resolved to stay with it, to stay with Alfred Eberhard.

In time, Eberhard did begin to have better luck with his propelled donor cells. He began using muscle cells rather than organ cells, and these were found to be slightly more durable—exactly equivalent to any other cell in terms of DNA content, their tougher protein coating made them better able to withstand the "dive" into the water drop.

Now that this hurdle had been overcome, Eberhard again set up his "targets"—the eggs were again suspended in the water drops, and the bizarre "shooting gallery" became active once more. According to the percentages, it would only be a matter of time before Eberhard achieved another hit.

This bull's-eye began exactly as the other one had—the shot cell moved slowly toward the egg, right on course, seeming certain of a collision. The collision did, in fact, occur. And when it did, there was the familiar deformation of the egg membrane. The egg pinched in, taking on a kidney shape in place of its former roundness. But all this had happened before, preparatory to the egg's recovery and its rejection of the donor cell. Would the cell gain admittance this time?

For an agonizing instant, nothing at all seemed to happen. The cell, its momentum apparently stopped, lay against the membrane of the egg. The egg did not spring back, nor did it open up. It hovered between the two as the incredibly minute but vital forces sought a balance within the water drop. And now, finally, it could be seen that the egg membrane was, in fact, tearing!

A tiny rent had opened up in it and the cell was slipping slowly but undeniably into the cytoplasm of the egg! In seconds, everything had happened—the membrane had parted, the donor cell had been taken in, and the membrane had healed again! The donor cell had penetrated the egg, penetrated it as surely as an enzyme-bearing sperm!

But what would happen now? Would the merger "take"? Would the presence of a full amount of chromosomal material start the egg dividing?

Feverishly, Alfred Eberhard stared through the microscope. For a long time (but what did time matter to him now?) nothing happened—nothing at all. The egg and the donor cell seemed to "ignore" each other. They each went about their metabolic business separately, as if they hadn't yet "realized" they'd been merged. Chemically, they had not yet begun to affect one another. But each seemed to be operating normally, healthily.

Beads of sweat formed on Eberhard's brow as he peered at the cell-within-a-cell. The grayish donor cell, perhaps a tenth of the size of the yellowish egg, moved lazily through the grainy cytoplasm, as if exploring. Claire Rogers moistened a washcloth and mopped her lover's brow—he was unaware of her presence, unaware of everything except the tiny speck of the universe which had been hugely enlarged under his relentless gaze.

After a time, the miraculous, the impossible, began to occur. . . . The donor cell came to rest very near the center of the egg. Its other metabolic processes could be seen to be slowing, as the cell gathered all its forces for the demanding chore of dividing. Eberhard's breath grew labored as, under the scope, he saw the chromosomes of the donor cell begin to line up at the midpoint of the nucleus. Every muscle in his body was clenched as he watched the brightly colored gene necklaces fall into their miraculously ordered phalanxes. He gasped as he saw the strands begin to stretch, to divide themselves into identical halves, each half equal in DNA content to the first existing cell.

But now came the all-important question: Would the egg divide along with the dividing cell? If it didn't, all that would be happening would be a simple mitotic division, an ordinary splitting of a single cell, which just happened to be using the egg as a nutritive medium. If, however, the egg divided along with the cell, that would signal the beginning of an embryo, the first stage of a whole new individual, the first cloned *mammal* ever produced.

"Come on, come on," Alfred Eberhard heard himself saying in a hissing whisper. His soul was in the dividing cell, all his yearnings were steered toward its fruition.

And now, as the chromosomes began to pull apart in the nucleus of the donor cell, it could be seen that the membrane of the egg was in fact beginning to cinch inward! The fold began about a third of the way down from the top of the circular egg—as was normal in the first division of a mammalian embryo. With agonizing slowness, the membrane moved in, seemed to halt, and then continued, splitting itself at last into two distinct parts, connected by a common membrane in between!

"It's there, it's there!" exclaimed Alfred Eberhard, still not daring to lift his aching eyes from the microscope tubes, for fear the egg would disappear if he took his nurturing attention away for even an instant.

Lovingly, with a fierce and burning love, Eberhard observed the unevenly divided egg. The top, smaller half, was known as the animal pole. The bottom, larger half, was known as the vegetal pole. Already, in his racing mind's eye, Eberhard could envision the further development of each of the two half embryos. He could *see* the various organs developing; he could *see* the entire life history of the rat which was forming before his amazed eyes.

In time, the cells of the embryo again divided. There were now four of them. Soon there were eight. And everything was going almost bizarrely well—nutrients could be seen filtering through the egg membrane; waste products could be seen making their way out into the water drop. . . .

But Dr. Eberhard knew that the embryo could not remain in its present environment for long. Unlike the frog, which develops outside the body even in nature, the mammalian embryo is infinitely fragile, requiring the regulated internal environment of the uterus, if it is to prosper. The embryo of a mammal must be fed by the bloodstream of a "mother"; its needs must be provided for by a host. Accordingly, Eberhard knew that the developing bundle of cells must soon be implanted in the uterus of a rat. To avoid the possible rejection of the embryo, it had to be the same rat from whom the egg had originally been "borrowed."

"Claire," he said, in a strained and mechanical

voice, "prepare number 406 B. Anesthetize her and lay out a tray of instruments. . . ."

Claire Rogers hurriedly found the rat in question, and, after checking her over to gauge her overall physical condition, prepared to anesthetize her. Within seconds, the rat had fallen limp, dead to all sensation.

Claire placed the tiny animal on the "operating table" and set about arranging the scalpels, sutures, and other implements which Eberhard would need to perform the implantation operation.

"Have you finished?" he asked, when he realized that her scuffling movements had stopped. He still had not lifted his eyes from the microscope.

"Yes, Alfred," said Claire. "Everything's ready."

"Good," said Eberhard. "We'll do this operation as carefully as if we were dealing with a human patient. We've got a healthy looking sphere of sixteen cells here—we may have one more split even while the operation is proceeding. We've got to be very very careful. . . . Claire, I want you to watch the embryo while I incise the rat—tell me immediately of anything even slightly irregular."

With great regret, Alfred Eberhard tore himself away from the microscope—how he would have loved to leave his eyes there, while his hands moved on to the next step of the experiment! His eyes were immediately replaced by those of Claire Rogers. Hardly a second had gone by in which the developing cells were not observed keenly, desperately.

Alfred Eberhard stood tall and godlike above the

tiny anesthetized rodent. How minute the animal was, and yet how rich in promise! Eberhard regarded the pink shaved abdomen, visualizing the nourishing organs within. "Oh, be kind!" he wanted to urge the organs of the hosting rat. "Give of yourself as I have given of myself, to bring this new creature to life!" He begged the rat to conspire in this parody of nature, to be the biological pawn of this unprecedented manipulation of genetic possibilities.

Eberhard seized the scalpel. Decisively, he made one small clean slash in the drugged animal's belly—crisscrossing the barely visible scar that was left from the incision Eberhard had made when he'd pirated the rat's fallopian tubes. The animal bled very little. Eberhard attached tiny clamps to the "lapels" of the severed flesh, exposing the genital tract. All his attention now focussed on the uterus, that fibrous, funnel-shaped organ so supremely well-suited for its nurturing function, so admirably equipped with blood vessels, with supporting muscles, with hormones.

Expertly, Alfred Eberhard sliced it. The whitish internal muscles offered more resistance to the scalpel's edge than had the pink exterior flesh. But the uterus had been opened now—there was a tiny lengthwise slit in it, a slit which, by applying slight pressure to the top and bottom of the uterus, could be made to open wide enough to receive the embryo-containing water drop. . . .

Now that the hosting rat had been prepared, Eberhard again turned his attention to the amazing activity taking place on the microscope slide. "What's going on, Claire?" he asked anxiously.

"We seem to be getting another split," she said.

Eberhard moved swiftly across the lab and rudely displaced Claire Rogers from her stool in front of the microscope. Greedily, he peered through the eyepiece, watching as each of the sixteen cells moved gracefully toward prophase.

"Well," said Eberhard, "we'd better let this next division take place before we go ahead with the implantation. The cells are especially delicate while they're splitting. Keep an eye on the host in the meantime, Claire."

She did as she was told, stifling a growing anger and a growing hurt. She realized now that she had never been regarded as an equal, that Alfred Eberhard, the man she loved, was incapable of regarding anyone as an equal. She wished she could say no to him; she wished there was something she could deny him. But she felt that she could deny him nothing. . . .

At length the cell division was completed and the embryo was temporarily at rest.

"All right, Claire," said Eberhard imperiously, "we've got to work fast now. I'm going to siphon off most of the water in the drop—it's too unwieldy to work with as it is. I'm going to leave just enough to adhere to the tip of the micro-dropper. That means we have very little time before the embryo runs out of nutrients and begins to dry out. Now, you'll have to open the uterus of the rat while I move in with the dropper—it should only take a few seconds. . . ."

Using an ultra-fine hypodermic as a suction tube, Alfred Eberhard drew off most of the water in which the embryo was suspended. Through the microscope, the shrinking of the drop looked like the sudden draining of a lake. Eberhard watched closely, making sure the zygote was not damaged in the draining process.

When most of the water had been removed, Eberhard probed the tiny droplet with a glass straw of incredibly narrow gauge. Because of surface tension (how handy it came in now!) the entire droplet—including the developing cells—adhered to the tiny dropper.

Holding his precious cargo with infinite care, Eberhard lifted the dropper and brought it to the counter on which the opened rat reclined. Claire was standing there, ready to part the slitted uterus of the animal.

When she was instructed to do so by Eberhard, she applied a gentle pinching pressure to the top and bottom of the funnel-shaped organ. Responding to the pressure, the muscular tissue parted at the incision, and, in an instant, Eberhard had plunged in with the dropper, depositing the embryo in its natural habitat. It was over in a matter of half a minute!

The microscopic embryo having been implanted, the uterus was sealed, and the abdomen of the rodent was sewn up again.

And now there was nothing to do but wait. Unlike the case of the frogs' eggs, where development took place outside the body, and thus could be closely observed at every stage, the mammalian embryo had to be tucked away within the body of a host, where it progressed—or failed to—with nerve-wracking secrecy. There were ways, of course, to monitor the progress of a mammal, but how much less precise, less immediate, less reassuring they were, than the moment-to-moment data that could be gleaned by staring constantly through the lens of a microscope!

For now, there was nothing at all that could be done. Alfred Eberhard and Claire Rogers kept a vigil over the anesthetized rat, waiting for it to begin to stir. And when it did wake up, what then? It would be some time before they could determine whether or not the embryo had become successfully implanted, whether it would begin to develop normally within the womb, or whether the transplantation would kill it, as trees are sometimes killed by moving into too-rich soil. There would be no way of knowing for some while—and the period of uncertainty could not help but be agonizing.

Eighteen

The gestation period of a rat is three weeks.

For three weeks, Alfred Eberhard barely slept, barely ate, barely spoke, except to ask questions and make utterances directly connected to the progress of his—hopefully—pregnant subject, laboratory rat number 406 B, who was—hopefully—bearing the first cloned mammalian embryo ever produced.

The health of laboratory rat number 406 B was a constant preoccupation with Alfred during those three weeks. He expended more energy worrying about that rat than the most doting husband ever wasted worrying about the welfare of his expectant wife. Was the rat eating properly? Was she resting? Was she becoming lethargic? And what of her weight—was she gaining, losing, holding steady?

In addition to these mundane questions, a more specifically scientific querying was always going on in the mind of Dr. Eberhard. He ran blood tests on the rat, tested for hormone content in the blood, searched for clues indicating that the tiny rodent was preparing to lactate.

All evidence seemed to point to the same astonishing, longed-for conclusion: Laboratory rat number 406 B did in fact, seem to be pregnant! She exhibited all the hormonal and metabolic symptoms—her estrogen was up, her kidney functions increased, indicating that she was also working at cleansing the tissues of another developing creature!

And not only did 406 B seem to be pregnant, but she seemed to be very healthily so. Her weight increased slightly and gradually. Her blood count seemed to be keeping pace with demands made on her circulatory system by the extra baggage of an embryo. Her nipples appeared to be developing—the first signs of pre-lactation liquid had been spotted on her fur. And laboratory rat number 406 B seemed somehow *happy*—happy with the instinctive expectancy of new life, of the natural joy of procreation.

How strange it was that this furry little creature, this four-legged signpost on the biological road that led to man, could be manipulated so, could be impregnated with a man's *idea*, and could bear that unnatural notion as if it were a natural one, feeling nothing but the animal fullness of new life stirring within! Number 406 B was blissfully ignorant of implications, pre-ethical, memory-free, aware of nothing but the physiological reality which was herself.

For Drs. Eberhard and Rogers, the situation was not so simple. For them, there were other issues besides the mere birth of a baby rat. Alfred Eberhard, having been immersed in the various stages of the cloning project for almost ten years now, had thought through every implication of his

work—and he had chosen to ignore those implications which might offer moral objections. He
had simply stopped thinking about certain things,
about the potential abuses, the potential horrors.
Claire Rogers, however, newer to the project and
less obsessed with it—or let us say, obsessed at one
remove, since it was Eberhard she was obsessed
with, rather than the project itself—had clearer
eyes about the possible upshots of these experiments: After a rat, what next? And what of the implicit *elitism* of cloning—who decides which genes
are worth replicating?

There were a thousand questions that needed
answering, all raised by the simple riddle incubating in the belly of lab rat number 406 B. . . .

But what was the condition of the fetus within
that belly? Was it developing normally?

That was impossible to know with certainty—a
fact which tormented Dr. Eberhard. Accustomed
to the instant verifying power of the microscope,
he felt frustrated and helpless now that the mystery
was out of his range of vision. It was, of course,
possible, by amniocentesis and various other methods, to gain some information about the fetus.
First of all, there was no question that the fetus—
whatever form it had taken—was alive. Second, an
analysis of the amniotic fluid indicated that, hormonally, conditions inside the uterus were normal.
These were encouraging signs, but still—who
could say what possibly monstrous mutation or
freak might be developing in that ravaged womb?

Alfred Eberhard's eyes grew increasingly shadowed through those three long weeks of waiting.

He lost weight, and his lean handsomeness now became a spectral and skeletal haggardness—he had the look of a mad prophet. And he had the thoughts of a mad prophet. Made unstable by lack of sleep, his mind formed weird conjectures, weird analogies—a frog, a rat, a man, a race of men—was there a difference? A woman, a uterus, tubes, pipes, eggs ripe for the plucking. . . . The tiny vulva of a rat, the large-scaled vulva of Claire Rogers. . . . Anything seemed possible to Eberhard in his prophetic exhaustion. Claire Rogers feared him now, even as she loved him.

No longer did she make attempts to comfort him, to stroke his shoulders, to mop his brow. She sensed that he was beyond the reach of those modest, natural comforts. She waited, instead, for him to come to her with his needs, for him to take what he wanted. In his suite at night—she essentially lived there now, though, for form's sake, she kept her own room in the researchers' dorm—she would submit to his embraces, enjoying them even though she felt they were only incidentally directed at her. And she wondered what grave, silent thoughts were wracking her lover. She yearned for the success of his plans and yet—just as John Goodwin had done—she could not help partly hoping that the fetal rat would die, or be deformed, that the experiment would somehow fail. A failure, she knew, would not comfort him—but a success would surely goad him on.

The experiment, however, did not fail. At the end of the standard gestation period, laboratory rat 406 B gave birth to a perfectly normal-appearing offspring. The only unusual thing about the birth was that it was singular, rather than the usual multiple litter of rodents. Other than that, the delivery was normal, the ratlet was normal—furless, closed-eyes, its tiny feet curled and kicking.

Alfred Eberhard and Claire Rogers stared down at the newborn creature, scuffling helplessly through the sterile shavings at the bottom of the cage. Instinctively, as if it were a natural offspring, the ratlet nestled into the belly of its "mother," seeking warmth and nourishment—and 406 B suckled the infant as if it were her own, as if, in fact, she had contributed something of herself. Yet she had contributed nothing—none of her own DNA informed the tissues of the baby rat. The ratlet had only one set of genes. . . .

For a long time Drs. Eberhard and Rogers mutely stared at the newborn. Neither could speak. Suddenly, Claire Rogers' eyes misted over with tears—whether from happiness, or relief, or a kind of creeping dread, she herself could not have said.

Finally, Alfred spoke. He turned toward her, and in his face was a poignant blend of triumph and exhaustion, a heartrending awareness of the price at which victory comes, and perhaps a sad preknowledge of where victory would lead. When he spoke, his words were the last words that Claire Rogers expected to hear from him, then or ever— but especially then, at such a moment.

"Claire," he said, "will you marry me?"

Nineteen

Alfred Eberhard and Claire Rogers were married several weeks after the birth of the world's first cloned mammal. A birth that was still a closely guarded secret.

The marriage came as no surprise to most members of the Brookside community, who had long been aware of the associates' unofficial arrangement. John Goodwin, however, *was* surprised—and pleased. He'd thought that his old friend would never marry, that he would hold himself aloof from the "average" pleasures and stresses of domesticity forever. He viewed Eberhard's decision to marry as a sign that perhaps he was mellowing, perhaps his fierce Selfness was melting somewhat with age. And, thought John Goodwin, Claire Rogers was the most worthy choice he could have made.

After the enormous strain of their long experiments on the laboratory rats, the newlyweds deserved a vacation. They took a week off for a motor trip through the hills surrounding the research center. It was spring—spring of 1973—and the foliage was lovely. Alfred Eberhard could not remember the last time he had been away from the

laboratory for any length of time. He felt refreshed, rejuvenated—and yet it could not really
be said that he was relaxed. . . . No, Alfred Eberhard was never relaxed, all appearances to the contrary. Part of him was always clenched, always eager
to push on—even at the same moment as he cradled his new wife in his sinewy arms, even as he
placidly drove through the countryside, the leaves
rustling, the radio playing.

Claire Eberhard, on the other hand, was genuinely relaxed, and ecstatically happy, through the
days and nights of that longed-for honeymoon.
How wonderfully shocked she'd been when Alfred
had proposed to her! How instantly his proposal
had soothed all the little hurts she'd received in
the course of working with him! How miraculously
it had restored her confidence in herself, a confidence that had been whittled away for so long by
Alfred Eberhard's professional and personal arrogance. All that was different now. By asking her to
marry him, Alfred had assured her that he had
loved her all along—implicitly. He had apologized
to her for all his little unfairnesses, and had made
them up to her in the most glorious way imaginable! She knew he'd come round when the pressure of the project was off; she'd known he would
show himself for the kind man he really was.

For the whole of that grand week, Alfred and
Claire never once spoke of their experiments. In-
wardly, Alfred was being torn to pieces with worry
and curiosity about the progress of the cloned
ratlet. But he would not allow himself to speak of
it. And Claire did not even allow herself to think

of it. Why think of that dreary lab when there was all of nature to look at, and all of Alfred to reach for?

But vacations—much less honeymoons—are temporary, and the Eberhards soon found themselves back at the facility. For a few days, there was a certain excitement in the air, as Claire Eberhard moved her things into the director's suite, thereby making official and permanent the merger of her life with Alfred Eberhard's. In a short time, however, with her things moved in and the basic routine of the working day re-established, it began to seem that things had always been the way they were right now, it was almost as if the two doctors had never been away.

In the lab, the cloned rat was flourishing. As it matured, it was seen to resemble its donor—or clonor, as Eberhard coined the term—more and more. Identical in genetic makeup, it proved to be identical in every visible detail. The markings on the fur were the same, the shading of the eyes matched exactly. The experiment was a huge success, there could be no question of that now.

And yet, Alfred Eberhard again elected not to publicize the results of his pioneering research. He and Claire conferred on this matter several times. Claire—like John Goodwin before her—favored full disclosure, as an ethical responsibility to the scientific community. Eberhard, however, protested, invoking the possibility of interference, annoyance from the press and so forth. As usual, it was Claire who eventually capitulated.

"All right, Alfred," she said finally. "We'll do

what you think best. But can't we at least tell John? After all, he was in on the project at the start—he has a right to know. And you can trust him, if you don't want it to go any further."

Alfred Eberhard carefully thought over his wife's request. He had to take several factors into account before giving his reply. First of all, it was very important that he not anger his wife, that he stay on as good terms with her as possible—that was absolutely essential for the success of his long-term plans. But was there a danger in letting John Goodwin know that a successful clone had been done on a mammal? Might he then suspect . . . ?—No, some new story would be invented, John Goodwin could be put off the track easily enough. But how troublesome it was, thought Alfred Eberhard, to have so many things to weigh, to have to proceed so cautiously.

"Very well, Claire," he said at last. "We'll tell John—but no one else."

Accordingly, John Goodwin was invited to the director's suite for a drink, and to hear the momentous news. Needless to say, he was impressed—and yet in his reaction there was a certain ambiguity, a certain fearfulness.

"Alfred, Claire," he said, "that's wonderful. Congratulations on an extraordinary piece of work!"

His congratulations were sincere—there could be no doubt of that—but it was equally clear, from the way he scanned the faces of Alfred and Claire Eberhard, that he was concerned. Were the two of them becoming too subsumed by their work? Had Claire become tinged by Alfred's brilliant but ruthless dedication? And then, of course, there was the inevitable question, the question that John Goodwin found himself trembling to ask. He tried to make his voice light and conversational, but there was a quaver in it. . . .

"Well," he said, "and where do you intend to go from here?"

And now it was Dr. Eberhard's turn to strive for naturalness in his voice. He had anticipated Goodwin's question, of course, and had rehearsed his answer a hundred times. But now it had to come out sounding perfect. Goodwin must be convinced—and, equally important for now, Claire must be convinced. Neither must guess yet. . . .

"We're really not sure yet, John," said Eberhard with a studied casualness. "We'll observe the cloned rat for awhile, of course, and see what we can learn from it. After that, we'll see. To tell the truth, John"—and here came the part that he had to put across—"I'm pretty tired of this whole thing. My enthusiasm for the whole cloning project is just about used up. I've put in too many years on it—I'm almost forty! Claire and I haven't really spoken about it yet"—this, at least, was true—"but my inclination is to terminate the clone project after studying the rat and then turn back to cancer research. After all, as you've told me more times than I care to remember, that *is* what we're here to do."

Having finished speaking, Alfred Eberhard furtively studied the faces of his listeners, trying to interpret their reactions. John and Claire both looked relieved. And when John spoke, it was in an unequivocally positive voice, no longer the strained, ambivalent one he had used before.

"I'm glad to hear that, Alfred," he said. And then he added with a smile, "and not just because you're telling me that you've finally come to agree with me. But hell, that was powerful stuff you were dealing with, and I'm really glad to see it dropped. It smacks too much of science fiction to me, always has. Let's try to cure cancer, and leave the creation of robots and mutants to scientists from Transylvania!"

"Now, John," Alfred said in a teasing voice. "Don't be so hard on me when I'm finally giving in. We did, after all, come up with some pretty interesting things along the way."

"That's right, John," said Claire. (The ploy had worked—he had enlisted her support, made her the advocate of the cloning experiments!) "That work taught us more about embryology and about the growth patterns of hormone-stimulated cells than any other project that I've ever heard of. Say what you will about the spookier side of it, but, theoretically speaking, it was a valuable body of work."

"I'm not denying that," said John Goodwin. "As a matter of fact, I'll propose a toast to it: To the cloned frog, the cloned rat and to the marriage that has somehow emerged from the whole crazy process!"

The three of them clinked glasses and laughed. All three of them had reason to be happy. John Goodwin was relieved to see that his old friend had seen the light—his marriage must be doing him good. Claire was happy for having seen the gentle, fault-admitting side of her husband—something she had never seen before. She was glad to support him, to help him however she could. And Alfred was pleased because his friend and his wife would come away from this evening thinking exactly what he wanted them to think. . . .

For several months, Alfred and Claire Eberhard worked uneventfully in the private sector of the lab. They traced the growth and development of the cloned rat. Eberhard feigned lack of interest in the project, although his fascination never, in fact, flagged. With a secret passion, he stroked the furry little creature, held it in his hand and caressed it as if it were his own destiny, a map of his life, augur and substance in one.

At the same time, the husband and wife team was—apparently—working on a new theoretical schema on the basis of which to organize their next cancer-related project. Alfred Eberhard appeared to be working very hard in this direction—and yet he came up with nothing. To his wife, it appeared that Alfred had hit an intellectual dry spell—how agonizing it must be for him! She was doubly touched, therefore, that Alfred should be so good to her. He was gentle even in the midst of his enormous frustration. And when *she* made suggestions, he never scoffed at them or brushed them aside, as he used to, but heard her out and then gently and carefully traced for her the failings of her schemata. She loved her husband more than ever. He again seemed accessible to her comforts, and she pledged to lavish those comforts on him as generously as she was able.

Alfred Eberhard observed his wife and traced the curve of her emotions. He watched her love grow from day to day—so cool was he in his observations, that he might have been appraising a graph. . . . He knew his wife adored his gentleness, knew her affections swelled if he showed weakness or self-doubt. Accordingly, he showed her those things. He knew that what he had to ask of her could only be granted on the basis of a huge and selfless love. And so he had to cultivate that love. He needed something that he could not take, but would have to ask for, to beg for, if need be. He had to lay the groundwork for that question.

Several more months passed. It was now the end of 1973. Still there had been no breakthrough in Alfred Eberhard's "intellectual dry spell." Still there had come no glimmer of an idea for a new cancer project. Claire Eberhard commiserated with her husband, took his frustration unto herself, stroked his forehead—and marvelled at his continuing kindness, even in the face of his crushing lack of progress.

She was worried about him. He had seemed terribly depressed lately. His appetite had not been good. His sleep had been restless. He was obviously preoccupied. She would do anything to help him, but what was there that she could do? She felt so helpless. Tell her, only tell her, what she could do, and she would do it, she would do it gladly. . . .

The time was ripe, Alfred Eberhard knew, to ask his question. He had brought his wife around to the proper state of mind. . . .

. . . It was late at night. Alfred Eberhard could not sleep. His wife, fighting off drowsiness, stayed awake at his side.

"Alfred," she said, "what is it? Is it the work? Don't worry about it, darling. Ideas will come—they always come, in time."

"No," said Alfred Eberhard, clutching his head and wearing an agonized expression, "ideas won't come! They *can't* come! There's no room for them in my head! My head is too filled with other things, things I have tried so hard to ignore, to put aside. My head is too full of thoughts I've tried to get out of the habit of thinking. I've got space for nothing else—and that's why the new ideas won't come!"

"But dearest," she crooned, cradling her husband in her arms and rocking him gently, "what are those other thoughts? Tell me. Share them with me, and maybe then you'll be free of them."

And now Alfred Eberhard curled up more tightly against his wife, making himself seem as small, as fragile, as helpless as he could. He tried to speak—his voice caught; he tried again. . . .

"C—Claire," he said softly, "I—I want you to have my baby!"

A wave of relief and joy swept through Claire Eberhard as she heard these words. Was that all that was bothering her husband?! How strange that it should be the very thing that she herself was yearning for! The beginning of a family—how odd that it should be so difficult for her husband to say.

"Oh, darling," she exclaimed, "of course, of course! I'd love to. Why didn't you ask me sooner? Were you afraid the pregnancy would interfere with my work, or—"

"Claire," said Alfred Eberhard softly, "I'm afraid you haven't exactly understood me. I—I want you to have *my* baby—I want you to bear my clone."

For some seconds, Claire Eberhard was not at all sure that she heard correctly. She was horribly disoriented. Her awareness of language seemed to have evaporated. She had heard words, but she could barely make sense of them. But, yes, he had said them. Her husband, cradled in her arms, curled up, vulnerable, very like a fetus himself, had asked her to bear his clone! This, then, had been the cause of his quiet misery all these months. This, then, had been the obsession which blocked out all other thoughts, which rendered his amazing mind blurry and ineffectual. This was what her husband needed. And yet, Claire Eberhard felt a touch of nausea at the thought. . . .

In her mind's eye she saw the genital tracts of the incised rats—tubes and passageways, secret and perhaps holy, probed, pirated, opened and closed at will. She thought of her own woman-hood, her monthly tides, the blood-laden promise of increase within her. She visualized her own in-sides, the tiny ovaries ceaselessly forming their monthly eggs, pearls of vitality, pieces of herself. She saw the slow journey through the tubes, into the uterus—the uterus in its clever nearness to the vagina, the vagina which, intent on pleasures of its own, welcomed seed—seed which was blocked from its natural goal by artificial means. And yet, the life went on within her: The eggs coded to herself, the hormone-fed instincts and secret yearnings, the capacity for joy at the very thought of motherhood, of the passing on of Self. This idea—her husband's stubborn obsession—hurt her, nauseated her, and yet she wanted so to help him. She'd promised herself she would. She wrestled with herself. . . .

"Alfred," she said, after a long and excruciating pause, "I—I don't think—"

"I understand your feeling," he interrupted. He had to stave off her refusal at all cost. He had to interrupt, refute, cajole, convince, plead if necessary—anything to fend off defeat, now that he was so close to victory. "Claire, I understand the enormity of what I'm asking. Do you think I haven't thought this over a hundred, a thousand, times? You've seen me these past months. I've been a wreck, carrying this burden in secret for so long. I've been with you every day, feeling how precious you are to me. I've wondered what would happen first—would I finally unburden myself to you, or burst!

"Believe me, I've tried to rid myself of the thought; I've tried to get the project out of my mind entirely—just as I told John Goodwin that night. But the idea torments me. The possibility haunts me. And Claire, there's another thing—I'm very nearly forty. I'm getting old—and I'm frightened. I've seen old men. I've seen men fade, seen them weaken and become pathetic—and that terrifies me. If I had an image of myself to gaze on as I aged—a youthful image coming into maturity as I myself crossed over into oldness, it would be such a comfort, I would face it so much more easily, knowing that my strength would be passed on. . . ."

Claire Eberhard had begun to cry. Her husband's words wracked her. She was overwhelmed by the memory of the past months, by her husband's tenderness in the face of his ordeal. And yet, still some deep-seated natural biological impulse was revolted by his notion, some layer of feeling that lurked beneath the layer we call emotion was being flayed and wounded.

"But Alfred," she sobbed, "what of me? What of my rightful part? You'll have your own young image as a comfort, but I—what will I have? The fetus will pass through me—nothing more! I'll be a mere incubator, my body will be used simply as a conveyance! And there'll be nothing of me in the child! No shadows of myself, no glad reminders of my parents, my ancestry—nothing! Oh, Alfred, I love you more than anything, but I don't think—"

"Wait, Claire!" Alfred Eberhard interrupted again. "You *shall* have your share in posterity! Your genes will be carried on. You'll get to see the family traits you want to see! Only, you'll see them in the *next* child!"

"Next child?" said Claire Eberhard.

"Of course, my darling," said Alfred Eberhard. "I'm not asking you to give up your genetic future—you are far too richly gifted to deprive pos- terity of your genes! You're young, and full of chil- dren! Listen, Claire, after the clone we'll make a baby in the good, old-fashioned way—How does that sound? You and I, together, half and half."

"Oh, Alfred," sobbed Claire Eberhard, feeling the last of her resistance crumbling in the face of her husband's persuasive barrage. Could she deny the reality of his suffering these past several months? Could she fail to understand his obses- sion with the project that had taken ten years of his life? Could she not sympathize with his desire to see the project through to its logical conclusion? And could she not be moved by her husband's ac- knowledged terror of aging?

All that aside, there was yet another element ar- guing in favor of Alfred's startling suggestion. His genetic makeup was *worthy* of being replicated, of being kept intact, undiluted! Yes, Claire Eberhard told herself, her husband was something of a mir- acle, a trophy of nature. She had always known that, even before her adoration of Alfred Eberhard had really ripened. He was exceedingly intelligent. Physi- cally, he was strong, sound and attractive, every part of him well-formed and ample. He was articulate; he could be charming; he was sensitive. . . .

She could not say no to him, about this, about anything. She could not silence her qualms, yet she could not say no.

"All right, Alfred," she said in a whisper. "If you think it can be done, I'll go along with it."

Twenty

Alfred Eberhard did not merely *think* a human clone could be accomplished—he knew it. He knew it with a part of himself that was beyond intellect, beyond even the intuition of the scientist, he knew it with the part of him where visions are born, where glimpses of the future are startlingly offered.

Everything that his conscious mind knew confirmed this confident vision. After all, a clone had been accomplished in a rat, and, speaking in terms of the reproductive and gene-transmitting processes involved, a rat and a human being were the same. Alfred Eberhard knew every step of the process, from the removal of the egg, to its preservation, its impregnation, its re-implantation. All those steps had been carefully refined in the course of the rodent experiments. Translating them to the larger, more workable scale of a human body would be simply—bizarrely simple.

And yet, in dealing with a human being, there were certain non-physical factors to consider—"psychological factors," as Dr. Eberhard rather disparagingly phrased it to himself. The process might prove to be something of an emotional strain. Alfred resolved to keep a close eye on his wife through the course of the experiment. If she was too harshly affected, it might jeopardize her health, and the entire project would fail.

It did not take a clinical eye to see that Claire Eberhard *was* in fact affected, and dramatically so, by the very prospect of bearing the first human clone. On the morning after her fate-sealing agreement, she arose from bed looking quite different from the way she had looked the evening before. There was a certain pallor in her cheeks. Her eyes were strangely lusterless. Her movements were rather stiff, and she seemed uncomfortable in her skin, as if her ownership of her own body had become a questionable premise. And yet, she would not back down—she had agreed, for her husband's sake, and she would follow through on her agreement.

The two of them walked from their apartment, down the long bright corridors to the private sector of the lab. They had taken this walk a thousand times—but how different everything looked today! Claire Eberhard was no longer an experimenter— she was to be experimented upon; the private sector of the lab was no longer merely a room casually shut away from the others—it was a deep and lugubrious sanctum, a place where forbidden acts were performed, away from the light of day.

She walked slowly, woodenly. Her husband strode beside her, trying to remain calm and pleasant, trying not to be annoyed at the slowness of her pace.

When they reached the lab, Alfred Eberhard lost

no time in explaining his procedural schema to Claire. He'd had it all planned out for months. He said the words straight out, no hesitations, no pauses. She sat before him, vacant-eyed nodding now and then. It was not, it could not be, her husband who was saying these things to her; she was not, could not be, a wife, a natural wife.

"Now, dear," Alfred was saying, "no one must know of this. We must act as if we are still working on a cancer project. Accordingly, we can have no assistants. You yourself will have to help me prepare for when I operate on you to remove the egg—the surgery will be very minor, of course, and I'll do the anesthesia. I'll need you to lay out the instruments and so forth. Do you understand?"

Claire Eberhard could only nod weakly. To assist at her own operation. To lay out instruments for her own surgery. She could not reply except to nod. . . .

Alfred Eberhard continued speaking. "Good. We'll proceed as follows. We'll go in after the egg the very next time you ovulate—that should be in just a couple of days, if I remember right from the time of your last period." (Of course he remembered right! He had been studying every detail of her monthly cycle for the past four months, making sure to time his ploy correctly!)

"Now, based on the kind of luck we were having with the rats' eggs in the new chemical bath, we should have no trouble keeping the ovum alive for as long as is necessary—some of the eggs lived for weeks, and we shouldn't need more time than a couple of days. During those days, I shall be removing cells from myself, and attempting to shoot them into the egg by means of the air gun. At the same time, I shall be treating you with hormones, so that your uterus will be maximally receptive to the re-implantation of the 'fertilized' egg. Fortunately, I won't even need to open you up a second time—we'll simply dilate your cervix, and implant the egg with an instrument fed in through the vagina. Do you understand?''

Again, Claire Eberhard could manage no more articulate response than a nod. She felt that she had no comprehension anymore. She understood the words, of course—they were part of the clinical vocabulary she had worked with for so long. She recognized the cool tone, so necessary for the economical transmission of ideas. And yet, when applied to *her,* how utterly, horrifyingly *foreign* the language seemed. It connected with no reality, with no reality of flesh and blood, of liquid coursing through sensitive tissues, of instincts chemically stamped by memories of our earliest swamp-dwelling forbears. It connected with nothing.

Claire Eberhard looked at her husband without recognition. She loved him, but that, too, was a notion she seemed to have stopped understanding. . . .

Two days later, Claire Eberhard began ovulating. The blood tests confirmed it. But Claire had no need of blood tests to tell her what was going on within herself. She recognized the familiar signs— the swelling and tenderness of her breasts, the slight darkening of the skin around her nipples, the dull warm ache in her ovaries. Her body was pro-

ducing a fertile egg, a miracle! An egg which, in
nature's order, would be merged with a sperm, producing a new individual, half-mother, half-father,
and therefore wholly its own person, but which,
now. . . .

"We must move quickly, Claire!" Alfred said.
"Place the instruments in the autoclave. Prepare
a dose of sodium Pentothal. I'll prepare the chemical bath and get the incubator started. Hurry,
please, there's no time to lose."

Mechanically, with a numbed unawareness of
everything except the immediate actions of her
hands, Claire Eberhard began arranging the instruments for her own operation. She prepared
the hypodermic for her own anesthesia. She made
ready the electrodes which would monitor the condition of her own body! . . .

And then, when everything had been prepared,
she removed her lab coat and clothes, and prepared to pull on the turquoise smock of a surgery
patient. For a moment she stood naked in the center of the lab, as if making one last effort to understand what was happening to her, as if making
one last inner attempt at rebellion, at denial of her
husband's fierce wishes. She could not turn back,
she had no will left—she had strength, enormous
strength, but all that strength was geared toward
the survival of her ordeal, not its avoidance.

Looking down, she contemplated her own vulnerable nakedness. She was not yet ready for the
operation. She had to wash and shave. Mechanically, she moved to the stainless surgical sink. She
turned on the water and adjusted it to a comfort-

able temperature. She took the sterile surgical soap in her hand and began working up a lather. Then she brought her soapy hands down onto her vulva and began to soap her lower abdomen and her pubic hair, feeling a vague shame in doing so, as if she were touching herself where she should not be touched, preparing to remove the mysterious hair that should not be tampered with. But it had to be removed, of course—it was standard operating room procedure.

She took the scissors and began clipping away at her pubic hair. The soapy ringlets came detached in her hand. She dropped them in the wastebasket, contemplating them. When she had cut away all that she could, she started in with the razor, the blade gliding over the tender flesh, making her unaccustomed skin feel raw and irritated.

Carefully, with hands that did not tremble even at this tremulous moment, she brought the razor down further, onto the folds of her vulva. Gently, she trimmed the wispy hair from her labia, making herself as smooth as a newborn, a girl with no thought yet of womanhood, of its possibilities, its potential glories and abuses.

Eberhard, meanwhile, was frantically preparing the bath which would receive the extracted egg. With infinite care, he prepared the solution of hormones and ions and nourishing salts, the solution that had to keep the ovum alive. He made sure that the gamma-ray equipment was functioning properly, so that, upon its removal, the egg could be quickly and effectively irradiated, destroying its nucleus and leaving its cytoplasm ready to receive the sham fertilizing cell.

The cells—*his* cells—were flourishing in rich agar-agar cultures laid out in petri dishes. Eberhard had removed the cells from himself—unflinchingly, he had sliced into his own forearm with a scalpel, scraped a small portion of the subcutaneous tissue into the cultures. He had not winced, though he had performed this small self-surgery without an anesthetic. But he was beyond pain. He merely gazed at his own slashed tissue with a vast and frightening unconcern. He saw there the germ of a thousand versions of himself, a thousand replicas. . . .

Claire Eberhard let the front of her turquoise smock drop down over her naked vulva. "I'm ready, Alfred," she said, in a dull and haunted monotone.

"Fine," her husband said, trying to control the feverish excitement within him. "I'll be set in just a moment. Get up onto the table, Claire. Would you like a sedative before the Pentothal?"

"No," she murmured. "I'm all right."

She climbed up onto the operating table that had been improvised in the lab. On impulse, she stared at the frosted glass door, the locked door that shut her away from the rest of the facility, from the rest of the world. It occurred to her that now she would be forever shut away from that world, that, as soon as the scalpel entered her and ravished her insides, as soon as her egg had been removed and the experiment was underway, she would be shut out of the rest of life, separated out by the unnaturalness of her participation in her husband's fierce obsession. She lay down and closed her eyes. Suddenly, it didn't matter anymore. She felt totally indifferent, totally outside herself. . . .

She did not even hear her husband approach the operating table. She merely sensed his nearness, and when her eyes flew open, he was standing high above her, huge, dark, heavy-faced, leaning over like a mountain, his torso like the face of a cliff that dwarfed and frightened her. The hypodermic was in his hands.

"All right," he said. "We're ready to begin. It will not take more than twenty minutes. And by the time you wake up from the anesthesia, I will have done everything necessary for the preparation of the ovum. Are you set?"

She nodded. She even managed to smile.

"We must lift your smock, dear," Alfred said. "Come now, lift your hips."

Claire Eberhard raised herself slightly, allowing her husband to pull the smock up to her waist. She was ashamed now. Her legs were cold.

"There now," he said. "Now, a quick injection, and off to sleep. You'll remember nothing when you awake."

He attempted to give his wife a reassuring smile as he stabbed the hypodermic into the flesh of her forearm. His manic excitement, however, infected his smile, and it was not reassuring—rather, it seemed a grinning death mask, a horrible row of bared rapacious teeth, joyless, hungry, ready to strike. That was the fearful image that Claire Eberhard carried with her into the drugged sleep induced by the sodium Pentothal.

Eberhard checked his wife's pulse. It was slow and steady, the heartbeat strong. He raised her eyelid and examined her hugely dilated pupil. All was as it should be. He prepared to cut into her.

He moved toward the center of the operating table. He inspected the tray of surgical instruments, making sure he had everything he'd need. He drew the incubator which would receive the extracted egg closer to him. He had to minimize the time that the tender ovum was exposed to light and air.

And now he looked down and contemplated the naked belly of his wife. Wife? No more a wife to him than she would be mother to the child she would bear! She was a host, a receptacle—for two years she had hosted Eberhard's passion, had sheathed his robust manhood—and now she would be his duplicate, doubly deceived.

Eberhard looked down at her, at the lovely white belly, the well-formed navel, the shaved pubis. How girlish her sex seemed, how innocent, notwithstanding the womanly fullness of the labia. In a way, it seemed a shame. But no, he told himself, he could not allow himself to think that way! Great scientific advances often seemed like shames at first! He picked up a scalpel.

The handle of it was cool and familiar in his hand. He brought the instrument close to the pale flesh of his wife, gazing intently at her belly, as if he could see through her skin and discern the precise location of the organs he needed to probe. He could mark the slight rise and fall of her breathing. He held his own breath for a second, and struck. . . .

Silently, with no hiss of pain or any tearing

sound, the blade moved through the flesh. Eberhard made a clean diagonal incision, perhaps two inches long, a couple of inches below the navel, slightly off to one side. He repeated the incision on the other side. It was necessary to probe both fallopian tubes, as it could not be known which one would bear the egg at any given month. The twin slashes slowly overflowed with blood, staining the lower abdomen and the shaven vulva. Eberhard stanched the bleeding, and affixed the gentle flesh-clamps to the wounds.

The incisions stayed open now, small unnatural mouths, unlipped orifices leading into her steamy and lightless interior. Eberhard brought the surgical light in very close, and peered through the slashes into the mysterious cavern of a woman's body. He could see the ovaries, lobed and lined with capillaries, held in place by the sturdy bands of ligament, suspended in the abdominal cavity like tender fruits adhering to a branch. He saw the funnel-shaped fallopian tubes, not attached to the ovaries, but arching under them, their flower-like mouths belled outward to catch the dropping eggs.

It was here that he must strike, these were the precincts that he must ravage. Though, fortunately, in the case of a human being, it was not necessary to incise the tubes themselves—the mouths of the oviducts were large enough so that it was possible simply to plunge in with the scoop and take what was needed. Still, the operation was a delicate one—the linings of the fallopian tubes were very richly nourished with tiny blood vessels,

vessels which ruptured under the coarse scraping pressure of the scoop.

Again and again, Alfred Eberhard plunged into the depths of the tubes, coming out with small pink wads of bleeding tissue—an amalgam of clotted follicular fluid, shreds of the tube lining itself, and—hopefully—a human ovum, ripe and healthy. Eberhard turned from one tube to the other, making sure that he emptied the contents of both. Who knew where the egg might be? He had to be thorough. But his scraping was taking its inevitable toll—the flayed insides of the fallopian tubes were copiously pouring forth blood now, blood which overflowed the bell-like mouths into the body cavity, as well as flowing downward into the uterus itself. From the uterus, the blood entered the vagina, whence it dripped down through the vulva.

Eberhard watched the internal blood trickle down slowly from between his wife's legs. It formed a small pool on the sheet which covered the operating room table. There was no one to mop the blood, no assistant, no one to stanch the bleeding. The bleeding was not dangerous, Alfred Eberhard told himself, just a few more scoops. The precious contents of each scoopful were emptied into the chemical bath, awaiting examination. Claire's bleeding increased, the blood poured from between her labia in a grotesque parody of natural menstruation. Enough! Alfred Eberhard told himself. He had to stop now.

He put down the surgical scoop and began to sponge away the blood that covered his wife's opened belly. The tube bleeding would soon stop, he knew. That was mere epithelial bleeding; there were no major arteries there. Gently, efficiently, coolly, he wiped away the blood that his probing had brought forth. He made a final examination of the internal regions: The ovaries were undisturbed; everything was as it should be. And he prepared to close up the incisions.

With the flesh clamps removed, the parted flesh moved together, like a mouth closing slowly in the midst of sleep. There was a slight expulsion of air from the abdomen as the lips of torn flesh knitted together. Alfred prepared the sutures. Expertly, he forced the needle down through the skin of his drugged wife. He pressed the needle across the wound, below the level of the skin, and drew it outward on the other side. Drawing the thread taut, he could see the cut flesh surge together and lock, the miraculously functioning tissues already beginning to heal.

He repeated the process again and again, putting a half dozen stitches into each of the incisions. When, finally, the scalpel wounds were closed, Alfred Eberhard heaved a tremendous, torso-wracking sigh. Only then did he realize that his entire body was soaked in sweat; the perspiration had engorged his shirt and penetrated even to his surgical smock. Suddenly, he tasted blood in his own mouth—he realized that his lips were bleeding. He had chewed them raw, unawares, during the course of the operation.

He now turned to the task of cleaning up the external signs of the surgery. Gently, he dabbed away the blood that still oozed lazily from his patient's vulva. He tried to drain the puddle that had formed on the table beneath her. He covered her scarred belly with a sheet. He again checked her pulse and her eyes—she seemed all right. . . . But then, Alfred Eberhard said to himself, she had always been strong.

It would be several hours before the patient emerged from the anesthesia. During that time, he had much to do, and he lost no time in getting to it. Without allowing himself even a moment to wind down from the excruciating tension of the surgery he had just performed, he began examining the tissue which he had removed from the fallopian tubes of his wife.

It was a long and laborious process. Of the several grams of epithelium which Eberhard had scraped away, only the tiniest portion could be examined at a given time. The pink mass of tissue had to be subdivided again and again, and then placed on microscope slides in the most minute quantities—only then could Eberhard be sure that the sought after egg—one cell amidst so many thousands!—would not escape his vigilant gaze. The remaining tissue had to be left incubating in the chemical bath, nourished and preserved by the dissolved nutrients and hormones.

Eberhard sat down at the microscope and began looking at slides—dozens of slides. Each one had to be carefully scanned. He saw a wide variety of cells under the scope—the close-packed brick-like cells of the mucous membrane which lined the tubes; the saucer-shaped blood cells; the yellowish cells of the follicular fluid, which is expelled from the ovary into the tube at the moment ovulation takes place. The presence of the follicular fluid was a very promising sign—ovulation had, in fact, occurred. But where was the egg?

Had it already passed through the fallopian tube and on into the uterus, where it would be overripe and useless? Or had it perhaps been left behind in some cranny of the oviduct which Eberhard's probing had failed to find? No, Eberhard pleaded, let it be here, in this bath, on one of these slides! With growing frenzy, he moved on through the slides, his eyes aching with the yearning to spot the egg. A pile of discarded, fruitless slides stood on the lab counter next to him.

Holding his forehead in one hand, he worked the fine focus of the scope and searched, searched for the one cell that was different from all the rest, the one cell that had the mysterious capacity to generate a whole new creature. He searched for that mystic cell, round and full, bigger than the others, bursting with grainy, protein-rich cytoplasm, heavy laden with the promise of life. . . .

And at last he found it! There it was: a human egg, seemingly healthy, bobbing gently in its drop of chemical solution! Dr. Eberhard gaped through the scope, hardly trusting his overused eyes. He brought the egg in and out of focus several times, seeking to assure himself of its reality. And the egg always reappeared.

Moving even more quickly now, Eberhard discarded all the other slides. He swept them off the counter amid a cacophonous crackle of breaking glass. He concentrated all his energy on this one single slide, on this one single cell within the slide. Using a micro-dropper, he drew off the other, extraneous tissue, leaving only the egg and a small amount of the nourishing liquid. That was all that was needed until after the egg had been irradiated. Then it must be returned to the incubator and be placed in a new, pure, unshared solution. But first, the gamma rays. . . .

Alfred Eberhard, holding the precious slide in his uncannily steady fingers, moved across the lab toward the gamma-ray generator. Suddenly, there was a moan. It issued from the operating table on which Claire Eberhard lay. She was coming out of anesthesia. The moans were piteous, speaking not of pain, but of utter lostness, lack of memory. The patient coming out of anesthesia remembers nothing, is a stranger to the world. Only the most fiercely stamped impressions and emotions remain in the mind of the anesthetized patient.

Claire Eberhard moaned. And she called her husband's name. Alfred Eberhard stopped in his tracks, but he did not go to her. She called his name again. "Dammit!" he muttered. He had no time for her now! She called his name yet once more. . . .

Albert Eberhard put down the microscopic slide and moved to his wife's side. Weakly, her arm lifted up toward him. Alfred Eberhard grasped the arm and planted the hypodermic firmly into the flesh. The new, unneeded dose of Pentothal entered her blood. Her arm dropped back, limp. She won't remember waking, Alfred Eberhard assured himself.

He moved back across the lab and retrieved the egg-bearing slide. Lovingly, he carried it over to the gamma-ray generator. The gamma-ray generator was a large, lead-encased machine, which narrowed down to a cone-shaped tip, through which a thin stream of radiation was emitted.

Eberhard placed the precious slide at the base of the generator. Adjusting the radiation emitter by means of a geared handle, he lowered it to the proper height. He now set the generator to the proper dosage—a minutely small amount of radiation, to be administered for a mere fraction of a second. That was all it took to destroy the frail nucleus. That was all that was required to inactivate the infinitely subtle chemistry of the DNA-containing chromosomes. Once the radiation had taken effect, the complex double helix of the DNA molecules would begin to dissolve, to crumble into their constituent parts—adenine, thymine, guanine, cytosine—simple substances which would soon pass through the battered nuclear membrane and be digested by the metabolism of the outer cell.

Eberhard made the final adjustments in the generator. He moved behind the lead shield and flicked the switch. It was over in a fraction of a second.

And now there was nothing to do but wait. The radiation would take a certain amount of time to do its work. It had to be absorbed by the dense molecules of the nucleus, and then, once absorbed, it would begin to consume them, to destroy them by a corrosive process taking place at the atomic level.

Alfred Eberhard placed the irradiated slide into its chemical bath—the cytoplasm of the egg must be kept healthy, even as the nucleus withered. He stared at the slide as if he could see into it, as if it were not microscopic. But in fact he saw nothing, and his stare was vacant. He was exhausted, but there was to be no rest for him. There was too much left to do.

His work on the egg being completed for the moment, Alfred Eberhard turned his attention to his sleeping wife. Again he checked her pulse. She was doing fine. Eberhard decided to administer a drug to bring her out of sedation. Better to wake her up now, he reasoned, than to risk her chance awakening at another inconvenient moment.

Eberhard prepared another hypodermic and filled it with a stimulant which would counteract the sodium Pentothal. He injected his third dosage into his wife's forearm. She awoke almost immediately, awoke with the same baffled expression worn by all post-operative patients. In a few seconds, the baffled look gave way to a smile—it was as if Claire Eberhard had remembered she was alive, and was glad. An instant later, however, the smile was effaced, its place taken by a drawn and joyless look, as if, having recalled the mere fact of her aliveness, she had gone on to remember the specific circumstances of her life, and her native joy had been clouded over.

"Are you in pain?" were her husband's first words to her.

"In pain?" she said, in a voice which indicated she found the question a strange one, perhaps a stupid one. "No, Alfred, I'm not in pain. Are you?"

Alfred Eberhard let the question pass. He ascribed it to the lingering effect of the anesthetic. Clearly, she was not fully awake yet, to make such a strange reply.

"The operation went well," he told her, trying to smile, trying to sound warm.

Claire did not reply. It made Alfred uneasy. He continued talking. "I've managed to isolate the egg," he said. "It appears to be very healthy. I've irradiated it, and am waiting for the radiation to take effect."

"That's nice, Alfred," she said in a patronizing tone, as if talking to a young child who had just done well on a test at school. "Did I lose much blood?"

"No," he said. "Some, of course, but not much."

"That's good," she said. Her voice though sleepy and rather slurred, had a definite edge to it, an edge which her husband had never noticed before. "I would hate to become weak, Alfred. I'd hate to do anything that would prevent me from bearing your child."

Was she being sarcastic? Alfred Eberhard asked himself. It sounded as if she were, and yet that was so unlike her. . . . Perhaps it was just the drug, or the loss of blood, or his own strained nerves. Probably she meant nothing by that tone. Very likely she wasn't even really aware of what she was saying. Still, it made him uneasy.

He would have liked to give her a sedative, to put her to sleep for a few hours more. He wanted to be alone. He looked at his watch. . . .

"I've got to check the progress of the egg, dear," he said. "Shall I give you a relaxant? I'm sure a few more hours rest would do you good."

"No, thank you, darling," said Claire, with elaborate courtesy. "I'd like to be awake. I'd like to watch you go about your work."

Twenty-one

The massive expertise that Alfred Eberhard had gained in his long years of work on the cloning experiments now came fully into play. The years of work on thousands of frog eggs, the years more on thousands of rats—it was all culminating here, in this bold experiment on a *single* human egg, an egg extracted from a human female. There could be no mistakes now, no false starts. Claire Eberhard would not be ovulating for another month, and even then, even given the huge, manic presumptuousness of her husband, could she really be expected to contribute another ovum?

No, the clone had to be achieved with this one single egg, or not at all. Accordingly, Alfred Eberhard handled this egg with immense care, exaggerated care. He did not sleep. He did not leave the laboratory. He monitored the progress of the egg as it rested in its chemical bath. He observed it as the absorbed radiation gradually de-activated the nucleus. He stared at it under the microscope as the chromosomes began to split apart, dissolve and disappear into the enzyme-rich cytoplasm of the egg.

In the meantime, Alfred Eberhard treated his

wife with hormones, bringing her uterus to a state of maximum receptivity for the re-implantation of the egg. He regarded his wife's body now, the way a farmer regards his field: He saw it as having no pre-rogatives of its own, merely a passive object which must be nurtured toward its ultimate fruition. He dosed her with progesterone, the so-called preg-nancy hormone, which triggers the dramatic thick-ening and strengthening of the uterine walls. He insisted that she remain in the improvised bed which had been prepared for her in the lab, that she rest and allow her body to replenish its blood supply.

Claire Eberhard lay there in the lab, her body aching with dull all-over post-operative ache, her sense of time horribly scrambled, her sense of self bafflingly shaken. She closed her eyes and tried to doze, but a full sleep would not come. Annoyingly, she kept hearing the laboratory rats scuffling in their cages. Drowsily, she imagined it was she her-self who made that sound, exploring and com-plaining while she uncomprehendingly awaited the firm grasp of the scientist.

It was sometime in the middle of the night when Alfred Eberhard decided that the egg was finally ready to receive the donor cell. The nucleus was by now totally de-activated; the cytoplasm still metabo-lized vigorously. . . . Everything looked promising.

Alfred removed the egg from the incubator, re-taining only a drop of its nourishing solution. This drop he placed on a microscope slide. Next, he brought the air-gun mechanism into position. The pump was ready, the rubber tubing was affixed, the ultra-fine hypodermic had been sterilized and tested. Gazing through the scope, he assured himself that all was as it should be—the "cannon barrel" of the hypodermic was positioned perfectly, a mere hair's breadth away from the egg-containing drop. The egg itself bobbed lightly, its condition seemed stable and healthy.

And now Eberhard set about inserting his own body cells, one by one, into the muzzle of the hypodermic. Removing them from their cultures by means of the tiny capillary tube. He then planted them in the barrel of the gun and "fired". . . .

The cells shot out, deformed, flew across the empty space between muzzle and water drop, crashed into the drop, and began "swimming" toward the egg. As in the case of the rat experiments, most of the cells scudded maddeningly past the target, making no contact. Gazing through the scope, Eberhard saw the spheroid egg floating temptingly. And yet he could not hit it! But he was not discouraged—no, he would simply continue shooting cells at the egg until he scored a hit. And he had to score a hit eventually—it was a mathematical certainty. He had millions, billions of cells in his body. He would turn himself inside out, if necessary, to gain enough cells to assure a hit! He would literally empty his body in the attempt, if he had to.

Again and again, Eberhard loaded up his cell gun. Again and again he activated the pump, sending the cells plummeting through the viscous, grainy fluid in which the egg existed. And finally, there was a hit! One of the cells finally connected with the target. It came, crescent-shaped out of the hypodermic, and sliced into the water drop, begin-

ning its epoch-making journey. It progressed
across the drop, being slightly deflected here and
there by tiny collisions with molecules of protein.
But it continued onward, closer and closer to the
teasing egg, seeming more and more certain to
run into it . . . until, at last, it did!

The egg deformed in response to the impact of
the crash. It bellied in slightly and was knocked
backward through the medium, the small body cell
lodged against it, seeking to nuzzle its way in. Slowly,
with a surging, jellyish movement, the egg began to
resume its normal shape, seeming to repel the nestling body cell. At that moment, however, there appeared a minute tear in the membrane of the egg!
Through the scope, the tear appeared as a gash,
perhaps an inch long, though in actuality, it was a
micro-slot, barely the size of a molecule, much
smaller than the body cell.

Would the body cell be able to slink through it?
Eberhard held his breath, his fists clenched, his
teeth gnashed together. The egg continued its outward surge, and as it flowed, the slit opened wider
and engulfed the cell! Through the open membrane slipped the donor, and by the time the egg
recovered its former roundness, the cell was implanted within it, riding the cytoplasmic tides toward the middle of the egg!

Eberhard heaved an enormous sigh of relief as
he watched the successful merger. His relief increased as he saw the egg membrane heal itself—
hardly any cytoplasm had been lost, and the egg
still appeared perfectly healthy. His fierce attention now focussed on the donor cell within the

egg. Had it been damaged in its journey? How was it faring in the unfamiliar chemistry of the egg? Would it survive? Would it replicate?

Again, there was an awesomely tense span of waiting—the metabolism of the body cell could not but be temporarily disarranged by the trauma of its transplantation. It would take some time to be able to assess its long-term chances for survival and growth.

Alfred Eberhard never lifted his eyes from the eyepiece of the microscope. He saw without looking, he was in a sort of trance, a waking sleep, but a sleep in which he was attuned to the slightest change in the tiny scene which his eyes only half beheld. He was vaguely aware of the steady, peaceful sound of his sleeping wife's breathing—it seemed a foreign sound to him, less real somehow than the microscopic drama being played out on the slide. In his exhaustion, his sense of scale became confused—how big was a cell, how small was a man? He was confused yet preternaturally lucid. . . . It would soon be dawn. . . .

As the first rays of new light filtered in the lab window, the first unmistakable signs of zygotic development could at last be seen. The chromosomes in the nucleus of the transplanted body cell began lining up at the midpoint. The other, nonreproductive metabolic processes slowed down. And then, finally, the actual division of the cell began! How Alfred Eberhard's heart pounded at the sight of that familiar but ceaselessly mysterious process.

The nucleus began to elongate. The egg membrane began to cinch in, and then, in only minutes after the first sign of change, there were two cells where before there had been but one! The two cells formed an unevenly divided ball. Very little, if any, growth had taken place. All in all, these two new cells comprised no more total protoplasm than the single cell had contained. But the DNA content had doubled! The number of chromosome-containing nuclei had doubled. The vital, gene-bearing elements within the cell had already replicated. The world's first human clone had begun to develop.

Alfred Eberhard watched, dazed and giddy, as the cell division continued. Within an hour there were four cells; by eight o'clock there were sixteen. Everything was proceeding optimally.

Claire Eberhard began to wake from her exhausted, blood-drained sleep. She started when she awoke, unsure of where she was. Then she remembered—in the laboratory—and that remembrance brought back to her the other circumstances in which she found herself. Her head fell back against the pillow. Her insides ached. Her hair felt oily and unpleasant against her scalp. "Alfred," she said weakly. . . .

"Ah, my dear, you're awake," he said, his voice bizarrely cheerful and fresh. "How are you feeling?"

"Better," she said. "Only—only . . . I feel empty, strangely empty."

These were the words that Alfred Eberhard dreaded to hear. His wife was losing heart. He had to boost her up, had to make sure that she would see the project through.

"It's normal to feel that way after an operation, Claire," he said. "You've lost blood, and you're further depressed by the after-effects of the anesthesia. You'll feel better soon."

Claire Eberhard smiled weakly and retreated behind her closed eyelids. How stupid her husband could be at times! Telling her the textbook after-effects of surgery—as if she didn't know them! Was that his solution to her emptiness?

"Do you love me, Alfred?" she said. She asked the question in a flat and skeptical voice, as if to say she would not believe his answer in any case.

"Of course I love you," he answered. His tone was unconvincing, and even he himself realized it.

Well, what does it matter? Claire thought. If he loves me, I'll do what I'm doing for love. If he doesn't love me, I've already thrown my life away— I'll make the final gesture.

"Alfred," Claire said, "do you ever have doubts about your actions?" Her voice was clear and fully awake now—though her eyes were still closed and her head was flat against the pillow. The position gave her a strangely oracular air. . . . "Do you ever hesitate, think that maybe there are some things that *can* be done, but *shouldn't* be done?"

"That's not how science works," he said softly.

"No, maybe not science," said Claire Eberhard, "but how about life?"

"Claire," Alfred said, his patience fading, his nerves severely frayed, "I really don't think this is the time to discuss our respective philosophies of life and science! I've asked you to do something, as my wife and my associate. You have agreed to do it. We talked about it at the time I asked you, and we could have discussed it even further, had you wished. But you agreed, and now we are in the very middle of the project. It's not the time to discuss intentions or ethics—it's the time to see to the mechanics of the process."

Claire Eberhard had no reply. Her husband's voice was cold. In a way, he was right: she had agreed. She agreed under duress, but she had agreed. She could turn back, of course, but turn back to *what*? Not to marriage as she had known it—that would be impossible now, she knew. Back to being single, loveless, alone?

"All right, Alfred," she said. "Let's go ahead. I'm just upset. Can you understand it at least that I'm upset?"

"Of course, dear," he said, trying in turn to sound conciliatory. "And I don't mean to be short with you—my own nerves are very strained, too. Well, let us carry on then. . . ."

Alfred Eberhard turned away from his wife's bedside and moved toward the microscope. He made a secret grimace as he turned away from her, a grimace that belied his conciliatory tone. His clenched jaw bespoke all the tense restraint that had gone into preventing himself from losing his temper with her. It had even occurred to him that, had she balked, it might perhaps be necessary to anesthetize her and perform the implantation against her will. Hopefully, that would not be necessary; hopefully, she would listen to reason and see the project through.

The steadily growing zygote had undergone yet another division, and it now consisted of thirty-two nearly identical cells. The cells in the top, smaller section of the sphere were slightly more compact than those in the larger, bottom part. The top cells had slightly less cytoplasm, but the nuclei were all the same, every one contained the exact same genetic material as the original fertilizing cell, the cell that had been plucked from the flesh of Alfred's forearm! Every cell carried the promise of his intellect, his strength, his grace. His obsession? . . .

"Claire," he said, his voice harsh and metallic across the open space of the laboratory. "We've got thirty-two cells now! We really should see about doing the implantation."

Claire Eberhard did not reply. She was without will. She would let herself be used. Perhaps she even wanted it that way, perhaps she had wanted it that way all along. She didn't know anymore. It seemed to her that she had never known.

Her husband had moved quickly back to her bedside.

"Dear," he said, "let me give you one final injection of progesterone. Then we'll move you back to the table and we can proceed. There'll be no incision this time. All we have to do is a simple cervical dilation. You don't even have to be put under—unless you want to."

"No," she said in a soft but unwavering voice, "I want to be awake. I want to *see* you do it."

Eberhard tried to ignore the vaguely threatening tone of her voice. She was horribly overwrought. And the hormones—they made her feel as if she were menstruating—it figured that she would be on edge. . . .

"All right, then," he said, "we'll just give you a local. But first, the hormones."

Alfred Eberhard prepared the hypodermic containing the progesterone. He approached his wife and gently took her wrist. He looked down at her forearm, which was vaguely discolored because of all the injections she had received. He plunged the needle in. Claire did not wince, not even as the viscous fluid was squeezed in, stretching and displacing the yielding tissues of her arm.

"Well, now, let me help you up. We'll move you back to the table and do the dilation."

Claire Eberhard sat up in her makeshift bed and began to rise. She wanted to walk to the operating table by herself, without her husband's assistance. Upon rising, however, she became lightheaded and had no choice but to lean against him. Her limp body pressed against his, and she felt his strength, his animal warmth, his maleness. She loved him still, had to acknowledge it. He led her to the table.

The improvised operating table was not equipped with the usual gynecological stirrups. It was necessary, therefore, to tie Claire's ankles to the corners of the table, to prevent her legs from reflexively closing as her loins were probed. Gently but firmly, Eberhard affixed stout nylon straps to his wife's ankles. She felt the pressure of them, pulling her heels down hard against the table, restricting all her movements. She felt imprisoned, and strangely secure.

Her turquoise surgical smock was again lifted. Claire felt no shame this time when her husband turned his gaze to her shaven pubis. She was beyond shame; it didn't matter anymore. With an expert surgeon's eye, Eberhard appraised the sutured incisions in his wife's abdomen. They seemed clean, healing normally. He looked at her vulva. The labia were covered with dried blood, and slightly swollen by the passage of fluids through them.

Eberhard felt that he should wash his wife before proceeding with the dilation. He moistened a sponge with a mild solution of surgical soap and prepared to bring it down between her legs. He imagined that his wife would welcome the cleaning, would welcome the soothing feel of the warm water against her sex.

"What are you doing?" she exclaimed harshly, at the first feel of the sponge.

Eberhard, taken aback at the hissing vehemence of her voice, said meekly, "I'm only washing you, Claire. You must be clean before we open you up."

"Anesthetize me first," she insisted. "I don't want to feel it! I don't want to feel anything there!"

"As you wish," he said, striving not to be angry as he prepared the needle full of local anesthetic, an anesthetic which would totally numb the patient's pubic area, while leaving her other senses perfectly alert. The drug would affect only the nerves in the pelvic region, so that the patient could undergo the strain of the muscle-stretching dilation without discomfort.

Claire Eberhard stared down the length of her own torso as her husband got ready to plunge the needle into her abdomen. He injected the anesthetic in two installments, one on either side of the pubic bone, so that the numbness would spread over her evenly. She stared at the needle as it entered her, stared at her husband's hairy hand clutching the hypodermic. She saw the metal tip break through the surface of her skin—but she didn't feel it. She was numb already, drugged by her own psychic agony.

It took several minutes for the anesthetic to take hold. During that time, Alfred Eberhard moved nervously around the lab, checking on the progress of the cloned zygote, inspecting and re-inspecting the apparatus necessary for the dilation of the cervix and the re-implantation of the egg into the opened uterus. Claire's eyes placidly followed her husband's restless movements around the lab. Poor man, she found herself thinking, he will never know any rest. That is the one capacity he lacks—the capacity for peace. He will suffer even more than I.

At last the anesthetic took effect. Alfred Eberhard placed his hand on his wife's genitalia and asked her what she felt: She felt nothing. He again moistened the sponge and cleaned the blood from the labia. Washing her, he felt a sudden flood of tenderness—but what place, he asked himself, could tenderness have here?

He continued washing, a professional task, no different from so many others. And then he approached her with the vaginal speculum. Gently parting the labia, he inserted the tip of the instrument between them and introduced it into the birth canal. He pressed gently on the outer end of the speculum, forcing it in until it encountered the constriction at the mouth of the womb. At this point, he stopped and peered through the hollow tube of the speculum at the lighted area within. He saw the interior of his wife's vagina, and the ring of muscle, or cervix, that led into the uterus. It was this ring of muscle that needed to be gently pried open, thereby affording access to the womb. . . .

Having established the exact location of the cervix, Eberhard reached for the dilator. This was an instrument approximately nine inches in length, which fit *inside* the vaginal speculum. Thus, the inner area was still lighted, clearly visible to the physician's eye. . . . The dilator had a small, expanding metal ring at the end. It was inserted into the birth canal, until the metal ring fit just inside the cervix. At this point, the ring was made to expand by a spring device controlled from the other end of the dilator—that is, the end of the dilator that extended out of the woman's body. Thus, the ring of the cervix was greatly enlarged, and it was possible to reach the womb.

The insertion of the dilator proceeded without complication—except for the fact that Claire Eberhard was again bleeding. Some bleeding was to be expected, of course, but Claire Eberhard's insides, ravaged by surgery and elevated doses of hormones, were particularly sensitive, and she bled more heavily than would be usual. Her blood was on the instruments and on her husband's hands. Looking down, she saw it on his hands but was strangely indifferent to it. The blood did not seem like her own.

Finally, the cervix was fully dilated and the bleeding had been controlled. Now it was time to implant the egg, the first cloned human zygote! Now was the moment when the bundle of cells had to be introduced into the womb of its mother host, whose bloodstream would nourish it, whose muscle would carry it—and who yet would be no part of it.

Claire watched dispassionately as her husband prepared the egg for implantation. Gently, he drew the egg-bearing water drop into a sterile capillary tube and approached his wife's loins, holding the cloned zygote in his hand.

Claire Eberhard's labia was parted, her vagina was open, her cervix was dilated. She was ready to receive, ready in this parody of natural reception, of sex, of procreation. Her ravaged insides had been artificially nourished and artificially opened.

Her husband moved the capillary tube through the hollow of the dilator. It was in her vagina now, moving carefully toward the uterus. Eberhard pushed it up a little further, checking its progress through the speculum. His wife's insides seemed a furrowed mass of fertile red tissue, bleeding, nutritive, elemental. Further now, past the ring of the cervix, went the cloned cluster of cells—into the uterus, that miraculous organ of muscle and feeding vessels.

Yes, the clone was in her now, and then, at the proper moment, Alfred Eberhard released the suction of the capillary tube, and the egg-bearing micro-drop fell off into the soft furrowed flesh of the womb, where—or so he prayed!—it would take root, take root and flourish as if it were a natural birth, a biologically sanctioned union, and not the bastard offspring of a single self-loving set of genes.

Claire Eberhard gazed down along the length of

her pale belly. She had no sensations, and yet she felt, she *knew* how everything was proceeding by the fiercely concentrated look on her husband's face, by the purposeful movements of his hands in and out of her. She knew. . . . And when she saw the bloodstained dilator being drawn out of her, followed by the bloodstained speculum, and saw her husband again pick up the sponge and begin to dab off her bloodstained loins, she knew that it was over, that it had been done. The foreign cells had been planted in her; she had been seeded, cultivated, like a field, like a laboratory rat. It was *there, inside* of her, no longer a mere idea, no longer a mere obsession even, but a growing, life-sucking physical fact, a fact more intimate than any man, any inside-less being could ever conceive.

Claire Eberhard suddenly began to laugh. It was a laugh like a howl, a laugh more horrific than the most piteous of sobs. It was a body-wracking cackle, an uncontrollable fit of mirthless laughter, the laughter of disbelief, of shock, of enormities too great to be comprehended. Her body shook, her ankles strained against the holding straps, her heels ached from the pressure. And yet she continued laughing. . . .

And now she realized the purpose of the laugh—she was trying to laugh the cloned mass out of her; she was trying to shake it from her womb by this hysterical outburst, trying to drown it. She laughed harder, laughed till she could not draw breath. Her stomach heaved, and she bade it heave all the more, she wanted it to turn and spin and burst if need be.

"Claire! Claire!" shouted her husband. "Try to

get hold of yourself! You're bleeding again! You may hemorrhage!"

Yes, hemorrhage, thought Claire Eberhard—a floodtide of blood to wash the stain away. She laughed harder . . . howled. . . .

But now the hypodermic was in her arm again, full of sodium Pentothal. Her husband had rammed it fiercely in, determined to stop that laughter that was driving him mad, that was threatening to ruin everything.

Claire stopped laughing abruptly. She slept. And Alfred Eberhard again dabbed the blood from her genitals. Then he set about cleaning up the lab.

Twenty-two

Claire Eberhard did not succeed in laughing the cloned embryo out of her womb. She was pregnant, pregnant in a manner in which no woman before her had ever been.

And yet, to all appearances, the pregnancy was a perfectly normal one. Claire began to gain weight, very slowly and very gradually. In time, the morning sickness started. Gradually, there came the first barely perceptible distension of her belly. Nature had been fooled, had mistaken this mechanical implantation for the usual creation of a fetus.

As was understandable, the expectant "mother's" state of mind underwent enormous fluctuations during this time. Claire Eberhard only faintly remembered the traces of defiance she had voiced against her husband during those bizarre thirty-six hours in the lab. She remembered feeling very angry. She remembered feeling soul-drainingly certain that her husband did not really love her, that he had set her up. But that had been a horribly stressful time. Perhaps she had been too harsh. She wasn't sure. After all, she *had* agreed.

Even so, it was hard for her to trust her husband

now. Yet on the other hand, he did treat her wonderfully well now that she was pregnant. He was gentle, considerate, solicitous in every way. He took every precaution for her welfare, her comfort. And besides, it was wonderful to be pregnant! There was a simple, pre-emotional joy in the fullness of it, the ripeness. One felt happy, the way that a tree heavy-hung with ripe apples must feel happy! There was life inside her, new life. But—and here the joy spilled out of her and left her limp—this life—what was it? A freak perhaps? A clone! A being containing no part of her, a genetic hitchhiker, riding for nine long months in her womb, and for a lifetime in her mind. But even so—and now the simple animal joy reasserted itself—it *was* life! It was life, and it was *hers*, by the fact that she nourished it, fed it, gave it a home and a resting place!

There was never any end to these rampant fluctuations in her mood. She was happy, baffled, angry, in love, enraged, mistrustful, giving—all in one. She adored her husband. She may have hated him as well—but she adored him nonetheless. And she reveled in his attentions. The way he rubbed her feet for her; the way he massaged her lower back when the strain of carrying the fetus had begun to make her sore—they were wonderful attentions, and, even if her husband's real concern was not for her, but for the fetus, what did it matter? She still purred under his touch, she still delighted in the softness of his voice.

And it was true: Alfred Eberhard did outdo himself as a dutiful husband during those difficult months. He was constantly at his wife's side, he ca-

tered to her every whim. Why? Was it, in fact, love—
a love that Alfred Eberhard had never succeeded
in really feeling until he had witnessed the ordeal
through which he had put his wife in the service of
his obsession? Was it mere guilt, the stubborn ves-
tiges of a long-denied conscience? Or was it simply
a displaced and exaggerated concern for the fetus,
a love affair with the developing embryo, which
manifested itself in his unwonted affection for his
spouse? Eberhard himself could probably not have
pinpointed his reasons. He only knew that something astounding was going on in the womb of his
wife, and that he must make himself a part of that
amazing process in whatever way he could.

When Claire was in her fifth month, the Eberhards let the news of her pregnancy leak out
among the staff. Needless to say, the staff was given
to believe that the pregnancy had arisen through
the most normal of means—and there was no one
who had any reason to doubt that. Even John
Goodwin, who had known of Alfred Eberhard's
fierce interest in the earlier cloning projects, did
not for a moment suspect that anything was amiss
in Claire's condition. After all, Alfred had told
him, just about a year ago, that he intended to give
up the cloning research altogether; and even if he
hadn't, well this . . . no, it couldn't be suspected,
not even for an instant. John Goodwin regarded
Claire's pregnancy as yet one more sign that his
old friend was turning out to be "normal" after
all. His earlier excesses being played out, Alfred
Eberhard was now ready to be a devoted family
man. John Goodwin was happy for him.

And he told Alfred Eberhard so, on the evening he came to the director's suite, bearing a congratulatory bottle of champagne.

"Alfred," he said, after the cork had been popped and the first glass had been poured, "this is some of the best news I've had in a long time. I've always felt that you and Claire had a wonderful, rare marriage, and I know that this child will cement your relationship in a way that nothing else could do."

"Yes," Alfred said, trying to appear the beaming expectant father, "it's wonderful, isn't it, Claire?"

"Oh, yes," said Claire Eberhard, obligingly patting her slightly bulbous tummy. "It's wonderful."

"Well," said John Goodwin, oblivious to the slight strain in his friends' replies, "what do you intend to name the baby? Have you picked a name yet?"

"Yes," said Claire Eberhard. "We intend to name it Orin."

"Orin," said John Goodwin, thoughtfully, trying the name out to himself. "That's a nice name. It's got character to it. But what if the baby is a girl?"

"Oh," said Claire, "it won't be."

"You sound pretty certain!" said John Goodwin with a laugh. "Have you been practicing the positions that they say increase the chances of a male child?"

"Oh, no," said Alfred Eberhard quickly, not wishing to give his wife a chance to say something perhaps indiscreet. "Nothing like that. It's just a hunch we have."

"Well," said John Goodwin, raising his champagne glass, "here's hopes for Orin, and for a beautiful, healthy baby, of whatever sex!"

The three drank the toast, and chatted awhile longer. John Goodwin left well before midnight since Alfred was very concerned that his dear expectant wife should get all the rest that she and Orin needed.

In terms of outward incident, the second half of Claire Eberhard's pregnancy was uneventful. Her health remained excellent, the development of the fetus seemed to be progressing normally. On several occasions, Alfred Eberhard checked up on his unborn, cloned offspring by means of amniocentesis. Inserting a fine hypodermic through the flesh of his wife's belly and into her uterus, he withdrew small samples of the amniotic fluid. By analyzing the fluid, various hormonal dysfunctions could be detected; these tests, however, proved consistently negative—as far as could be determined, the fetus was doing fine.

And, physically, Claire was doing fine. She had never looked lovelier. Her complexion was rosy, her expression was infinitely gentle, madonna-like. Her breasts were full, her strong legs carried her without difficulty.

Emotionally, however, the latter stages of her pregnancy were a tumultuous time for the woman. Her fluctuations of mood, far from abating, intensified. Her ambivalence toward her husband became excruciatingly sharp—she adored him, she admired his determination, his courage, the fierce independence of his thinking; and yet, she wondered, how could he put her through this? But

what, exactly, was it that he was putting her
through? It was childbirth—a process perfectly
natural in itself. Only the means of her impregnation had been unnatural—and was that really so
monstrous? Claire Eberhard asked herself that
question again and again. Perhaps it only seemed
monstrous because it had never been done before.
Perhaps, in the near future, it would come to be
regarded as standard practice, perhaps women
would agree to it without flinching! Perhaps she was
overplaying the strangeness of it. . . .

She did, after all, feel like a mother. Whatever the
so-called maternal instinct was, even if it consisted
of nothing more than a hormonal soup which acted
upon certain sections of the brain, she was *feeling*
it. That could not be denied. Her maternal feelings
were triggered by the presence of the fetus within
her womb. So what did it matter how it got there,
or whose genes it contained? It was *hers* regardless
of whether it had been coded without her genetic
help, regardless of the fact that it necessarily had
to be male, an exact chromosomal duplicate of her
husband. Still, it was hers—she was resigned to bearing it—and, more than that, she *loved* it.

And perhaps her love for it might have remained
constant, as constant as any mother's love; and perhaps her ambivalence toward her husband might
at last have been resolved—had not the actual
birth of the cloned child been such an unspeak-
able ordeal for Claire Eberhard. . . .

Twenty-three

It was around ten-thirty on the night of January 25, 1975, when Claire Eberhard felt herself going into labor. She lay calmly in her bed, assessing the first mild spasms, making sure that the pains were real, that it wasn't a false alarm. Gradually, the pains intensified, the intervals between the spasms decreased—there could be no question of it now.

"Alfred," she said softly, "it's time."

Automatically, with a physician's instinct, Alfred Eberhard placed his hand on his wife's swollen belly. He felt the steady oceanic surge, and then he felt a sudden rolling contraction of the muscles.

"I'll call John," he said. "And I'll get the stretcher to roll you down to the O.R."

"I can walk, Alfred," protested his wife.

"No," he said, "I'll wheel you down."

Alfred Eberhard rose quickly and called John Goodwin on the intra-center phone. It had been arranged that John would perform the delivery, with Alfred himself assisting. The birth was to take place in the main operating room of the facility, where any complication could be dealt with immediately. Two obstetric nurses were to be present.

Everything was being handled publicly, openly, officially—after all, this was the birth of the child of the director of the center and his wife.

John Goodwin was already present in the operating room when Claire Eberhard arrived, perched on a rolling stretcher wheeled by her husband.

"Traveling in style, eh, Claire?" said Goodwin, seeking to lighten the mood with a witty infusion of bedside manner.

"I'll say," answered Claire Eberhard with a smile. The smile, however, was interrupted by a wince—the pains were becoming stronger now. Rather than the steady dull ache of muscular contraction, Claire now felt a trace of a searingly sharp pain, as if something were beginning to tear inside of her.

In a couple of minutes, the nurses had arrived. The entire cast was now assembled, and the time of waiting began. No one could tell how long the labor might be—two hours, twelve hours, longer?

The spasms intensified steadily. A watery, yellowish fluid flowed from between Claire Eberhard's legs. John Goodwin checked to see how far the dilation of the cervix had proceeded.

"She's only one finger so far," he said. "We may be in for a long siege."

The two doctors and two nurses looked compassionately down at the expectant mother. She writhed now, her back arched, cat-like, in response to the bursting pressure within her loins. She moaned. Beads of sweat appeared on her brow and on her upper lip. Time passed. . . .

Two hours later, she was still writhing and moaning. The sheet on which she lay was soaked with sweat. A local anesthetic had been administered to relieve some of the cramped agony of the cervical muscles. Alfred Eberhard stared down at his wife imploringly. Silently he begged her to be strong, to bring this child forth. His mouth was dry. Now and then, John Goodwin patted him on the back, trying to calm him. He was hardly aware of the action. Something seemed to be humming—was it the clock on the wall? No, that clock didn't hum. Perhaps it was an echo of his wife's shrill groans.

John Goodwin again checked the dilation of the cervix.

"She's up to three fingers, Alfred," he said. "She's getting there, though it does seem to be damnably hard for her. I can see the baby's head— it seems to be turned sideways—she's going to have to open considerably wider before we can manage to bring it out. We may have to use forceps."

"No, John!" said Alfred Eberhard. "No forceps!" The words escaped him involuntarily. But suddenly he was terrified, as if the forceps would be brought into play against *his own* soft, not-yet-knitted skull! He could almost feel the instruments pressing in against his head, exerting pressure on his very brain.

"Easy, boy," said John Goodwin comfortingly. "We won't use them unless we absolutely have to."

Two more hours went by. Claire Eberhard was becoming exhausted. The wracking spasms stubbornly continued, but the rest of Claire's body could not respond. She could push no harder. The blood had drained from her face. When a spasm hit her, her face flushed scarlet, the blood suddenly surging through her with a violent **urgency**. As soon as the spasm had passed, however, the blood immediately slipped away, leaving her a bit more pallid each succeeding time. Alfred Eberhard was growing frightened. John Goodwin, too, was increasingly concerned, though he tried to remain calm and confidence-inspiring.

"Should we put her under, John?" asked Alfred Eberhard frantically. "She's working too hard, it's costing too much of her strength."

"We'll see," said John Goodwin. "She can't help us if she's anesthetized. . . . Claire, can you understand me?"

Claire nodded, her eyes wild, her head bobbing from side to side.

"Do you want to be put under, Claire?" John Goodwin asked. "Or can you stay awake and try to help us?"

"Awake," Claire Eberhard gasped. And then, her face momentarily clearing, her eyes fixed squarely on her husband, she added, "I want to see, I want to see it happen!"

"All right, then, Claire," said Dr. Goodwin. "Try your best to push. Try . . ."

Again there was a lull, a timeless pause in which the pulses ceased and Claire Eberhard hung suspended between echoing clangs of pain. Alfred Eberhard looked down at her, sweating profusely. John Goodwin rubbed his hands against his surgical smock, trying to keep the palms dry. The faces of the two females grimaced and twitched in unison, as if, by sympathetic vibrations, they themselves were feeling the twinges that sprang through the very depths of Claire Eberhard's insides.

And then, finally, there came a scream, a screech of monumental suffering, a rending, inhuman wail that rang horridly against the walls of the operating room. The doctors and nurses looked down at Claire Eberhard's face, and what they saw there was something very little like a face, but more a twisted mask of pain, of fear, and of a heartbreaking certainty of something going very wrong. And then they saw the blood. It poured from between her parted labia. Looking into the cervix, John Goodwin could see that the blood was coming from *around* the fetus—the bleeding was occurring further up the genital tract.

"That blood shouldn't be there," he said, trying vainly to keep the panic out of his voice. "Not now, not like that! Something's wrong. She's ruptured something. We've got to move fast now! Nurse, we'll need an episiotomy—without it, she'll tear for sure. And have the forceps ready—she's barely conscious. I don't think she'll be able to push. . . . I'm sorry Alfred, but there may be no choice but to use the instrument. . . ."

The nurse placed a scalpel in John Goodwin's hand, and he lost no time in slitting the lower end of Claire Eberhard's vulva, enlarging the channel through which the fetus would eventually pass. This done, he turned his attention to the upper end of the birth canal. . . . Finally, the baby's huge, sideways-turned head had poked its way out of the cervix. . . . John Goodwin could not yet see the face, but the top part of the skull was clearly visible, and accessible to the extended reach of the forceps. . . .

"I've got to use the forceps, Alfred," he said. "She's losing too much blood. We've got to get the baby out as quickly as we can, to get the pressure off her."

Alfred Eberhard nodded helplessly as the nurse slapped the forceps into John Goodwin's waiting hand. Alfred Eberhard was weak in the knees. Never in his life had he felt dizzy, faintly nauseous, in an operating room. He tried to clear his mind; he knew he might be needed.

John Goodwin had plunged in now with the forceps. He had little difficulty in grasping the infant's head, but now began the slow, exacting process of pulling the child forth from the birth canal. One had to pull firmly, while exerting only the slightest pressure on the infant's soft skull, being careful always to pull at an angle that would not damage the child's half-formed bones.

Goodwin sweated. A nurse wiped the sweat off his forehead. Slowly, slowly, the child emerged from the gore-lined channel. And always, ceaselessly, Claire Eberhard was bleeding.

Finally, the infant, slime-stained, wrinkled, a look of precocious anguish on its face, had been coaxed out sufficiently so that the forceps could be removed and the extraction could be completed by the gentler means of human hands. The head protruded bizarrely from the vagina. Next, the shoulders appeared, shriveled, frail. The arms slipped out, then the abdomen, the umbilical cord still attached, carrying the last of the mother-borne nutrients. The tiny hips emerged, the legs, the incredibly small and tender feet. John Goodwin held the newborn by the ankles and slapped its backside. It cried, a single, shrill, complaining note, and Alfred Eberhard's eyes misted over with tears. He wanted to hold the baby, the clone! Himself! . . . He reached out his hands. . . .

But John Goodwin quickly handed the squealing child to a nurse. "We've got to see to the mother," he said.

And, of course, he was right. Claire Eberhard had lost much blood—an amount of blood that could become critical were it not stanched very quickly. And yet, maddeningly, John Goodwin had no way of determining the exact source of the bleeding. It was in the upper genital region, but where exactly? The ovaries, the fallopian tubes, the ligatures that held the whole miraculous arrangement together?

"I don't understand it!" he exclaimed, as he applied cotton wadding to the unconscious woman's vulva, trying to slow the bleeding by the simple process of impeding its flow. "It was a difficult birth, but still, this shouldn't have happened—not to a woman of Claire's age and excellent overall health. Unless there was a congenital weakness somewhere, or something in her medical history. . . ."

It was only then, staring down at Claire Eberhard's deflated abdomen, that John Goodwin noticed the two tiny scars on either side of her pubic mound.

"Alfred," he said, "these scars—what are they, do you know?"

Eberhard's mind reeled. He felt suddenly dizzy; his mouth was dry; he could not breathe. He struggled for the presence of mind to come up with a plausible answer.

"Those—well, uh, Claire told me that once, in her late adolescence, she started developing polyps in her fallopian tubes. She had to have them scraped. She said it was very painful at the time, but there had never seemed to be any after-effects."

"Hmm," said John Goodwin, appraising the scars carefully. Perhaps it occurred to him that the scars seemed fresher than Alfred's story would suggest; but then, with all the stretching and straining that Claire's abdominal flesh had undergone, it was natural that scars should appear more raised, more freshly pink. "Hmm," he repeated. "I don't know what to make of it, Alfred. Normally, in women of child-bearing age, the tissue of the fallopian tubes regenerates very well. If she was scraped, say, five years ago, the lining should have had more than enough time to replenish itself. But perhaps not. . . . Alfred, I'm afraid that Claire has ruptured her tubes. That's what the symptoms indicate, and with the added evidence of this history—I'm afraid that's what it is."

"Will she—" began Alfred Eberhard weakly, his heart pounding.

"She'll be all right," said John Goodwin comfortingly. "The hemorrhaging has stopped, and she's out of danger. But Alfred, I doubt she'll be able to conceive again. I'm almost sure she won't.

You should be very grateful that the child you have appears to be a healthy, normal one. It's the only one that Claire will ever bear."

Alfred Eberhard raised his hands to his eyes. How weary he suddenly was! He rubbed his eyes hard, wanting to see nothing but the random fleeting patterns that appeared from the pressure of his rubbing. At last he opened his eyes and looked down at his wife. She was unconscious, perhaps asleep, and yet her look was not reposeful. A nurse approached him. She held the infant, washed and wrapped in a soft blue blanket.

"Dr. Eberhard," she said deferentially, "would you like to hold your son?"

Mechanically, Eberhard reached his hands out to receive the living bundle that the nurse handed to him. The bundle weighed almost nothing. Alfred Eberhard peered inside the blanket at the boy child, expecting to recognize himself. But he did not. He saw only a baby, well-formed, though with the forcep marks still visible in the skull. The baby was dark-haired, dark-eyed, the eyes deep-set and solemn. Alfred recognized the infant as his son— but as himself . . . ?

Twenty-four

It had been decided, between Drs. Eberhard and Goodwin, that Claire should not be told of her condition until after she had recovered her strength. What was there to be gained by telling her sooner, they reasoned. It would only upset her and deepen the emotional trauma of the difficult birth.

But Claire was not dependent upon the diagnosis of her husband and her friend to inform her that something had gone profoundly wrong within her. She knew it, as a scientist and as a woman. Perhaps she had not yet realized that she was permanently, irreparably sterile, but she knew that something wasn't right, that this childbirth had cost her something infinitely precious to her.

Probably—or so it seemed to John Goodwin—that was why the new mother acted so strangely toward her child. She refused to suckle it—she claimed weakness as an excuse, but John Goodwin perceived a less physical motivation for her refusal. She seemed disinclined to have the child near her at all. She insisted that the child's crib be placed in a room separate from the one she slept in—the room she had occupied alone, in a single bed, ever since giving birth.

In the early weeks of the child's life, John Goodwin had tried, as a family friend, to probe Claire Eberhard's feelings.

"Claire," he had said, "I understand that the birth was difficult and painful for you. I understand and I sympathize. But the pain you suffered was not the child's fault. It's not fair, and it does no one any good, for you to be so distant from the baby—it isn't healthy, Claire."

"I know all that," Claire had answered, trying not to lose her temper with her well-intentioned friend. "I know it isn't fair, and I know it isn't healthy. But I can't help my feelings. And there's more to it than you know, John—there's more to it than you'll ever know."

John Goodwin had let this cryptic statement pass. It was not his place to plumb the depths of Claire Eberhard's psyche. If there were profounder questions to be asked and answered, they could only be handled *within* the marriage—or by a psychiatrist. A family friend—or even a family doctor—could only go so far.

And so John Goodwin had withdrawn from the domestic crisis that was making the Eberhard household such an inhospitable place for the development of a newborn child. Before bowing out, however, he had urged Alfred Eberhard not to wait too much longer before informing his wife of her sterility.

"My guess," said Goodwin, "is that Claire's aversion to the child stems from anxiety. She is vaguely aware that something is wrong with her, but she's not *sure* and that makes it impossible for her to relax. Perhaps, if you tell her after the initial trauma wears off, she'll be able to resign herself to the situation, and begin to be a mother.''

Alfred Eberhard had nodded gravely, assenting to his friend's advice—but dammit! How could anyone's advice be of any value, if no one knew the *real* reason for Claire's actions? Alfred realized sadly that he had placed himself beyond the pale of all human assistance. His secret scheming had left him totally alone, alone with a wife who now clearly seemed to loathe him, who would not nurture his son.

The child was several weeks old now, and his mother had barely touched him! Eberhard himself had taken care of the feeding, the changing, the coddling and the cuddling! He hesitated bringing a nurse into the apartment, for fear of having his domestic troubles become a universal topic of conversation—but, God, how long could this go on?

Seemingly forever, as far as Claire Eberhard was concerned. Two months had now gone by since the birth of the child. Externally, at least, the mother's health had returned—her cheeks were pink again, her weight had stabilized; she still did not know of the trouble inside her, though she still had her creeping suspicions. And she still ignored little Orin. He barely existed for her. She was deaf—or seemed to be—to his cries in the night. It was the father who always got up to feed, to comfort. Every night, Alfred Eberhard would be roused from his bed—in which he now slept alone—to rock the child, to sing to him.

Eberhard was growing increasingly exasperated. His exasperation was twofold. On the one hand, it was his own disturbed sleep, his own impatience with the domestic chores, that was driving him to distraction. But on the other hand, he was hugely concerned for the well-being of little Orin, the creature that Eberhard had worked so hard and so long to bring into being. Could he allow him to be scarred, psychically wounded, by the cruel inattention of his mother? No, he had to try to make Claire understand the selfishness of her actions. A confrontation was inevitable, that was all.

And then it happened one evening when Claire and Alfred Eberhard were having dinner. They still had dinner together, though there was rarely any conversation at the table. Orin was sleeping—or should have been sleeping—but at some point he awoke, and, as always, he awoke crying.

And, as always, Claire Eberhard made no response whatsoever; she did not even seem to hear the piercing, shrill peals. That was her husband's affair. She knew exactly what he would do: He would put down his knife and fork, wipe his hands and mouth on his napkin, and then, perhaps giving her one quick reproachful glance, he would leave the table and see to the baby.

But this time, Alfred Eberhard did not respond. He made no movement—he was as still as his wife. The baby cried again—neither "parent" budged. It was a war of nerves, and, inevitably, having so much more at stake, Alfred Eberhard lost. The baby cried a third time, and finally Eberhard slammed his utensils down on the table and turned a furious gaze on his wife.

"Goddammit, Claire!" he hissed. "Will you please see to the baby!"

Claire raised her eyes to him very slowly, and her eyes said that, as far as she was concerned, there *was* no baby. She said nothing more.

Eberhard was beside himself. He wanted to grab his wife by the neck. He wanted to shake her violently. When he spoke again, his voice was ugly with rage, the blood seemed to gurgle in his throat. His face was scarlet from the pulsing pressure of his anger.

"Don't you see what you're doing?" he said. "Aren't you aware of the horrible damage you're causing? What chance does that child have of being normal, if his mother ostracizes him?"

"Normal?" said Claire Eberhard softly, relishing the morbid irony of the word. "That's rather a strange way to put it, Alfred."

Claire's urbane indifference was more than Alfred could bear. His rage redoubled, he felt a pounding in his temples, a hotness in his cheeks.

"Listen, Claire," he said, his voice threatening, "use whatever words you like, or don't use any words at all, if that suits you better. But the fact remains, I can't go on playing both mother and father to that infant."

Claire Eberhard began to laugh. It was a gruesomely hollow laugh, mirthless and ghostly. "But Alfred, you *are* both mother and father to the infant. . . ."

Alfred Eberhard could listen no more, neither to his wife's words nor to the continued crying of little Orin. He sprang from the table and stormed into the baby's room. He fed the infant and saw to its disgusting change of diapers. He was revolted and furious; his hands shook with rage. Changing the diaper, he pricked the baby's side with the safety pin. He trembled, unsure whether or not it had been accidental. Silently he rehearsed angry words to his wife, found the taunts and jibes which would break down her cool and mocking reserve.

But when he stormed back into the kitchen, his wife was no longer smiling or cool or reserved. She was whimpering piteously, like a wounded animal, inconsolable. She slumped in her chair, her face lined with tears. Eberhard stopped in his tracks when he saw her. His rage did not disappear, but took refuge deep within him. He felt a sudden urge to cry himself, to cry from helplessness.

"Alfred," she said weakly, "Alfred, tell me what's wrong inside of me."

Alfred Eberhard steeled himself to make his reply. He urged himself to be gentle, to be sympathetic, and yet his anger seethed within him, he could not fight down a certain spiteful tone which crept into his words.

"Claire," he said, "your fallopian tubes ruptured during the childbirth."

"And that means . . ." said Claire Eberhard falteringly.

"That means," continued her husband, "that you can't have any more children."

Claire's tears came in torrents now, her worst

fears confirmed. "Any *more* children, Alfred?" she said bitterly between sobs. "No, I can't have *any* children, no children of my own."

Her voice was lost in sobs. No more words came out, though there was much more she would have liked to say. Alfred Eberhard stood mutely before her, unable to meet her searing gaze. Then he turned and left the room. Little Orin was crying again. . . .

The inescapable confirmation of the fact that Claire Eberhard had been made sterile by the bearing of her husband's clone, brought about a dramatic and unforseeable change in her attitude toward the child. No longer did she shun the infant, no longer did she regard it with the seeming indifference that was actually covering up her horror; on the contrary, she now became an extremely attentive—even doting—mother, tending to the baby's every whim, responding to its every whimper.

This startling turnabout in her behavior took place with a bizarre suddenness. It began on the very night of the confrontation, in fact.

Late that night, when Orin woke through crying, his father, as usual, sprang up from his bed and went to the cribside. When he got there, however, he found that, for the first time, his wife had reached the cradle first. Her back was to him, and he saw only her rounded shoulders as she caressed the baby and rocked it in her arms. Never did she so much as turn around toward Alfred Eberhard, never did she even acknowledge his presence. She just stood with her back to him, rocking the infant, cooing to it—and hiding it from the sight of its father with the gentle breadth of her back.

For some moments, Alfred Eberhard looked on in silence. He was touched, and more than that, he was relieved, relieved that his wife was finally assuming her rightful share of the responsibilities of having a child. He knew she would come round, and yet, he thought, there was something a little disconcerting in the way she refused to turn around toward him, in the way she used her own body as a shield placed between the father and the son. Better not to worry about that now, though, he told himself. Better just to look forward to the barely remembered pleasure of an uninterrupted night's sleep.

The next day, without consulting her husband, Claire Eberhard moved the baby's crib into her own room, placing it very close to her narrow, single bed. She wanted the child near her, wanted to hear the sound of its breathing, to smell the milky smell of its breath. She played with the infant that entire afternoon, dangling brightly colored birds in front of him, delighting in the alert expression on his face, in the eager grasp of his tiny, wrinkled hands. She took him on her knee, held him in her arms, laid her cheek against the incredible softness of the baby's tummy. Little Orin laughed at that— his mommy's hair tickled him.

It is probable that Claire Eberhard was not yet aware of the incredibly complex series of motivations which had prompted the remarkable change in her. She knew that she loved the baby now, but

did she realize the subtle desperation in her efforts
to become a part of this child, to stamp this infant—who was not her own—with the indelible imprint of her own feelings and affections? This was
to be her only child—genetically, she had been
cruelly robbed of even a surrogate immortality—
but there were other ways besides the chemical tyr-
anny of chromosomes, to form another being in
one's own image.

There was the day-to-day formative power of
teaching, of playing, of love. But it was not simple
love that motivated her to expend such huge attention on little Orin. Hatred also played a part,
though Claire Eberhard may not have acknowledged this as yet. It was a growing, moldering,
seething hatred for her husband, whose selfish arrogance had robbed her of the chance to carry
herself on, who had subjugated her will to his own
at each and every juncture.

Yes, somewhere in the depths of her unconscious mind, there was an indissoluble link between Claire's love for the cloned infant and her
hatred for the adult original. She would see to it
that those two beings, genetically identical, would
never harmonize; she would do all she could to
assure that her husband's prideful dream of self-
perpetuation turned into a mocking nightmare of
daunted hopes and cruelly ironic inversions.

It must be remembered, of course, that these
grim thoughts did not intrude on Clair Eberhard's
suddenly sunny consciousness. No, life, for her,
had become a glad adventure of nurturing, of

watching little Orin develop from day to day. She
bathed him, she stroked him, she sang to him.

Alfred Eberhard could not have been happier
about this whole turn of events. He again was able
to sleep through the night. His conscience—that
vestigial organ—was soothed, now that Claire
seemed so happy. Alfred was troubled, to be sure,
about the way his wife ignored him—but that
would pass. And if it didn't, he had gotten what
he needed from her. They could always evolve
some sort of new arrangement.

It sometimes annoyed Alfred that his wife allowed
him so little access to the child. She always seemed
to get to him first, to monopolize him. But, thought
Eberhard to himself, that was certainly preferable
to the former state of affairs! Alfred admitted to
himself that, though he made a wonderful donor,
he probably wasn't much good as a father anyway.
He was too preoccupied; his patience was limited.

Did it ever occur to Alfred Eberhard that his wife
was trying to take the child away from him? Perhaps it did—but Alfred did not for a moment believe she could succeed. He was a man of
science—he knew the awesome power of chemistry! That was a power that could never be undone!
That was a link that could never be broken. The
child was *his,* of that Alfred Eberhard was sure.

And so it did not trouble him when Claire announced that she would not be going back to the
lab, but had decided to stay at home and devote
all her time to the baby. That was fine with him.
He himself initiated a new cancer project, a rather
lackluster affair in which he took only a lukewarm

interest. But that too was all right with Alfred Eberhard. Some of his old passion was gone—no, not gone, but prematurely transferred to his cloned infant son.

He was forty. His hair was beginning to go gray at the temples. He became fatigued more readily than he used to. He was still fit, but he was slowing down. The first faint glimpses of mortality had begun to appear. But Eberhard faced them with equanimity—or with relative equanimity at least. He was comforted by the knowledge that an exact duplicate of himself was at every moment maturing, that there would be another being exactly like himself—no, not *like* himself: *himself!*—moving in to complete whatever remained to be done, to fill his place exactly. In those early months of Orin's life, Alfred Eberhard never doubted that this would be so.

Twenty-five

Our narrative now skips ahead five years, into a new decade.

It was 1980. Orin Eberhard was five years old. He had grown into a healthy and well-formed boy, with thick dark hair and piercing deep-set eyes. He seemed in all respects normal, except perhaps in his rather exaggerated attachment to his mother. But that was understandable—his mother had been his almost constant companion since the earliest weeks of his infancy, while his father seemed a mere vague presence who came and went, who disappeared after breakfast and did not come back again till Orin was almost ready to go to sleep.

But it was not only this disproportion in the amount of time that Orin spent with each of his parents that accounted for the pronounced inequality of his feelings for them; somehow, with a child's wordless understanding, Orin had come to know that his mother did not like his father. She never said as much, and of course Orin had no other grown-up couples to gauge by—but still, he somehow *knew* it. And if his mommy didn't like his daddy, then neither, really, did he. His mommy must have a reason. . . . But, just as Claire Eberhard never spoke of her aversion for her husband, neither did little Orin ever speak of his secret dislike for his father. It was a private and rather puzzling feeling he kept to himself.

Orin Eberhard no longer slept in a crib. He was a big boy now, and slept in a bed—a bed that was placed very near his mommy's. He liked it that way. Daddy slept in a whole different room. This, too, added to Orin's conviction that the *real* family consisted of his mommy and himself. His father was something of an intruder.

Not that Alfred Eberhard did not make efforts to enter into a more intimate relationship with his son, to win the boy's affection. He made overtures quite often, but they were always repulsed, repulsed in that deflating and uncombatable way that children have of fending off unwanted attention. Alfred Eberhard tried to interest Orin in the things that *he* had been interested in as a child. He was constantly on the look-out for shared proclivities, for things that, chemically, they *had* to have in common.

Alfred tried to interest his son in music. He went so far as to purchase a piano, which Orin staunchly refused to play. Why, thought Orin, should he sit all by himself at the piano, when he could be playing with his mommy, doing something that was more fun, and not feeling lonely in the meantime? Eberhard could not understand his son's balking. He *had* to be gifted! It could not be otherwise. If he, Eberhard, had been a near prodigy at Orin's age, it was inconceivable that Orin should not also

be one! Why wouldn't the little bastard sit down
and practice! Eberhard was frustrated no end by
his cloned son's truculence.

(The final irony in this business of the piano was
the fact that Orin *was,* in terms of sheer ability, a
prodigy! When he glanced over the music, written
by Bach and Mozart, he immediately understood
its structure; he immediately grasped the mathematical and formal elements which made it what
it was. But Orin himself saw nothing remarkable
in his ability to penetrate, at the age of five, all the
subtleties and nuances of this great art. As far as
he knew, *anyone* could do it, and what was there to
get excited about? So then, he *had,* inevitably, in-
herited his father's talent—he simply didn't have
his *inclination*—that was where chemistry fell short,
where other factors came into play. . . .)

Daunted again and again in his efforts to break
his wife's monopoly on the affections of "their"
son, Alfred Eberhard understandably looked forward to the day when little Orin would enter kindergarten. *Then* his wife's influence would finally
begin to be diluted. *Then* Orin would find himself
in a more natural situation, and his native tastes,
talents and excellences, would begin to really show
themselves. . . .

To some degree, this did, in fact, occur, but not
nearly as totally as Alfred Eberhard would have
hoped. True, when Orin found himself in a class-
room full of ordinary children, it did begin to
dawn on him that he was somehow smarter than
they were. When certain students fumbled over a
task as ludicrously simple as counting from one to

ten, it did strike him as strange. It seemed unusual to him that sometimes a little boy or girl did not remember how to say a word that had already been explained to them once.

But, though he was slowly becoming aware of his potential academic excellence, this awareness did not lead Orin into the intensely precocious sort of mental life that his father might have hoped for— that his father had lived through. When Orin came home from school at the end of the day, he did not bury himself in fifth and sixth grade books, as his father had done as a kindergarten pupil. Rather, Orin asked his mother to read *to him*—and the books he preferred were the simple ones.

To be sure, Orin was *capable* of reading his own books, and of comprehending far more complex things than Dick and Jane—but simple stories, read aloud, were what he *preferred*. The simplicity of the stories left Orin's mind free to weave a thousand variations of his own; and he loved the sound of his mother's voice reading to him. It was the sound he loved best in the whole world, the sound he associated with every comfort and every kind attention.

Needless to say, the fact that Orin did not immediately "come round" when he began attending school, added yet another note of frustration to Alfred Eberhard's feelings. Here he was, forty-five years old, graying, with a ruined marriage, beginning to physically weaken. He had pinned all his hopes on this cloned offspring. (Almost like a pious man, who foreswears the pleasures of this world for the greater pleasures of the next, Alfred

Eberhard had devoted the time of his own greatest strength to the development of someone to come after.) And what was this cloned offspring turning out to be—not himself, but a parody of himself, a creature different from himself, whose difference mocked Alfred by his *ability* to be the same.

Angry and despairing, Alfred Eberhard felt the need to talk to someone. But always, he was blocked from meaningful confidence by his awful secret. Truly, he was beyond the reach of human help. He resolved to speak with John Goodwin— not, of course, to tell him of the true circumstances of Orin's birth, but to state the situation *as if* Orin were a normal offspring. Perhaps, even by mere analogy, John Goodwin might have something useful to offer.

"Listen, Alfred," John Goodwin said, as the two old friends sipped a beer in the researchers' lounge, "it's understandable that you're upset. No parent likes to feel closed out of his child's life. But try to regard it *scientifically*—Orin is going through the Oedipal stage. Try not to worry so much—it's *normal.*"

Normal! How that word galled Alfred Eberhard! What did it mean? What relevance did it have? Of what use was it to him? No use at all. . . .

"You're right, of course, John," said Alfred miserably. "But still—well—" No more words came to him. How he ached to spill his secret! What a relief it would have been! But he didn't dare. He only shrugged and tried to smile.

John Goodwin perceived the intensity, if not the true cause, of his friend's misery. In a way, he was

glad to see it. It confirmed his feeling that Alfred
Eberhard had always been, at heart, a deeply feeling person.

As time passed, the situation with Orin did not
improve. If anything, it grew worse. As the child
grew older, and more verbal, his defiance toward
his father became more outward. It showed itself
in the most everyday exchanges—as if Orin, with
some bizarre intuitive awareness of his own engendering, was intent on proclaiming himself different from his father in every detail. If, at table, Orin
balked at eating a certain food—string beans, let
us say—Eberhard might try to persuade him by
announcing how much he himself enjoyed string
beans.

"That doesn't mean I have to like them," the
six-year-old clone would respond. And that exchange would be enough to insure that Orin
would carry a long-term aversion to string beans.
(After such an impertinent reply, Orin would always glance secretly at his mother, seeing if she
approved of his slighting behavior toward Daddy.)
Claire was careful not to overtly encourage Orin—
and yet the child was fairly confident he saw a hint
of gratification there.

Needless to say, Alfred Eberhard's dissatisfaction
with his son did much to increase the already excruciating tension between himself and his wife.
On several occasions, Eberhard had been reduced
to pleading that Claire relent in her destructive
monopolization of the boy. Claire had looked at
him wide-eyed, as if she wasn't even faintly aware
of what he meant! Further frustrated by her reac-

tion, he would move on to threats—but what had
he to threaten her with? Divorce? Claire Eberhard
would be only too glad to grant her hated husband
a divorce—provided, of course, that she was given
custody of their child!—and *that*, Alfred would
never in a million years agree to. Could he
threaten her with physical violence? She would
probably welcome that—it would be her final
trump card in assuring that Orin would be turned
against him forever!

No, there was no way out. Alfred Eberhard was
stuck with his wife, and with her treatment of his
son. She had him blocked in every way. It was her
victory.

But what sort of victory was it? For Claire Eberhard, it certainly was not an unequivocal one. In
bearing Orin at all, she had lost something infinitely precious of herself, irreplaceable. And yet,
even beyond that biological loss, there were other,
psychological tolls that Claire paid in exchange for
her monopoly of her son's affections.

She knew, somewhere deep within herself, that
her treatment of the boy was destructive. She was
depriving him of the chance to know his father.
She was—unintentionally but helplessly—causing
him to be emotionally one-sided, as if the emotional one-sidedness could in some way balance off
his genetic one-sidedness. But in her heart of
hearts, Claire knew that this notion was selfish and
wrong—and, secretly, she punished herself for it.
She came to realize gradually that she was *using*
Orin to get back at her husband, and that though
her love for Orin was real—indeed, the most real

thing in Claire Eberhard's cruelly truncated life—
it was a smothering, misguided love, an unnatural
love.

Claire loved her "son" with a jealous, exclusive
passion, a kind of love more appropriate to a mis-
tress than a mother. And, secretly, she was ashamed
of herself. The huge enjoyment she took in her
little boy was always tinged with a note of ineffable
sadness, the endless melancholy of hurting a loved
one by one's very love. . . .

And what of little Orin himself? How did he fare
amidst this awful tangle of love and hate and frustrated hopes?

To some extent, he was protected by his ignorance. Having no knowledge of other families, the
utter strangeness of his own never occurred to
him. And, needless to say, he had no notion that
he was different from everyone else—from everyone else who had ever been born! Didn't he have
one head, two arms, two legs, just like everybody
else? There was no reason to suspect that his conception had been any different. And there was far
less reason to suspect that Orin was a duplicate of
his father! For what did the two of them have in
common, beyond the superficial traits of hair and
eyes and breadth of forehead and a hint of cleft
in the chin? No, as far as Orin was concerned, they
weren't alike at all! They didn't even like the same
foods. And Daddy "liked" to be by himself and
not to talk to Mommy much, while Orin was just
the opposite. No, this man, tall and big and sad-
looking, was a stranger to Orin. And though Orin
didn't know it yet—for now, that strangeness was

a funny puzzle, a kind of game—that strangeness was leaving him with an excruciating, unfillable emptiness at the middle of himself.

Several more years passed. The bizarre paradox of Orin Eberhard's development grew more and more pronounced—in every genetically determined detail of physical appearance and native mental ability, he uncannily resembled his father; however, in every environmentally determined trait of temperament and taste, he grew away from him more and more.

Like his father, Orin had shocked the psychologist who administered his I.Q. test. Owing to refinement in statistical techniques, Orin did not run off the scale, as his father had done—but he was well up into the genius category—further up the "unusually gifted" scale than any child in the whole of the psychologist's experience.

But, contrary to his father, Orin did not seem inclined to gear this ability toward great success in school. He was not intellectually lazy—far from it—but his interests ran along different lines than the cut-and-dried stuff of mathematics and science. Orin preferred to daydream, to think in images, to inhabit the gentler realm of the non-specific.

Like his father had done, Orin was growing into a tall and well-built boy. But, contrary to his father, he showed little interest in athletics, liking neither the competitiveness nor the structure of playground games.

Like his father, Orin had the raw traits of leadership—the articulateness, the physical presence. But, contrary to his father, he had no taste for bringing those strengths to bear. He had neither the need nor the confidence to lead.

It is always a wrenching thing for a father to admit that he is disappointed in his son—but how much more so if the son is a clone! Then there is no diluting influence to blame, the boy's weaknesses could not be ascribed to the mother's genes, an inferior strain infused by unlucky chance!

Day by day, it grew more and more painful for Alfred Eberhard to confront his boy, this mock duplicate of himself. It had been bad enough when Orin was five: then he was a mere toddler; there was something almost cute in his defiance. But now he was ten, approaching puberty, frighteningly recognizable in physical appearance—and still so damnably, relentlessly, different! He seemed to have no backbone! He seemed not so much a replica of Eberhard, as an anti-replica—as if Orin was the empty space that existed when Eberhard moved from somewhere!

It was agonizing, and Alfred Eberhard could no longer avoid showing it. No longer did he make affectionate overtures toward his boy, as he used to. No, he had been put off too many times. No longer did he mask his disapproval of the way his wife handled the lad. Now he came right out and told her she was ruining the boy, perhaps had ruined him already.

As for Claire Eberhard, the guilt that she had always dimly felt about her fierce monopolization of the boy, had, over the years, been building into

a frightful self-loathing. Yes, she regarded herself
as monstrous, a spider of a mother, devouring her
young, feeding on him for her own twisted needs.
She was aware of Orin's warped growth, like a
plant lit only from one side, and she took the pain
of it into herself. Yet she was incapable of relaxing
her grip on the boy. Perversely, her guilt made her
clasp him all the tighter. Hating herself, *he* was the
only thing she loved.

And Orin, too, was beginning to become aware
of the awesome unhappiness of his surroundings.
His father-as-stranger game had turned sour. His
love for his mother now made him uneasy sometimes. And he had seen enough grown-up faces
now to know that other people did not look at
each other the way his parents did, and other
mothers did not look at their sons the way his
mother looked at him. And other fathers looked
at their sons more often than his father ever
turned his eyes his way.

The three of them were locked in a horrible situation that was spiraling further downward with
every passing day. They had long ago passed the
point where a psychiatrist should have been called
in. (But, thought Alfred Eberhard with hopelessly
grim humor, what good could a psychiatrist do
them? Could the highly respected Dr. Alfred Eberhard approach a colleague and say, "You see, I've
cloned a son and things aren't working out, and I
need your help"? No. Again, the necessarily secret
means of his son's engendering put him beyond
the reach of help, beyond the reach of all humanity. . . .)

Alfred Eberhard, fifty years old, drained in body and spirit, constantly mocking himself for his futile pridefulness, tried to ignore his domestic problems and go about his work. (But his work meant nothing now.) Claire Eberhard stayed home and lavished attention on her son (knowing that her attention was bad for him). And Orin Eberhard, the first cloned human, unaware of his own secret, wondered if all families were like this (secretly praying that they weren't).

The three of them were slowly going mad.

Twenty-six

When Orin Eberhard was fifteen, his father decided that he must be sent away to prep school, to the same prep school which he himself had attended. It was the first time that Alfred Eberhard had ever absolutely insisted on having his own way where his son was concerned; always before, fearing a scene or the boy's own defiance, he had given in to his wife's coddling judgments. This time, however, he was determined to prevail: The confrontations could not go on, the horrible strain of the domestic situation had to be broken.

There was nothing about the Eberhard homelife that was not unnatural and grotesque. The parents slept in separate bedrooms; the morbidly fierce bond between mother and son existed, as did the lack of communication between son and father. There was the secret loathing of everyone involved—it could not go on! Orin had to be got away from the house, and there was only one place where he could logically go—St. Paul's the same place where Eberhard's mind-set had been largely formed. They would make a man of him, if anyone could. They would show him the true pleasures of the mind, and of manhood!

Alfred Eberhard made his proclamation at the dinner table, one evening in July 1990, fully expecting a pitched battle to ensue. But no protest was issued. On the contrary, everyone seemed rather relieved. Claire Eberhard was secretly glad that her son would be taken out of her destructive clutches—though she had no idea how she would fill the awful emptiness of her life once he was gone. Orin, though he never would have had the nerve to suggest it himself, was glad of the chance to get away from home. It would be an adventure— and besides, he was getting old enough to realize that he wasn't happy where he was. Alfred Eberhard's own relief was perhaps the greatest of all— no longer would he have to daily confront his folly of follies, the visible evidence of his hubris and his failure.

So then, it was decided: Orin would be enrolled for the fall term. He would leave right after Labor Day. . . .

The six weeks between the making of this decision and Orin's actual departure, however, were a poignant and tension-filled time.

Now that his son's departure was imminent, Alfred Eberhard again yearned to establish some meaningful connection with him. He wanted to *talk* with the boy, not just make chitchat, but to have something *said*. Why was it so difficult? Why wouldn't the boy respond? His mind always seemed to be elsewhere. Either he was daydreaming, or his mind was skipping ahead to the time when he would be free of his father's burdensome company, and be back in the happy presence of his mother!

But, in truth, if the adolescent Orin did repel his father's overtures, it was really not by choice. He, too, had a yearning for that contact, that confirming exchange with the being who looked so much like him, who was equipped like him. But he simply could not relax around him. . . . With his mother, it was different—he knew the rhythms of her speech; he knew how to reply. With his father, it was too frightening, he simply had not had enough practice at it. . . .

Alfred Eberhard no longer became angry at his cloned son's rebuffs—now they only made him sad. They made him yearn to hold the boy in his arms, to give him, in one long moment, all the affection for so long thwarted and withheld, comforting them both—both?—how strange to speak of both! . . . To comfort himself—in both bodies, the fifty-three-year-old body, dimming, and the thirteen-year-old body, painfully growing into its own. How sad and how futile it all seemed now to Alfred. He had sought two bodies, two lives, and had found only two sadnesses, the sadness of age and the sadness of youth; the sadness of self and the sadness of not-self.

And there were yet other sorts of sadness that wracked the Eberhard family during those trying weeks. There was the sadness that Claire Eberhard felt, as the irresistible power of a certain notion grew in her. Yes, she *would* do it. She had tried to dissuade herself, but she was too weak. She had

come to hate herself too much. She could not resist this one last supreme piece of loving violence
which she would wreak upon her son in the name
of his father.

It was a repulsive idea, but there was a gruesome
beauty in it, an inevitable perfection. And why not
give in to it? She was not, after all, the child's
mother. That was a myth, a hateful lie. She would
never be anyone's mother. She would never hold
a child in her womb—except. . . . The idea was
sweet with a maddening sweetness. She wished that
she might die before she did it—Poor Orin! . . .
But she would do it. . . .

Orin, meanwhile, was trying to form some idea
of what it would be like to be away from home.
What would it be like sleeping in a big dormitory
filled with other boys? And what would the teachers be like? And how often could he come home
to see his mother? He knew that he would miss
her terribly.

He was to leave for school on Labor Day of 1980.
On the night before, a Sunday night, very late,
Claire Eberhard slipped silently into his bedroom.

Orin was asleep on his side, his body loosely
curled. His breathing was slow and even. The light
summer blanket had been shaken off his shoulders, and for some moments, Claire stood at the
boy's bedside, staring at him. Broken shafts of
moonlight filtered in through the drawn blinds.
How lovely he looked! His hair was black and
curly, his skin was smooth and luminous. Through
his cotton pajamas, his boyish shoulders looked
delicate and sculptured. His neck was a thin stalk,

its curve lovely and floral. The youthful form made a sweeping curve in the twisted fabric of the blanket.

Slowly, carefully, cautious not to wake him prematurely, Claire Eberhard lay down at his side. She did not touch him, but only absorbed his nearness, his warmth, the sleepy smell of his breath. She found herself trembling. Her hand reached out and touched the back of his neck; she caressed the lowest fringes of his tousled hair, There was a slight hitch in his breathing—but he did not awaken. . . .

Claire was ashamed and excited. It had been so long. . . . Heat passed between the two placid bodies, through skin, through cotton, through the soft nylon of her nightgown. She stroked his back, felt the indentation of his lower spine and the rise of his boyish buttocks. She turned softly on her side, facing him, letting her warm knees rest against his. Her hand cupped his waist, she felt the slender curve between ribs and hips.

Orin's eyes opened. She met his eyes, fearful, sure. He was confused. There was a warmth in him, a warmth under the blanket with him. "Mommy?" he said.

"Yes . . . no," said Claire. "Let me hold you, darling."

Her arms came out around him, drawing him against her. His cheek was against her chest. He felt her bosom swelling against his throat. Her breath was warm and hurried against his hair. Her leg came up and covered his own—it was pleasantly heavy on top of him; he could barely move, he didn't want to. Something was happening to him now, something that had happened before, but only in secret. He was ashamed—it was something that no one should know about. Would his mother be mad if she knew?

Claire's hands were lost in the boy's curly hair, she drew his face down harder against her breasts. And her hips began to sway, began to move in an almost forgotten pattern. Her loins found the solidity of youthful thighs to rub against, she pressed herself, showing her own secret to the boy, so shy of his. She was engulfing him, surrounding him, making him her own. Baffled, dreaming, needful, he allowed himself to be moved, squeezed, kneaded. . . .

Her hand, at last, slid down along his back and past the flimsy waistband of his pajamas, down over the disconcertingly cool skin of his buttocks.

What was this? he wondered. How strange to be touched there! Gently, insistently, she coaxed the pajamas down over his hips, exposing him. Why? he wondered. For what? Her nightgown was bunched around her waist. Below, she was naked, and ready, and aching, and ashamed, and determined.

She pulled the boy on top of her. He followed, trusting, dreamy, willing to share his secret now. How nice it was to let his weight down on her belly, to feel her soft tummy underneath him, to ride on it! Her hand came down and held him, gently—but still, for a moment, he was frightened.

His hips twitched, trying to escape. Her hand was on his back, restraining him. . . . But now he saw there was no need of escape, none at all.

Claire's eyes rolled back, her breath failing her.

How like a man he felt! Trembling, she drew him in. He allowed himself to be led, unaware of destinations. What was it, so warm, so strange, so unlike her body, her cool dry skin? He rocked on top of her, but it was not him who was rocking now. No, it was something outside of him, propelling him on, whispering advice—no, orders!—to him, sweet orders to be followed, learned. And she rocked, his mommy rocked him, swayed, bounced him on her soft belly. . . .

She had him in her womb again—by her choice, this time!—not planted there, but drawn gently in! A child was in her womb, yes, and when he was expelled he would be hers, stamped by her. She would give birth again!

. . . Afterward, they lay together. Orin was frightened. He cried.

"Mom?" he asked. "Is it all right, what we just did?"

"Yes, darling," said Claire Eberhard. "It's all right."

"Do other people do it?" he asked.

"It's different for us, Orin," she said.

"Why?" he asked.

"You'll understand some day," she said. "Did you like it?"

"Yes," said Orin, nestling against his mother's shoulder. "More than anything."

"So did I," said Claire Eberhard. "But Orin, this must be a secret between us. No one else can know. Okay?"

"Okay," he said. "I love you, Mommy."

Twenty-seven

The next day, after accompanying her husband on the forlorn errand of taking Orin to the train, Claire Eberhard got undressed and got into bed. She did not get into her own bed, but into Orin's, which, in the rush of the morning's preparations, had not yet been made.

She lay in that bed for the entire rest of that day and night. She did not eat dinner. Her husband, realizing how upset she was, and fearing a sarcastic reply, made no comment on her behavior.

She did not get up for breakfast the next morning. Her husband only casually noticed her absence before going off to the lab. But when, upon returning, he found her still in Orin's bed, still in her rumpled nightgown, having still not eaten, he began to be worried. He looked at her. Her eyes were vacant, the expression on her face was empty but tense; she seemed barely aware of his presence.

"Claire!" he said.

She made no reply.

"Claire!" he repeated. "Answer me! You can't lie here forever! Orin is gone—but he's only at school, for God's sake! Come on now, pull yourself together!"

But Claire Eberhard did not respond. If she heard her husband's words at all, she didn't show it. If she felt anything about those words, it was only a dim, grim sense of victory that she was stronger than the words were. The words couldn't make her leave the bed. . . .

Alfred Eberhard looked helplessly at his wife. Part of him could not help but take a spiteful pleasure in the fact that she was crumbling, that her constant, bitchy scheming to take his own son away from him had led to this! But thoughts like that, he knew, did no one any good. What if she really *were* crumbling? What if she were having a breakdown? What might not she say? What harm couldn't she do if she began telling family secrets? Though, of course, Eberhard reasoned, who would believe her—if she were crazy, that is. That was a comfort, that no one would believe her, that she had no proof. Eberhard tried to keep himself calm by thinking of that. Still, he did not sleep very well that night.

Claire Eberhard did not get out of Orin's bed the next day either. Though she did not know that it was the next day—time was not working in that orderly a fashion for her. For her, no time had passed since Orin had left—or, more specifically, no time had passed since the moment she had laid down next to Orin in this very bed. That had been an excruciatingly long moment. It had contained her maddeningly sweet, forbidden intercourse with the boy, her infinitely lonely and soul-whipping walk back to her own bed afterward; it contained all the rest of that sleepless night, the re-living, the self-blaming, the insistent gladness; it contained Orin's face the next morning, his face asking, What now, Mommy?—and her with no answer. The moment contained Alfred in his bizarrely cuckolded ignorance, his backfired plan making him old and bitter and pathetic. That was the endless moment that had brought her to his bed, Orin's bed, where time no longer passed, where everything was re-living and thinking-over, an infinity of time in which to study that one long moment.

Claire Eberhard began thinking aloud. "I was right to do it," she said. "He's not my son—he's Alfred's son! Oh, *Alfred,*" she scolded herself, making an ugly face, "don't say that name!"

A long time passed within Claire's endless moment. "No!" she suddenly screamed. "I was *wrong!* I had no right! Oooh, I was so wrong—I raped him! And all because my insides are ruined—all knotted and gnarled and ugly—like Alfred!" And she began to laugh, a mad, cackling laugh that echoed off the walls of her empty room. "Yes," she howled, "like Alfred! Knotted, gnarled and ugly! Like Alfred! Like . . . like . . . me. . . ." The laughing abruptly stopped. Claire Eberhard began to make horrible cat-like screeches. Her hand tightened into a claw. Suddenly she reached up, as if taking herself by surprise, and tore out a clump of her hair. She dragged her nails along her cheek and brought forth blood. Cruelly, she twisted at her nipples through her nylon nightgown, the same one she had worn when. . . .

"But no!" she insisted. "I was right! Orin was my only baby—I remember he hurt me—he hurt me so badly! But I forgave him, welcomed him back! That was good of me, to welcome back Alfred. No, not Alfred! Orin! . . . Yes, Orin. Alfred is old and knotted and gnarled, like me, oh, like me. . . ."

Alfred Eberhard came home from the lab that evening, not knowing what to expect. He hoped that his wife would have shaken off the stupor she'd been in, but he realized that she might perhaps need some more time. She had been terribly upset at Orin's leaving—he must be prepared to bear with her for awhile.

But he was not prepared to face the gruesome spectacle that confronted him when he entered Orin's room. His wife was still in the bed. But was it his wife? Her face was horribly distorted, stretched out of shape by a tormented grin-grimace. Her eyes were wild, seeing nothing or too much. Her nostrils flared; the corners of her mouth twitched uncontrollably. And she was besmirched with filth. She had defecated in the bed, had smeared herself with her own feces. It was everywhere—in her hair, on her cheeks, drawn across the bodice of her nightgown in fierce, self-hating streaks.

Alfred Eberhard mutely stared at her, his knees going weak under him. Claire Eberhard looked back at him, a taunting smile on her face, slowly bringing her fingers to her lips. . . .

Alfred Eberhard, sickened, bolted from the room. He needed to get help. He needed to get someone to come and take her away. . . .

Twenty-eight

Alfred Eberhard had succeeded in keeping a great many secrets from the Brookside community-at-large—the hospitalization of his wife, however, was one grim and mortifying event which he could not prevent from becoming public. The arrival of the ambulance, marked with the insignia of the state facility, the frowning bustle of doctors and assistants—it was all painfully visible. And, though Alfred Eberhard managed to mask the sight of his besmirched wife from the general gaze, it was not long before the story, in broad outline at least, was being whispered and modified throughout the Institute.

Though, of course, the story that circulated was lacking in the most important details—no one knew the origin of Claire Eberhard's breakdown. No one knew the secret of her "son's" engendering; no one, except John Goodwin, who was utterly discreet, knew that Claire had been made sterile in giving birth to Orin.

All that the staff knew was that Claire had been a thoroughly devoted mother, and that she must have been mind-stricken by the departure of her boy. But, murmured some of the more gossipy members of the staff, what did that say about the Eberhard marriage, if a husband was helpless to comfort a wife, to help her through what was, after all, a perfectly normal event in a mother-child relationship? Something deeper must be wrong there—but what?

No one knew. Strangely enough, not even Alfred Eberhard knew of *all* the factors leading up to his wife's collapse. He did not know of his wife's seduction of his cloned son. No one except Orin knew of that—and yet Orin was, or course, ignorant of the fact that he was cloned—the unnatural fertilization that had begun this whole extended nightmare.

No one knew the whole story—no one except Claire Eberhard. And the weight of the whole story had driven her mad, had reduced her to the pathetic, phantom-filled inactivity of the catatonic schizophrenic.

She had not resisted the doctors when they tried to coax her into the strait-jacket. Her muscles had been rigid, her limbs difficult to manipulate—but that was not because of willful defiance, but rather the morbid muscular tension that was the counterpart of her emotional fixedness. She had let them take her away from Orin's bed, for what did it matter? Anywhere they took her would still be Orin's bed. And as long as it took to get there, it would still be that one long moment, that moment when Claire had lured the baby back into her womb, committed that mythic outrage, that act of fierce anger and possessiveness and revenge. She let them take her. . . . She didn't know she was going.

Alfred Eberhard rode along in the ambulance. He was disgusted and panic-stricken. Would his wife reveal anything? How would Orin be affected? The psychiatrists tried to comfort him, knowing how awful it must be for a devoted husband and father to be put through such an ordeal as this.

At the hospital, Claire Eberhard was taken into an emergency admitting ward, where she was cleaned thoroughly, examined, and then put under sedation. This completed, her husband was brought into consultation with Dr. Irving Sexton, chief diagnostician of the state facility.

"Dr. Eberhard," Dr. Sexton said, "since you are a medical man, I can dispense with all the nonsense I usually have to say. You know what schizophrenia is, you know the characteristics of a catatonic stupor. And you know, as well as we do, that curing it is a very hit or miss affair. We don't even know the causes. We can guess at the *emotional* causes, but those aren't the final ones. It's the *chemical* causes that elude us—the changes in the mind chemistry that are brought about by the emotional changes. That's what we don't yet know. So, we've got to start with emotional causes. Has your wife been under any undue strain lately?"

"Our son left for boarding school two days ago," said Dr. Eberhard. "They were very attached and had never been separated before. I suppose that's the immediate cause of my wife's breakdown."

"Perhaps," said Dr. Sexton skeptically. "But it hardly seems like sufficient cause for the state your wife is in."

"No, of course not," said Dr. Eberhard, trying to keep his composure in the face of the psychiatrist's probing. "You see, my wife became sterile in giving birth to our son. That may account for the virulence of her attachment to him."

"Ah," said Dr. Sexton, without emphasis. He made an entry in a little book. "Now we're getting somewhere. Becoming sterile can often be a horrible trauma for a woman—its effects sometimes don't surface for decades. Now, did your wife want to have a large family? Was that very important to her?"

Dr. Eberhard hesitated. He was acutely uncomfortable, as if his body had been opened and a chill breeze was blowing on his insides. "N—no," he said finally. "I don't think she wanted a big family. But I know that it was important to her to have at least one more child."

"And why was that so important to her?" asked Dr. Sexton. His voice was scrupulously neutral, and yet Eberhard imagined that there was an insinuation in it, as if Sexton possessed knowledge he could not possibly possess.

"Well, uh, she wanted to be sure that Orin had a playmate, that he wouldn't be an only child."

"Ah, yes," said Dr. Sexton. "Many women feel that way. . . . But still, Dr. Eberhard, there seems a remarkable disproportion between the possible causes we've spoken of, and the massiveness of the effects we can see. Are there any other factors that might perhaps throw some light on the situation?"

Alfred Eberhard hesitated. How much should he tell? How long would the questions go on?

"Dr. Eberhard," continued Sexton, after a pause, "as a medical man, I hope you will realize that I am not trying to pry unduly, but can you tell me, please—on what sort of terms were you and Mrs. Eberhard?"

"Not very good terms, Dr. Sexton," said Eberhard weakly, raising his eyes to the psychiatrist, looking for a visible reassurance as to his discretion.

"Well," said Dr. Sexton coaxingly, "what exactly does 'not very good terms' mean? Did you fight? Were you having normal marital relations?"

"We did not fight," said Dr. Eberhard. "Or not much, at least." And now Dr. Eberhard steeled himself for the inevitable confession, the confession that shamed him, as if his own manhood were being aspersed. . . . "But we had not had relations for some time."

Dr. Sexton nodded sagely, making another entry in his book. "For how long, Dr. Eberhard?"

Bizarrely, Alfred Eberhard felt himself blushing. He tried to speak, but for some seconds words would not come. "Not since Orin's birth," he whispered at last. Then, as if to clear himself: "She became frigid after that. She felt too badly about becoming sterile, the thought of sex became repulsive to her. . . . I have never touched her since the birth."

Dr. Irving Sexton sat back in his leather chair, letting the eraser of his pencil rest against his upper lip. For some moments he regarded Alfred Eberhard, gauging his strength, trying to decide how much he could bear. Should he tell him what he knew?

"Dr. Eberhard," he said at last, "perhaps it is wrong of me to tell you this, but given the gravity of your wife's condition, I feel that nothing must be withheld—on either of our parts. Doctor, your wife was given a thorough examination as soon as she was brought in. The exam includes an internal . . . Traces of semen were found in her vagina."

Eberhard was stunned. He could not make sense of the words. It was too astonishing. He felt nothing but a faint nausea, the physical grip of a simple animal jealousy. But how could it be?

"Dr. Eberhard," continued Sexton, "I'm sure that this is horribly upsetting for you, and I have no wish to make it worse. But we must do all we can to reconstruct your wife's state of mind. We must try to define every factor. Dr. Eberhard, did you know your wife had a lover?"

Were he not feeling so intensely sick, Eberhard might almost have laughed! A lover! His wife had barely left the apartment all these years, except in the company of Orin. She had broken off all her social contacts completely, wanting no distractions from the pleasure of her little boy. A lover! It was unthinkable! And yet, there was the undeniable evidence, the residue of a man's love within her body.

"Doctor," Alfred said, "I—I really don't know what to say. I knew nothing. It seems impossible to me even now. She was always with my—our son— She saw no one. All her warmth and all her affection were reserved for him."

And now a grotesque, a horrific thought began to take possession of Alfred. No, it could not be! It was too bizarre. . . . But she had seen absolutely no one else in the days before Orin's departure, of that Alfred Eberhard was sure. And when she had become catatonic, she had taken to *his* bed, she had laid there on *his* pillow. No, it couldn't be! But there was no other answer. . . .

"Doctor," gasped Alfred Eberhard, "I think I'm going to be sick."

Desperately, clumsily, Alfred Eberhard bolted from Sexton's office, trying to hold down the acrid burning weight that was surging upward from his stomach. He barely made it to the lavatory before vomiting.

Afterwards, he washed his face with freezing cold water and tried to clear his head. He suddenly knew with absolute certainty that it was true. It was the only possibility powerful enough to account for the horrible collapse of Claire.

He tried to collect himself and returned to Dr. Sexton's office. The psychiatrist was calmly seated at his desk.

"It seems we've reached the same conclusion," he said.

"Yes," said Dr. Eberhard. "Not a very pretty conclusion."

"No," said Dr. Sexton. "But we're not dealing with esthetics here. Pretty or otherwise, we have to see if we can help your wife overcome the debilitating shame she must be feeling. Her self-hatred must be enormous at this point."

"What about the boy?" interrupted Alfred Eberhard.

"Yes," said Dr. Sexton, "the boy will unquestionably have to be considered at some point—but not right now. He's at boarding school, you say?"

Dr. Eberhard nodded.

"My advice is that you let him stay there. Monitor his progress as closely as is practical—if there are signs of trouble, let me know. But in the meantime, I think it's best if he's not told of his mother's condition; if he learns how much his mother is suffering because of her transgression, he's likely to feel that, having shared the transgression, he must share the suffering. But if he doesn't know—or doesn't know until he becomes equipped to handle it better—perhaps he can escape the self-torment.

"Youth is remarkably resilient. Children can rebound from almost anything, if they are allowed to, if the horrible weight of adult guilt is not laid on them, to crush them. Try to shield him, and, above all, don't let him know that you know what he has done—or what's been done to him. As the boy's father, your imagined anger could be deadly to the boy. As it is, he may imagine he's killed you by possessing his mother—his guilt at that thought would be boundless! We must watch him closely. In the meantime, we'll do everything we can for your wife."

Dr. Sexton rose, extending his hand to Dr. Eberhard. Automatically, Dr. Eberhard came to his feet, and automatically, he turned to leave Sexton's office when the handshake was concluded. But though he performed these social rituals with seeming ease, Alfred Eberhard was horribly dazed and disoriented. There was so much he had not foreseen, so much that could not be accounted for by his elegantly logical chemical schemata. Incest—but was it incest, could it truly be called that? . . . Madness—that word, at least, could be unequivocally applied. . . . And how about *evil?* Did that word fit? Had Eberhard's scheme been evil? He had not thought so—truly, he had not thought along those lines at all! Good, evil—no, he had thought in different terms: Possible, impossible; self, not self. Only now did Eberhard begin to realize that he had left something out.

He was dazed, dizzy—so much so that it took him some moments to recognize John Goodwin, who had been sitting in the hospital waiting room, and who now walked toward his old friend with resolute steps and an expression of sadness and concern on his face.

"Alfred," he said, "I came over as soon as I heard. How is she?"

"Hmm?" said Alfred Eberhard, his eyes taking a long time to focus. "Oh, John, I don't really know how she is. Not good. She's sleeping."

John Goodwin looked closely at his friend, reading the strain in his face, the barely maintained coherence in his thoughts. "Alfred," he said, "you should get some rest. Let me take you home. There's nothing you can do here."

Alfred Eberhard shrugged, glad, for once in his life, to surrender his will to another, to have someone tell him what he should do. How weary he was, how sick at heart. . . . His eyes were red, and deeply circled black. His hair was speckled with silver strands. How much older he looked than

John Goodwin—how much more he had put himself through, and how much more he had put others through in the process.

The two men reached John Goodwin's car and began the ride home in silence. There was so much that John Goodwin wanted to ask, so much he wanted to be sure of. But he could not bring himself to prod Alfred on to talk. Still, he wished he would say something.

Goodwin communed with his own thoughts about Claire. He was terrifically fond of her. At one time, in fact, he had feared that he was in love with her! He had tried to laugh that feeling off, and had largely succeeded. Still, he'd always admired her. There had been a fine warm strength about her, a vitality, a zest—but where had it gone? What had gone so utterly wrong in her life that she had been transformed from a spirited, daring young woman, into a catatonic, the most poignant manifestation of a spirit giving up, of confronting a horror too great to battle against?

He yearned to know. He recalled images of her: the first time he'd met here, sweet and perky, so obviously enthralled by Alfred . . . in the early days of their marriage, so assiduously helping Alfred with his cloning experiments . . . and then, a painful image—the image of her in the throes of an agonizing childbirth. He saw it so clearly—the tormented expression on her face, the violent heaving of her belly, the blood pouring from her, the white stretched scars on her abdomen.

The scars! John had not remembered them until now. The scars—old scars, but new-looking from the stretching trauma of birth. But who had told him that the scars were old? Not Claire herself! Alfred had told him! And the rupturing of the tubes—that should not have happened, if the scraping Alfred mentioned had taken place years and years before! But perhaps it had been done only months before, nine months before! . . . Why had nothing come out of the supposed cancer research that Alfred purported to be doing in the months following the experiments with the cloned rat? Alfred had never gone that long without something significant to offer. Why did they stay in the private sector of the lab? They could just as easily have moved back into the main laboratory if they were doing cancer research!

Could it be true? John Goodwin hoped that it was not: He pictured little Orin. Could he find one feature that resembled Claire? Hair color, eye color, shape of face—it was all Alfred. And they'd been so sure that the child would be a boy.

John Goodwin felt an empty burning in the pit of his stomach. Claire Eberhard had been driven mad, perhaps permanently. She had been made sterile, never having had the chance to reproduce herself, to pass along her own genetic structure. She had been robbed of even that meager sort of immortality; and now she had been robbed of her reason . . . if, that is, John Goodwin's surmise were true. He prayed it wasn't.

Unconsciously, he turned to face Alfred Eberhard. Somehow, he knew that meeting his colleague's eyes would give him the answer. Alfred's face was turned away from him, his eyes staring blankly out the car window, but Eberhard felt the weight of Goodwin's eyes on him. He knew it would be disaster to meet those eyes, but he could not resist meeting them. Slowly, his head turned. Their gazes locked. . . . John Goodwin beheld a man ravaged by warped ambitions gone sour, devouring him from within. He *knew*. . . .

"Oh, Jesus, Alfred," was all he could say.

Denial was useless, Eberhard knew. And besides, he no longer had the stomach for denial! No, what he needed now was catharsis, a manic, morbidly ecstatic proclamation of the secret he had held inside so long: "Yes!" he shouted, his voice strained and metallic from the fierce constriction of his throat. "Orin is a clone! The first ever! Congratulate me, John! Never thought it could actually be done, did you? Well, I did it! I plucked an egg from Claire—yes, dammit, weakening the lining of her tubes in the process—and re-implanted it after it had been fertilized. And there you have it!"

"And she agreed to it?" gasped John Goodwin.

"Of course she did!" exclaimed Alfred, a mad self-mocking pride in his voice. "She adored me, John! You told me that yourself. She would have done anything for me. And it all might have worked out, if it wasn't for the damned difficulty of the birth! I'd promised her that we could make a normal baby afterward. How was I to know it wasn't going to work out?"

"But Alfred," John said, "even if it *had* worked out, what of the presumption, the *arrogance*, the unnaturalness of making an exact copy of yourself?"

"Goddammit, John, you're a scientist! Cut out that moralistic horseshit! It was *arrogant* of Galileo to maintain that earth wasn't the center of the universe! It was *arrogant* of Einstein to suggest that Newton's scheme fell short! Every new idea is arrogant!

"And why shouldn't I make an exact copy of myself? Have you looked around you lately? Have you seen what most people are like? Have you gauged the quality of their minds? And how about the soundness of their bodies? What do they understand, what do they appreciate, what are they *worth?* John, I happen to have been a very fortunate accident—that's not conceit, you understand—I acknowledge that it was an *accident.* I claim no credit! But let's be objective—let's look at what I've got. . . ."

"I *know* what you've got," John grated, "but that's not the issue. Are you trying to pass yourself off as a benefactor of the race? Are you trying to tell me your intention was to upgrade the human stock by spreading some of your genes around? That's a repulsive idea, fascistic and hateful. But I don't believe that that was your intention, in any case. I don't believe you could really carry the idea that far away from *yourself.* You wanted to be carried on, that's all. You wanted two shots at life—twice as many chances as you're entitled to."

"No," Alfred said hoarsely, an insane gleam suddenly glinting in his eyes. "Why say *twice* as many? Why stop at two? You accuse me of all these things, this massive selfishness—and then you think I would have stopped at two? Who knows where I would have stopped! Ah, but it's all gone wrong. I've been thwarted."

"You've been thwarted!" screamed John Goodwin, full of wrath and pity for Claire Eberhard. "What of your wife? You have the nerve to say that *you've* been thwarted, when your wife is in a mental hospital, every vestige of her will to live drained out of her because of what you've subjected her to—"

But now it was Eberhard's turn to respond in anger. "No," he hissed. "Claire is not put away because of what *I* did to her! She's there because of what she did to herself! John, she seduced my son! She went to his bed and took him! And now he's got to live with that!"

John Goodwin fell silent. There was no more he could say. He was overwhelmed by the unnaturalness of the life that Alfred Eberhard had built and had subjected his family to. John Goodwin felt as if he was drowning, being pulled down into a bottomless pool of slime. He would say no more; he would hear no more.

He took Alfred Eberhard home and helped the exhausted man into bed. He gave him a sedative. Then he went to his own apartment. But he couldn't sleep. He knew he would never again sleep soundly in that place. He had to get away.

Twenty-nine

The next morning, John Goodwin came to Alfred Eberhard's apartment, to tell him of his intention to leave Brookside.

"I can't convince you to stay?" said Eberhard, rubbing his unshaven chin, sipping his coffee, trying hard to rouse himself from lingering sleepiness and an awful depression.

"No, Alfred," the man said, wistfully shaking his head. Then, after a pause, he added, "I want you to understand that I am not leaving out of anger. It's just that I feel I've seen too much. All these years, even while I've been immersed in my own work, I've been, in some sense, more interested in *your* life than in my own. Even during our periods of estrangement from one another, I've thought about you, about the seeming *largeness* of everything you undertook. In some ways, I've envied you—though I hope without rancor. I feel that I've shared much of your life—and now I feel that, if I stay here, I'll have to share your burden, the incredible weight of responsibility for what you've done. And I just don't think I can do that. I think it might very well drive me crazy."

"Hmm," said Alfred Eberhard, with a slight, mirthless smile. "Yes, there does seem to be a lot of the stuff of madness in the situation, doesn't there? That's something I really didn't figure on. But since you're leaving, and since we may as well be frank with each other at the last, I'll tell you that, if I had it all to do again, I'd do it all the same! Do you think that's horrible of me? . . . Perhaps it is. But still, the idea is so intoxicating! And if the birth hadn't been so difficult . . ."

John Goodwin recoiled a bit, shocked and dismayed by the ungodly stubbornness of his friend's obsession. "Well, Alfred," he said at last, "you *don't* have it to do over again. You've got to pick up the pieces and go from here. What will you do?"

"I don't know," said Eberhard with a helpless shrug. "It largely depends on what becomes of Claire, when or if she recovers. In the meantime, the psychiatrist has advised me to keep the truth from Orin. That will take some ingenuity, but I suppose I can do it, for awhile at least."

"And what about you, Alfred? What will you do?"

"Me?" said Eberhard, as if he found it strange that his own intentions should even need to be questioned. "I shall go on working. I'll develop a new project, find something to bury myself in. I'll be all right. And what about you, John? What do you intend to do?"

"First, I'm going to take a long vacation—very long. And then I'll see. Maybe I'll take a hospital job. I'll miss the research, though. Well, I have to go. Goodbye, Alfred."

"Goodbye, John," he said.

The two old friends clasped hands warmly. Though not quite warmly enough. With Alfred Eberhard, it was never quite warmly enough.

The next several months were a pathetic time in the life of the Eberhard family.

Claire languished in the mental hospital. She did not respond to treatment—to any sort of treatment. Nothing seemed to penetrate the self-loathing isolation in which she had enclosed herself. She did not seem to hear the doctors' words. Drugs threw her into a stupor but gave her no meaningful relief. She lay in her bed, talking to herself, arguing with herself, playing over and over again the sweet forbidden moment when she had taken Orin in her arms.

Now and then she thought of Alfred. His image brought out the cat-like screams, the tearing claws, the murderous moments of utter fury. But then, Orin's image would replace Alfred's (those images so uncannily alike), and Claire would grow calm again, retreating into her gruesome parody of tranquility.

After a time, Alfred Eberhard had his wife transferred to a private facility very near Brookside. It seemed that she was in for a long confinement. She should at least be made physically comfortable.

Meanwhile, letters arrived from Orin on the average of once a week. The letters were always addressed to Claire. Alfred was hardly ever mentioned in them, except for an occasional, "Say hello to Daddy," which, in the context of the rest of the letter, seemed perhaps facetious. To his mother, Orin wrote the most affectionate things. He reminisced about the time they had spent together, about the old stories his mother had read to him years ago, about how much he looked forward to vacations.

He talked relatively little about school, and what he did say, seemed to indicate that he didn't like it much. If he took any real interest in his classes, the letters didn't reveal it. If he had any real relish for the vigorous maleness of the athletic and social life of the school, he didn't mention it. The tone of his letters was backward-looking and somehow effeminate. He sounded like an exile.

Alfred Eberhard, in order to hide from Orin the grim truth about his mother, was faced with the forlorn task of answering the boy's letters in *her* handwriting, trying to mimic her tone, trying to trump up within himself the ability to express a love more powerful than any he had ever felt.

How strange it was to be writing in a woman's voice! And yet, Alfred Eberhard knew his wife's mannerisms so well—hadn't they driven him up the wall for years, as he watched her pamper the boy, as he listened to her cooing in his ear!—that he found that he could ape her tone quite convincingly. Week in, week out, he responded to Orin's letters, trying, half-consciously, to raise the boy's opinion of his father, to put some new ideas into his one-sided mind.

The correspondence between "mother" and son continued all through the fall, and, around the middle of November, the central subject of Orin's letters began to be his eagerness to be home for Christmas. This threw Alfred Eberhard into a bit of a panic—he didn't want Orin home yet; he didn't want to face him. Finally, he decided to tell the boy that he should see if he could make some other arrangements for vacation, staying with a friend perhaps, as Mommy and Daddy had an important conference in Switzerland and would be out of the country for several weeks.

Thus, there was a lapse of some time in the correspondence. And when it started again, early in January of 1991, it was never quite the same. Orin was cooler, more reserved, the letters came less frequently. Had Orin been hurt by his "mother's" refusal to see him? Or was he simply busier with school, more wrapped up in his own life? Whichever it was, Alfred Eberhard was relieved. He hesitated to admit it to himself, but the less he had to do with his family, the happier he was. Their very existence mocked him, reminded him of his follies. Nothing had turned out the way he wanted, and he would just as soon have forgotten that any of it ever happened.

Bizarrely, Orin, who was an exact chemical duplicate of himself, seemed to have *nothing* to do with him—less than nothing! Far from comforting Eberhard as he grew older, Orin's existence served to remind him of his lonely uniqueness—his *mind* had not been duplicated, his *personality* had not been copied. He'd been duped by his own ambitions.

It was a bad time for Alfred Eberhard. He had great difficulty losing himself in his work. He attended to the administration of Brookside more lackadaisically than he ever had. He felt old, tired. He felt that the active, the worthwhile part of his life was over, and that now he was enduring a rather dull and restless denouement. At moments, he positively wished that it was over with, that the mortality he so feared would descend and blot him out.

But then, suddenly, all that changed. . . .

It had to do with a woman, a young woman. Her name was Jean Stafford. She appeared in Eberhard's office one morning, having been sent from Washington as part of a new research team doing work in cryogenics. She was the liaison between the team itself and the regular Brookside staff, and it was her job to work with the administration, to arrange for space, material and so forth. Her first task was to get on terms with the director, to acquaint him with the goals and methods of the cryogenics project, and to enlist his support and cooperation.

Eberhard barely looked up when Jean Stafford first entered the office. He didn't mean to be rude, he just couldn't muster much interest. And when he *did* look up, he barely saw her—Eberhard had all but stopped noticing faces. He couldn't imagine that there were any *new* ones.

It was true that Jean Stafford's face was not unlike other faces he had seen—the high intelligent forehead, the restless dark eyes behind stylish, glinting eyeglasses, the pert nose and mobile mouth, the rather aggressive chin. It was the face of so many women scientists, with its played-down prettiness, its disconcerting mix of scrubbedness and sensuality. Eberhard regarded it with huge detachment.

The meeting began in a formal and businesslike way. Dr. Stafford offered her hand and sat down.

Eberhard welcomed her to Brookside, rather un-
convincingly. (What was the source of the grand
sadness in this man? wondered Jean Stafford. What
was the secret sorrow that made those heavy-lidded
black eyes so melancholically beautiful?) And then
they began to speak of the business at hand.

"Dr. Eberhard," said Dr. Stafford, in a rather
husky but soothing voice, "I assume you've long
been aware of the growing interest in cryogenics.
It's an amazing field, and the possibilities of it are
just beginning to be explored. The reason we are
at Brookside is to research the specific application
of freezing temperatures to the treatment of cancer. As you know, cryogenic treatment is already
being used on certain non-cancerous tumors, such
as those which cause Parkinson's disease. Our purpose here is to find ways to broaden the use of
cryogenics."

"Yes," said Dr. Eberhard, rather mechanically.
"It sounds like a fascinating project."

The strained cordiality of Eberhard's reply did
not escape Jean Stafford. Far from being offended
by his minimal response, however, the young
woman was intrigued by it. What were the depths
that underlay his lugubrious manner? Intuitively,
Jean Stafford sensed that Dr. Eberhard was neither
dull nor lazy—on the contrary, his understated
manner seemed to come from an *excess* of energy,
of energy turned inward on itself, turned bitter
and poignant and strangely appealing.

"Yes," echoed Jean Stafford, wishing to prolong
the interview, to remain in Eberhard's presence a
while longer, "it is a fascinating field. To me, the

most exciting thing about it, is that it almost stops time."

Involuntarily, Eberhard's face tightened at the mention of this idea. The response was immediately noted by Jean Stafford, and she plunged on.

"At temperatures as low as those we're now able to maintain, time all but stops! As you know, the pace of chemical reactions is partly dependent on the temperature at which they take place. The warmer the medium, the quicker the reaction; the cooler the medium, the slower it is."

"Yes, of course," said Dr. Eberhard, his interest beginning to be pricked. "That's the whole reason for, say, refrigerating food, to slow down the chemical reactions which lead to its spoilage."

"Exactly," said Jean Stafford. "Though, in cryogenics, we deal with temperatures that are much, much colder—temperatures that approach absolute zero—the temperature at which every substance becomes a solid, and virtually nothing happens! Now, if we apply these temperatures to human tissues—theoretically, at least—all the chemical processes that constitute aging slow down, almost to a standstill. We can create the state that the old comic books used to call 'suspended animation.' "

"Yes," said Eberhard, "the only problem would be bringing the tissue out of the deep freeze, and restoring it to normal function."

"True," agreed Jean Stafford, "and that's exactly the problem we're working on. We've already got the freezing chambers—those steel cylinders where the temperature can be controlled with amazing exactness. Now, all we need is the know-how to bring the 'suspended' tissues back into time, without damaging them in the process."

"And will you be able to do it?" asked Eberhard.

"I don't see why not!" Jean Stafford said with exuberant confidence. "The theory behind it is perfectly sound—we just have to work out the mechanics."

Now, for the first time, Alfred Eberhard really *looked* at Jean Stafford. And, looking at her, he realized that he had not looked at anyone or anything in months. He saw her features with a tremendous freshness of appreciation, as if he were a blind man, just given back the use of his eyes. He gazed at her raven-black hair, the texture of her complexion. What was it that made him wake up so suddenly? Perhaps her final statement—so like the fierce confidence of Eberhard himself, in his former, less jaded days! Yes, he thought, there was something hard and fine about this young woman! There was something bold, undeflectable, heedless of consequences. He saw in her a kindred spirit, a being more like himself than that horrible parody of himself which he had created.

Jean Stafford was pleased and flattered at the obvious change in Dr. Eberhard's mood and bearing. She had touched something in him, she knew.

"You *are* interested," she could not help remarking.

"Yes," said Eberhard with a smile—a smile not warm, but joyous nonetheless, "I am. I like the way you put it—the idea of stopping time. I tried to stop time once myself."

"Oh, really?" she said, hoping to gain some insight into this dark and ferociously attractive man. "How did you do?"

"Oh," he said casually, "not very well. . . . But listen, Dr. Stafford, be assured that I will assist you and your colleagues in whatever way I can. The staff and facilities of Brookside are at your disposal. And, if I may, I'd like to come down and observe your work sometime."

"Whenever you like," said Jean Stafford. "You're always welcome, Doctor."

The two of them shook hands again, with considerably greater enthusiasm this time, and Jean Stafford left the office.

When she had gone, Alfred Eberhard tried to analyze the excitement within himself. It was something he had not felt in months—no, years. It was a thorough aliveness, an eagerness to be doing things, a passion. But what, he wondered, was the passion for? Was it for the new idea he'd just been exposed to, or for the woman who had presented it to him? Eberhard could not be sure, but no matter, it was a distinction he had never quibbled over.

Thirty

About a week after his initial meeting with Jean Stafford, Dr. Eberhard went down to the sector of the lab which had been set aside for the cryogenics project.

Dr. Stafford gave the director an enthusiastic greeting, and introduced him to her colleagues on the project. Then she began to acquaint him with the mechanics of the work itself.

"The gadgetry is simple," she said, with calm expertise. "The principle is exactly the same as in a commercial refrigerator. A refrigerant is constantly passing from a liquid to a gaseous state, and back again. In the process of vaporizing to a gaseous state, it draws off a tremendous amount of heat from its environment—the heat of vaporization, as it's called—thereby cooling its surroundings. Now, in a regular refrigerator, the substance used is freon—here, it's liquid nitrogen, which changes state at roughly two hundred degrees below zero."

Alfred Eberhard only half listened as Jean Stafford continued her brief tour of the cryogenics lab. He glanced politely at the frozen frog cultures, at the extracted tumors that had been de-activated by the application of extreme cold, but his concentration focussed on Jean Stafford herself. She had not been off his mind since their first meeting. She had reawakened things in Alfred Eberhard that he had long forgotten. (How agonizing, in retrospect, had been those years of being closed off from his wife's bed! He seemed to have accepted it at the time—in the early months, he had occasionally visited one of the prostitutes in town; but soon, he had given up even that meager satisfaction. He had simply let that part of himself become inactive, growing to believe he could do just as well without it. But now, since meeting Jean Stafford, how sharply he had been reminded of the cravings which assail men and women! How strange to be awakened in the middle of the night by one's screaming carnal hunger, to have, at Eberhard's age, no recourse but to relieve oneself like an adolescent. . . .)

He stared at Jean Stafford, and she knew it. His hunger fed her own. She wanted this sad attractive man as badly as he wanted her. She wanted to plumb the depths of his intriguing sorrow as intensely as he yearned to plumb the recesses of her body, her young body which had renewed him.

But on the surface, all that was happening was a professional tour of the lab, in the company of colleagues. "And here we see . . ." "And so, Doctor, as I was saying . . ." Eberhard nodded politely, wondering if he was succeeding in keeping the lascivious look from his face. Jean Stafford droned on, fearing that her cool professional voice was fading to a bedroom whisper.

When, at last, the tour was over, Eberhard summoned all his presence of mind, and told Jean Stafford's colleagues how glad he was to have met them all. He wished them luck on their project. Then, bidding his voice not to quaver, he said, "Dr. Stafford, can you come to my office for a moment? There are papers from Washington about the new appropriation, and I could use your help in going over them."

Jean Stafford looked up at him, with no surprise in her face. She knew. Perhaps everyone in the room knew—the sexual tension was that palpable. But Eberhard did not care. Never in his life had he felt so reckless, so exigent—not even in the wildest transports of his youth. Jean Stafford had touched something in him, a part of his sexuality never touched before, the part that is the cousin of madness and death. Jean Stafford knew that aspect of sexuality very well. She cultivated it in herself, she acted according to its dictates.

"Yes, Dr. Eberhard," she said, meeting his eyes in a locked and goading glance, "of course."

The two of them left the laboratory. They walked stiffly, their movements made unnatural by the powerful tensions within them. As soon as they reached the corridor, they turned not toward Dr. Eberhard's office, but toward the resident wing— no words needed saying. Jean Stafford followed. (Though in another way, it was she who led. . . .) Their hands were on each other even now. Eberhard placed his hand in the small of her back—he had forgotten the feel of a woman's flesh, the welcome warmth of it which seeps through clothing into the reaching hand. His broad palm felt both the hollow of her back and the gentle rising of her rump. She walked close to him, swaying slightly, allowing her hip to rub against the outside of his thigh, scissoring as they walked.

They reached Eberhard's apartment (that haunted place to which, before today, Eberhard had always dreaded returning). The door was barely closed behind them when they fell into each other's arms. Greedily, Eberhard pressed against Jean Stafford, rejoicing in the resiliency of her youthful flesh. Wonderingly, his hands probed her, rediscovering woman through her, feeling all the throat-closing joy of returning to a much-loved place.

He kissed her mouth and cupped her breasts, needing to assure himself of every part of her, and he felt a giddiness rising within him, a simple unquestioning joy that he had not known in as long as he could remember, and perhaps had never known. It was an uncalculating, un-thought-out gladness that there was someone to make love to. Here was someone who would feel good to be next to.

Jean Stafford returned his embraces, reaching around his broad, strong back, encouraging him with her quickening breathing against his neck. Warmly, she coaxed the joy out of him, drew it forth the way a slap brings blood to the surface. She wanted to delve through that joy and learn his sorrow, wanted to open for him, and by opening, open him, and penetrate to that core of sorrow where she would reside with him, where they would be together.

Wordlessly, they moved into the bedroom (the bedroom in which Eberhard had for so long slept alone—so long that Claire's impression was no longer in the bed or in his body). Their clothes still on, they tumbled downward, Eberhard riding that giddy crest of joy, that glad relieving sense of nothing-matters-except-these-bodies-at-this-moment. He pulled her hair and bit her cheeks—he knew he could do anything—he could even be gentle perhaps. She bucked beneath him, urging him on.

And finally she reached between his legs, focussing all his mad releasing energy there, squeezing him, not gently, goading him on, putting the dare to him with hard eyes in which he recognized his own. Yes, he recognized his own eyes in hers, and he recognized his own probing coolness in the way she took him, recognized her better than he recognized himself in this mad abandoned satyr state. It was she who was after secrets now, and he would give up anything just to have this grateful release, just to have these thighs to nestle into.

The clothes were off them now, and Alfred Eberhard was rising high over her to take her. Their eyes locked, fierce, scalding like dry ice, and even before he moved down into her, those eyes had made a pact, a pact as between murderers or gods, never to back down from the mad intensity of this linking, never to deny this bond, this frightening similarity-of-soul between them. And then, to seal the pact, he entered her, knowing that, in entering, he was being entered, in a way he had never allowed himself to be.

. . . From that day forth, Alfred Eberhard and Jean Stafford were lovers. It was a relationship unlike any other that Alfred had ever known. He'd never *felt* this way before. He'd never loved—he realized that now. . . .

The nature of Eberhard's love for Jean Stafford (as hers for him) was a strange one, though, perhaps a morbid one. There was desperation in his love—the love of a person who has given up on all else and concentrated all his yearning on a single object. But there was a certain *purity* in the feeling. The love did not *connect* with anything, was not a means to any end, was not even a part of a coherent life scheme: The love simply *was*. It was the sole gain to which Alfred Eberhard dedicated all his life's myriad losses.

And he was happy, happier than he had ever been. Or perhaps it would be more correct to say, he *thought* of himself as happy for the first time. He hadn't thought along those lines before. He'd thought in terms of productivity, of getting something done, accomplishing something that no one before him had accomplished. Now he thought only of having Jean's face and her husky voice and her young body at the end of the day. That constituted happiness; that was his ambition. And in light of this happiness, the memory of his disappointment; his tragedies, dimmed. They seemed to belong to a different life, to be the karmic baggage of another person. A cloned son? A wife in a mental hospital? Eberhard could barely connect those things with himself now. . . .

There were, of course, reminders. There were Orin's letters, still addressed to his "mother." Eberhard still answered them, secretly, though his replies were briefer and less frequent. And there was evidence of Claire around the apartment, little touches she had put in in the early days of their marriage. And then there was the bed in Orin's room, the bed in which Claire had seduced her sleeping boy, the room in which the unnaturalness of their lives had reached its gut-wrenching climax. Eberhard could not ignore those things. Or could he? How much was it possible for a person to put behind himself? How thoroughly could a person make himself over?

If there was anything that could make a man forget, it was the love of a woman such as Jean Stafford. It would be wrong to assert that Jean Stafford loved Eberhard more than Claire had, and yet there was something in her love which lent it a far greater, white-hot intensity. Jean had the capacity to be cruel, to be devouring. She could be masterful even in the midst of sexual submission. She could revel in her own cool strength even in the midst of situations that most women would regard as subservient, perhaps even degrading.

For her, sex was inextricably linked to the probing of her own and her partner's innermost depths, those secret nooks of sorrow and ambivalence which one normally hides from the outside world, and perhaps even from oneself. She was a priestess of the psycho-erotic—and she came to Al-

fred Eberhard at precisely the right moment, the
moment when, his catastrophic past behind him
and the first glimpses of oldness and weakness in
front of him, he was ripe for a searing passion, a
self-losing love that would offer him the illusion of
starting fresh. Jean Stafford, so much like himself
in her icy strength and amoral boldness in thought
and action, was the only woman whom he could
have trusted to lead him along that ecstatic road.

It had been late winter when Alfred Eberhard
and Jean Stafford met. Now it was spring, spring
of 1991. In the few short months of their relationship, the two of them had grown very close. Jean
had all but moved in with Alfred. They made no
effort to keep their affair a secret—they had no
energy to waste on discretion. (Needless to say, in
the gossip-loving world of the facility, this left Eberhard open for a lot of pseudo-indignant criticism:
How could he? the stodgier members of the staff
whispered among themselves. And with his poor
wife gone only these few months! If they only knew
the grim parody of married life Eberhard had lived
for fifteen years!)

But, though Alfred Eberhard had no compunction about flouting public opinion, he did feel
himself to be in a rather touchy position with Jean
herself. How much should he tell her? She already
knew, of course, that Eberhard had a wife, and that
his wife had had a nervous breakdown. She'd
known that before she'd even gone to bed with
him (and who can say, given Jean Stafford's predi-

lections, if that hadn't been part of what drew her to him?). But the nature of the Eberhard marriage, and the bizarre circumstances which had led to Claire's collapse—no one knew of that, except John Goodwin, and he was gone. Of those grim facts, Jean Stafford knew nothing.

But she wanted to know, and as she and Eberhard grew closer, she began to probe. Had Eberhard loved her very much? Did he love her still? What was it like for him to see her fall apart? And what was their son like? Was he more like the father or the mother? What sort of relationship did Eberhard have with the boy?

These questions were understandably painful for Alfred Eberhard, and he often tried to fend them off. But Jean was not to be denied. For her, the probing was too central a part of the passion. So Eberhard began to answer, and, in time, there came to be a certain perverse satisfaction in talking about those awful things. They were painful, but there was a certain pleasure in the pain, as in the pain of a loose tooth, which oozes the pleasant salty taste of blood into the mouth.

Of course, Alfred still chose to lie in many of his answers. He was not yet prepared to reveal to Jean that his son had been cloned, or that the immediate cause of his wife's catatonia had been a quasi-incestuous linking with the boy. No, there was desperation in Eberhard's love, but he would have to become a good deal more desperate before he spilled those terrible secrets.

For now, he parried the questions, giving partial answers, stopping short of full disclosure. Yes, he had loved his wife, but not like this. No, he did not love her anymore—she had become too pathetic a figure for him to love. Physically, their son resembled him, but otherwise he was far closer to the mother. They did not have a close relationship. He had been closed off by his wife's possessiveness. Please, Jean, no more questions now—let me make love to you again. . . .

Thus, their affair deepened and intensified. Eberhard began spending some of his days in the cryogenics lab, though he was not, technically, connected with the project. He wanted to watch Jean work. (Never had he placed anyone else's work before his own.) He performed his own tasks without relish, as if they were the most mundane chores imaginable. And, occasionally, he reflected on the folly of his seeking immortality through the cloning of a son. What did immortality matter? What mattered was to have one rich life, a life such as at the age of fifty-six he was just beginning to live, a life of passion and fire! . . . How beside the point all the rest of it seemed—how rightly the lack of resemblance between Orin and himself bespoke the aridity of the whole idea! The thing to hope for was not a mere physical copy, but a soulmate, such as he had found in Jean.

As May advanced, Eberhard began to realize that some of the energy he had been directing toward his lover, had to be deflected toward dealing with a very real and unavoidable crisis: Orin would be coming home for the summer. How should he be handled? What should he be told? How shattering would his response to his "mother's" condition be? And how would he react to the new situation in the Eberhard home?

(Grimly, Eberhard reminded himself that he would be dealing with a flesh-and-blood adolescent—not a mere mental concept which he had now disclaimed. Eberhard found himself wishing that this inconvenient duplicate of himself did not exist! This cloned replica, which represented the crowning achievement of Eberhard's intellectual life, was proving to be the bane of his *real* life. How simple, how joyous, his life would be, if there weren't one too many of himself.)

Jean Stafford, even with her limited awareness of the boy's real situation, was equally concerned about what would happen when he arrived home. She and Eberhard discussed it on several occasions.

"So then," said Jean. "he knows nothing at all of his mother's condition?"

"No," Alfred told her, "nothing at all. Every precaution has been taken to prevent his finding out. I've even been forging letters from her all year long. But he'll have to find out now."

"How will you tell him?" she asked. "Will he face her? Will you take him to the hospital?"

"I've consulted the psychiatrist about that," said Alfred gravely. "His advice is that I tell Orin first, and give the news a little time to sink in. After that, I'll give him the option of seeing her or not. It might be horribly wrenching for him, but it might, in a way, do him good. And it might do Claire good as well. But who knows? It's impossible to foresee how they'll react to each other."

"What about me?" asked Jean. "How do you think he'll respond to me?"

"Frankly, I'm worried about that," said Eberhard. "He was very attached to his mother—too attached. And I can't help fearing that he'll bristle at the idea of anyone even remotely taking her place. If he loved me, it might be different. He might realize that someone else was important to me, and he might go along for the ride, however grudgingly. But I don't think he loves me."

"Really?" said Jean. "You don't think he loves you at all?"

"If he does," said Eberhard, "I don't think he knows it. He seems to be a rather extreme case of a son who needs to forge his own identity by setting himself up as opposite to his father in every way."

". . . And that makes you sad," Jean said.

"Of course," he said, nodding wistfully. "Though I feel I'm resigned to it now. For the longest time, I wasn't. It made me miserable to see him growing away from me, branching off in different directions—it was as if my own youth was going askew in memory, becoming something I could no longer recognize. I felt that it was my wife's doing, and I was terrifically angry with her. She had a very strong need to make her mark on the boy, a morbidly strong need."

"And why was that need so strong?" asked Jean.

"Because—" said Alfred Eberhard, "—because . . ." And now he felt his forehead start to prickle as he wavered between confession and the continuation of his sham. "I guess because Orin resembled me so closely. And because Claire became sterile in giving birth to him."

"Ah, yes," said Jean, "you've told me that. It's an unfortunate set of circumstances. Well, for my part, I shall do what I can to make Orin like me. If he hates me, I'll handle it the best I can. And I'll try to help you with him as much or as little as you think best."

"Thank you, Jean," said Eberhard. "I love you."

There was a pause. Eberhard scanned Jean's face, wondering if she would say "I love you" back to him. But she waited—it was a way she had of asserting her power over him. And when she finally replied, she did not say the expected thing: "Alfred," she said, "you've never needed anyone before, have you?" She asked the question softly but imperiously, certain of the answer.

"No, dear," he said. "Never." He felt a sweet reluctance in submitting to her. Then she rewarded him.

"I love you, Alfred."

Thirty-one

Orin came home from boarding school in early June. His father went along to meet him at the station. When the train pulled in and the passengers began disembarking, Eberhard spotted his boy immediately. Orin had grown taller—he was just barely shorter than his father now. His features had taken on a manly squareness, his complexion darkening with the beginnings of blue-black facial hair. And he was strong—one could tell that by the way his suitcase bobbed in his hand, by his sure firm step as he climbed down from the train. . . .

It took Orin some moments to recognize his father. He'd been scanning the platform for another face.

"Where's Mom?" were the boy's first words when the two Eberhards had moved together and shaken hands.

"She, uh, couldn't be here," said Eberhard uneasily. He wished to postpone the traumatic moment at least until they had reached their car and were out of public view, but for Orin, the traumatic moment had already come—he knew that something must be very, very wrong if his mother was not there to meet him.

Sensing his father's hesitancy, he did not immediately press him for an explanation—but there was a horribly milky feeling in Orin's arms and legs as he walked toward the car. His field of vision was blurry at the edges. He was terribly afraid. . . .

Mechanically, Orin threw his suitcase into the trunk. The two of them got into the car and Eberhard started the engine. Slowly, he moved through the parking lot. The suspense was agonizing to Orin, every second oppressed him more and more. Finally, he asked in a strained whisper, a voice already close to tears, "Father, why isn't Mom here? What's wrong?"

And now Alfred Eberhard steeled himself to give the explanation he had rehearsed so many times and still so dreaded giving. "Orin," he said, "your mother is very sick. She's in the hospital."

"What's wrong with her?" Orin asked, his stomach churning, his eyes filling up. (Though, beneath the melting surface of his eyes was a layer of unflinching, accusing hardness toward his father, as if the real question were: What did *you* do to her?)

"Orin," said Eberhard softly, "soon after you left, your mother had a nervous breakdown. Her doctor advised me not to tell you before now—there was nothing you, or any of us, could have done. We just had to stand aside and hope that she'd get better by herself."

"But she hasn't," said Orin, a kind of grieving fury in his voice.

"No," said Alfred Eberhard. "She hasn't. Not yet, at least."

"But she wrote to me all those months!" said

Orin, a lack of comprehension compounding his pain. "How could she have written to me?"

"*I* wrote to you, Orin," said his father. "I thought it was best that you thought things were all right—at least until you were settled at school and—"

"You *tricked* me!" interrupted Orin.

"Yes," said Eberhard, somewhat disconcerted by the boy's readiness to confront him. "I spoke to the doctor about it. We thought it was for the best. Are you angry with me?"

"That doesn't matter," the boy said. "Why did Mom have a nervous breakdown? Why did it happen?"

This was the question of questions, the one that cut cruelly across the interlocking secrets that defined the unique madness of the Eberhard family. Why, indeed! Whose "secret" was to blame? Was it the fact that Alfred had manipulated her into bearing the first human clone? Or the fact that Orin had made the forbidden re-entry into his "mother's" womb? (And what of that secret, in its relation to *Orin's* mind? How had he borne it all these months? Did he even remember it—or had he perhaps repressed it, denied the astounding reality and come to think of it as simply a naughty dream, something which could never really have happened?)

"No one knows why it happened," Alfred told his son, wondering if Orin would push him further. "Sometimes things go wrong in people's brains. The brain is just like any other organ—its health depends on many things. Sometimes things go wrong."

Orin did not reply. He could not talk anymore. He did not know what else to ask, and besides, there were no answers that could have comforted him. For a few minutes he sat silently, staring out the window with glazed eyes that saw nothing. Then he began to whimper, softly, sporadically, like a puppy. Alfred Eberhard reached his hand across the car, laying his palm on his son's shoulder. Orin squirmed away, pressing himself against the door.

Orin did not speak for the whole rest of that day. At home, he unpacked in silence, and then he lay in his bed (the bed that Claire had taken to in that long moment of passion and despair) and read. He declined to eat dinner. He read until he fell asleep.

At breakfast the next morning, he asked if he could see his mother.

"Of course," said Alfred Eberhard. "But Orin, you must realize that she is no longer like she was. She has changed a lot."

"She's still my mother," said Orin, a hint of reproach in his voice.

"Of course she is," said Eberhard, trying to maintain the gentleness in his tone. "But you must be prepared to face her. She may not acknowledge you; she may not recognize you. The doctors say that she takes almost no notice of the outside world."

"She'll recognize me," said Orin firmly. But there was fear in his face now. If she didn't recognize him, that would be the worst thing he could think of.

Directly after breakfast, the two of them headed for the hospital, neither knowing what to expect. It had been some weeks since Eberhard had looked in on his wife, and the last time he had seen her, she had shown the same discouraging reaction as on all the previous occasions: no reaction at all. She had seemed not to notice him, and had simply gone on mumbling to herself, her ashen face contorting grotesquely as her mouth formed arcane words. Eberhard dreaded the moment when his son would have to confront that sight.

At the hospital, Alfred and Orin Eberhard were met by Dr. Raymond Sachs, who had been Claire's physician since her transfer to the private facility. Sachs was a youngish man with sandy hair and horn-rimmed glasses. He had, of course, been informed of the history of Claire Eberhard's malady—including the strong conjecture that incest had been involved. For this reason, he was especially concerned about Orin's reaction to the sight of his mother. Previously, he had even suggested to Alfred Eberhard that the boy should perhaps go into therapy himself, to work out the conflicts inevitably engendered by all he had been through. The two doctors had decided to wait on this idea, and to act according to Orin's reaction.

Dr. Sachs made a friendly attempt to let Orin know what to expect. Orin cut him short, saying he had heard all that before—he simply wanted to see his mother, please.

Drs. Eberhard and Sachs exchanged a concerned look.

"All right, Orin," said Dr. Sachs. "We'll take you to her right now. Come along with me, please."

The three of them began walking down a long, brightly lit hall. The hall was lined with doors, and every door was closed. Finally, near the end of the corridor, Dr. Sachs stopped. Orin watched, rapt

and fearful, as the psychiatrist's hand closed
around the doorknob. It seemed to take forever
for him to pull the wooden door open. And then
he motioned Orin and Alfred inside.

The first thing Orin saw was sunlight slanting in
through half-closed blinds, making parallel strips
of brightness across the foot of a large disheveled
bed. There was a woman in the bed, a woman
whose hair was wild and whose face would not stay
still and whose hands gestured frantically in front
of her. But where was his mother? And why was
this woman here? Had Dr. Sachs made a mistake?

Orin was afraid. He wanted to turn and run out
of the room. But he couldn't do that. He had to
stand there and look and recognize his mother. He
saw her a little better now, recognized a little of the
old softness in the eyes, at the moments when the
eyes were not flashing secret rage. He recognized
the hands, though the hands looked so tense now,
so gnarled, curled and rigid like talons.

His mother didn't look at him. She looked at
nothing; she talked to herself. Finally, Dr. Sachs
approached her. "Claire," he said, "your son is
here. Your son, Orin."

For a fraction of a second, Claire Eberhard's face
seemed to take on a frightening lucidity, as if she
had understood, and then *willfully* chosen not to
understand, to retreat behind her madly fluttering
hands. Her face became a blank again, a busy blank
that spoke of nothing.

Orin Eberhard moved toward the bed in a
trance-like way. His father moved to stop him, but
Dr. Sachs motioned him away. "Mommy?" said the

boy. Claire's face flashed another excruciatingly short-lived moment of clarity. "Mommy," he repeated. "It's me, Orin."

Claire Eberhard looked away from him and cackled. "Alfred," she said, "you're Alfred! You're playing a trick on me! Orin is here," she said, pointing to her belly, making a grotesquely parodied gesture over it, as if she'd just had something good to eat. "Orin is inside me; he's in my belly, waiting to be hatched."

And then Claire Eberhard drifted off into incoherence, seeming to go back and cover up her tracks, as if, even in madness, she feared she'd said too much. Orin retreated from her bedside, his cheeks streaked with tears. His father held out his hands to the boy, but Orin moved directly toward the door.

The two men followed him out of the room. In the hall, Dr. Sachs looked compassionately at Orin and asked him how he felt. Orin only shrugged.

"I understand how you feel, Orin," the doctor said gently. "It's a very, very hard thing to see. Would you like to talk to me about it sometime?"

"There's nothing to say," said Orin.

"Well," said Dr. Sachs, "if there's anything that you do want to say, will you call me?"

"Yes," said Orin. But he had no intention of calling. If they couldn't make his mother well, then there was nothing he wanted to say to them.

Thirty-two

Orin had now been home for about a week. Since visiting his mother, he had been morose and quiet. When he spoke to his father at all, he tended to be slighting. But mostly he ignored him and went his moody way, reading, walking outdoors, brooding.

Alfred Eberhard found his presence quite unsettling. The boy was a constant goad to him, a constant mocking, blaming goad. Eberhard tried to be nice to the boy. He offered him the use of the car. He tried to engage him in conversation; he tried to talk with him about school—but always he was rebuffed. He tried not to be angry. He tried to analyze the reasons why the boy made him so distinctly uncomfortable. There was, of course, the disconcerting physical resemblance. Eberhard often had the feeling that he was looking into a time-warp mirror when he glanced at the boy. And of course there were the various questions of conscience to be dealt with.

But more than anything else, concluded Eberhard, the boy made him uneasy because he was so *normal!* Not psychologically normal, after all he'd endured, but physically normal. Even though he was not a normal boy—he was a clone, a laboratory specimen! Why didn't he walk more like a robot? Why were his movements so annoyingly like the rather ungainly movements of any tall sixteen year old? Why was his complexion as mottled as that of an average adolescent? Why wasn't Orin more *special*, even if his specialness were in the direction of freakishness?

Alfred found the whole thing rather deflating. He'd attempted to construct a *new type* of creature, and he'd ended up being saddled with a mere *human*, with human failings and human conflicts—a mere variation on the same old dreary theme.

There was also another, more immediately graspable, reason for Eberhard's resentment of his son's presence: He had not seen Jean Stafford in a week. Oh, he had stopped by briefly in the cryo lab, but he had spent no nights with her. He had not had sex with her since Orin's homecoming. This had been a concession to the boy's delicacy, but it could not go on. Eberhard resolved to talk to Orin, to acquaint him with the situation. He would do it at dinner that very evening.

He wanted to be tactful. "Orin," he said, breaking the gloomy silence of the dinner table, "I know that, for you, the news of your mother's sickness is still fresh. I understand that, and I respect your feelings. But for me, her absence is a long-established fact. She's been gone almost a year now. And it's been very lonely for me. So, I, er, want you to know that I—uh—have a new friend."

"That doesn't surprise me," said Orin, without looking up from his plate.

"Well," said Eberhard, trying to hold his temper, "I'm not trying to surprise you, or not surprise you. But I think that, since we live here together, you and I, and since I would like to have my friend here sometimes, that the two of you should meet, and, well, try to be friends."

"Father," said Orin, "if you want to have your 'friend' here, that's your business. But I really don't think that I want to meet her."

"Why not, Orin?" Alfred asked. "She's very nice, and—"

"I just don't want to meet her, that's all," he said.

"You're not being fair, Orin," said Eberhard, his temper beginning to rise. "I'm trying my best to take your feelings into account, and you're totally disregarding mine."

"Look," Orin said, "you're not taking my feelings into account. If you were thinking about my feelings, you wouldn't talk to me about bringing your whores—"

Alfred Eberhard's hand was in motion before he realized what was happening. It landed with a resounding smack against Orin's cheek. The boy flushed, but he neither cried nor complained. He simply got up and left the table, giving his father a final, strangely satisfied glance. No doubt the little bastard thinks of it as a victory, thought Eberhard, his hand trembling—just like Claire would have. . . .

Later that evening, Eberhard went to Jean Stafford's room in the residence wing. He went to her full of desire and frustration and rage, and he took her without a word.

Afterward, he told her what had happened with Orin.

"It's a difficult situation," she said.

"No," he said, "it's an impossible situation."

"No situation is impossible," Jean said. "Give the boy some time. It's natural that he hates the idea of having anyone in his mother's place. But I'll win him over, you'll see. But, you should go home now, Alfred. It's no good to let the boy feel that you've abandoned him. Go to him."

Alfred Eberhard could not help letting out a groan. But he went. When he reached his apartment, he found Orin lying in bed, reading. He didn't even look up from the book when he heard his father enter.

. . . Jean Stafford's confidence that she could win Orin over turned out to be ill-founded. The lad was absolutely intransigent in his loyalty toward his mother, and in his nasty defiance toward anything having to do with his father.

Jean had smiled warmly at their first meeting, eager to make a good impression. She extended her hand to him and said, "It's nice to meet you, Orin. I've heard so much about you."

Orin had done nothing except to stare down at Jean's extended hand, which came to look rather silly as it grasped the air.

The next time they met was on an evening when Alfred Eberhard had asked Jean over for dinner. The three of them sat at table, Jean Stafford trying, on repeated occasions, to engage Orin in conversation. Orin answered in monosyllables. And finally, when Jean's perfectly civil questions had become too much for him, he said, "Can't you see that I really don't want to talk to you?"

"Why not?" she asked.

"Very clever," said Orin with a sneer. "You ask me why not, so I'll talk to you about it. But I've just said I don't want to talk to you. So I won't tell you why not—and that's that."

And that ended the attempts at conversation for the evening. But Jean Stafford stayed over at the Eberhard's apartment that night. Alfred insisted on it. He was tired of being bullied by his son! He was tired of incommoding himself because of the stubbornness and incivility of the boy! If Jean Stafford's presence bothered him that much, then so be it! At his, Eberhard's, age, one did not throw away nights of happiness because of the neurotic manipulations of an adolescent!

And the nights that Alfred Eberhard spent with Jean Stafford *were* nights of happiness, even given the strain that Orin's presence caused. In the warmth of her arms, Eberhard found solace and forgetfulness from all his failures and frustrations. Talking with her—in her peculiar, exciting, all-is-permitted way— he opened up and aired himself. Yes, he would have her here, regardless of Orin's tantrums!

Jean Stafford gladly went along with her lover's feelings. She had been quite miffed at Orin's snubbing of her. She had tried, but she quite simply did not like the boy. He was snide, bratty, selfish and cunning. If he wanted to get on terms, he would have to come to *her.* And yes, she would be happy to warm Alfred's bed, regardless of the lad's feelings.

It was not an auspicious beginning to the summer.

And, as the summer progressed, the tensions among the three people who stayed at the Eberhard apartment only grew more pronounced. Orin seemed to grow ever more ingenious at annoying his father. His father seemed increasingly inclined to answer Orin's jibes with cruel retorts—he knew he was acting childish when he did that, but he could no longer help himself.

Orin grew more and more open in his insulting attitude toward Jean Stafford. He often made references to his mother, references designed to make it perfectly clear to Jean that she was an unwelcome intruder. And Jean, for her part, no longer even tried to be the boy's ally. Her pride had been wounded by Orin's refusal to be won over, and now she turned a coldly analytical, merciless eye on the entire situation.

One night, after making love, when Alfred was again bemoaning his lack of communication with his son, she interjected simply, "Let's face it, Alfred. He hates you."

To a degree which surprised him, Eberhard found that he was upset by these words. He'd thought he was beyond the point where his son could hurt him, but these words stung. He tried to deny them, to explain them away.

"No," he said. "It's not that, it's not nearly that simple. He has conflicts. He's terribly attached to his mother. And there are still other factors, factors you don't even know about."

"That may be," said Jean coolly. "But what it boils down to is that he hates you. All those fancy explanations are just a smoke screen that psychiatrists put up because families aren't supposed to hate each other—it's not a pretty idea. But face it, Alfred, no matter what *reasons* you point to, the fact is that he hates you."

"But—" Alfred began, groping for a way to refute Jean's icy logic.

"—And what's more," continued Jean in a soft but savage voice, "you hate him!"

"No!" he protested, a sort of primitive terror taking hold of him as he confronted this idea. "I don't hate him! He's difficult, it's true, and we don't get along very well, but—"

"Nonsense!" she hissed. "Don't hide behind those pathetic family fallacies! You hate him! You can't admit it, because it's supposedly a horrible thing for a father to hate his son. But you *do* hate him! It shows: I see it when you look at him. You hate the whiny sound of his voice, the prissy look of his movements. You hate him for not being more like you. And you hate him for not *liking* you, as if you feel he's passing judgment. . . ."

Alfred Eberhard could not reply. The words landed on him like blows. He tried to deny the truth of Jean's accusations, he tried to shout them down—but he could not. They were true. He did hate Orin. Hate was not the only thing he felt for the boy—but it was one of the things he felt—and perhaps the central one. It was ugly, but it was true! And what did it mean? It was ghastly enough, deadening enough, for any father to hate a son—but what if the son were a clone, an exact genetic copy? Then the hatred must inevitably be self-directed, an awful confrontation with one's own unsavory possibilities! How could one deny one's sins, one's faults, one's mocking ambivalences, when they confronted one daily, clothed in flesh?

This was the awful burden that Alfred Eberhard had to bear once he acknowledged that he did hate his son. And the only person who could help him bear that burden was Jean Stafford, a searingly cold woman who gnawed at Alfred Eberhard even as she soothed him.

In addition to—and partly brought on by—these psychological woes, Alfred Eberhard began to suffer from physical illness as the summer wore on.

At first, he had tried to ignore the symptoms—the slight burning in his loins could have been caused by any number of things. The increasing frequency of his urination might have been due to simple urethritis, caused by the dramatic increase in his sexual activity. The lower back pains were something that affected almost everyone at one time or another.

But as the weeks passed, the symptoms intensified, growing harder and harder to ignore. It began to be painful for Alfred Eberhard to have sex. At first, the pain was only a slight twinge which actually added to his arousal; but soon, the twinge crossed the plateau into undeniable discomfort. Blood began appearing in his urine. The dull ache in the small of his back sharpened to a sporadic, wrenching burn. By the time Alfred Eberhard admitted to himself that he had better take a blood test, he already knew that his kidneys had begun to dysfunction. The elevated level of urea in the blood only confirmed it.

The awareness that a disease, of as yet undetermined seriousness, was percolating within him, threw Alfred Eberhard into a quiet but undeniable panic. He had never been ill in his life. His organs had always worked together in perfect harmony. And now, what was this? Cancer? Pyelonephritis? Or, less dramatically but no less horrifyingly, was it simply a vague but irreversible renal slowdown, the first domino to topple in a series of organic failures which would lead gradually to weakness, debility, all the humiliating precursors of inevitable death?

Alfred did not mind the pain. He would gladly have borne the knife-like slash of hurt that seemed to wind through all his tubes and channels, if only he were allowed to keep his strength! How cruelly ironic it was that his body should be mutinying now, now when he had just begun to really live, just begun to know passion! Feeling the loss before he had even lost her, he thought of Jean Stafford, so youthful, so strong, so addictingly exciting—he *had* to stay strong for her! He had to fight off the gruesome treachery of age, of worn-out parts of fading powers. . . .

For weeks he hid his pain from her. He could not bear that she should know of his debility. He diagnosed himself, conducting tests in secret. The uremic toxins continued to rise in concentration, there were signs of pus now, of undeniable infection. And there was the pain, the shameful pain that Eberhard frantically endeavored to hide, to keep out of his face and out of his voice.

And then, finally, in mid August, Alfred Eberhard's illness betrayed him. It was not the pain that gave him away, but rather the gruesome sight of the blood which, engorging his uro-genital tract, had mingled with his semen, turning the ejaculate a morbid, ghastly pink.

Jean Stafford was frightened at the sight of it. And Alfred was ashamed, ashamed that his secret had been spilled. And now, with the secret out, all his fears and rage at weakening, his defiance of death—and terror of it—came pouring out. He was frantic, desperate, nearly hysterical. . . .

"Alfred, darling, what is it?" Jean asked, holding him and rocking him and stroking his feverish brow.

"Something is wrong with me!" whispered Eberhard, his voice choked with shame and horror. "My kidneys. . . . I've been in pain . . . terrible pain. . . . And I don't know what it is. I don't want to know! I don't want to grow old and weak. I've seen people wear out, first one organ going and then another. I won't go through that! I love you, Jean, and I want you, and I want *myself,* do you understand?—my strength, my body, my abilities."

Jean Stafford held her lover in her arms. She loved his anguish, his struggle, his fierceness. Only, he must not become pathetic, he must not allow himself to become pathetic. She stroked his head, she coaxed him on to reveal the full depths of his desperation.

"Jean," he rambled, "do you ever think of immortality? It's a horrible thing to think of, and yet everybody does. I've thought of it quite a lot myself. I remember an old Greek myth about a man who asked the gods for immortal life, but he didn't think to ask them for immortal *youth*. Well, they let him live forever, and he went on, getting more decrepit every day, pieces of him wearing out, becoming useless. He was the most miserable man on earth. And that's how I feel with this sickness working on me. Perhaps it isn't even anything that serious. But even if it isn't, it's the first grim downward step!

"I'm fifty-six years old, Jean! Maybe that thought wouldn't horrify me so, if it weren't that I have your youth so close at hand, for contrast. Perhaps, without your youth, I'd be serene. But no, that would be worse, infinitely worse. What's that poem—'Do not go gentle into that good night'?"

Eberhard lay back on the bed. He was sweating profusely. He was in pain, and the pain fed his desperation and pushed the words out of him, more words than he'd intended to say, more truth than he'd intended ever to tell to anybody.

"People think far too much about immortality," he grated. "And about stopping time. Jean, do you remember, I think it was the first time that we met, you were telling me about your work, and you said the most interesting part of it was that it was of stopping time?"

"Yes, Alfred, I remember," she said.

"And I said that I had tried to stop time once, but I never told you how I tried to do it. Do you remember?"

"Yes, darling. All you said was that you hadn't done it very well."

"Yes," said Eberhard, with a ghastly little laugh. "That's true, I didn't do it very well. I did it in the form of a son who hates me, with whom I have nothing in common, a son who is less like me than, than *you* are!"

"But Alfred," said Jean Stafford, looking for words to soothe him, "that happens to so many people—so many people try to live again through their children. And the result is bound to be ultimately sad."

"Jean," said Eberhard, "you don't understand me. Other people don't know what I've done. Other people don't mold their children the way I molded Orin."

"What are you saying, Alfred?" asked Jean, a look of baffled conjecture on her face.

"I'm saying," he pronounced slowly, "that Orin was not produced as other children are produced. He is not a natural offspring—he's a clone. . . ."

Involuntarily, Jean Stafford's hand shot up to her mouth. She rubbed her chin fiercely, trying to absorb what she had just been told. It was astounding! And yet it fit, it made so many things so much more understandable! The uncanny physical resemblance, of course; but, beyond that, the passionate bond that existed between father and son—even if it was a bond of mutual disdain! It had an amazing valence, the valence of a bitter conflict within the self! And Claire Eberhard's madness—it was all of a piece. She had been driven insane by the part she'd been made to play in this unprecedented psychodrama. And her domination of the boy was an understandable attempt at compensation for her genetic exclusion from him. It all made sense now, a warped but horribly consistent sense.

Jean Stafford tried to speak. It was some moments before she was able to form words.

"Does—does Orin know?" she asked.

"No," said Eberhard. "We've been careful not to let him find out—we'd hoped that he might turn out *normal* if he didn't know." Again Eberhard let out that ghastly, mocking laugh.

"Alfred," she said, "it occurs to me that perhaps Orin *does* know, and perhaps that accounts for his thorough, inevitable hatred of you."

"But he couldn't know," protested Eberhard. "There's no way."

"I'm not suggesting that he *knows* in the usual way," Jean interrupted. "I'm not saying he *consciously* knows that he has sprung from you, and you alone. But I wonder if some pre-conscious 'brain,' operating in each and every cell of his body, does not recognize its affinity with every cell of *yours*—and I wonder if that agonizing recognition, the recognition that he is not *original,* that his entire being has been only *borrowed,* is not the source of his hatred. Perhaps in some unconscious way, Orin is aware that he does not truly *exist!*"

"But Jean," Alfred protested, "of course he exists! You can see him, hear him. He moves, he talks."

"Yes, she replied, "but so does a shadow, so does an echo, so does a mirror image—or at least they all *seem* to! But none of them has an existence apart from the *other,* the *real* being that informs them. . . ."

"Those things you mention have no choice but to *follow* their original—they have no *will,* no life of their own. But Orin, to put it mildly, goes his own way, makes himself totally different from me."

"Not merely different," said Jean Stafford coolly, "but *opposite*—opposite in the way that a mirror reverses right and left, or the way a shadow makes a vertical form seem horizontal!"

"All right, all right," he said. "I'll admit you've drawn a good analogy. But what does it mean? I'm sick of theory! What does it matter? I cloned Orin out of vanity, out of a misguided urge to go on forever, and I've ended up with an opposite who mocks me, whose very being goads me as I grow older, who does me no good—*that's* what matters."

"Alfred!" said Jean Stafford, softly but insistently. "The theory matters because it has its applications. Now listen, Alfred, and be strong." (Jean Stafford's face now took on the unworldly fixity of an oracle; her voice was the riveting monotone of a hypnotist. . . .) "You created Orin, as undeniably as a man creates his shadow. The shadow is secondary, subsidiary, with no prerogatives of its own. You created Orin to make yourself immortal—but you know now that that was futile—as soon as Orin had clothed himself in a body that seemed to be his own, he developed a *personality* of his own, a personality opposite to yours. And that's when you realized the glaring naivete of what you had attempted.

"You may be able to create innumerable *bodies* from the one body you begin with, but personality is unique! Too many things go into the formation of it, too many millions of uncontrollable accidents go into making it what it is. You, Alfred Eberhard, in the body you have now, the fifty-six-year-old body which is beginning to fail you and which you are beginning to hate, are the only Alfred Eberhard who will ever exist! You are the sole repository for the personality, the mind, which *is* Alfred Eberhard. The other bodies which may arise from you will inevitably house grotesque parodies of that mind . . . parodies which you will hate, and which will hate you."

"Yes," he said, with a gut-wrenching groan, "I know that, and that is why I mock myself."

"But you can use those other bodies to feed the personality you have. You have created those bodies, have given of yourself—if only a single cell—to make them. And you can take them back, Alfred! They are yours, and you can take them back to replenish the body you have now, the only body which will ever house the personality that is Alfred Eberhard."

"Jean," Alfred gasped, "what are you suggesting?" But already he had begun to realize what she was suggesting. His skin had begun to prickle with the realization, and he hovered in a near-mad state between ultimate horror and the unquenchable greed of living.

"Alfred," she said, "you are growing old. You know it and you fear it. You are in pain and there will be far worse pain. Your mind yearns to go on living and your will yearns to remain strong, but your body is fading. Yet, you have another body, a body which is just now coming to maturity. That body is called Orin—but it is only a shadow of yourself. You created that body, and you can take it back, as you need it, piece by piece."

"No!" gasped Eberhard, protesting helplessly, as in a dream. "It's impossible!"

"It's not impossible, Alfred," said Jean Stafford

with ungodly composure. "Every part of him is genetically coded to yourself, every organ of his is
interchangeable with your own. Why shouldn't you
take what you need? He hates you, and you hate
him. Why not rescind the existence you have
loaned him, to save yourself?

"Your kidneys are beginning to fail you. Soon,
the poisons that accumulate because of your failing kidneys will choke off other organs. But what
if you had new kidneys? And what if, in time, you
would have other organs to use as replacements as
old ones faded—a new heart, new lungs, new
glands to keep you virile. Think of it, Alfred. . . ."

Alfred Eberhard held his head in his hands and
rocked spastically on the bed. How devastating the
notion was, how seductive, how grotesque! And yet it
was a species of immortality, an immortality based on
murder, on scavenging organs from other bodies in
order to keep a single body alive. How the idea
pricked him, how Jean's cold voice tormented him.

"But how? How?" he said weakly.

"Remember how *I* stop time, Alfred?" said Jean
Stafford. "With cryogenics. With temperatures so
cold that aging all but stops, that life processes come
almost to a halt, that organs are preserved. Now
what if Orin were to disappear, to come to be
thought dead? We could take a kidney from him,
and implant it into you—that would solve your present problem, wouldn't it? After that, we could
freeze Orin, and put him in a place that no one
knew of. He would go on living just fine with his
single kidney, and he would barely age at all.

"We could go back to him, Alfred, whenever

there was anything we needed! We could disassemble him part by part to keep you youthful, and when his supply of organs began to be depleted, or if we had to take something he couldn't live without, we could clone another body for you, and another, and another. Alfred Eberhard could go on and on."

Arcane images swam brilliantly through Alfred Eberhard's mind, iridescent streamers of giddy thought that was near to insanity; yes, he *could* go on and on. His being could outpace the generations, could baffle death—but at what cost?

"No!" he said, "I can't! It's madness!"

"You will grow old, Alfred," Jean said.

"I'm growing old already."

"You will fade and suffer," she argued.

"Yes, I know."

"And you will lose me, Alfred. You will lose everything, and you will lose me!"

"Jean," said Eberhard miserably, "don't torment me."

"Then don't be a coward!" she said savagely. "You have come this far. You can't stop short."

Eberhard began to sob. There was infinite sadness in his sobbing—but no remorse. He sobbed out his weakness, and was left with nothing but resolve—he *would* go on.

"All right," he said. "I'll do it. But how?"

"How?" said Jean Stafford. "Oh, we'll work out *how*. That's only a question of method, of procedure. The details will all fall into place, I'm sure."

Thirty-three

In the days that followed, while maintaining the appearance of professional and domestic normalcy, Jean Stafford and Alfred Eberhard evolved the details of their bizarre scheme. The plan was formed carefully, detail by detail, with an unearthly cool-headedness—a cool-headedness which even Alfred Eberhard, working alone, would not have been able to maintain. It was Jean Stafford—motivated by what? by love? by a manic desire to push science to its limit? by a simple and inexplicable compulsion to plunge into the forbidden?—who provided the driving force. But Alfred Eberhard, once he had taken his grim resolve, never wavered.

How strange it was to confront Orin during those secretly conspiring days! How disconcerting it was to watch him walk across the room, to see him reading a book, or going to the refrigerator for a glass of juice! How bizarre to see him performing all these small, everyday acts, as if he really were what he appeared to be, a sixteen-year-old youth, himself, original, unique! To think that he was a shadow, and a doomed shadow at that!

But Orin did nothing during those fateful days

to win his father's sympathy. On the contrary, he
did everything he could to antagonize the elder
Eberhard, as if, as Jean Stafford had hypothesized,
there really was some sort of *molecular* antipathy
between them, a hatred so far below the level of
consciousness, that it could never be fathomed or
relieved. Orin spoke in the whiny voice he knew
his father detested; he moved in the rather effeminate way that made his father cringe. And he was
sure to be especially slighting to Jean Stafford, to
make her uneasy in whatever way he could.

These ploys of Orin's, which, in the past, had
driven his father to distraction, now were a kind
of balm to the older Eberhard. Whatever remnants
of conscience might still have held sway in Eberhard's ravaged mind, were silenced by Orin's
manifest dislike of him. Let the boy be surly, sullen,
rude—that only made things easier. If he was so
clearly unhappy, so obviously maladjusted, perhaps
even tinged with his "mother's" madness—all the
more reason to do away with him!

For really, reasoned Eberhard, what did Orin
have to live for? To all appearances, the only person
he loved in the whole world, was his mother—and
she was crazy, locked away, a horrifying spectacle.
The boy had no spark, no ambition, he was unso-
ciable, mopy, morose.

Fortunately for the ease of his resolve, Alfred
Eberhard never gave a thought to his cloned son's
inner life, that hidden playground full of images
and shreds of music, that secret stage where Orin
enacted all the fun and all the love he could not
bring to the outside world. Alfred Eberhard never

considered the stories that played in Orin's mind, in subtle counterpoint to the stories that he read, or the friendships he entered into with the people he met in books, or the thoughts that came to him when he drove through the hills—when he drove, not as other teenagers drove, in raucous clusters of friends, but by himself, lonely, the radio turned off, only the sound of tires on asphalt to pace the rhythm of his thoughts. . . . Could Alfred Eberhard have cut him open if he had even once allowed himself to think of those things?

Bit by bit, the plan was formed. Eberhard and Jean Stafford talked it over in Eberhard's bed at night. They discussed it after making love, their bodies still flushed from the heat of passion, the bedclothes damp and tangled under them—lust and murder and relentless intellect blended in a mad concoction.

"But Jean," said Eberhard, "how can we explain the fact that Orin will suddenly disappear?"

"He'll disappear," Jean said in a soft-cold voice, "because he'll be presumed dead. And dead people generally disappear, don't they, darling?"

"Yes, of course," he said. "But there is generally a body around to prove they're dead."

"There *will* be a body," said Jean Stafford. "Only it won't be Orin's. It'll be one of the cadavers that we have on hand for research—that'll be an easy enough switch."

"But what about identification? It'll be *seen* that the cadaver isn't Orin."

"Alfred," she said, "have you ever seen a body

that's been trapped in a burnt-out car? They all look rather alike."

"But there are ways of checking." protested Alfred. "Dental records, for example."

"And where are Orin's dental records?" Jean asked.

"Right here at the institute, of course," said Eberhard. "All the staff medical and dental services are provided right here."

"Precisely," she said, with cool triumph in her voice. "So then, it shouldn't be much problem to gain access to those records, should it? And to make the necessary adjustments?"

"No," said Eberhard, "I suppose not."

"Well, then, that part is settled. Now, about arranging the 'accident.' . . ."

Jean Stafford went on in her diabolically methodical way. And as she talked, a strange ambivalence sprang up in Alfred Eberhard. He almost hoped that some insuperable obstacle would present itself, he almost wished that they would be thwarted. He knew that, if a plan could be arranged, he *would* do it. And yet, he knew that he would feel relief and a kind of gratitude if their planning came to nothing. He would almost have preferred the creeping specter of age and death to the prospect of robbing Orin's body. But there were no snags in Jean's thinking, no easy way out for him.

". . . And so," she said, "we'll place the cadaver in the car *before* we remove the kidney from Orin's body. That way, a minimum of time will be wasted *after* the operation. Once the kidney is removed,

Orin will be placed directly into the cryogenic chamber. The cryogenic chamber will then be moved to the private sector of the lab. The kidney will be frozen separately, and kept on hand to be re-implanted into *you*.

"And then, the accident—we'll take two cars, of course. You will ride with the cadaver, and I'll follow you, alone. At some likely spot among the hills, some suitably treacherous curve, we'll nudge your car over the edge, douse it with gasoline and set it ablaze. 'Orin' will be found at the wheel, charred and lifeless. By the time the accident's discovered, we will have made it back to the Institute, put everything in order and gone to bed."

"But still, there are so many factors. . . ." Alfred protested dully.

"And every factor is accounted for!" said Jean Stafford. "As head of the cryogenics project, I can easily obtain the freezing apparatus. As director of the facility, you have sole access to the private sector of the lab. We'll perform the operation on Labor Day weekend, when no one will be here but ourselves. It's a well-established fact that Orin takes those aimless solitary rides at night. A young driver, on those curves— an accident is very understandable. It's airtight, Alfred—unless, that is, you're losing your nerve."

The words stung Eberhard. He steeled himself by thinking of his own pain, present and future, and by picturing Orin in his smirking unpleasantness. He forced himself to feel a sudden surge of grave dislike for his son, and his courage returned. "No," he said, "I'm not losing my nerve. I only want to be sure that we've got everything right."

"Everything *is* right, Alfred," she said. "And now, will you make love to me again? I always want you after we've talked. . . ."

Thirty-four

On Sunday evening of Labor Day weekend, 1991, Orin Eberhard began to do his packing. He'd be leaving to return to school in just a couple of days, and he preferred not to save everything for the last minute. Besides, he had nothing else to do. He seldom had had anything to do that summer. He'd been bored and unhappy most of the time. He wished he got along better with his father. Oh, Orin knew that he wasn't very pleasant most of the time, but that was because he couldn't help it. Couldn't his father see that he didn't *want* to be acting that way? How much nicer the summer would have been if he and his father could have done more together. Or even if Jean had struggled through to being friends with him.

It was his own fault, Orin told himself. He didn't know why he acted like he did. He sort of knew, but not in a way that did him any good. Maybe he *should* have called that psychiatrist from his mother's hospital—he had seemed like a nice man. But he was too connected with that horrible image of the mad woman in the bed. Orin would not have been able to detach him from that image.

But maybe Orin would talk to someone when he got back to school. Wouldn't it be a nice surprise for everyone, thought Orin, if he could get to understand things better while he was away, and then return and be nice so that everyone could get along? Maybe next summer would be that way.

It was shortly before midnight when Orin got into bed. He was very tired, but he decided to read awhile. Reading helped to fend off the image that always assailed him before he went to sleep. Sometimes, if he read until his eyes closed by themselves, he could escape the image altogether. But sometimes, if he escaped it then, it would come back to him in dreams—a mad woman in bed, gesturing frantically, not recognizing him.

Alfred Eberhard moved stealthily through the darkened halls of the research institute. He carried a flashlight, which threw a single shaft of fugitive brightness through the empty corridors. His own footfalls were the only sound.

He went down the single flight of concrete stairs to the morgue. Opening the door, his flashlight shone on the far wall, the wall which was composed of various "drawers," which slid out on their oiled bearings to reveal their grisly contents—human corpses, expertly catalogued, preserved with formaldehyde, patiently awaiting the researcher's knife. Eberhard's breath caught at the sharp and sour smell of the embalming fluid. He reflected grimly on the ironic fate of one of these people who had "left his body to science"!

Eberhard approached the wall of drawers. On each drawer, there was a card describing the sex, height, weight and the age at death of the cadaver within. Eberhard scanned these grim legends, looking for as close an approximation of Orin (of *himself*, in every respect but age!) as he could find. At length, he found one. He slid the drawer open and he shone his flashlight at the yellowish, waxen face that appeared. (Bizarrely, the corpse almost seemed to *squint* under the flashlight, as if disturbed in sleep by sunshine coming in through parted curtains. Eberhard slid the drawer out further, revealing the rather sunken torso, the shriveled sex, the delicately sculpted legs, with folds of yellow skin above the knees.

Eberhard unhinged the drawer and slid the body from off of its rolled slab. He maneuvered it onto a stretcher, struggling against the body's weird rigidity, its comic grotesque resistance to a change of posture. He took the body out of the morgue, and brought it upstairs, to his car.

Wrestling the cadaver into the front seat (the sour smell, the waxy feel of dead limbs, the dull sheen of a corpse's hair), Eberhard noticed that Jean Stafford had thought to put a pair of Orin's sneakers on the floor. That was good, he thought—the sneakers probably wouldn't burn entirely, there'd be some trace of them left, a fringe of lace perhaps, a piece of half-melted sole.

Jean Stafford, meanwhile, had wheeled the cryogenic chamber into the operating room. She loved the cold steel gleam of the body-sized cylinder, with its network of conducting tubes, carrying refrigerant, carrying messages from the frozen body. The dim lights glinted off the curved window built into the steel cylinder. There was nothing behind the window now, but soon there would be—a face, Orin's face, so much like Alfred's: a frozen face, a body waiting to be pillaged. Unconsciously, with secret pleasure, Jean Stafford let her fingertips play along the icy metal surface of the chamber. She loved it—it was the coldest thing on earth.

It was approximately one A.M. when Alfred Eberhard and Jean Stafford met back at the director's apartment. Eberhard had already prepared the initial anesthetic. The stretcher on which Orin was to be wheeled to the operating room was waiting in the hall.

"Well, Alfred," she said, regarding him with a goading, unflinching eye, "are you ready?"

Eberhard swallowed painfully. He stared at her. He could not get past her chrome-cold surface.

"Yes," he said, "I'm ready. . . ." Then, after a pause, he added in a strangely boyish, almost imploring voice. "Jean, when this is done, you'll stay with me, won't you? You won't leave me, will you?"

"No, Alfred," she said. As always, her voice was cold, but there was passion in it. "I'll stay with you—and I'll stay young for you. Because, Alfred, there will be other operations, you know. I'm not doing this only for your sake. If it can be done, *I* shall do it, too! And I don't even need a conspirator—I can bear my own! My own replica! From my body to my womb to the world—and back to my body! I can do

it, and I will do it! The two of us can go on forever!
But now, Alfred, let us see to Orin.''

Silently, the two of them crept into Orin's bedroom. Eberhard clutched the hypodermic full of
sodium Pentothal. They approached the bed. Orin
was asleep, lying on his back, the sheet draped over
him in sculptured disarray. His mouth was slightly
open, his breath was slow and even. Dim moonlight
filtered into the room, giving his black curls a silver
cast, giving his face a subtle porcelain-like sheen.

They were at the bedside now. Eberhard hesitated. He glanced at Jean—her expression im-
pelled him to go on. He reached down and gently
grasped his son's forearm. (How soft the skin was!
How firm and lovely the muscles underneath! Alfred Eberhard felt a sudden urge simply to *hold* his
son, to touch him, to know his young and fleeing
beauty. . . .)

He plunged the hypodermic through the skin,
and squeezed the anesthetic into the boy's receptive tissues. At the first prick, the boy winced ever
so slightly—but then he drifted off into a deeper,
unnatural sleep, a sleep that would be his permanent state for a suspended infinity of frozen time.

Alfred reached down and lifted the limp body
from the bed. A sharp pain tore through his lower
back at the strain of it. He threw Orin over his
shoulder, the boy's hands dangling loosely down
his father's back, his head bobbing numbly with
his father's steps. He carried the drugged youth
through the apartment and placed him down on
the stretcher in the hall.

It was Jean Stafford who wheeled the body to the

operating room. Alfred Eberhard was winded, his heart was pounding violently. The sound of his labored breathing came as a haunting counterpoint to the slight squeaking of the stretcher wheels as the grim procession made its way through the empty silent halls. Jean Stafford never slackened her pace. One of Orin's arms slipped over the edge of the stretcher and fluttered grotesquely from the motion.

And now they had reached the scrub room. Jean Stafford cut Orin's pajamas away from his body, and washed him. His flesh was warm and placid under the pressure of her scrubbing. It was a pleasure to touch his skin, to feel the textures of the different parts of him. She shaved his pubic area. And then she covered him with two sterile sheets, one for his legs, the other for his chest, leaving his middle exposed, marking the place where the surgeon would strike.

When the body had been prepared, Eberhard and Jean Stafford scrubbed, and then got into their turquoise surgical smocks. The masks were affixed, the sterile paper slippers were put on. And then the three of them moved through the several sterilizing chambers—each set of sliding doors excluding one more layer of contamination, one further chance of infection—till at last they entered the operating room itself.

It was nearly two A.M. by now, and there was still much to be done. There was still the introduction of the urinary catheter, the tube that had to be inserted through the boy's urethra to the bladder, draining off the urine, so that the bladder would not become distended and interfere with the surgeon's access to the other organs. There was still the attachment of the various electrodes from the instruments which would monitor the patient's metabolism—the heartbeat, the brain waves. There was still the final sterilization and laying out of the surgical instruments, the knives, shears, probes, the clamps which retracted the flesh and left the body cavity gapingly open.

Jean Stafford saw to these tasks while Alfred Eberhard examined the cryogenic apparatus, making certain it was ready to receive the newly sewn up body. Eberhard activated the electroencephalograph and the electrocardiogram, making sure that their read-outs were accurate. He tried to keep himself occupied with these practiced mechanical chores. He did not want to have time to think; he was afraid to let his mind run free.

But his mind began to detach itself from the tasks his hands were performing, and Alfred Eberhard grew quietly but distinctly frantic. He began to be oppressed by a certain humming sound, a soft but inescapable sound that seemed to come from the electric clock on the wall. Stopping time, thought Alfred Eberhard—if you could stop time, you could stop the humming, that awful droning hum that burned right into the very center of the brain. But no, he thought, that humming isn't from the clock—the clock doesn't hum. The humming was from inside him.

Trying to dispel the hum, Alfred Eberhard glanced around the operating room, upward at the empty amphitheater, downward at the spotless floor, over at the gleaming steel cylinder near the operating table. But the hum persisted—perhaps the hum would never stop. Well, then, one had to proceed even in the face of it.

"Is everything ready, Jean?" he heard himself say.

"Yes, Alfred, everything." The voice broke through the hum, comforting and goading. "Brain waves and pulse are normal. Respiratory functions are satisfactory. The freezing mechanism has been activated, and is ready to receive the organ as soon as it's removed. We can begin whenever you are ready."

Alfred Eberhard inhaled deeply, trying to steady himself. He stood perfectly still, only his eyes—deep-socketed, dark, unearthily sad—darted restlessly from thing to thing. And always, the hum. . . .

Slowly, with the heavy step of a doomed man, Alfred Eberhard approached the operating table. He glanced one last time at the clock on the operating room wall. He could not have said exactly why, but he wanted to know the precise time when he had approached the anesthetized patient. It was 2:34:18. . . . Eberhard watched the clock for some seconds—each second was precisely the same—time was calm.

He now stood alongside the operating table and regarded the section of naked torso in front of him, and a change came over him—he was calm now, professional. He began to palpate the body, determining the exact locations of the various organs, deciding exactly where he must strike. In his mind, he had already traced out the smooth arc that he must cut in that flesh to gain access to the organs underneath, to reach that rich repository of youth. He had succeeded at last in switching off his mind— only his hands, the surgeon's hands, were thinking now—and the hands heard no hum, they heard nothing at all.

Alfred Eberhard extended his gloved right hand. In an instant, Jean Stafford had slapped the scalpel into it. Even through the glove, Eberhard could feel the coldness of the metal. His scalpel-wielding hand edged forward toward the body. The tip of the blade was only inches away from the flesh, the soft flesh that rose and fell ever so slightly with the rhythm of Orin's breathing. The scalpel moved slowly forward, until it just touched the restraining skin, the skin that even now began to pucker slightly around the encroaching blade. But no, something was wrong. . . .

"Jean!" said Eberhard in a cool professional tone. "Why have you covered the patient's face? The face should not be covered in abdominal operations—it interferes with breathing, and for no reason."

"But Alfred!" Jean said. "The face . . . it . . ."

"I know very well," said Eberhard. "It's kind of you to try to spare me. But Jean, you and I shall go on forever, and we must not spare each other anything! I will spare you nothing! And I will allow you to spare me nothing! Lower the sheet, please!"

At this demand, Jean Stafford's immense composure seemed, for the first time, to crack. Her hands trembled ever so slightly. But she complied. And the face was revealed. *Eberhard's* face, forty years younger; the high forehead, sadly shadowed eyes, the broad full mouth, the slightly cleft chin. Eberhard stared as his own face was laid bare before him. He devoured the sight of it, drank in the horror with a kind of twisted gratitude. The sight of the face brought back the hum, the relentless whining hum that threatened to drive him mad.

But Eberhard was glad for the hum now—it was a sort of penance, a burden he agreed to bear for all eternity in exchange for this intimate robbery he was about to commit. Suddenly he thought of Abraham and Isaac, that near-murder by a father of a son. Would Abraham have heard this humming? Eberhard wondered. Would Abraham, goaded on to murder by his God, hear this same relentless humming that Eberhard, goaded on by *his* God: himself, was hearing?. . . . But Abraham had stopped short—his God had relented. Eberhard would not.

He looked down at the scalpel still clutched in his hand. A glint of light glared off of the blade, echoing the hum. And Eberhard again approached the body. For one brief moment he wavered—the voice of Jean Stafford urged him on.

And now the point of the surgical knife was again pressed against the torso. The skin—so fragile, so thin!—battled against the piercing blade for an endless instant, but finally, inevitably, it burst, giving entrance to the cold, intruding steel. There had been a slight moist popping sound as the skin had finally been punctured, a sound like biting into a plum. And then had come the blood, a thin line of red that first had traced out the curving course of the incision, and finally had overflowed, spilling down over the shapely hollows of the torso in scarlet rivulets.

Jean, her hand clutching a surgical sponge, reached out to dab away the blood. Alfred Eberhard held her wrist, restraining her. He wanted to gaze at it, to watch the way it thickened moment to moment, the miraculous attempts at healing which began almost immediately. How strange it all was!

A body, here, with Eberhard's face, incised, bleeding, yearning to seal itself, to preserve the life inside it, to maintain the awesome integrity of the realm within its skin! Life, in that moment, seemed infinitely mysterious to Eberhard, a man who knew every aspect of the chemistry of it, a man who had manipulated its secrets and its possibilities as no man before him had ever done. He watched the red streams trickle down Orin's side, he stared at the halves of his sundered flesh, pink and oozing. And, watching, he heard the hum within him rise in pitch and volume to a piercing shriek. . . . The shriek rang out inside his head, blotting out all else.

Deafened by this silent screech, Alfred Eberhard did not hear the tiny sound of footsteps scuffling in the chamber outside the operating room. But Jean Stafford heard it, and her body went rigid at the sound. Her breath caught and she found she could not move. She could only swivel slowly and stare with a locked expression at the sliding doors.

Alfred looked up to see her stiff and staring, and he fearfully followed the direction of her eyes. The scalpel was still in his hand, his body was wet with perspiration beneath the surgical smock. And Orin slowly bled. . . .

"What was it, Jean?" whispered Eberhard.

"I thought I heard someone!" she gasped. Eberhard could barely hear her through the hum.

"There's no one here," said Eberhard.

He turned back toward the body. Reluctantly, Jean Stafford took her eyes from the seam of the sliding doors.

"The clamps, Jean," said Eberhard, "I'll need the clamps."

Her hands trembling now, she reached down to the surgical tray and picked up the flesh retractors.

But now there was an unmistakable sound—the electric buzz and the metal clang of the sliding doors slipping open! The clamps fell from Jean Stafford's fingers, the scalpel dropped from Eberhard's hand. Quickly, silently, their faces contorted with fear, they turned their eyes toward the opened door.

There, just inside the doorway, stood Claire Eberhard! She was wearing her hospital nightgown, white and virginal. Her hair was awry but bizarrely beautiful. Her eyes were vacant, the eyes of a sleepwalker, and as she began moving into the center of the operating room, her motion was the motion of a sleepwalker, the stiff steps exactly measured, the bare feet seeming hardly to be in contact with the ground. Eberhard and Jean Stafford, terror-stricken, could neither speak nor move.

"Ah, Alfred," Claire said, her voice a breathy and trance-like whisper, "I was looking for Orin. Have you seen him? It was a year ago today that I crawled into his bed—did you know that? Yes, a year ago today. I wouldn't have remembered except that it was a holiday and everyone was talking about the holiday. And I thought that if it was a year ago today, it would be nice if I could visit him. I told the doctor, but he didn't think it was a good idea. I had to climb out the window to do it! (And here she gave a haunting little laugh.) I haven't done that since I was a little girl. Oh, and who are you?" she asked, apparently noticing Jean Stafford for the first time. . . .

"I don't know you, do I? You have a hard face—it frightens me. But Alfred, what I was saying was that I wanted to see Orin. I walked here and I went to the apartment and I looked for him in his bed, the bed I found him in last year. But he wasn't there and I was very disappointed and confused. I started wandering around and then I could see that there was a light on here. But Alfred, it's Orin that I'm looking for, and as usual, it's only you I find. Do you know where he is, Alfred?"

Alfred Eberhard battled against the screaming noise in his head and the awful reeling sensation in his body, and he tried to find a voice to answer. But no words came. Nor could Jean Stafford speak, but she at least could move her limbs, and she subtly slid herself between Claire Eberhard and the operating table, so that the mad woman might not catch sight of Orin.

But Claire's eyes, cat-like, followed the surreptitious movement. Her suspicions aroused, she moved forward with an unexpected quickness, between Eberhard and Jean Stafford, straight toward the stretcher on which her "son" lay.

"Ah," she said, seeing only the boy's placid sleeping face, "here's Orin! Alfred, why did you want to hide him from me? It's I who was always hiding him from you! But that's all right now. Here he is. How handsome he looks! Much more manly than when I saw him last. . . ."

Alfred Eberhard and Jean Stafford eyed each other helplessly. If only they could quickly give her an injection! If only they could get rid of her somehow.

Claire Eberhard continued to hover over her darling boy. She cooed to him, kissed his lips, and now she began to run her hand down his torso, over the pale green sheet her fingers played, down over his shoulder, his chest—and then when she reached his solar plexus, the sheet ended, and her hand was on his skin, warm soft skin. . . .

But oh! What was this? . . . Something was wrong! Something was wet and sticky here. Claire could not prevent her fingers from exploring this mystery. Slowly, unstoppably, her fingertips slipped into the channel of the body's sundered flesh. She felt the tissue rising up on either side, she felt the steamy warmth within! Her fingers penetrated to that warmth, she felt the lips of his opened flesh closing on her fingers like a ghastly kiss.

And suddenly, in an excruciatingly lucid instant, she realized what had happened; she realized what she was doing. With a horrible howling scream, she recoiled from the body, she looked down at her bloodstained hands. And then she stared at her husband, cowering alongside the operating table, unable to move. Her stare was murderous, wrathful, avenging. Eberhard's knees went weak under him, his bowels loosened, his teeth began to chatter.

Claire's stare moved for a moment to the face of Jean Stafford who met her gaze, impassive, stony.

Savagely, her head craned forward, her face set in undeflectable resolve. Claire grabbed a scalpel from the tray of surgical instruments. Jean sprang back several steps. But Alfred Eberhard could not budge. He would not have moved even if he could have. The hum was too much. He didn't care anymore.

"Alfred!" The single word resounded crazily from the walls of the operating room, and in that word was concentrated all the horror and grief of a lifetime. Claire Eberhard sprang forward, and in one quick cruel slash of the scalpel, she opened Eberhard's jugular.

The blood pulsed forth in torrents. Eberhard slumped to one knee, instinctively trying to stanch the bleeding. Claire cut him on the other side, and now the twin streams soaked the dying man's surgical smock and the floor on which he lay. In less than a minute, his body had emptied itself.

Now Claire looked up. Jean Stafford had fled, regaining her ability to move at the first sight of Alfred's blood. Claire knew what she had to do. She let the scalpel fall from her hand. She moved toward the operating table. From the surgical tray, she reached for the needle and the sutures. She had to stitch up Orin and bring him out of the anesthesia. Orin had to live. Orin was her baby.

AMANDA HAZARD MYSTERIES
BY CONNIE FEDDERSEN

DEAD IN THE CELLAR   (0-8217-5245-6, $4.99)

DEAD IN THE DIRT   (1-57566-046-6, $4.99)

DEAD IN THE MELON PATCH   (0-8217-4872-6, $4.99)

DEAD IN THE WATER   (0-8217-5244-8, $4.99)

Available wherever paperbacks are sold, or order direct from the Publisher. Send cover price plus 50¢ per copy for mailing and handling to Penguin USA, P.O. Box 999, c/o Dept. 17109, Bergenfield, NJ 07621. Residents of New York and Tennessee must include sales tax. DO NOT SEND CASH.

THE MYSTERIES OF MARY ROBERTS RINEHART

THE AFTER HOUSE   (0-8217-4246-6, $3.99/$4.99)

THE CIRCULAR STAIRCASE   (0-8217-3528-4, $3.95/$4.95)

THE DOOR   (0-8217-3526-8, $3.95/$4.95)

THE FRIGHTENED WIFE   (0-8217-3494-6, $3.95/$4.95)

A LIGHT IN THE WINDOW   (0-8217-4021-0, $3.99/$4.99)

THE STATE VS.   (0-8217-2412-6, $3.50/$4.50)
ELINOR NORTON

THE SWIMMING POOL   (0-8217-3679-5, $3.95/$4.95)

THE WALL   (0-8217-4017-2, $3.99/$4.99)

THE WINDOW AT THE WHITE CAT
                         (0-8217-4246-9, $3.99/$4.99)

THREE COMPLETE NOVELS: THE BAT, THE HAUNTED
LADY, THE YELLOW ROOM
                         (0-8217-114-4, $13.00/$16.00)

POLITICAL ESPIONAGE AND
HEART-STOPPING HORROR....
NOVELS BY NOEL HYND